HIS FATAL LEGACY

HEATHER ATKINSON

Boldwood

First published in Great Britain in 2023 by Boldwood Books Ltd.

Cover Design: Alice Moore Design

Cover Photography: Shutterstock

A CIP catalogue record for this book is available from the British Library.

Paperback ISBN 978-1-80415-804-3

Large Print ISBN 978-1-80415-803-6

Hardback ISBN 978-1-80415-802-9

Ebook ISBN 978-1-80415-805-0

Kindle ISBN 978-1-80415-806-7

Audio CD ISBN 978-1-80415-797-8

MP3 CD ISBN 978-1-80415-798-5

Digital audio download ISBN 978-1-80415-799-2

Boldwood Books Ltd
23 Bowerdean Street
London SW6 3TN
www.boldwoodbooks.com

1

ALARDYCE HOUSE, JUST OUTSIDE EDINBURGH,
SCOTLAND, MARCH 1897

Sir Henry Alardyce regarded his wife Amy with a worried frown. She was slumped at the dining table, staring miserably at her breakfast. Ever since her eldest son Robert had got married and moved out, she'd been quieter, more sedate. Her large blue eyes had lost their sparkle and there was a little grey appearing in her glorious chestnut hair. Even her skin was paler. They'd thought it would be a relief that a monster was no longer living under their roof; however, the worry of what he was getting up to now he was no longer restrained by his parents was a constant torture for Amy. She especially feared for Jane, Robert's sweet, innocent wife. Amy blamed herself for not doing more to stop them from eloping to Gretna Green and marrying over the anvil after both families had vetoed the wedding, but Henry thought she was taking too much on her shoulders. When Robert wanted to do something, no one on God's earth could stop him.

Henry covered his wife's hand with his own. The fingers on both her hands were twisted and bent after his mad brother Edward had tortured her, thick reddened skin where the nails used to be. Whenever they were out in public, she wore gloves to hide them as the deformity repelled a lot of people, but not Henry. He loved every sweet inch of her.

'Shall we go out somewhere today?' he asked her.

She raised her head and smiled, eyes wide and sad. 'I don't feel up to it.'

'Come on, Amy, this isn't like you. Where's all that fire of yours?'

'I think it's gone out.'

'Oh, no, it hasn't, it just needs stoking again.'

Her lips twitched. 'Really? What did you have in mind?'

'Well, I was thinking of catching a play or dining out, but if you have a better idea, I'm more than willing to go along with it,' he smiled, leaning into her, brushing her lips with his own.

Husbands and wives didn't usually kiss at the dining table, but Amy and Henry had long ago discarded convention, preferring to show their deep affection for one another rather than hide it beneath an austere front like their contemporaries. Besides, they'd been ousted by society years ago for their scandalous and very bloody family history, which had the unexpected side effect of allowing them to live life on their own terms. Their servants were used to their ways and didn't blink at this public show of affection.

'There's a new programme of music and varieties at the Empire Palace Theatre,' he added.

'Sweet Lord, save us from varieties,' she replied, wrinkling her nose.

'Or we could dine out?'

'I'm not sure I could restrain myself if people started pointing at us and whispering behind their hands. I might be tempted to throw bread rolls at them.'

'I knew it,' he smiled. 'Your fire still burns brightly.'

'Sorry, I have been a bit of a misery lately. You're right, I need to shake myself out of it, but not with dinners and theatres.'

'How about we take a holiday, get away from it all for a while? We could go to the Lake District, like we discussed?'

As much as Amy loved living at Alardyce House, the thought of a change of scenery made her beam. 'You know, I think that could be just the thing. I'm sure the children would love it.'

'Shall I make the arrangements?'

'I'll do it. I need something to occupy my time.'

'And I'll send word to have Riverwood aired.' Riverwood was the small mansion house their family owned half a mile from Ullswater.

She kissed him. 'Thank you, Henry. This is just what I need.'

He smiled as he watched her rise from her chair with much more energy than she'd had just a moment ago and bustle to the door, calling for her maid, Hazel.

Only when she'd gone did he turn his attention back to the newspaper and to the disturbing article he'd been reading. It was about a woman who'd been attacked in the New Town, a maid heading home after finishing work that evening. She'd been dragged down an alleyway, sexually assaulted and badly beaten. It was the second attack in two months. The poor woman had been found crumpled on the cobbles, bleeding and sobbing. Physically she would be fine, but her mental recovery would be much harder.

When Henry had read about the first attack last month, he'd tried to ignore that nagging voice in his head that said Robert was responsible. He lived not far from where the attack had taken place, but Henry had managed to convince himself that anyone could have done it. The city had a dark side and could be a violent place, especially for women walking alone at night.

Now this second attack had happened close to where the first had been perpetrated and he could no longer ignore that nagging voice. What if his stepson was responsible? Confronting him would be useless, he would simply deny it. On top of that, Robert knew Henry's secret, the one he'd kept from Amy their entire marriage and which could shatter their relationship if she ever found out. When his younger brother Edward had been executed for almost killing her and for the murder of four other women, Henry had used his influence to have his body turned over to him and had him placed in the family vault. He and Amy hadn't been together then, so it hadn't felt like he'd betrayed her, but he should have told her when they'd got engaged. However, he hadn't, and now it was too late. Robert was enjoying his hold over him far too much to tell his mother but one day he would, it was inevitable. Henry had to tell her before that day came in order to save his marriage, but Amy had been so down lately he hadn't had the heart. They would take their trip to the Lake District, it would raise her spirits and hopefully when they came home, he would be able to break it to her gently and beg for her forgiveness.

He'd just finished reading the disturbing article for a second time, attempting to glean from it some clue proving Robert was responsible, when Amy returned to the room, the sparkle back in her lovely blue eyes.

'I've told the children and they're very excited,' she smiled.

They had three other children – six-year-old Lydia, five-year-old John and four-year-old Stephen. Robert wasn't Henry's biological son. He was the product of an affair Amy had with a footman when she'd first come to live at Alardyce eighteen years ago after the death of both her parents. Robert's real father, Matthew Crowle, had been a rapist and murderer, unbeknownst to Amy at the time, and his son was turning out to be as big a monster as he'd been. Matthew was dead, killed saving Amy from Henry's mad brother Edward, who had stabbed him in the stomach. However, he'd survived this initial wound. Amy had torn the blade from Matthew's belly so she and Robert could be free of his poisonous influence, a fact Robert had only recently discovered and which had sent him over the edge.

'They could use the break as much as we could,' Henry told his wife. 'Things have been so tense lately.'

'Lydia asked if Robert and Jane were coming but I said no,' she replied. 'They're newlyweds and need to spend time together. I didn't like to say they're the reason we need to get away.'

Henry considered showing her the article in the newspaper before rejecting the idea. After Edward had attacked her, the entire sickening story had become public knowledge and the newspapers had seized on it. Amy had vowed never to read a newspaper again after the horrible lies they'd printed about her, so there was no risk of her reading about the attacks. As they'd both been rejected by society, there was no one to tell her about them either. Let her live in blissful ignorance just a little longer. He had the feeling Robert's sickening urges would soon raise merry hell.

* * *

Robert sat at his dining table like a king. How he loved finally being his own master and he was only seventeen years old. Most of his friends still relied on their parents' purse strings to survive, but Robert had his own money. His mother had given him £20,000 from her personal fortune that had not been absorbed into the Alardyce estate, something Henry had insisted on when they'd wed because his own mother had plotted against Amy when she was a girl and thrown her into Matthew's arms to trap her and take her money from her. Henry had refused to allow his harridan of a mother to be victorious from beyond the grave, which was the only reason why Robert still had any respect left for him. Since his elopement with Jane, the close relationship he'd enjoyed with his stepfather had been destroyed.

Now Robert was master of his own grand home in the very desirable Drummond Place in the elegant Edinburgh New Town, with a beautiful wife and hopefully a child on the way soon. He glanced at his wife from behind his newspaper. She sat at the opposite end of the dining table, nibbling a piece of toast.

'You should eat more,' he told her. 'Especially if you're going to be with child.'

'I've never had much of an appetite in the morning,' she replied, forcing her sweet smile.

'You don't have much of an appetite at any other meal. I never noticed before how little you eat. No wonder you're so thin. I want you to start eating more, Jane.'

'But I eat what I need.'

'Then eat more. Last night in bed, your elbow kept digging into my ribs. You seem to get pointier every day.'

Her cheeks flushed and her lips pursed. 'That's my natural shape, Robert, it's how I've always been.'

'Corsets conceal so much,' he sighed as though he were hard done by.

Jane blinked away the hot tears. Robert had always called her beautiful but the last couple of weeks he'd started making digs about her figure, saying he preferred women with more meat on their bones, and it hurt. It wasn't as though she purposefully ate as little as possible. They'd known each other since they were children and he'd never been cruel to her like this before.

'Your comments hurt me, Robert,' she said.

'Hmmm?' he replied, studying the newspaper.

'I said your comments hurt me,' she repeated, louder.

Finally she had his full attention and he lowered the newspaper, appalled to see her eyes were shiny with tears.

'I'm sorry,' he said, dumping the newspaper on the table, getting to his feet and hastening to her side. He knelt by her chair and took her hands. 'I'm being very thoughtless.'

'Yes, you are. You've started saying cruel things to me lately, Robert. Are you bored of me already?'

'No, of course not.' He looked to the footman standing sentry at the back of the room. 'Leave us.'

'Sir,' bowed the man before leaving, closing the door behind him.

Robert looked back at Jane. 'How could I get bored of you? I love you.'

'Then why do you keep saying cruel things?'

'I don't mean to be cruel, I'm just worried about you. I heard about my friend's sister, who was thin. She died during childbirth because the baby was so large. I don't want that to happen to you.'

'I know who you're referring to – Emily Saunders. What you perhaps don't know is that she was always sickly, right from being a child. I, however, am very healthy.'

'Yes, you're right,' he said, kissing her fingers. 'I just couldn't bear to lose you.'

Joy filled Jane. She'd been thinking he was fed up of her, and all the time he was worried about her. She took his dear face between her hands and smiled. 'You won't lose me, I promise.'

He kissed her. 'Good. Why don't I take you shopping? I remember you mentioning something about a sapphire necklace.'

'But it was dreadfully expensive.'

'Nothing but the best for my wife.'

'Don't you have business to attend to?'

'I do, but it can wait. You're more important.' Her smile touched his heart. He was relieved something still could.

'If you're sure?' she said, bristling with excitement.

'I am. We can have some lunch too.'

'Wonderful. I'll go and get ready,' she said, kissing him before rushing out of the room and upstairs.

Feeling very pleased with himself, Robert returned to his seat and picked his newspaper back up to continue reading the story of the maid who had been attacked just a few streets from his house, heart racing with excitement.

* * *

Amy was afraid something would happen to stop them from leaving for the Lake District, some emergency to do with Robert or Jane, but nothing occurred and the family left in their carriage for the train station. The servants accompanying them followed in a second carriage piled high with luggage.

They were deposited at Waverley Station and the servants and porters hauled their luggage onto the train while Henry, Amy and the nanny did their best to keep the children, who were thrilled by this unexpected trip, in line.

'Stephen, please calm down,' sighed Henry when they were finally ensconced in their first-class carriage, the servants in second class. 'Don't hit the window,' he added. 'You're giving me a headache.'

Stephen stopped slapping the glass with his palm and turned to playing with his beloved toy horse instead. Amy smiled as she watched him play, recalling when Robert had been so innocent. In her heart, she knew her other sons wouldn't turn out like their older brother because they both had Henry's goodness, it shone out of them. Robert was the one who bore the curse.

Amy smiled when Henry took her hand. She rested her head on his shoulder as the train pulled away from the station.

'Do you think Robert and Jane will be angry that we left without telling them?' she said.

'To be perfectly honest, I couldn't care less,' he replied. 'We've earned this holiday.'

'Yes, we have,' she smiled, enjoying watching the city whizz by.

2

Riverwood lived up to its name, situated as it was on the edge of a thick, dark forest on the banks of a river not far from the village of Pooley Bridge at the northern end of Lake Ullswater. The house had been built from the traditional grey stone so popular in the Lake District. It was smaller than Alardyce, more of a large manor house than a grand estate, tucked away from view of the road by the trees. Henry's father had bought it as a country retreat for his family and it had been passed on to Henry when he'd inherited everything.

Amy and Henry left the children to run off their enthusiasm, which not even the long train journey had managed to dampen, in the garden, the nanny watching over them, and went inside the house.

The interior of Riverwood was very cosy, with a country cottage feel. The fires had been lit by the staff from the village who had aired the house and cleaned it before their arrival. Their own servants – Amy's maid Hazel, Henry's valet Donald, the first footman Frederick, the cook Mrs Clapperton and the kitchen maid – set about organising tea and sandwiches for the family.

Amy and Henry headed upstairs together, shutting themselves away in their bedroom.

'This was a wonderful idea of yours,' smiled Amy, sliding her arms around her husband's neck as he pulled her to him.

'You look so much better already and we've only just arrived,' he replied.

'God forgive me for saying this about my own son, but it's a relief being far away from him.'

'Let's not think about him or Jane while we're here. Let's just relax and enjoy ourselves.'

'Is that your idea of relaxing?' she smiled when he kissed her neck.

'Can you think of a better way?' he murmured into her skin.

'Perhaps not,' she breathed.

They jumped when there was a knock at the door.

'My lady,' called Hazel's voice. 'Do you require me to assist you to change?'

'No, thank you,' she called back. Amy smiled at her beloved husband, feeling the stress draining out of her. 'I already have help.'

Henry laughed as they fell back onto the bed together.

* * *

'I can't believe you bought me this necklace, Robert,' beamed Jane, her gloved hands continually stroking the fabulous jewel around her neck as they walked the city streets.

'You're worth it,' he replied. 'Just be careful to cover it with your coat. You don't want to get robbed.'

'Oh, yes, quite right,' she said, fastening the top button of her plum-coloured fur-lined coat to hide the jewel. 'We must show Aunt Amy, she'll adore it.'

'If that's what you want to do, then we'll go. Let's have lunch first, though, I'm famished.'

'Me too. Why don't we go to Paterson's?'

Robert's smile faltered. Paterson's was a new tearoom that had sprung up on Princes Street and was frequented by the most fashionable of Edinburgh society. Robert loathed the most fashionable people. They'd rejected his family because his mother had an affair with a footman and then was almost killed by her insane cousin. For a reason he'd never been able to fathom, fashionable society had decided she'd brought it on herself with her loose morals. He was also looked down on because he was the son of a servant and not just any servant but Matthew Crowle, confidence trickster, rapist and murderer. It was only thanks to Henry's considerable wealth and influence that his family was gradually being accepted back into society, but Robert knew he'd never be fully accepted because he would always be the son of a footman. But he didn't want to let Jane down.

'Paterson's it is,' he said, forcing a smile.

As they weren't far from the tearoom, they walked there. Robert was dismayed to see it was busy. There were only a couple of tables free, so they were seated at the back of the room. They ordered tea and sandwiches, Jane looking around for someone she knew while they waited for their order to arrive.

Jane wasn't a stranger to Edinburgh society because of her close connection to the Alardyce family and the frequent trips she'd made to the city over the years from London, but it was the first time she'd become a part of it. Her natural sweetness and openness had endeared her to even the harshest of her family's critics and she'd made more progress in two months than Robert's parents had in years in reintroducing their family back into the society that had rejected them. Robert cared nothing for the good opinion of strangers, he was like his mother and stepfather in that respect, but he knew it was important to Jane and for any children they might have, as well as his young siblings, so he was attempting to make the effort. But always at the back of his mind was the thought that they were all looking down on him, making it difficult for him to get along with anyone.

'Look, Robert,' smiled Jane. 'There's Tilda Warburton,' she added with a wave in the direction of a small wisp of a girl in a hideous green dress that made her look ill.

The woman in question smiled and waved back before returning to her conversation with the matronly woman sitting opposite her. Once again, the progress Jane had made astonished Robert. Only last year, no one had been willing to acknowledge an Alardyce in public.

'Mary Walker's here too,' said Jane.

Robert couldn't help but admire the beautiful brunette as she strolled into the tearoom, the picture of elegance, skin like fresh cream. She was accompanied by two men – her husband and brother. Her husband was a quiet, serious man who rarely bothered anyone, but Robert loathed her brother, who was a preening, idiotic fop draped in different coloured silks and satins, his hair crimped and curled. He even wore rouge and powder. Their family was immensely wealthy, one of the richest in not just Edinburgh but the whole of Scotland; however, Benjamin Richardson was living, breathing proof that money could not buy intelligence. He was a constant embarrassment to his family, who spent a fortune cleaning up after his gaffes and paying off his gambling debts.

Mary spotted Jane waving at her and walked over to their table, Robert getting to his feet out of politeness.

'Jane,' she smiled. 'How lovely to see you.' Her eyes widened when she saw the jewel around her neck. 'Is that the necklace from Samuel's Jewellers?'

'It is,' she beamed back. 'Robert bought it for me.'

'How exceedingly generous of him. I was considering purchasing it myself, but it suits your colouring so much more. It looks like it was made for you.'

'Thank you,' replied Jane, delighted by this compliment from one of the most fashionable beauties in the city. 'That's so kind of you, but it would have looked lovely on you too.'

Genuine warmth filled Mary's eyes. Jane had a natural flair for making people feel good about themselves and they always loved her for it. 'It's such a shame there aren't more tables free or we could have joined you.'

'Another time, perhaps,' replied Jane.

'Hugh and I are hosting a fancy dress ball next Friday. You must come. Everyone's going to be there.'

Robert wasn't sure who this mysterious 'everyone' was. Usually it was the people the Walkers deemed worthy of gracing their home.

Jane was both astonished and overjoyed. Alardyces didn't get invited into other people's homes. 'We'd love to come, wouldn't we, Robert?'

'We'd be delighted,' he said flatly. How he loathed socialising with anyone other than his disreputable friends at Vivienne's establishment.

'Lovely,' said Mary. 'I'll send one of the footmen round with an invitation.'

'I adore fancy dress balls,' said Jane. 'I'll have to think about my costume.'

'You should wear the sapphire. It will be the talk of the evening.'

'I will,' she smiled.

Robert, who had retaken his seat, glanced up at Benjamin, who was smiling down at him with contempt in his eyes, large nostrils flaring.

'And how are you, Robert?' said Benjamin in a voice that, in Robert's opinion, was far too high-pitched for a man.

'I'm excellent, thank you,' he replied icily. 'Especially after marrying the most beautiful woman in the world.'

Jane beamed at her husband, her eyes sparkling.

'It must be love,' smiled Benjamin. He turned to Jane. 'I can't think of any other reason why such a lovely, intelligent woman as yourself would voluntarily take the name Alardyce.'

Robert shot to his feet and thrust his face into Benjamin's, who merely looked amused.

'Take back that insult right now,' he snarled.

'It's not an insult,' replied Benjamin with a disdainful arch of the eyebrow. 'I merely said what everyone's thinking but is too polite to say, my own dear sister included.'

'That is not true,' said Mary, cheeks heating, aware that everyone in the tearoom was watching them. 'Don't pay any attention,' she told Jane. 'My brother's always saying outlandish things simply to get a reaction. Come away, Ben,' she said, tugging at his arm.

He refused to move, staring back at a furious Robert, a sardonic smile playing on his thin lips. Mary looked around for her husband to assist but he was seated at a table studying the menu, oblivious to what was happening, too concerned with his stomach.

'Apologise at once,' growled Robert, jaw so set with fury he could barely speak.

'I don't apologise to the progeny of servants,' retorted Benjamin.

'Ben,' exclaimed Mary, grabbing his arm with both hands and pulling him away. 'Jane, Robert, I'm so sorry.'

Robert grabbed his other arm and held on, forcing Mary to release her brother.

'I might be the son of a footman,' said Robert, 'but I'm the one living in his own home with his beautiful wife and a fortune of his own. You're the one still living with his mummy and daddy who are forced to do everything for you because you're too incompetent to manage it yourself.'

'How dare you,' began Benjamin.

Robert released his arm and his sister dragged him to the table where her still oblivious husband sat.

With one last glare at Benjamin, Robert straightened his cuffs and retook his seat, running a hand through his thick dark hair. He was surprised to see Jane was smiling.

'Are you all right?' he asked her. 'I thought that fool would have upset you.'

'He did,' she replied. 'Until you put him in his place. Then I realised how inconsequential the silly little man is. I'm so proud of you and, to be honest, relieved.'

'Relieved?'

'You looked so furious, I thought you would throw him through a window, but you turned the situation on its head and he was the one who looked foolish.'

He smiled and covered her hand with his own. 'We're having a nice day. I refuse to let anyone spoil it.'

'I quite agree,' she smiled. 'Oh, good, the sandwiches are here.'

One of the many things Robert loved about Jane was her ability to recover from things quickly. She was always able to let an insult go, unlike him, who clung onto every single one and brooded endlessly over it. The only time insults seemed to bother her was when they came from him.

He glanced sideways at a smirking Benjamin Richardson. He would get him back and Robert swore it would be painful.

* * *

After finishing their tea and sandwiches, Robert and Jane left the tearoom and caught a Hansom cab to Alardyce House. By this time, Robert had simmered down after his altercation with that moronic peacock, enjoying how excited Jane was about showing her parents-in-law the sapphire.

As they descended from the carriage, Robert assisting his wife down, the front door opened and Rush himself shuffled out.

'Good afternoon, sir, madam,' said the butler, bowing from Robert to Jane. 'You weren't expected.'

'I wasn't aware that I had to make an appointment to see my own parents,' replied Robert coldly. This old fool had interfered in his affairs once too often. Rush was aware of his proclivities. He also knew that he was a killer. The only other people who knew that were his parents. Not even Jane knew and he hated it that a mere butler had a hold over him, not that he'd ever use it. Rush was far too proper, but Robert loathed anyone having an advantage over him.

'It's not that, sir,' said Rush. 'I'm afraid the family's gone away.'

'What?' said Jane. 'You can't be serious?'

'I'm afraid I'm perfectly serious, madam.'

'Where have they gone?'

'Riverwood. They left this morning.'

'Why would they go and not tell us?'

'It was a last-minute decision. Sir Henry was worried about Lady Alardyce's health.'

'Why, what's wrong with her?' said Robert, panicking.

'Nothing specific, sir, just a depression of spirits. He hoped a change of scenery would do her some good.'

'Was my mother happy to go?'

'Oh, yes, sir. She was very excited, as were all the children.'

'Why didn't they tell us?'

'It was a bit sudden, sir. There wasn't time.'

Fury and a little panic shifted inside Robert. That morning, the story had been printed in the newspapers about the attack on that stupid little maid, an attack he was responsible for. Had his parents put two and two together and decided they needed to get away from him?

'This is so strange,' said Jane. 'Why would they leave without telling us? I don't understand.'

'I really couldn't say, madam,' replied Rush.

'Perhaps we should join them at Riverwood?' said Robert, black eyes narrowing with slyness.

'Lady Alardyce did say she required peace and quiet to help her recover,' said Rush.

'She can't get any peace and quiet with John and Stephen constantly running around, yelling. I think some fresh country air could be just what we need after spending a few months in the city. Don't you agree, Jane?'

'I don't know, Robert,' she replied. 'They didn't tell us they were going. Maybe they want some privacy?'

'Nonsense. We're family too.'

'But we've been invited to that fancy dress ball next week.'

'We can be back in time for that.'

'I'm really not sure. I'd hate to turn up uninvited. We can go another time.'

Inwardly, Robert was seething. First Benjamin Richardson and now his own family. Everyone seemed determined to slap him in the face today and he was getting sick of it. He wanted to punish his parents for this insult.

Rush could see Robert's thoughts run through his mind and he wanted to protect his employers from him. 'Please don't take it as a personal slight, sir. It was simply spur of the moment, some excitement to break the monotony. I wouldn't advise travelling down there because they don't intend to be there for long.'

'So it's just a weekend trip?' said Jane.

'I anticipate they'll be back within the next few days.'

'There you are, Robert, it's not worth our while travelling down there. We can see them when they get back. Why don't we go away somewhere ourselves? We were talking about visiting Bute on the west coast. We could take one of those steamers.'

He smoothed out his frown. 'What a wonderful idea, darling. Let's go home and discuss it.'

Taking her arm, he led her back to the waiting cab.

Rush was relieved when the carriage left the grounds. He'd thought it would be harder to get rid of them.

3

Robert threw himself into a chair at a table where his three closest friends were gathered in Vivienne's establishment, so annoyed he failed to respond to a cheery greeting from April, his favourite of all the girls in the brothel.

'What on earth is wrong with you?' said Andrew Charteris, his closest friend.

'What makes you think something's wrong?' muttered Robert.

'Apart from the fact that your eyes are darker than the blackest pit of hell? Your jaw is so tense you can barely speak and your muscles look so taut they could snap your bones. You have everything you've ever wanted – your own home and fortune and you're married to your china doll, so what could possibly be wrong?'

'My parents went to the Lake District without telling me.' His scowl deepened when his friends burst out laughing. 'What is so amusing?'

'Aww, have Mummy and Daddy gone away without telling you?' giggled a drunken Daniel, his dark, swarthy good looks marred by the haziness of his eyes and floridity of his cheeks from an excess of wine. 'Diddums.'

'Do you want a bottle smashing over your head?' snarled Robert.

Daniel went silent and held up his hands, although he was grinning.

'Why so angry?' said Thomas, his blond hair ruffled and blue eyes as hazy as his friend's. 'I'd be delighted if my parents left the country.'

'They've only gone to get away from me.'

'Why would they do that?' said Andrew, raising his glass to his lips with an elegant white hand. He was the only one of Robert's friends who wasn't in his cups, but Andrew didn't like to lose control and he was far more intelligent that Daniel and Thomas.

The knot of muscle at the base of Robert's jaw throbbed. 'I don't know.'

'Oh, I think you do, you just don't want to tell us.'

Robert glared at him before pouring himself a glass of claret and downing the contents.

'And what does your china doll have to say about it?' pressed Andrew.

'I do wish you wouldn't call her that,' he sighed. 'Her name's Jane.'

'I apologise. What does Jane have to say about it?'

'That we should forget about it and go to Bute on a steamer.'

'Why don't you?'

'Because I will allow no one to best me.' His big hands curled into fists. 'No one.'

Robert was the youngest of their group but Andrew, assessing him with the detached professional eye of a trainee medical student, thought how much older he looked than his seventeen years. Since getting married, he'd gained a natural air of authority, his boyishness falling away to reveal the hardened man beneath. He could easily be mistaken for a man in his early twenties or even older, but these childish tantrums did mar the effect.

'So, what are you going to do about it?' said Andrew.

'I don't know yet, but I'll think of something. I'm also going to punish that idiot Benjamin Richardson. He insulted not only me but my whole family in Paterson's.'

'Good. He needs punishing. That fool thinks he can get away with murder.'

'He's not going to get away with this. Jane and I have been invited to his sister's house next week for a fancy dress ball. It will be the perfect opportunity.'

'How did you get invited to the Walkers' house?' said Thomas. 'I've been trying for months and nothing.'

'Because you tried to seduce Mary's younger sister,' retorted Daniel.

'Only her father walking in on the pair of you in the drawing room saved her honour.'

'Oh, I forgot about that,' he said before belching. 'She was a beautiful piece too, with skin like the ripest fruit.'

'I hope you don't mean blotchy, like a banana,' giggled Daniel.

Thomas's look was withering. 'You're an idiot.'

'Our family is slowly being allowed back into society,' said Robert. 'And that's all thanks to Jane.'

The three men released a collective groan.

'What?' frowned Robert.

'You don't want to get involved with all that nonsense,' said Thomas. 'All convention and gossip and boring balls. It's much more fun here,' he added, slapping the backside of one of the scantily clad women who passed their table. She flashed him a wink and a smile before continuing on her way.

'I agree but Jane does and it's good for my brothers and sister, but that doesn't mean I have to put up with clowns like Benjamin Richardson.'

'Robbie,' smiled April, plonking herself down on his lap and wrapping her arms around his neck. 'You haven't visited me in weeks. What's wrong?'

Robert smiled. He was the only man who'd ever given April sexual pleasure, which had happened the last time he'd visited her. He hadn't been with her since because he was trying to be faithful to his wife, something he was failing at, especially with his nocturnal forays into the city and also because he enjoyed her torment. April wanted to feel that pleasure again, he was the only one who could give it to her, and his refusal was torture for her. He'd even throttled her the last time they'd had sex, but with his charm, he'd managed to persuade her it had been an accident and she seemed to have forgotten all about the incident.

He kissed her and April groaned into his mouth. He could feel her heart pounding against his chest as his hand slid up her thigh, disappearing under her skirts.

'Robbie,' she breathed, eyes sliding shut.

He kissed her neck, moving lower to her large creamy breasts, bursting out of their corset. How he wished Jane's were like this, it was what he liked, not her flat chest. If only she was larger up top, she would be absolutely perfect.

'Do you like that?' he breathed in her ear as she grew warmer and wetter around his fingers.

'Yes,' she rasped, cheeks flooding with colour. 'Oh, Robbie.'

His three friends looked on in astonishment, mouths hanging open, glasses halfway to their lips.

'There are rooms upstairs, you know?' said a disdainful Andrew.

'Shut up,' Daniel hissed at him, fascinated by this display. No one had seen April exhibit genuine pleasure before. Her acting skills weren't very good.

With one last kiss, Robert tipped her back onto her feet. 'On you go, I'm talking with my friends.'

She stamped her foot in fury. 'Robbie.'

'What?' he said with an innocent smile.

'You can't keep doing this to me. I am not a toy.'

'No, but you are a prostitute. I'm sure you'll easily find someone who can pick up where I left off.'

'Yes, but...'

'But what?' he said when she trailed off.

'No one makes me feel as good as you do,' she announced before racing out of the room, sobbing.

'That was cruel, Robert,' said Andrew.

He took a satisfied swig of claret. 'You looked to be rather enjoying the show.'

'No, I wasn't. I'm not a desperate pervert like these two,' he said, nodding at Daniel and Thomas. 'The least you could do is finish what you started.'

'I enjoy winding her up into a state of unbearable tension.'

'Sadist.'

Robert shrugged. 'When did you suddenly become prudish? If you hadn't noticed, this is a brothel.'

'I have noticed but all that goes on upstairs, not at the tables.' He almost added the comment, *how common*, but managed to stop himself just in time. Robert would take that as an insult about his parentage and would no doubt respond by driving his fist into his face.

'I'm sure you'll recover from the shock one day,' said Robert.

Daniel shook himself out of his surprise. 'So, what are you going to do about your parents?' he drawled, putting his feet up on the table, nearly knocking over the bottle of claret.

'Show them that I'm not easily got rid of,' Robert replied with a satisfied smile. 'Henry will no doubt be very pleased with himself. I'm looking forward to wiping the grin off his smug face.'

'Andrew hasn't been able to stop enthusing about how divine your mother is,' smiled Thomas. 'According to him, she's the perfect specimen of womanhood. It makes me curious to meet her.'

Thomas had expected this comment to enrage Robert but, on the contrary, he merely smiled. 'You should try, it would be amusing to watch her grind you into the dust. My mother is unlike any other woman.'

'So Andrew says. Apparently, her figure could rival that of Venus herself.'

Andrew slammed down his glass. 'I never said anything of the sort. You're making things up to get me into trouble.' He glanced nervously at Robert, whose black eyes were fixed on him. 'I didn't Robert, honestly. I admire and respect your mother but that's as far as it goes.' Sweat broke out on his back as Robert's stare became more intense.

Andrew sighed with relief when Robert drained his glass, breaking the tense moment.

'Leaving already?' frowned Daniel when he got to his feet.

'I promised Jane I wouldn't be out for long, plus there's something I need to do first.'

He left the lounge area and walked into the hallway to find Vivienne comforting April. Usually, the madam was very strict with her girls and a slap to the face was enough to snap them out of any tantrums, but she'd always felt very maternal towards April.

'I'm sorry,' said Robert. 'Have I made my little April shower cry?'

She released a hurt sniff and turned away from him.

Robert handed Vivienne some coins and took April's hand. 'You didn't really think I'd be so cruel, did you?'

April beamed at him before they rushed upstairs together.

'I think I'm going to have to start paying *him*,' Vivienne commented to Costigan, the doorman, as she watched them go.

Andrew, Daniel and Thomas all looked up at the ceiling when the light fitting above them started to sway and April's cries of release filled the building.

'I don't know why everyone says the Alardyces are cursed,' Andrew commented to his friends. 'From what I've seen, they have the luck of the devil.'

* * *

Amy underwent a transformation at Riverwood. The gloom that had hung around her lifted and all her vivacity returned. She charged about the garden with the children, laughing and playing and paddling with them in the river. Henry watched her from the comfort of a deck chair, smiling at how happy and carefree she looked. She hadn't been able to recover from the shock of seeing her own son murder someone right in front of her at Alardyce. He'd feared that if she'd continued on the path she'd been on, she would have fallen victim to another of her fevers, which always seemed to strike her down when she was subjected to intense emotional stress. She'd barely survived the last one, which had hit after she'd discovered her eldest son was a violent pervert. If it hadn't been for the skills of Magda Magrath, the local healer, she would currently be in the Alardyce crypt. Henry's eyes narrowed at the thought of the crypt where the body of his younger brother rested, the brother who had nearly killed her. He resolved to tell her about that on their return to Alardyce, he had no wish to set back her recovery.

'All right, boys,' said Henry, getting to his feet when they produced bats and balls to play with. 'Let your mother sit down, she's been running around all morning.'

'Aww,' they whined.

'Your father's right,' panted Amy. 'I need a rest and a cold drink. You can play with Lydia.'

'But she's drawing,' moaned John.

'Then play together, there's two of you. That's all you need for bat and ball,' she told them breathlessly before sinking into the deck chair beside Henry's.

'Having fun?' he smiled, as Frederick poured her a cool glass of lemonade.

'I certainly am. Thank you,' she told Frederick when he handed her the glass. Greedily she drank down the contents. 'That's better,' she said, reclining in her chair, smiling as she watched the boys play bat and ball for five seconds before Stephen accused John of cheating. 'I don't have the energy I used to, though.'

'Neither do I. It is rather depressing when you start to slow down.'

'I've noticed it since that last fever. Sometimes I feel like an old woman.'

'Amy, you've been running around with the children in the sun for the last hour and a half. An old woman you are not.'

She took his hand and beamed. 'Thank you, that does make me feel better. You've been sitting in the shade for the last hour and a half like an old man.'

'Charming,' he smiled, raising her hand to his lips to kiss it. He frowned when he spied a carriage climbing the drive towards the house. 'Oh, who can that be?' he sighed, not wanting their idyll ruined by unwelcome visitors.

'It's probably Mr and Mrs Romer from the house down the lane. They said they'd stop by.'

'How wonderful,' he sighed. 'We're going to be saddled with a bore with a perpetual cough and a shrieking shrew who talks of naught but hats and gowns.'

'That's a bit unfair. They're a perfectly nice couple.'

'You mean boring.'

'Well, maybe a little bit. We'll tell them we're taking the children into Windermere this afternoon, so they won't stay long.'

'Knowing that pair, they'll come with us, then we'll be forced to leave our haven.'

She patted his hand. 'Don't worry, I'll handle them. You carry on relaxing here.'

'You're an angel,' he smiled, before settling back in his chair to watch the children play. Lydia had joined in with the boys' game and had managed to stop them from fighting with each other.

Amy got up and exited the garden by a small gate onto the gravelled drive. She fully expected either Mr Romer's enormous bulk to descend from the carriage or his wife's fragile, sparrow-like frame, but instead she was confronted by a pair of angry black eyes.

'Robert,' she breathed.

His smile was wicked. 'Hello, Mother.'

4

'What on earth are you doing here?' Amy demanded of her eldest son. She could sense the rage gathered around him, which he wore proudly like a cloak.

'We went to visit you at Alardyce, but Rush kindly informed us you'd come to Riverwood. He said your departure was rather hasty. We were worried, so we wanted to check you were all right. Sorry, dear,' he told Jane, who was waiting to descend from the carriage. He held out his hand to help her. 'Why isn't there a footman here to assist us?' he demanded.

'We only brought one footman and he's working in the garden.'

'Why on earth have you got a footman gardening?'

'He isn't gardening, he's serving drinks. You're young and strong, I'm sure you can get out of a carriage on your own,' she said a little bad-temperedly.

Jane's cheeks were flushed with embarrassment. 'I'm sorry, Aunt Amy, it was very rude of us to turn up unannounced. I did say we should go to Bute on one of the steamers, but Robert's been so worried about your health. He was afraid you were having another attack of fever.'

Amy knew Jane really believed that but looking into her son's eyes and seeing the smugness there, she realised he hadn't been worried at all.

They'd come here without inviting him or even mentioning it and this was their punishment.

'As you can see, I'm fine,' she sighed.

'Do you want us to go?' said Jane.

Before she could reply, the boys and Lydia spotted their older brother and came racing over to the fence, cheering.

'At least someone's pleased to see us,' smiled Robert before striding through the gate to greet them.

'I did tell him this wasn't a good idea,' Jane told Amy. 'But he was just so anxious.'

Amy patted her hand. It wasn't her fault. 'That's all right, you're most welcome. We've plenty of room.'

'We could take a cottage somewhere...'

'Really not necessary,' she said, forcing a smile before linking her arm through Jane's. 'You must be parched after your journey. I'll arrange some refreshments. It really is unusually warm for the time of year. You can sit with us and enjoy the sun.'

Amy was aware she was wittering, but she was desperately attempting to hide her dismay. She should be pleased she had all her children around her and the fact that she wasn't made her feel guilty.

As she returned to the garden with Jane, she saw Henry getting to his feet, eyes full of surprise and annoyance. She was willing to wager he wished their visitors had been the Romers now.

Robert stalked across the garden to greet his stepfather, thrusting out his hand to him.

'What on earth are you doing here?' said Henry, shaking his hand with little enthusiasm.

'Careful, Father,' replied Robert. 'Anyone would think you didn't want us here.'

'But...' Henry trailed off, so many questions, he wasn't sure where to start.

'Jane was itching to show you the sapphire necklace I bought her,' announced Robert. 'I hate to see her disappointed, so I thought we should come at once.'

'It could have waited, Robert,' blushed Jane, looking at the ground.

'We did go to Alardyce to show you,' he continued, unabashed. 'But Rush informed us you were here. We found it so strange that you ran off without a word that we felt something must be wrong, so we came to make sure you were all right.'

'As you can see, we're fine,' replied Henry stonily.

'Are you staying with us, Robert?' Lydia asked him, dancing about excitedly.

'Why not?' he smiled. 'It'll be fun.'

Lydia and the boys cheered.

'We really should find somewhere else to stay,' said Jane, very sensitive to Henry's darkening mood.

'Aww, no,' said Lydia. 'I was so sad when you left home, Robert. It will be fun living with you again.'

'In that case, how could I refuse?' he smiled, hugging her.

Robert's genuine affection for his siblings reassured Amy that he could still feel real emotion. After blaming her for his biological father's death, she knew some of his feelings for her had faded, as would his love for Jane when he began to tire of her. She hoped and prayed his brothers and sister could stop him from getting completely lost in the monster. She watched him play bat and ball with them, his eyes warm with happiness. Her boy had been so sweet once, but that had been eroded away ever since she and Henry had discovered his disgusting proclivities, which had replaced his goodness with arrogance and an insufferable smugness. Becoming master of his own home seemed to be exacerbating it.

'Jane, do you like my shoes?' Lydia asked her. Lydia held Jane's opinion of fashion in very high regard.

'They're very pretty,' she smiled.

'Thank you,' grinned Lydia, giving her a little twirl.

'And covered in mud from running about the garden,' replied Henry.

'They've got to let off some steam after being cooped up in grim Alardyce House all winter,' replied Robert.

'Alardyce is not grim,' retorted Henry. 'It's a beautiful family home.'

'You should come and stay at our house in the city, Lydia,' Robert told her. 'It's so busy and exciting.'

'Can I, Mama?' Lydia asked Amy. 'Can I stay with Robert and Jane?'

'Let's get this holiday out of the way first,' she told her. 'Now let Robert and Jane rest after their journey.'

Lydia and the boys returned to their games while the adults took a seat in the garden.

'Where is the footman?' frowned Robert. 'I'm parched.'

'Taking your things up to your room,' replied Amy.

'Well, how long is the fool going to take? If we'd known things were so spartan here, we would have brought one of our own servants. Naturally we assumed you were adequately provisioned.'

'I'm sure you can last a few more minutes without bursting into a ball of flames,' said Henry.

'Hazel will be out in a minute,' said Amy. 'She can arrange tea and sandwiches.'

'It's too hot for tea,' said Robert. 'This will do nicely,' he smiled, pouring himself and Jane a glass of lemonade from the jug on the table. He took a sip and grimaced. 'It's warm.' His eyes narrowed at Henry's mock gasp of horror.

'How long do you intend to stay?' Amy asked them.

'We don't know yet,' said Robert. 'There's no rush for us to leave, is there?'

'We have been invited to that fancy dress ball at Mary Walker's,' said Jane. 'I want to be back in time for that.'

'When is it?' said Amy.

'Next Friday.'

'That's short notice for a ball. Will you have your costume ready in time?'

'I have one I wore to a ball in London, so no one up here has seen it.'

'Oh, good, and Robert, what will you go as?'

He smiled. 'Jack the Ripper.'

'What a horrid thing to say,' said Jane, tapping his arm.

'Jane's right,' said Amy. 'That's not funny.'

'Did you lose your sense of humour when you crossed the border into England, Mother?'

'I do hope you didn't come all this way just to be rude?' Henry asked him.

'I came here to spend time with my beloved family. Oh, at last,' he said when Hazel emerged from the house carrying a tray laden down with treats.

Hazel hesitated when she saw Robert, so surprised she feared she'd drop the tray. Robert, for his part, wished she'd stop gawping at him. He hadn't been near her since he'd eloped with Jane. He'd only used her to get information about his mother because, as her personal maid, she was privy to a lot of secrets. Physically he found her repulsive.

'Hazel, are you all right?' said Amy.

'Yes, my lady,' she replied. 'Sorry, I was a little dazzled coming into the bright sunshine from the house.'

This explanation seemed to satisfy Amy and mercifully everyone's attention was drawn to the food and drink.

Hazel trembled inside as she stood beside Robert. Part of her was relieved that her affair with her mistress's son was over. It had tortured her with guilt because Hazel was extremely fond of Amy. However, she missed his expert caresses. Very few men had been interested in her and her affair with that beautiful, vibrant young man had brought a lot of colour into her life. The guilt had gone, but life was so much duller now. It hurt when he didn't even look her way, his attention taken up by his radiant bride, not that she could blame him for that.

Once all the food and drink had been placed on the table, she rushed back to the house, head bowed. No one noticed.

'That's better,' said Robert when he'd downed a full glass of cool lemonade. 'It shouldn't be like this in March,' he added, loosening his collar.

'You could always go back to Scotland where it's cooler,' replied Henry, causing Robert's eyes to narrow.

'So why did you flee down here then?' said Robert.

'We didn't flee,' said Amy. 'We wanted a break, that's all. There's nothing sinister about it.'

'You could have sent us word. We were worried.'

'You're a grown man now with his own household. We don't need to inform you of every little thing. That's what happens when you fly the nest, Robert.'

'I thought you were trying to avoid me.'

'Not everything's about you,' she snapped in exasperation. She'd been feeling so much better and already he was ruining it. Amy could feel the strength she'd just got back being sapped from her limbs.

'It was a misunderstanding,' said Jane, ever the peacekeeper. 'Let's leave it at that.'

'I think that's an excellent idea,' said Henry. 'So, have you taken your own cottage?'

'No, we thought we'd stay here,' replied Robert. 'You've got plenty of room. Besides, Mother's already said it's fine.'

Amy flashed her husband an apologetic look when he glanced at her.

An idea occurred to Henry, and he had to repress a crafty smile. 'Actually, it's rather fortuitous you showed up.'

'What do you mean?' said Robert.

'Your mother and I planned to spend the night at a lovely little hotel in Bowness-on-Windermere. We need some time together, just the two of us, so you can help the nanny look after the children.'

'How lovely,' said Jane, spotting a chance to redeem herself and her husband for turning up uninvited. 'So romantic. We'll take care of the children, don't you worry. Go and have a nice time together. Make it two nights if you want.'

'Really?' smiled Henry, enjoying Robert's black look. 'What do you say, Amy? Shall we make it two nights?'

'Why not?' she replied. 'We deserve a treat.'

'It's settled then,' smiled Jane, getting to her feet. 'Children, Robert and I will be staying with you for the next two nights while your parents take a trip away.'

'Yay,' they all cheered, although Stephen did run up to his mother and fling himself at her.

'I'll miss you, Mama,' he said.

'I'll miss you too, darling,' she smiled, hugging him.

Robert watched them enviously. Once he'd been the apple of his mother's eye, the centre of her world. Now she fled halfway across the country to avoid him. 'Why do you need us to look after the children when you have a nanny?' he said icily.

'Well, the children are a handful and we didn't bring the under-nanny,' replied Amy.

'But you were still planning on spending a night away together with just one nanny.'

'One night she could manage, but now you and Jane are here, we can make it two,' she said, releasing Stephen, who flung himself at his father next to tell him how much he would be missed too.

'It's fine,' said Jane. 'Go and enjoy yourselves. We'll look after the children and ensure they're kept occupied.'

'Thank you,' smiled Amy, getting to her feet. 'In that case, we'd better arrange for our things to be packed.'

'You're leaving today and you're not packed?' said Robert. 'I thought the servants would have already seen to that if they know you're leaving.'

'They haven't had time. As I said, we only brought a skeleton staff and they've been so busy unpacking and preparing the food.' With that, she left the table and headed back to the house, calling for Hazel.

'I'd better see how my valet progresses,' said Henry, getting up too and following his wife, feeling Robert's eyes burn into his back the entire way.

Once Amy and Henry were alone together in their bedroom, they both laughed.

'Well, that put Robert in his place,' said Henry. 'Fancy coming down here uninvited.'

'I know,' she sighed. 'He wasn't worried, he only did it to punish us for daring to leave without his permission. That boy's ego grows by the day.'

'We certainly knocked it down a peg or two.'

'Or we made him determined to punish us some more.'

'We can but see.'

'You don't think he'd take it out on the children, do you?'

'Actually, I don't. He has a lot of affection for his siblings. I don't think he'd ever hurt them or you.'

Amy gazed into her husband's eyes and took his hand. 'But you fear he'll hurt you?'

'I have absolutely no fear of that boy, but I'm the only one he'd intentionally harm.'

'That doesn't make me feel better.'

'Nevertheless, that's how it is and we both know it, but I do believe the children are safe with him. Besides, the nanny and Jane will be here too.'

'Yes, you're right.' She shook her head. 'I hate having these awful thoughts about my own son.'

'He's no one to blame but himself. Let's forget about him for a little while. Where do you want to stay?'

'How about Windermere Manor? The Romers said it's wonderful.'

'Let's hope they're not there. At least the season hasn't started yet, so they should have a room for us.'

'What if we can't find anywhere with a vacancy?'

'The weather's very mild. We can always stay in the carriage if there's no other choice, or we could lie beneath the stars, safely cradled in mother nature's arms.'

'Name me one night when you haven't been in a huge comfortable bed with servants to attend to your every need.'

'All right, I haven't, but I have been on picnics.'

Amy giggled. 'That's hardly the same thing.'

'It could be exciting,' he said, sliding his arms around her waist. 'We could romp in the grass, the trees providing us with privacy.'

'As well as insects and other beasties. Call me unadventurous, but no, thank you. I'm sure we'll find a hotel.'

Within the hour, they were packed and ready to leave, Hazel a little astonished by it all, wondering what on earth was going on. She watched the family gather together to wave off the master and mistress as they got into their carriage accompanied by no servants. The only one who didn't seem pleased about this unexpected trip was Robert, who looked sulky as he watched them leave, arms folded across his chest. He might be a married man with a household of his own, but right then he looked like a spoilt brat who hadn't got his own way.

There had been whispers among the servants that there was something strange about Master Robert. First Daisy had suddenly left, and she had been very nervous for the few days before her departure, then Winnie had been found bleeding in the garden with her back striped. For some reason none of them understood, the housekeeper Mrs Grier had attacked her mistress and run across a frozen lake, which had cracked beneath her weight and she'd drowned. Then Robert had eloped with Miss Parke because both their families had suddenly gone against an engagement that they'd been all for. It was what had happened to Winnie that made some of the staff suspect that perhaps Master Robert took after his biological father. This suspicion had only been strengthened when Rush had taken over hiring the maids and was careful to choose the very plainest of girls. The housemaids at Alardyce were now so plain that Hazel felt attractive in comparison. She found it hard to believe that the sweet boy who had showered her with gentle caresses could be the monster they purported him to be, but watching him glare with his jet-black eyes at his parents' carriage as it headed down the drive, she began to wonder...

As though he'd sensed her watching him, Robert's head snapped her way and for a moment, she found herself pinned by a pair of hellishly furious eyes, so ferocious it made her jump. It was brief, the impression gone before she could even be sure it had really happened and the corner of his mouth curled into a smile, sending heat flooding through her body while Jane and the children remained oblivious, frantically waving to the departing carriage.

Hazel turned and hurried back into the house, torn between fear and excitement. Part of her was desperate for him to come to her, the other part wanted him as far away as possible. Worst of all, with his parents away, there were no restrictions on him. Until they returned, he was effectively master of the house, master of them all.

* * *

To Henry's surprise, Amy broke into fits of giggles once they were out of sight of Riverwood.

'Amy, are you well?' he said, concerned.

'I'm fine,' she smiled. 'It was Robert's face. He thought he'd got one over on us and you turned the tables on him in a moment of genius.'

'I'm glad you approve,' he smiled, wrapping his arm around her.

She nestled into him, the black shadow of Robert's presence lifting and with it all her strength and happiness returned.

5

Robert stalked Riverwood, dissatisfied and annoyed. He hated anyone getting the better of him and his parents had run rings around him. Jane was playing with the children in the drawing room and the sound of their laughter and chatter was getting on his nerves, so he'd feigned a headache to escape the noise for a while.

He hunted the house for Hazel, hoping she could give him some useful titbit of information. No doubt he'd have to give her something in return, but he told himself it was more of an exchange, like handing over money for a purchase, nothing more.

He smiled when he found her in one of the spare bedrooms. He folded his arms across his chest and leaned against the doorframe to watch her make up the bed. From the back, she could be considered attractive. As she'd never had children and she was on her feet most of the day, she had a fine figure. It was when she turned around to reveal that dopey frog face that the illusion was shattered.

'There you are,' he said.

Hazel jumped and whipped round to face him. 'Master Robert,' she gasped, heart thumping.

'I thought you were hiding from me,' he said, walking into the room and closing the door.

She backed away from him as he advanced on her, holding the pillow-case she was clutching onto before her like a shield.

'No, sir,' she replied. 'I have to make up the room for you and Mrs Alardyce, that's all.'

She grimaced when she reached the wall and banged her back against it. Robert snatched the pillowcase from her hands, tossed it over his shoulder then planted his palms against the wall either side of her, penning her in.

'I missed you,' he said.

'You're married to one of the most beautiful women in the country. Why would you miss me?'

'There's more to a person than their looks,' he breathed, dipping his head to kiss her.

Hazel's eyes closed with longing, until she recalled her mistress's trusting face. She ducked under his arm and rushed to the other side of the room.

'You're playing hard to get all of a sudden,' he frowned.

'Things have changed. You're a married man now. Before it didn't feel like we were hurting anyone but now... I just can't.'

'Jane will never know,' he said, advancing on her again.

'You only romanced me to get information about your mother,' she said, reaching behind her for the door handle.

'That's not true, Hazel. I adore you. You're different to the other women.'

'How can you speak to me like this with your wife downstairs?'

'Forget about her.'

'You might be able to, but I can't. Whatever happened between us is over. You don't care about me.'

'Hazel, that's simply not true. I know you still desire me, I can see it in your eyes and the flush of your cheeks. Don't you want more of the plea-sure I can give you?' he said, voice lowering to a sultry whisper.

'Pleasure like you gave Daisy?'

Hazel couldn't quite believe she'd said it. She blinked at him, numb with shock, before panic set in, her heart hammering and stomach churn-ing. The transformation in Robert was astonishing. The shadows in the room seemed to gather around him, as though he was master of them too and his black eyes took on a disturbing gleam.

Hazel squeaked with fear, tore open the door and ran out, gasping with panic when she heard pursuing footsteps.

A low deep laugh rolled towards her, so chilling she was frozen to the spot. Looking back over her shoulder, she saw Robert had stopped halfway down the corridor, lips curled into a half-grimace, half-smile, eyes bright with malevolence.

I see you, she thought to herself. Now I really see you.

Hazel rushed downstairs so fast she almost fell, longing for the welcoming warmth of the kitchen and the redoubtable Mrs Clapperton. At least one positive thing had come out of that terrifying encounter – her desire for Robert Alardyce had been completely eradicated.

* * *

'This is heaven,' said Amy, who sat on the balcony overlooking Lake Windermere, Henry beside her. 'I love our children but it's wonderful just the two of us.'

'It certainly is,' he smiled. 'No yelling, for one thing.'

'Did you yell a lot when you were the boys' age?'

'No. I was always a very quiet child. Mother saw to that. Any loud noise or normal childish behaviour was mercilessly crushed.'

Amy felt sad for him and thought it a wonder that he'd grown into the good man he was today. Other than her father, he was the only man who'd never hurt her, and she knew he never would.

'What about you?' he said, his smile dispelling the shadow of his past. 'Were you permitted to tear about the house yelling and playing as we allow our children to?'

'I was, more so, in fact. My father used to call me a wildcat.'

'Now that I can imagine. You still are a wildcat, my dear.'

'I've been feeling more like a lame old cat lately.'

'And now?'

Her eyes sparkled, reflecting the setting sun. 'The old mischief's returning.'

'Now that is interesting,' he smiled, leaning over to kiss her. 'What is it?' he said when her eyes widened.

'It's the Romers.'

'Where?'

'Down there, just getting out of their carriage.'

They peered over the balcony to see the feared neighbours themselves, Mr Romer waddling towards the door, his wisp of a wife floating alongside him.

'Quick, inside,' said Henry, taking Amy's hand and pulling her back into their room. He closed the doors, locked them and drew the curtains. 'What on earth are they doing here?'

'They like to dine here,' replied Amy.

'Right, we'll eat in our room tonight. If they find out we're here, we'll never be rid of them.'

'I've just had a thought – they often call on us at Riverwood after they've dined out. Robert and Jane might have the pleasure of their company later.'

Henry's smile was wicked. 'Oh, I do hope so. Now then, wife, let's make the most of your mischievous mood.'

'What do you have in mind, charades?'

'God, no. I only play that dreadful game because Lydia screeches like a plucked hen if we refuse. I was thinking of more adult games,' he said, unlacing the back of her dress.

He removed her clothing piece by piece, enjoying taking his time. Despite having four children and the passage of so many years, her figure was still fine. She would always be so beautiful to him, even when she was an old woman.

She sighed with pleasure, leaning back against him as he kissed her neck, his hands caressing her large creamy breasts. She turned in his arms to face him and pushed his jacket off his shoulders. Amy's eyes were so full of spark and life, she could still have been that seventeen-year-old girl he'd fallen in love with.

* * *

Jane could only stare in astonishment at the couple who had practically barged their way into Riverwood. The small, thin woman was twittering on about a hat she'd bought and the large, obese man didn't seem able to stop coughing. As it was so late, too late to make a call, the nanny had already taken the children upstairs to put them to bed and how Jane envied them. What was she supposed to do with this pair?

'Ah, Robert,' she said when her husband finally strolled into the drawing room. 'Sorry if you were disturbed, dear, I know you have a headache,' she added, hoping this couple would take the hint and leave.

The woman's eyes widened. 'My, Robert Alardyce. I hardly recognised you. What a man you've become.'

'Thank you, Ginny,' he replied with his most charming smile, kissing her cheek. 'How wonderful to see you again.'

'I heard you got married. And this is your beautiful bride?'

'Yes, this is Jane.'

'We thought your parents would be here,' said Mr Romer. 'We heard they were back in residence.'

'They are, but they've gone to spend a couple of nights at Bowness-on-Windermere.'

'A holiday in a holiday, eh? I say, how lavish.'

'Mother's health hasn't been too good recently and she needs peace and quiet, so Jane and I offered to watch the children so she could have a rest.'

'How wonderfully thoughtful of you, Robert,' said Ginny, gazing up at him with watery grey eyes, resting her hand on his arm.

'Thank you,' he smiled magnanimously. 'We would invite you to stay for drinks, but nanny's putting the children to bed and if they discover you're here, they'll insist on coming down to say hello and they won't want to go back up again.'

'We'll go,' said Ginny. 'We don't want to cause a fuss.'

'My parents will be back the day after tomorrow. You must return then and bring your collection of train timetables, George. My father has developed his own interest in them. I'm sure he'll find your collection fascinating.'

'Really?' he smiled, chubby face lighting up. 'How wonderful to finally find a fellow collector. I'll bring the lot.'

'Excellent, and Ginny, I know Mother would love your advice on hats. She wants to buy her summer wardrobe and isn't sure about this season's fashions.'

'I'll certainly do my best to advise her,' beamed Ginny, who loved dispensing her wisdom to others, whether they wanted her to or not.

'How wonderful,' said Robert, smile broadening. 'They'll be absolutely delighted.'

'We'll return the day after tomorrow then, about four?'

'Perfect, and I insist you stay for dinner.'

'Oh, we will.' Ginny ran her hand up Robert's arm, the lasciviousness in the older woman's eyes shocking Jane. 'We'll look forward to it,' she said in a breathy purr.

Jane supposed she couldn't blame her for admiring a man as beautiful as Robert when she'd been saddled with the wheezy windbag beside her.

'As will we,' smiled Robert, enjoying his revenge. 'I can't wait to tell my parents.'

'Why did you invite them back?' said Jane when the Romers had gone. 'Your parents can't stand them.'

'That'll teach them to dump their children on us and swan off.'

'That's not fair. They deserve some time alone together. You can't punish them for that.'

'I'm not punishing them, but I admit I will enjoy seeing their faces when they find out. Oh, don't fret,' he added when she opened her mouth to argue further. He took her face in his hands. 'It'll be fine, I promise.'

He silenced her with a kiss.

'Robert,' she said when he pushed her back onto the couch and buried his face in her neck. 'We can't do that here.'

He raised his head to look into her eyes. 'Why not? We must snatch every opportunity to make our baby.'

'We might have already succeeded. Time will tell. We should go to bed if we want to do that,' she added when he started pushing up her skirts.

'We don't have to be confined to a bed, you know. We can do it in other places.'

'But we never have.'

'Then it's time we started getting more adventurous. What's the problem?' he pressed when she still looked uncertain. 'The children and the servants are in bed. No one will see us.'

She gasped when his hand slid under her skirts, her eyes rolling shut with pleasure.

'Let's try something different,' he said. 'Mother once told me the secret to maintaining a healthy marriage is the element of surprise, keeping things fresh.'

Jane's eyes flew open. 'I do hope you don't think our marriage is going stale after two months?'

'No, of course not. That's not what I meant at all.' An impish smile spread across his face. 'Besides, doesn't this feel a bit naughty?'

'Yes,' she smiled back, feeling wicked just for admitting it.

Hazel walked into the drawing room and gasped when she saw Robert and Jane together on the couch. Despite how he'd frightened her earlier, she couldn't take her eyes off his beautiful, muscular body. Judging by the noises Jane was making, she was enjoying his attentions, her bare thighs wrapped around his waist. In fact, the only thing she was wearing was her beloved sapphire pendant.

Robert lifted his head from his wife's neck, those black eyes of his burning. When he saw Hazel watching them, his face split into a grin. Her presence didn't seem to deter him in the slightest because he didn't miss a stroke, Hazel fascinated by the way his hips moved. He looked sinuous, like a snake.

Recalling how he'd been earlier, when she'd seen the real man, she turned and left, quietly closing the door behind her. Robert turned his full attention back to his wife, who had noticed nothing.

6

The two nights away alone with her husband had done Amy the power of good and she returned to Riverwood ready to face Robert. When their carriage rolled to a halt outside the house, he was waiting to greet them with Jane and the children.

'Hello, darling,' smiled Amy, kissing her eldest son's cheek. It was the first time in weeks she'd managed to go near him without replaying in her head the moment he'd murdered Hobbs. 'I hope the children behaved for you?'

'They've been as good as gold,' he replied, winking down at Lydia, who beamed up at him.

'Jane, sweetheart,' said Amy, turning to kiss her. 'Thank you for watching over them.'

'I enjoyed it,' she replied. 'They're wonderful children.'

'Any problems?'

'None whatsoever.'

'Excellent.'

'How was the trip? Did you enjoy it?'

'It was lovely,' smiled Amy, linking her arm through Jane's and walking with her back to the house. 'I feel so much better.'

'Oh, good,' she smiled, pleased.

'Mother seems much improved,' Robert commented to Henry.

'She does,' he replied. 'She just needed some quiet time.'

'So she doesn't know about Edward's body in the crypt then?'

'No, she does not,' said Henry, glancing around to make sure no one had overheard, but the children had already returned to their games and Amy and Jane were out of earshot. 'Why on earth are you bringing that up now?'

'I'm wondering when you're finally going to do the right thing and tell her that the body of the man who tortured and almost killed her is resting in the grounds of her own home.'

'As I've already said, I'll tell her when the time is right. You've seen how much improved she is after weeks of being miserable. I will not ruin that.'

'The longer you leave it, the worse it will get. You have to tell her.'

'I see what this is – we came here without letting you know and you don't like it, then you got even angrier when we went away for a couple of nights and you're bringing this up to try and get your own back.'

'Nonsense.'

'No, it's not, but I'll tell you what I will do – if you reveal my secret, I'll reveal yours.'

'What do you mean?' said Robert, panicking a little as he thought about the two maids he'd attacked.

'I wonder what Jane would think of you if she found out you'd killed three people?'

Robert's skin turned white. 'You wouldn't.'

'Why not? A sweet, innocent girl like her wouldn't take news like that very well.'

'She wouldn't believe you.'

'She would when both I and your mother told her.'

'Jane didn't believe either of you when you tried to tell her I was a monster and she won't believe that either.'

'So you're saying your wife didn't think there was anything strange about that night?'

He hesitated before saying, 'No.'

'What about the cuts and bruises to your body after that brutal fight? Did she not comment on those either?' He smiled when Robert failed to reply. 'You'd lose her forever, but I guarantee Amy and I would overcome our particular crisis. So please, go ahead and tell your mother, make her feel miserable again, but if you do, I will tell your own wife some home truths.'

'You know, Henry,' said Robert, standing nose to nose with him, 'one day, I will get the better of you and when that day comes, my mother will see you for what you really are.'

'And what is that? The man who has done nothing but love her from the moment he met her. I've never hurt her like you have. Do you know why we took this holiday? Because you broke her heart and she needed a little bit of time away to put herself back together again, and you couldn't even give her that, so don't you dare start making threats. You should be going down on your knees before me and thanking me.'

'What?' he spluttered.

'I helped her recover. I will always be there to help her pick up the pieces after you've smashed her to bits again, because you will. I read in the papers about those two attacks on those maids in the city.'

Robert's face turned to stone. 'It wasn't me.'

To his surprise, Henry's expression softened.

'It makes me sad how far we are from each other now. I loved you like my own son and I still do. It's true,' he added when Robert snorted. 'I admit I've been hard on you, but I'm afraid for you. Continue on this path and you will end up like Edward and Matthew. I don't want that for you. They were too far gone but I still think you can be saved.'

Henry watched a struggle take place within his stepson as his hard front briefly disintegrated, revealing the scared boy beneath. 'I don't know what to do, Father,' he whispered.

'Are you coming in for tea?' Amy called to them.

'Yes, in a moment,' replied Henry before turning back to Robert. 'We'll talk again this evening, when Amy and Jane are in bed. I'm sure that, between us, we can come up with a solution.'

Robert nodded and ran an agitated hand through his hair. 'I do hope so. I don't want to hang.'

Henry clapped him on the shoulder. 'I won't allow that to happen. Now let's join our wives.'

'Yes, all right,' he replied, smirking at Henry's back, all trace of scared innocence wiped from his face. It really was too easy.

* * *

The rest of the day passed in relative peace. Amy even managed to enjoy herself in her older son's company. Those two nights away from everyone had given her the breathing space she'd needed to recover from the trauma. It was only striking her now how much it had affected her. If she'd continued on the path she'd been on, she would have succumbed to another fever and she might not have had the strength to fight it off.

Amy retired early to bed, feeling happy and at peace. Jane went up not long after her. The children were already asleep, exhausted after a day of playing, leaving Henry and Robert to talk before the drawing room fire. Despite the warmth of the day, the nights were still cold.

'So, Father,' opened Robert. 'Do you want to start or shall I?'

Henry tore his gaze from the flames, cradling a glass of whisky in his pale, slender hand. 'Why don't you start?'

'All right,' he said, taking a deep breath. 'You're right, I did attack those maids.'

He'd expected censure, but Henry merely sighed. Clearly this news hadn't surprised him.

'It's a compulsion I can't control,' continued Robert. 'It rises inside me and possesses me completely. I'm helpless against it.'

'I can't decide if you're the victim of some disorder or just plain evil.'

'I am not evil,' Robert replied passionately.

'Edward was. I could see it so clearly inside him. It always amazed me that no one else could, not even your mother, who is one of the most astute people I know. I don't see the same thing in you, although I've no doubt you're capable of the same atrocities.'

'Was Matthew evil?'

'Part of him was, but there was still something good inside him. I will be forever grateful to him for saving your mother's life, even if she was only in Edward's house because of him, so I can't bring myself to think entirely badly of him. Have you heard of Julius Koch?'

The sudden change in topic puzzled Robert. 'No.'

'He's a German psychiatrist who studied the psychology of criminal behaviour. I've been reading about his work, it is rather fascinating. He says that some individuals are compelled to commit crimes. Koch coined the word *psychopath*, which means suffering of the soul. Does your soul suffer, Robert?'

'You're being rather melodramatic, aren't you, Father?' said Robert, with a roll of the eyes.

'Not at all. It made me wonder if psychiatric help might cure you of this impulse.'

Robert shot to his feet, knocking over his chair. 'So that's your game – you want to have me locked up in a lunatic asylum.'

'Don't be ridiculous, of course I don't.' Henry's expression hardened. 'Don't stand there glaring at me with those black eyes, they do nothing to intimidate me. Sit down and let's talk like reasonable human beings.'

Robert huffed out a breath, righted his chair and slammed himself back down into it. 'Are you suggesting dragging me to Germany so this Koch can prod and poke me?'

'Not at all. Besides, he retired last year but there is someone in Edinburgh...'

'Already you're plotting to have me locked up. Well, you can't, Father. I'm my own man now. You no longer control my destiny.'

'Will you please let me finish? And keep your voice down, we don't want Jane and your mother overhearing. That's better,' he said when Robert remained silent. 'Dr Campbell is a respected physician and psychiatrist with very nice offices at Morningside Place.'

'Morningside Place? That's where the Edinburgh Lunatic Asylum is.'

'Yes, it is. Campbell is Physician Superintendent there, but he also sees private patients, most of them very wealthy, who never set foot inside the hospital. I feel he could be the one to help you. He specialises in people with your... inclinations.'

'And if I tell him what I've done, he'll have me locked up.'

'You don't tell him what you've done, you'll only tell him that you're having disturbing fantasies.'

'Isn't lying to the man who's supposedly going to help me counterproductive?'

'Better that than being arrested and hanged, which will happen if you continue with your activities. The police aren't fools. One day, they will catch up with you.'

'I'm far smarter than any dolt of a policeman.'

'Arrogance like that leads to a downfall. I'm trying to help you, Robert, and this is the only way I can see. Koch believes mental aberrations such as yours can be treated.'

Robert swelled with fury. 'I do not have a mental aberration.'

'What would you call it, then? Because it's certainly not normal. You should also stop visiting that brothel. It's not very respectful to Jane. How would you feel if you gave her the pox?'

'How do you know I've been going there? Have you had me followed? You have, haven't you?' he thundered when Henry failed to reply.

'Unless you want your wife and mother to overhear this sordid conversation, lower your voice.'

'It was Knapp, wasn't it? You had the odious creature follow me.'

'I set him to watch you after I read about the first maid you attacked in the city. I had hoped marrying Jane would settle you down, but sadly it didn't. Unfortunately, he wasn't shadowing you when you attacked the second maid. How I wish he had because he could have saved that poor girl. He really was furious with himself for that. I shudder to think what he'd do to you if he caught you attempting to attack another woman. Not even I would be able to stop him. You're a physically powerful man but you couldn't stand up to Knapp, as you well know. It's one reason why you hate him so much.'

Robert was so shocked he was unable to speak. He thought back over the last few weeks, attempting to recall any sense of being followed, but there was nothing. It could all be a bluff on his stepfather's part. Henry already knew he frequented Vivienne's establishment. He could be trying to scare him into behaving, but Henry wasn't one for blind bluffs. He always made sure he was on very solid ground before making any tactical move and he had the means to pay an army of people to follow him for the rest of his life.

'I hope you understand I don't enjoy this,' pressed Henry when Robert remained silent. 'You're your own man now, married with your own home and fortune. I shouldn't have to keep watch over you any more. I feel, if you could rid yourself of these proclivities, you could be very successful. You invested your money as I advised and you're making an excellent living. You have a good head for business despite your youth and you could have a wonderful life with the woman you love. Don't let your darker half destroy all that.'

Finally, something his stepfather said spoke to Robert, and when he looked at Henry, it was without wrath. 'I want that life, Father. You don't know how much.'

'Then talk to Dr Campbell. It can't hurt. I swear you won't be locked up. This will be a friendly chat in his very nice office, just the two of you. If you prefer, I can accompany you.'

'Will Knapp be there?'

'Most certainly not.'

'And there won't be any orderlies waiting to cart me off?'

'I swear on your mother's life no one will attempt to have you committed and you will be free to leave at any time.'

Robert knew Henry would not make such an oath unless he meant it down to his very bones. This could be a way to get back into his stepfather's good books. There was also the possibility that Dr Campbell could cure him, then he could finally live a normal life with Jane. Together they would fill their house with lots of children and he would make an enormous fortune for them to inherit. He would buy a vast estate like Alardyce and become a laird. It was a nice future and he wanted it.

Hope rose in Henry's breast as he watched his stepson consider his offer. For the first time since Robert had attacked Daisy and this nightmare had begun, he looked like the boy he used to be. For once, his dark eyes weren't full of slyness and conceit, they were bright and hopeful. The goodness in him hadn't been entirely swallowed by the darkness. He just prayed this help hadn't come too late.

'All right, Father,' Robert eventually said. 'I'll see your quack, but one whiff of treachery and I'll leave and I won't go back.'

'I wouldn't do that to you or your mother.'

Robert nodded. 'I know.'

'Good. Well, I'm glad that's settled. You're doing the right thing, for yourself as well as the rest of the family.' Henry drained his whisky glass and set it on the table. 'Now, I'm off to bed. Goodnight, son.'

'Goodnight, Father,' replied Robert, turning to gaze into the flames as Henry left the room, wondering if he could be saved or if he would be consumed by the wildfire that raged inside him.

7

Robert decided that now he was finally getting back into his parents' good books and his mother was once again relaxed in his company, he would deter the Romers from visiting. He sent them a note telling them not to come because the children were ill with something contagious. He knew it would keep them away, as they had a morbid fear of illness. All day, he fretted that somehow they wouldn't get the note or would ignore it and come anyway, but thankfully they were a no show and he relaxed.

He and Jane stayed at Riverwood for another two days, which passed peacefully, and the family enjoyed each other's company. Then it was time for them to return to Edinburgh for the fancy dress ball.

Before he left, Robert spoke privately with Henry again, who told him he would arrange an appointment with Dr Campbell upon his return to Alardyce. In the meantime, he warned him to stay away from Vivienne's and his nefarious friends and not to roam the streets alone at night. Already Robert had been put off from doing either because he didn't know if Knapp would be following him. The mere thought doused his criminal ardour. He'd been pummelled by those fists before and had no wish to endure it again.

* * *

'Robert, you look so handsome,' smiled Jane as he descended the stairs in his fancy dress costume.

'Don't sound so surprised,' he replied with an amused smile.

Robert wore a costume his tailor had pretentiously named 'Night'. It was all black, with black trousers, shirt, waistcoat and a short black cape. A black mask with gold edging framed his eyes, which glittered beautifully, highlighted by the gold flecks in the mask. His dark hair had been slicked back, accentuating the sharp planes of his face, making him look beautiful and dangerous.

'I didn't mean it like that,' she replied. 'You always look handsome, but that costume only highlights it.' She slid her arms around his neck and kissed him with more passion than she usually would in front of the servants. The footman waited at the door, looking snooty and po-faced as any good footman should.

'You look divine,' Robert smiled down at his wife.

He'd purposefully chosen an all-black costume to complement hers, which was called 'Winter'. Her dress was large and flouncy, all white with tiny diamonds sewn into the bodice to represent snowflakes and a white fur wrap around her shoulders, giving her a fairy-tale appearance. Her blonde hair had been arranged into a complicated pattern of interwoven plaits and a white veil hung down her back. Even though she was fair, all the white didn't drain her colouring, in fact it enhanced it. The only colour she wore was her prized sapphire, as she felt the blue was in keeping with her chosen theme.

He kissed her again, Jane enthusiastically responding, until they were interrupted by the footman informing them their carriage had pulled up outside. They didn't need a carriage to take them to Mary's house as it was practically around the corner from their home on Drummond Place, but they didn't want to appear paupers by turning up on foot and Robert snatched every chance to show off his wealth.

'To be continued later, my beautiful little snowflake,' Robert whispered in Jane's ear before kissing her neck, making her giggle.

Together they headed outside to the carriage, the footman assisting Jane to climb in, hampered as she was by her layers of skirts. She was all excitement, the invitation clutched tightly in her hand, as though she was terrified she would lose it and be denied entry.

They pulled up outside the Walkers' grand townhouse and Robert stared at it enviously. Although superficially it wasn't much different to their own, Northumberland Street was even more exclusive than Drummond Place and he had aspirations to move here one day. Then he thought how a huge estate like Alardyce, which would one day become John's, would be even better, and his jealousy moved in another direction.

Four liveried footmen waited at the front door to receive the guests. Even to Robert, so many footmen was an extravagance. Clearly the Walkers were enjoying parading their wealth.

One of the footmen lowered the steps of the carriage and assisted Jane down, Robert following. Her hand resting on his arm, they made their way up to the front door where they were received by the butler, who took the invitation from them and announced their arrival in a deep, booming voice.

Naturally the infamous Alardyce name attracted a lot of attention and everyone turned to look their way. Jane swallowed nervously before treating them all to her sweetest smile, while Robert strode alongside her, looking dark and brooding.

'Jane, how wonderful of you to come,' said Mary, hurrying out of the drawing room to greet them, wearing a floor-length burgundy Rococo-style ballgown that ballooned out at the waist. On her head was balanced a towering, curled silver wig adorned with flowers. 'What a beautiful costume, it positively glitters in the light. My, the sapphire matches it perfectly.'

'Thank you, Mary,' said Jane, her cheeks blooming with joyous colour. 'But I don't look as lovely as you. Is that a Marie Antoinette dress?'

'Yes, although I'm regretting my choice now. There's at least six Marie Antoinettes here already, her costume really is all the rage. You're obviously blessed with much more imagination.'

'I wouldn't say that,' said Jane, her blush deepening.

Mary turned to Robert. 'You cut quite the dramatic figure. How clever of you both to coordinate your costumes. I tried to get Hugh to dress up as

Louis XVI, but he flatly refused. He wanted to be Henry VIII instead. We look ridiculous together.'

'You're so lovely, Mary, you could never look ridiculous,' said Jane.

Mary's eyes filled with genuine fondness, not because of the compliment, she'd received plenty already that night, but because Jane really meant it. Honesty shone out of her eyes. She truly cared about people and everyone she spoke to felt that.

'That's very sweet of you to say.' Mary's eyes slipped to the door when more guests were announced. 'Don't let me keep you chatting in the hallway. Please, feel free to mingle and enjoy the food and drink.'

'Thank you,' said Jane as Mary bustled to the front door to greet more guests. She looked to Robert. 'Shall we go into the ballroom? I want to dance.'

He smiled and held out his arm to her. 'Of course, if that's what you want, then that's what we shall do.'

With an excited smile, she took his arm and they progressed through the house towards the ballroom. Nerves fluttered inside Jane as all heads turned their way, some people whispering behind their hands. She wasn't concerned for herself but for Robert because she knew a lot of the guests were thinking it scandalous that the son of a servant was being allowed to mingle with the cream of society. However, she noticed a lot of the women were regarding Robert with interest and their glances were more appreciative than scathing. It wasn't surprising because he looked so handsome. There was something magnetic about him that spoke to the primal part of a woman. She knew because she felt it every day living with him.

It was something that had blossomed inside him since he'd become his own master. Robert was a powerful man and, unlike every other man here, he needed neither wealth nor title to prove it. It flowed through his very veins, and it seemed the female guests were sensing that. This phenomenon was even more remarkable because he was only seventeen, very soon to be eighteen. He for his part paid them no attention, striding through the house as though he owned it, so self-assured everyone moved out of his way.

Jane paused on the threshold of the ballroom to admire the scene, taking in the elaborate costumes, the flash of jewels adorning wrists, necks and fingers, the dazzling effect of the lamps ranged around the room lighting up the scene as the guests moved about the floor. Laughter and chatter filled the air, and the room was bursting with happiness and pleasure. It was a heady mixture, as though the tight restraints of society could snap at any moment and anarchy would reign.

'It's wonderful,' she breathed.

Robert escorted her into the middle of the ballroom and held her in his strong arms. Jane marvelled at him because he was acting as though everyone wasn't staring at them. This was their first foray into society, and she was terrified she would do something embarrassing that would ruin this chance, not only for them but for the rest of their family and any children they might have.

Feeling her shake in his arms, Robert smiled down at her. 'Just look at me,' he whispered. 'It's just the two of us in the whole world and they don't exist.'

She smiled and nodded as they moved together. They were both elegant dancers and, although everyone watched them closely, Jane felt herself start to relax. No matter what happened, she was determined to enjoy tonight.

She whirled around with her husband, who was by far the handsomest and most graceful man in the room, his eyes dancing with pleasure. Perhaps they could make a success of tonight after all? This hope was strengthened when she overheard a pair of dancers close by discussing what an elegant couple they were, and she found she was disappointed when the dance ended.

The moment it did, Jane was approached by three men, all of whom asked her for the next dance. She looked from one to the other in consternation before looking to Robert and seeing the jealousy shining in his eyes. Wanting to reassure him, she took his hand and squeezed it.

'Mr Alardyce,' one of the men politely said. 'I do hope you don't mind if I dance the next with your lovely wife?'

Robert assessed the man, who was twenty years older than Jane, greying and portly. Determining that he was no threat, he nodded magnanimously. The delighted man held his arm out to Jane, who accepted it. She continually looked back at her husband as she was led away, communicating to him that he was the only man she was interested in.

The other two disappointed men wandered off and Robert suddenly found himself surrounded by ladies of all ages. Looking through the gaggle of women, he saw Jane frowning at the scene, ignoring her partner, who was talking to her. This pleased him. She was feeling jealous too. It wasn't unusual for married people to dance with others, in fact a refusal was deemed rude, but they weren't used to sharing each other and they were both finding it difficult.

Keeping his wife's feelings in mind, he took the hand of one of the plainer girls, who appeared thrilled to have been chosen. She grinned back over her shoulder at her disappointed friends. As they danced, the girl prattled on endlessly about nothing in particular. In fact, he couldn't have repeated what she said because he didn't listen, too busy watching his angel float about the room, being admired by every man present. Her eyes kept flicking to him and when their gazes caught, she would give him one of her radiant smiles. Those who had determined to watch the infamous Alardyces very closely were forced to admit that it did seem to be a love match.

When the dance ended, Robert released his partner and bowed to her before attempting to walk over to Jane, but another man asked her for a dance. Jane, always impeccably polite and never wanting to hurt anyone's feelings, found she was unable to refuse, casting Robert an apologetic look as she was swept into another dance.

'Your wife is popular tonight,' said a voice behind him.

He turned to find Mary Walker staring up at him, her ridiculous wig balanced on top of her head.

'May I have this dance?' she said.

Robert politely bowed and took her in his arms.

'It seems your debut here tonight is a success,' said Mary as they danced together. 'One half of the room wants to dance with Jane, the other half wants to dance with you.'

'We are both very appreciative of you inviting us.'

'You're welcome. Truth be told, I had an ulterior motive.'

'Oh, yes?' he said, his mind only half on the conversation, still watching Jane.

'Let's discuss it in private. Meet me upstairs, third door on the left.'

Finally, she had his attention and he frowned down at her. 'Excuse me?'

She leaned in closer to whisper, 'You're an extremely attractive man, I've always thought so. It's why I invited you here tonight.'

Robert frowned. 'I thought you were fond of my wife?'

'I am. Jane's a lovely girl but let's face it, that's what she is – a girl. A man like you requires a real woman.'

'Jane is everything I need.'

'That's sweet of you to say, but I can offer you delights you've never even imagined.'

'I doubt that.'

Her sultry smile fell. 'Are you turning me down?'

'Yes.'

'It wouldn't be wise to displease me. I can smooth the path for your entry back into society or I can break the pair of you with a single word.'

'If you're representative of so-called civilised society, then I want nothing to do with it.'

'How dare you...'

His grip on her tightened when she attempted to stomp away from him.

'Let go of me,' she said, vainly struggling.

'I wouldn't do that, unless you want all your guests to realise something is going on, and believe me when I say I will have no problem telling them the truth.'

'You wouldn't dare,' she said, although she did cease her struggles.

'If you knew me at all, you'd realise how ridiculous that statement is. Now be quiet and listen. I am not interested in you in the slightest. Jane is everything I want.' As he spoke, he tried not to think about April or the maids. 'You will use all your influence to ensure we are welcomed back into society. Not for myself, I couldn't care less if this house burned down with all of you inside, but I do care about my wife and our future children. If you don't, then I will tell not only your husband but every member of influential society how you propositioned me. I might even put an advert in all the newspapers.'

'You're bluffing.'

His smile was malicious. 'Why not push me and see? But I warn you, I never bluff.'

'No one would take your word over mine.'

'We're surrounded by spiteful gossips. Even if they didn't believe it, they would certainly enjoy talking about it again and again, whispering behind your back. It would drive a woman like you mad.'

'Listen, you little brat...' She winced when he squeezed her again.

'As you said, I'm a man, and like a man, I will go to any lengths to defend my wife. Just keep smiling, pretend to be my friend, be a genuine friend to Jane and not a single word will pass my lips. Agreed?'

She glowered up at him. 'Agreed.'

'What wonderful timing you have, Mrs Walker. The dance has ended,' he said before releasing her.

He gave her a stiff bow, which she returned with a haughty curtsey before stalking off. Robert was aware of a woman waiting to dance with him, but he pretended he hadn't seen her and made his way towards Jane, who had just been released by a man who was young and handsome.

'Shall we get a drink?' he said, taking her arm before anyone else could claim her.

'Yes, please,' she smiled up at him. 'How are you enjoying the ball?'

'It's wonderful,' he said, trying to find some enthusiasm, for her sake.

'I'm having a lovely time. Everyone's so friendly and pleasant. I saw you dancing with Mary. It was so kind of her to invite us, wasn't it?'

'Very,' he said tightly. Sometimes his wife's innocence broke his heart. She seemed too special for this grubby world. She was certainly too special for him.

They were served punch by a maid. The blood thundered in his head as she handed him a glass. She was petite and pretty, dark-haired with smoky eyes. When she realised he was staring, she flashed him a coy smile. In his head, her smile morphed into a grimace of terror, her high-pitched scream piercing his brain as he beat her naked back...

'Robert, are you all right?' said Jane.

Her hand on his arm snapped him out of it. 'Sorry, I was miles away. It's all the noise, it's giving me a headache.'

'In that case, you shouldn't have the punch.'

'You're probably right,' he said, dumping the glass on the table, taking Jane's hand and leading her away from the maid. Why did maids fascinate him so? Was it because his own mother had an affair with a servant? Could it be something passed down in the blood? Or perhaps it was just that maids were lesser, more vulnerable.

'Champagne, sir?' said a voice.

Robert turned to face what he at first thought was a footman, until he realised it was Benjamin Richardson in footman livery. He carried a silver tray holding glasses of champagne. Worst of all was the smirk on his face.

8

As Robert and Jane stared at Benjamin in astonishment, the room erupted into laughter.

'I take it you approve of my costume?' said Benjamin, having to shout to be heard over the din. 'I thought of all the guests, you would appreciate it the most, given how your father was very partial to wearing the uniform.'

Fury coursed through Robert, darkening his eyes, hands snapping into fists. The laughing faces around him seemed to whirl until they blurred into one, the sound filling his ears. He looked down at Jane and was appalled to see her cheeks bright pink with embarrassment, eyes shiny with tears. She'd been having such a nice time and this prancing clown had ruined it. Well, he was going to do something about that. It would be very easy for him to tear Benjamin limb from limb, but he managed to rein in his temper. There was a better way to put him in his place.

'So you want to be a footman, do you?' said Robert, surprised by how calm he sounded. 'Footmen have to clear up the mess. Did you know that? Of course not. People like you barely notice those who actually have a purpose in life.' He knocked the tray out of his hands, sending glasses and champagne flying. 'Clean it up, servant.'

Benjamin's eyes widened with surprise. He'd expected the Alardyces to run out, cowed and humiliated, leaving him to bask in the adulation of his wonderful idea. He looked to the other guests, who were no longer laughing. In fact, they appeared to be rather uncertain and were waiting to see what happened next.

'What are you waiting for, servant?' pressed Robert, voice ringing out loud and clear through the now silent room. 'Clean it up.'

'I...' Benjamin looked around for assistance, with no idea how to handle the situation, but no one was stepping forward to help. Over the years, he'd annoyed and insulted every single one of them and malicious pleasure shone in all their eyes.

'Are you refusing to clean up the mess?' Robert asked him. 'Disobedient servants need to be punished.'

Benjamin yelped when Robert grabbed his right arm and twisted it, forcing him to his knees.

'Clean it up,' he told him.

'Robert,' began Jane. 'That isn't necessary.'

'Yes, it is,' he replied, staring down coldly at the grimacing Benjamin. 'What are you waiting for, servant? Clean it up.'

'All right, all right,' he squealed when Robert twisted harder. He produced a silk handkerchief from his pocket with his free hand and began dabbing at the champagne on the floor.

The laughter started up again, small titters at first that quickly morphed into roars, only this time they weren't aimed at the Alardyces but rather at the cringing Benjamin, while Robert stared down at him with malicious pleasure.

Jane tapped his arm. 'Robert, please,' she whispered. 'That's enough.'

He nodded and released Benjamin, who gasped with relief and slumped to the floor.

'This really is the highlight of the evening,' announced Robert. 'Benjamin Richardson grovelling at my feet.' His lips curled into a smile. 'My father would be so proud.' Robert removed the mask he was wearing and dumped it on a table before holding his arm out to Jane. 'I'm bored. Shall we leave?'

She took his arm and smiled. 'Yes, please.'

They progressed to the door, holding their heads high, everyone standing aside to allow them to pass. One person began to applaud, and everyone swiftly joined in.

As they left, Robert spotted a sullen Mary watching from the side of the room. He wasn't sure if she'd put Benjamin up to this or if the fool had done it off his own back with her blessing. Either way, she didn't look very happy.

They climbed back into their carriage, Jane slumping into the far corner, looking miserable.

'Are you all right?' he said, wrapping an arm around her.

'Everything was going so well,' she replied. 'We were having a lovely time and then that idiot spoilt it.'

'I put him in his place. You don't think I went too far, do you?'

'At first I did, when you were twisting his arm, then I thought how mean he was trying to be to you and he deserved it.' The tears she'd been suppressing finally spilled down her cheeks. 'Why do people have to be so cruel?'

'Because they enjoy it. The important thing is we left with our heads held high and Benjamin was the one who was left looking the fool.'

'I suppose you're right. It could have been worse. I just had such high hopes for tonight.'

'Well, Mary Walker did tell me when we were dancing that she's going to do all in her power to help introduce us into society.'

Her tears dried up. 'Really?'

He smiled. 'Really.'

'I suppose after what happened to her brother, she won't want to do that.'

'Oh, I think she will,' he said with a sly smile.

'I don't care about all those people,' she said, nestling into him. 'I have you and that's enough for me. Aunt Amy and Uncle Henry don't need society and neither do we.'

'You'll always have me,' he said, hugging her.

'Let's go home and keep trying for our baby.'

'Again?' he said, tilting her face up to his. 'Mrs Alardyce, you're becoming insatiable.'

'Because, Mr Alardyce, you are the handsomest man in Edinburgh.'

She kissed him and rested her head on his chest. 'You're all I need, Robert. I'm content with that.'

She smiled when he wrapped his arms around her and kissed the top of her head, he made her feel so safe.

Robert's gaze turned to the carriage window. He'd started to consider the city to be his hunting ground but tonight had made him remember that Jane was the most precious thing to him in the whole world. He'd been propositioned by one of the most famous beauties in the city and her offer hadn't moved him in the slightest, in fact he'd been more stirred by her pretty maid. From now on, he would be a changed man. He would stop going to Vivienne's and stop stalking the streets at night. He would visit Henry's doctor to try to rid himself of his dark compulsions. He would be the husband Jane deserved and a good father to their children. He would have the nice life he had always dreamed of, and he would rub everyone's noses in it, especially the Richardsons.

* * *

Robert climbed into Henry's carriage the moment it rolled to a halt outside his house in Drummond Place.

'Good morning, Robert,' smiled Henry as he settled himself on the seat opposite. 'I'm glad you came. I did think you might back out. Well done for seeing it through.'

'I want to do this,' he replied as the carriage set off. 'I've realised that Jane is the most important thing to me and I want to be the husband she deserves. I want to get better.'

'Excellent,' he smiled. This time, the boy did seem to be truly genuine. Robert thought he could pull the wool over his eyes, but Henry always knew when he was being disingenuous. 'What brought about this change?'

'The fancy dress ball at Mary Walker's house.'

'Yes, I heard about that.'

'You heard about Benjamin Richardson too?'

Henry nodded, eyes dancing. 'That fool's had it coming for a long time.'

'I thought you'd be angry.'

'I was angry. At him. By all accounts, you put him in his place rather firmly.'

'How do you know about this? You don't socialise.'

'A business acquaintance of mine was there. He couldn't wait to tell me at our next meeting. He said he hadn't had such a good evening in years. Benjamin has upset a lot of people over the years with his antics, including my business partner, and the consensus is that he got what he deserved. In fact, you've become quite the local hero.'

'I have?' Robert said, eyes shining with wonder.

'Oh, yes. Everyone's saying you conducted yourself in a very manly way.'

'So that's why we've received three invitations in as many days. I thought it might be a joke.'

'Most certainly not. You're the man of the moment and everyone's saying Jane conducted herself with grace and dignity. Congratulations to you both. Keep this up and the name Alardyce will no longer be anathema to polite society.'

'The Richardsons will want revenge.'

'I doubt Benjamin has the brains.'

'Perhaps not, but his sister does.'

'Mary? I thought she was friends with Jane.'

'Friends,' Robert spat. 'The odious woman propositioned me while we were dancing. She wasn't very happy when I turned her down.'

'You should get used to offers like that if you're going to be part of society. It happens more than you think. The veneer of respectability is extremely thin.'

'Have you ever been propositioned?'

'Yes, in my younger days, usually by married women. Not since your mother and I were ousted from society, which, to be honest, was a relief. I suppose I'm too old to attract that sort of attention now anyway.'

Robert didn't agree. Henry barely looked any different to when he'd first met him nine years ago. Slightly greyer, just a little more weight, but he was still fit and striking-looking. Robert could only hope he aged so well.

'It was an insult,' said Robert. 'As if any woman could compare to Jane.'

'I hope you remember that the next time you think about going to the brothel.'

'I've already decided I'm not going back there, and I'll prove it,' added Robert when doubt filled his stepfather's eyes. 'Get Knapp to watch me day and night. I won't go near the place again.'

'And will you see your doubtful friends any more?'

'That's where it gets a little complicated.'

'In what way?'

'Andrew knows what I've done.'

Henry's pale skin turned even paler. 'How much does he know?'

'Most of it – Daisy, my urges, Mrs Grier.'

'Dear God,' Henry sighed. 'You told me no one else knew.'

'I know, and I'm sorry, but I thought you should know. I want to do the right thing, honestly, Father.'

'It's all right,' he said more gently, recognising that for the first time in a long time, Robert was being sincere. Getting angry at him might cause him to pull away again and relapse back into his old ways, something he was not willing to risk. 'Does he know about the last two attacks you committed, as well as what happened to your grandmother and Hobbs?'

'No, I swear.'

'I believe you. Do you think Andrew might use this as a blackmail opportunity?'

'I wouldn't put it past him. He's not short of money, his family sends him plenty and he's very careful with it, but he might if he thought it would amuse him or get him something he wanted.'

'Then we must prepare for such an occasion, just in case he tries it.'

'How?'

'Leave that with me.'

'That's why I don't want to cut him out of my life completely. I fear if I insult him, then he might use what he knows against me.'

'Fight fire with fire. I'll find something on him that he'll be anxious to keep quiet, then, if he does attempt to blackmail you, he'll find himself checkmated.'

'Good idea, Father. You should start with the hospital where he's studying. There was some scandal involving a woman that he was so anxious to keep quiet he refused to tell even me the details.'

'Thank you for the tip. There does seem to be a new maturity about you, Robert. Perhaps if this thing is tackled early enough, it can be stopped.'

'I do hope so,' he sighed. For months, he'd resented his stepfather, but what if he was actually his saviour? Would Matthew still be alive if he'd had someone like Sir Henry Alardyce to help him? He should be grateful to the Walkers. Even though they'd propositioned and insulted him, they'd helped mould him into a man.

Robert allowed a tiny bit of hope to enter his heart. Perhaps he wasn't damned? This might just be a phase that he could overcome.

'Here we are,' said Henry when the carriage rolled to a halt.

They descended into a quiet leafy lane. Robert looked over his shoulder at the Edinburgh Lunatic Asylum, looming over him like a bird of prey. The architect had attempted to bring some aesthetic pleasure to those who were forced to look upon it on a regular basis. It had been built in the neo-classical style and the intention had been for it to resemble a pleasant country house, but in Robert's opinion, they had failed miserably. It looked exactly what it was – a pit in which to throw the detritus of society. The asylum had been split into four blocks to accommodate different classes, so the wealthy wouldn't have to mix with the paupers, but madness made no such distinctions. One block might be more pleasant to dwell in than another, but the real prison was in the patient's own mind.

Robert shivered as he thought that his own actions could one day land him in that grim institution, pounding at the walls, desperate to be set free while the mad ranted and wailed around him. Hanging would be preferable to such a fate.

9

'This way, Robert,' said Henry, putting a gentle hand on his shoulder and steering him inside a pleasant three-storey townhouse.

As he walked inside, Robert tensed, ready to fight should anyone be waiting to take him away and lock him up, but the only person there was a pinched-faced man writing at a desk. He looked up when they walked in.

'We're here to see Dr Campbell,' said Henry.

'Of course, sir, he's expecting you. Please go in.'

'Thank you.'

Robert followed his stepfather up to the next floor and into a spacious office, the furniture all dark oak and beautifully polished. The window looked out over the asylum, which made Robert feel uncomfortable.

A large middle-aged man with bushy grey sideburns and a tartan waistcoat got to his feet with a cheerful smile. He resembled an overstuffed sofa.

'Sir Henry,' he beamed. 'Good to see you.' He turned to Robert with the assessing eye of the professional. 'And you must be Robert.'

'I am,' he retorted a little hostilely.

'No need to look so worried, I don't bite, unlike some of my patients.'

Robert thought this an odd statement but took the seat Campbell indicated.

'So, Robert,' said Campbell. 'Your stepfather tells me you've been having some problems.'

He just nodded, starting to feel embarrassed.

'Would you feel better talking if your father waited outside?'

'No, he can stay. He knows everything.'

'Very well, then. In your own time.'

Robert had expected to be relentlessly interrogated, but Campbell just stared at him expectantly.

'Well,' he slowly began, glancing at Henry, who gave him an encouraging nod. 'I've been having these fantasies.'

'What sort of fantasies?' prompted Campbell when he went silent.

'Violent ones,' he mumbled to the floor.

If this statement shocked Campbell, he certainly didn't show it. 'And what form does the violence take?'

Robert sighed. 'Do I have to spell it out?'

'If I'm to help, then yes.'

Another sigh. 'I imagine beating women,' he muttered. 'And they scream.'

'Have you actually lived out any of these fantasies?'

He shook his head, keeping in mind Henry's advice.

'Have you ever been tempted to beat your wife?'

His head snapped up. 'No, never.'

'How long have you been married?'

'Two months.'

'And when did these fantasies start?'

'I'm not sure, to be honest. They seemed to creep up on me, but I don't remember having them before I was sixteen.'

'You're seventeen now, soon to be eighteen?'

'Yes, in November.'

'Were you in a relationship with your wife when it started?'

'We've been friends since we were children, but yes, they started when we realised we were in love.'

Campbell nodded as though something made sense to him. 'Are you in good health?'

'Yes, very.'

'Any medical history?'

'None at all. I've always been fit and healthy.'

'And tell me, Robert – in your fantasies, what exactly do you do to the women?'

Robert took a deep breath when his heart started to thud with excitement. 'I beat them,' he replied, mumbling to the floor again.

'With your hands or an implement?'

Campbell spoke matter-of-factly and without embarrassment, which made Robert feel even more uncomfortable.

'With my hands. Sometimes with a big stick.'

'And in your fantasies, how does the woman react? Does she enjoy it or not?'

'She doesn't like it. She screams.'

'Do you like her screams, Robert?'

He nodded, keeping his eyes on the floor, unable to look either of them in the eye.

'In your fantasies, does the woman ever resemble anyone you know? Your mother or your wife, for instance?'

'Certainly not,' he snapped. 'She's just sort of faceless.'

'So it doesn't matter whether she's blonde, brunette, short, tall?'

'No.'

'So it's the screams that are important to you? Her reaction to your violence?'

Robert glanced at Henry, who was regarding him impassively. There was no judgement or disgust in his eyes and Robert felt some of the respect he'd lost for him returning. 'Yes,' he replied. 'The screams are important.'

'They arouse you?'

Robert's cheeks burned as he nodded.

'How are sexual relations between you and your wife?'

'That's private,' he scowled.

'I know I sound like I'm being nosy, Robert, but I need to establish if you're able to sustain a normal sexual relationship without the need for violence.'

'I am. I'd never do anything like that to Jane, it's always beautiful and tender between us.'

'So you're able to ejaculate without hearing the screams?'

Robert turned a violent shade of crimson, eyes glittering with outrage. 'Excuse me?'

'I can assure you that nothing will go beyond these four walls, Mr Alardyce,' said Campbell. 'And if it helps, I've heard much worse in my time. During the course of my career, I've been told things that would make your hair curl. This really is nothing and I can't help you unless I know everything. So please be as frank as you can.'

Robert looked to Henry, who nodded encouragingly. 'I have no trouble at all,' he sighed. 'We're trying for a baby and we're enjoying trying,' he said a little petulantly.

'That's good, Robert. So, you have healthy relations with your wife?'

'Yes, very much so.'

'Have you ever wanted to ask her if she could indulge your fantasies?'

'No, and I never would because she would never countenance it and because I could never hurt her, I love her so much.'

'Excellent,' he smiled. 'Well, I don't think there's much to worry about.'

'You don't?' said a surprised Henry.

'Not at all. I think these fantasies are Robert's way of learning to cope with becoming a man and all the new emotions and feelings that entails. You're recently married, master of your own home. Everything's very new and going it alone in the big wide world can be frightening. I'm not afraid to admit I found becoming sole provider for a wife and then my children rather daunting. Things have changed so rapidly, you're afraid of losing control, and these fantasies are your psyche's way of regaining control.'

'You don't go in for all that new-fangled nonsense about psyches and ids, do you?' frowned Robert.

'I most certainly do. The unconscious mind is a deep and mysterious thing that we are only starting to scratch the surface of. It uses symbolism to communicate to us our deepest fears and I believe that is what yours is doing. These fantasies are a way for you to reassert your masculinity and overcome the fear all the huge life changes you've gone through have stirred up. This is confirmed because it all started not long before you fell in love and with that came all the powerful urges of the adult male.'

'You're right, it did,' said Robert thoughtfully.

'The important thing is that you don't act on those impulses.'

'How do I do that?'

'With a vigorous physical regime that allows you to expend all your aggressive energy. What sports do you play?'

'I enjoy riding and hunting.'

'How often do you ride and hunt?'

'I used to do it all the time when I lived at Alardyce, but now I live in the city, hardly ever.'

'You need to get back into it on a regular basis.'

'He's always welcome at Alardyce to hunt and ride,' said Henry.

'Excellent,' said Campbell. 'And may I recommend a contact sport? Rugby and boxing are good ways to purge oneself of aggression. If you go for the latter, avoid the bare-knuckle fights. Marquess of Queensberry rules only.'

'Actually, I rather like the sound of boxing,' smiled Robert.

'Keep a diary of when these fantasies strike. Do they occur when you've not had any opportunity for physical exercise? Do they occur after eating certain foods or when you've been mentally aggravated? There may be a pattern you've not noticed, and if there is, then you might be able to stop the fantasies before they happen.'

Campbell's words buoyed Robert's hopes even more. If his father hadn't been Matthew Crowle, he would have been convinced he could overcome this. However, Campbell didn't know the whole story. His diagnosis might be very different if he knew he'd actually attacked three women and killed three people, including his own grandmother.

'Try to avoid over-using stimulants too, Robert,' said Campbell. 'Claret is good for the blood, but limit yourself to two glasses a day. Scotch is fine too, but everything in moderation. Eat plain, simple foods, lead a quiet, wholesome life and give yourself time to adjust to your new situation.'

'Yes, I will,' said Robert.

'Excellent. Any questions?'

'Er, I don't think so.'

'Right, well, on you go then.'

'That's it?'

'Yes, unless there's anything else you'd like to add?'

'No.'

Campbell got to his feet and extended his hand to him. 'It was a pleasure meeting you, Robert.'

'You too,' he replied, a little confused. 'Thank you,' he added, shaking his hand.

'Sir Henry,' said Campbell, shaking his hand too.

'Thank you for your time, Charles,' replied Henry.

'You're very welcome. I'm always here if you need me.'

'That's good to know.'

Henry and Robert left the office, neither of them speaking until they were back in the carriage.

'Well,' said Henry. 'What do you think of what he had to say?'

'Other than the embarrassment he put me through?' replied Robert.

'Yes, other than that.'

'I liked what he said about sports and avoiding stimulants. His words about losing control made sense to me. I know when I eloped with Jane I said I wanted to become a man, but I hadn't realised how overwhelming it would be. Growing up, I always had Mother to protect me, then you. I was so busy thinking of how wonderful it would be to strike out on my own that I hadn't considered the weight of responsibility. But what use are Campbell's recommendations? What would he have said if he'd known everything I've done?'

'Maybe he wouldn't have said anything different.'

'We both know that's not true. He would have called his orderlies and had me locked up in his asylum.'

'You don't know that.'

'The outcome of that appointment would have been very different had he known.'

'Perhaps. If you really feel the need, you could go back and tell him everything.'

'No, thank you.'

'Then you must take his advice – plenty of activity and lead a wholesome life.'

'I intend to. Did you mean what you said about me coming to Alardyce to ride and hunt?'

'Absolutely. We used to do that a lot together and I miss it.'

'As do I. I'd like to try boxing too. A man should learn how to defend himself properly.'

'Judging by what you did to Benjamin Richardson, you already know.'

'A scrawny fop is hardly a challenge.'

'Very well. You could try my boxing club.'

'You have a boxing club?'

'Yes. I was nineteen when I first joined.'

'I never knew that.'

'I could take you along as a guest and if you like the look of the place, you could become a member.'

'Could we go there now?' said Robert, excited at the thought.

'Yes, if you like.'

Henry wound down the window and redirected the driver to a street in the New Town.

'How good a boxer are you, Father?'

'Well, I'm not one to blow my own trumpet, but there were very few who could get the better of me in the ring.'

Now Robert understood why he'd always felt wary going up against Henry and how he'd knocked him onto his backside the one time he'd punched him. He could certainly use skills like that.

10

'Thank you, Rush,' smiled Amy as he placed the tea tray on the table beside the armchair she occupied in her sitting room, a book in her hands. Not that she'd managed to read a single word, she was too busy wondering how Henry was getting on with Robert.

'You're welcome, my lady,' he bowed. 'And may I say how glad I am to see you looking so much better. The air in the Lake District must have been very healing.'

'It was indeed. It's a beautiful part of the country. Have you ever been to the Lake District, Rush?'

'I've been to Riverwood on three occasions when the late Sir Alfred took me along. I found it a very restful place.'

'Then we must take you with us the next time we go. We're planning another trip in the summer, only you won't be working, you'll be relaxing.'

'My lady,' he said, scandalised. 'I really couldn't.'

'Oh, yes, you can and you will. When was the last time you had a holiday?'

'I had three days off last year when my sister passed away.'

'Then you're due another holiday. Think of it as a thank you for your service to us, particularly recently, when you cleaned up the conservatory after all that... unpleasantness.'

The unpleasantness in question was when she and Robert had been attacked by Hobbs – Matthew's right-hand man – and Robert had murdered him while he'd been lying injured on the floor. Henry and Robert had got rid of the body while Rush had cleaned up all the blood and he'd never mentioned it since.

'I don't require any reward for that, my lady. You and Sir Henry will always have my loyalty.'

Amy beamed at him. He was due to retire next year and she would be very sad to lose him. Henry had already gifted him a small cottage on the estate to live in rent-free for as long as he needed it. He would also be paid a very generous pension. He and Amy intended to look after him for the rest of his life, it was the least they could do.

'I know, Rush, but you deserve a holiday. Life shouldn't all be about duty and work. You should be able to relax and enjoy it too.'

'I enjoy my lot in life, particularly since you and Sir Henry took over Alardyce. It's such a happy, pleasant place now. Before, it was a house of darkness and shadows.'

'Yes, I remember,' she said quietly.

'I did want to tell you that Master Robert came here while you were away.'

'I know. He turned up at Riverwood with Jane.'

'Oh, my goodness. I'm so sorry, my lady, it's my fault for mentioning where you'd gone, but I couldn't bring myself to lie.'

'Of course not. You did the right thing, Rush. We actually ended up having a nice time together. It felt good to bring our son back to us again.'

'I'm very glad to hear that.'

'I really think Robert's turning a corner. He can be saved, I'm sure of it.'

'Yes, my lady,' was all he replied, but Rush knew that boy was beyond saving. He was as bad as Master Edward, he'd been just the same at Robert's age, before the evil had entirely swallowed him. The late Sir Alfred had moments of hope that his son could be redeemed, just as his mistress had about her own son. It made his old heart ache that she would have to endure the same pain when she finally realised her boy was doomed. 'Can I get you anything else?'

'No, thank you.'

His eyes flicked to the window. 'Sir Henry's home.' He couldn't help but smile at the way her eyes lit up. Whenever the late Sir Alfred came home, Lady Lenora would usually groan and roll her eyes.

Rush left to greet his master. A couple of minutes later, Henry strode into the sitting room and Amy rushed into his arms.

'How did it go?' she asked him.

'Very well. Robert responded favourably and decided to take on Dr Campbell's recommendations.'

'Such as?'

'Living a life of moderation, and he also suggested sports to allow Robert to vent his energy and aggression.'

'They sound like good recommendations, but will they be enough?'

'Only time will tell. I've already taken him to my boxing club at his request and he's become a member.'

'That does sound positive,' she smiled. 'And did Dr Campbell suspect he'd done anything more? I was afraid he'd link Robert to those attacks that have been reported in the newspapers.'

'I don't think so. He seemed to think it was all down to Robert's psyche attempting to regain control of a life that has got out of control due to all the recent changes – leaving home, getting married, becoming his own man.'

'That does make sense. My goodness, our boy could be saved.'

'Robert does seem very determined to curb his unnatural appetites. He's going to come to the estate to hunt and ride more, like we used to. Today it felt like I was getting my son back.'

'Oh, Henry,' she beamed, throwing her arms around his neck and kissing him.

'We will save him,' he said as she clung onto him. 'We will.'

* * *

Robert did indeed throw himself wholeheartedly into the suggestions Campbell had put forward. He attended the boxing club four times a week, in fact, he had a great flair for the sport. Twice a week, he'd head over to Alardyce to hunt and ride with Henry and the two began to rebuild their close relationship. When they had finished riding, Robert would return to the house with Henry to sit and talk with his mother for a while. Then he would go home to Jane to spend time with her, eating only plain foods and having just a glass of claret or a Scotch before retiring to bed early with his wife to continue trying to make their baby. He also managed to stay away from Vivienne's and his disreputable friends. On top of all that, his investments were all going well, and he made four thousand pounds in as many months.

Every night, before retiring to bed, he would write in his journal, dutifully noting the day's activities and everything he'd consumed. He was dismayed when, after two months, the fantasies still continued, but on the bright side, he had managed to stop himself from going on the prowl at night and, with nothing else happening, the news of the two attacks on the maids was quickly forgotten as more recent news took its place. In Auld Reekie, there was always something happening – murders, assaults, robberies, especially in the Old Town, which was populated by the poor, drunks and addicts while the wealthy hid away in the clean, elegant New Town.

Then came the day he and Jane had been waiting for – she discovered she was with child, four months after they married. A delighted Robert invited the whole family round for dinner to break the news. He invited Andrew too, as he'd been offended by Robert's recent lack of contact.

Andrew was the first to arrive, handing his hat and coat to the waiting butler before he was shown into the drawing room where Robert and Jane waited.

'I was starting to think you were avoiding me, Robert,' said Andrew, shaking his hand.

'Not at all,' he replied. 'Why would you think that?'

'Because I've hardly seen you. Hello, Jane, you look radiant, as always,' he added, kissing her cheek.

'Thank you, Andrew,' she replied. 'Would you like a drink?'

'Scotch, please,' he said, and the footman set about pouring his drink. 'So, am I the only guest or are we expecting company?'

'My family are joining us,' replied Robert.

His eyes lit up. 'Does that include your delightful mother?'

'It does and you'll behave yourself.'

'I don't know what you mean.'

'Oh, yes, you do.'

They were interrupted by the doorbell ringing and a minute later Lydia, John and Stephen tore into the room, hurling themselves at Robert and Jane. Amy and Henry followed them in, their smiles faltering when they saw Andrew standing by the fire cradling his whisky, a cheerful smile on his face.

'Hello,' he said. 'Lovely to see you all again.'

They responded with curt nods.

'Are you going to do some magic tricks, Andrew?' Lydia asked him.

'I will after dinner, if you really want. I've got a new one with a coin.'

'Can't you do it now?'

'Why not?' he smiled, producing a coin from his pocket, all three children gathering around to watch.

'Congratulations on your investment,' said Henry, shaking Robert's hand while Andrew amused the children with magic tricks. 'That is a massive amount of money to make, especially when you've only just started out in business.'

'We're very proud of you,' said Amy, kissing her son's cheek.

Robert beamed. This was the life he wanted – happiness, success and his parents liked him again.

'Robert is very clever,' said Jane, standing beside her husband.

He smiled down at her. 'Shall we tell them now? I can't wait a second longer.'

'Yes, why not?' she smiled back.

'If I could have everyone's attention, please,' he called.

Andrew had just finished his magic trick, the three children applauding before turning to face their brother.

'We were going to announce this at dinner,' said Robert, wrapping an arm around Jane. 'But I can't keep it in any longer. I'm very happy to announce that Jane is with child.'

'Oh, that's wonderful,' beamed Amy. 'Congratulations,' she said, kissing Jane's cheek before hugging her son.

'Yes, really wonderful news,' said Henry, shaking his stepson's hand.

'With child?' repeated a confused Lydia. 'What does that mean?'

'It means I'm going to have a baby,' replied Jane.

Lydia clapped excitedly while her brothers still looked puzzled.

'For dinner?' said John.

'What a disturbing notion,' commented Andrew.

'I have a baby growing inside my tummy,' said Jane, pressing a hand to her abdomen.

'How did it get there?'

'There's a question for your parents,' smiled Andrew, sipping his Scotch.

'Your brother put it there,' Henry told John.

'Robert or Stephen?' he replied.

'Robert,' he quickly replied while Andrew chuckled.

'How did he put it there?'

Henry's mouth opened and closed as he became increasingly flustered, Andrew grinning like a Cheshire cat.

'I'll tell you when you're older,' was his reply.

'Why?'

'Because it's grown-up knowledge.'

'Why?'

'The curious minds of the young,' smiled Andrew. 'How about another magic trick, children?'

Henry exhaled with relief when John turned his attention to Andrew. At least the reptile was of some earthly use.

After dinner, they retreated into the large private garden at the back of the house for drinks, the evening dry and mild.

'Andrew is surprisingly good with children,' said Amy, her arm linked through Robert's as they watched him run around the garden with the boys, Lydia eagerly chatting to Jane about the baby.

'I know you have a low opinion of him, but he does have some good qualities,' replied Robert.

'I'm unwilling to condemn someone so young. We all make poor decisions in our youth.' She glanced sideways at him. 'And I am not referring to you, darling.'

'I know,' he smiled, patting her hand. 'You seem much more comfortable around me now. It feels like how it used to be between us.'

'Doesn't it?' she smiled. 'That's because you're much happier, much lighter. The darkness that seemed to live inside you has lifted.'

'I feel so much better. All those urges are still there, I won't lie to you, but they don't rule me any more. With everything going on, I hardly have time to even think about them. I'm really enjoying boxing too. It relieves a lot of my frustration.'

'I'm so proud of how far you've come. You're very strong. I knew you could beat it, and now you're going to be a father.'

'I can't wait,' he smiled, gazing at Jane.

'You'll be a wonderful father, you're a natural with your brothers and sister, they adore you. Everything's going to be all right.'

It sounded like she was telling herself that as much as him, but he decided not to comment on it. Finally, they felt to be back to how they used to be, and he loved it.

Andrew was the essence of propriety, remaining polite to Robert's family and refraining from flirting with Amy, although he did continue to admire her from afar, particularly her misshapen hands. How he adored them. He would love nothing more than to stroke and caress them and for them to touch him in turn. He lapsed into this pleasant daydream while standing in the garden. The children had given him some respite and he watched Lady Alardyce, who appeared rather ethereal in the fading light, which highlighted all the varying colours in her hair. Unfortunately, Lydia noticed the shiver of pleasure that ran through his body.

'Are you cold, Andrew?' she asked him.

The sound of her voice snapped him out of it. 'I'm very well thank you, Lady Lydia.'

'Silly Andrew, I'm not a lady,' she grinned before mercifully abandoning him to his thoughts.

Andrew ensured he was the last to leave so he could talk to Robert in private. Henry seemed rather reluctant to leave his stepson alone in his company, but he had little choice, as Robert was master of this house.

Jane retired to bed after the family had left, leaving the two men alone
to talk.

'I do hope your china doll didn't retire early to escape my company?'
Andrew asked Robert once they were alone together by the fire in the
latter's study.

'Not at all,' he replied. 'The pregnancy just means she tires more
easily.'

'Well, I have to say well done, Robert,' said Andrew, leaning forward in
his seat to clink his whisky glass against the one his friend held. 'You have
everything you ever dreamed of – Jane carrying your child, your own
home, wealth and success.'

'Thank you.'

Andrew tilted his head to one side. 'But it's still not enough, is it?'

'What do you mean?'

'I read about those attacks in the papers on those two maids. That was
you, wasn't it?' The corner of his mouth lifted into a smile when his friend
failed to reply. 'You don't want to admit it out loud and I can certainly
understand that, but I know it was you. It seems getting all you ever desired
hasn't cured you.'

'I'm doing much better. The urge to attack has gone, although the
fantasies still remain.'

'As long as they remain in your head and don't intrude on your physical
life, I suppose that would be all right. What brought about this sudden
change?'

'I spoke to a professional. I didn't give him all the details, of course, but
he gave me some advice that has proved to be effective.'

'Such as?'

'Taking up sports to rid me of some of my aggression, so I took up
boxing, which I'm enjoying and have a flair for. I also go out hunting and
riding more. Plain foods, minimal alcohol, that sort of thing.'

'Sounds rather dull.'

'Well, it's not, and it's working. Hopefully all that's behind me now.'

'And was avoiding me part of your good doctor's advice?'

'No, but avoiding the brothels was. I'm sorry if it seems like I was
avoiding you, but we always met at Vivienne's and I couldn't risk going

back there. That's why I invited you here tonight to share in our good news, so you'd know that you are still very much my good friend.'

'And I appreciate that. It's been a very pleasant evening.'

'I noticed you didn't flirt with my mother as you used to.'

'Because I didn't think it would be very well received.' What he didn't add was that the memory of her knee connecting sharply with his groin had never left him and he had no wish for a repeat performance. 'I'm glad I acted so prudently now I know you've taken up boxing, but I do still greatly esteem that majestic woman.'

'And her hands too?' frowned Robert. 'I noticed you kept looking at them when we were at the dining table.'

'Her hands are just some of the many parts that I admire about her. Don't glower at me, Robert, I mean no offence. Anyway, you've broken poor April's heart. Every time I go to Vivienne's, she asks if I've seen you. Your absence is driving the girl to distraction.'

'She'll have to get used to my absence because I'm never going back. I mean it,' he added when Andrew raised a sceptical eyebrow.

'Whatever you say,' he smiled, taking a sip of whisky. 'So, your lovely wife fulfils all your needs?'

'Of course. I need no one else.'

'You do know that when a woman gets heavy with child, sex is the last thing on her mind, and for quite a while after the birth too. Some women never want it ever again if the ordeal of childbirth is too much.'

'Stop it, Andrew.'

'Stop what?'

'Stop putting obstacles before me that don't exist.'

'I'm doing nothing of the sort. I'm simply preparing you. Forewarned is forearmed, isn't that how the saying goes? You must prepare a contingency if it does occur because I fear your darker compulsions may well overtake you if you have no outlet for your desires.'

'I only want Jane,' said Robert firmly.

'Yes, you've already said, but a man has the right to indulge in his manly desires and if his wife, for whatever reason, is incapable of accommodating him, then he has the right to seek it elsewhere.'

'I can imagine my mother's reaction if you said that in front of her.'

'Your mother is ahead of her time. One day, things will change, but as they stand now, you have that right.'

'I want to be true to Jane.'

'It's a bit late for that, you've already been untrue. A little more won't do any harm. Just think about it, Robert. A visit to Vivienne's establishment might be worth it if it stops you from taking up your bad habits again. It's certainly the lesser of two evils.'

'Yes, thank you for your advice,' sighed Robert. 'Now can we please change the subject?'

'Very well. I have news of my own – I took my exams and passed with flying colours.'

'That's wonderful. Congratulations,' said Robert, raising his glass in a toast. 'So you're officially a sawbones?'

'I am so much more than a blood-soaked sot with a saw,' sniffed Andrew. 'I'm a member of the Royal College of Surgeons. So, if you ever need something lopping off, I'm your man. I'm also particularly interested in hygiene reform.'

'Isn't that hypocritical, coming from a man who spends most of his time in a brothel?'

'Not most of my time, actually, and they're the ideal places to start. The spread of venereal disease is an absolute scourge and the treatments damaging and downright dangerous. Just think how wonderful it would be if we could not only control the spread of infection but eradicate it altogether, specifically syphilis and gonorrhoea.'

'So you're saying all the time you spend at Vivienne's is actually research for the betterment of mankind?'

'Exactly.' He frowned when Robert snorted.

'I don't want to finish off a lovely evening discussing venereal disease,' said Robert.

'Fine, let's change the subject. I heard about what you did to Benjamin Richardson.'

'Hasn't everyone?' said Robert, lips curling into a smile at the memory.

'I know that cretin of old. We have sparred in the past. All I'll say is watch your back. He will want revenge and he's a sly snake who may try to take it in an unexpected way.'

'You're full of grim warnings. It's very depressing.'

'I'm sorry, but I would hate to see you ruin this nice life you've built for yourself.'

'That won't happen. Everything's under control.'

'Just ensure it stays that way. The worst falls always come when you're flying highest.'

11

As the months passed, Jane's belly swelled with child. Despite all Robert's fears, her pregnancy progressed smoothly, other than some morning sickness in the early months. Robert hadn't thought his wife could be any more beautiful, but as she neared the end of her pregnancy, she transcended from a mere mortal into a glorious goddess-like figure who he felt he didn't deserve. He wanted to protect her and their child from the whole world. It was a relief when she finally went into confinement.

Jane wanted to go into confinement at Alardyce rather than remain in the city, although that would have been more usual; the Alardyces were never ones for convention and Jane wanted the comfort of her Aunt Amy. She had also decided that she wanted Magda Magrath to attend her rather than a male doctor. Having a renowned witch in attendance was another substantial breach of etiquette, but after two of her friends in London had died in childbirth with supposedly renowned medical men present, she decided to put the well-being of herself and her child before convention.

Although Robert loathed the witch because she could see his darker half, he knew she was a miracle worker who had saved his mother's life.

When Jane was just two weeks off giving birth, she and Robert temporarily shut up their townhouse and moved back to Alardyce, taking only the valet and lady's maid with them. Robert's old bedroom had been prepared to receive them. Amy had gifted Jane her own lightweight bed for the birth. It was tradition to pass the birthing beds on to the next generation.

They arrived at Alardyce just in time for Christmas and there was an air of excitement. The entire household, the servants included, were looking forward to welcoming the new addition to the family. Amy watched Robert very carefully. He seemed more thrilled than anyone, taking such tender care of his wife it brought tears to her eyes. How could a real monster behave like that? Finally, she thought he'd overcome his demons.

Robert, however, was hiding a secret. As she was so heavy with child, Jane no longer felt like sex, something Robert respected. To him, in her state, she was too exalted to indulge in such a base pleasure, even if it was a way for them to express their love. She would allow him to hold her in his arms and shower her with kisses but anything more was beyond her, and they both knew it would be that way for several weeks after the birth.

Andrew's words came back to haunt Robert as his dark urges started to rise again. Fortunately, Rush had maintained the tradition of hiring only the plainest maids, so there was no temptation there. Jane's own personal maid was very pretty, until she opened her mouth to reveal crooked yellow teeth that made him feel nauseous, so there was no temptation there either. His fantasies were becoming even more violent and he would dream about them, jumping awake in the middle of the night bathed in sweat and with an erection. The sight of his angel fast asleep beside him would soothe him and he would settle back down, gently stroking her swollen belly, but he knew if he didn't do something soon, it would slip out of his control again.

* * *

'Robert, calm down,' yelled a deep, savage voice. 'For Christ's sake, someone pull him off him before he kills him.'

Strong arms wrapped around Robert's chest and he was hauled backwards across the ring away from his opponent, who was a bloodied mess on the canvas.

Robert struggled to get back at him, desperate to unleash more of his pent-up frustration, but he was dragged out of the ring. He only started to calm down when he was staring up into the mashed, scarred face of Jackson Kinnaird, an ex-professional boxer who had set up this particular club. Robert was ashamed of his behaviour as he genuinely respected and admired this man who had taught him so much and who had complimented his skill.

'You calm now?' barked Jackson.

'Yes, sir,' replied Robert. 'Sorry, I got... carried away.'

'What the fuck's up with you?' Jackson had never let the fact that only gentlemen attended his club mellow his rough language and harsh ways. Once he'd even struck a duke for backchatting him. He cared naught for wealth and class, which was another reason why Robert so admired him. Jackson didn't care that his father had been a footman.

'I needed to vent some of my frustration,' said Robert.

'Frustration?' snapped Jackson before understanding crept across his face. 'Your missus is up the spout, isn't she?'

'She's due to give birth in a couple of weeks.'

'Now I get it. Well, take my advice, son, and piss off to a brothel to get rid of all your frustration,' he said, mashed lips curling into a leer.

'I can't do that to Jane.'

'If she cannae gi'e it to you then someone has to before I end up scraping brains off my nice canvas. Now piss off out of it and don't come back until you've emptied yourself into some wee lassie.'

Jackson's massive hand clamped down on the back of his neck and propelled him towards the door. 'You're no' the first man I've had to do this to, it's for your own good. And fucking nice right hook by the way, you made me proud,' he said before shoving him through the door into the changing room.

After leaving the boxing club, Robert prowled the streets, his dark fantasies growing in his mind. He glanced at women he passed by, imagining their backs striped bright red and bleeding, their screams filling his ears as they uselessly struggled beneath him. He was tempted to visit Dr Campbell, but he was too afraid of him seeing the evil that dwelt in his heart and throwing him into his hospital. Neither could he confide in his parents. He didn't want to pollute Alardyce with his putrid thoughts, it was where his angel was going to give birth to their child.

The urges swept through his body, making his fingers twitch, stirring feelings in his breast and belly so potent he wished he could plunge his hand inside himself and pluck them out. As thoughts of screams and blood whirled more violently in his head, he realised there was no choice, he had to relieve his frustration, but he resolved to keep the violence locked up inside himself. He would not release that on another woman.

He wound his way to Vivienne's and experienced some sadness as he gazed up at the grey stone frontage of the brothel. He'd done so well and now he was left with no choice, but it was for the greater good. If he didn't do this, then he would do something worse to an innocent woman and he refused to lose his nice life.

The middle of the afternoon was a quiet time for the brothel, although Corrigan was still on guard duty, looking as angry and scarred as ever. He nodded once sharply at Robert as he entered the establishment. Due to the hour, not even Vivienne was there to greet him and it was Corrigan's gruff call that beckoned her out of her parlour.

'Robert,' she beamed, looking as stunning as ever in her traditional crimson dress, fiery hair piled atop her head. 'It's been a while since we saw you.'

'Is April in?' he said quickly.

She frowned. 'Robert, you're sweating. Are you all right?'

'Is April in?' he repeated more urgently.

'No, sorry. Her mother's sick, so she's gone to look after her. Millie's in, though.'

'I don't want her,' he replied. With her blonde curls and blue eyes, her resemblance to Jane would make him uncomfortable.

'In that case, I'm afraid that only leaves me. Don't get upset, Corrigan,' she added when the doorman growled. 'Robert's one of my best customers. Besides, I'm curious after April's been singing his praises.' She looked back at Robert. 'Would I do for you?'

He grabbed her and kissed her, thrusting his tongue into her mouth, which she eagerly received.

'You'll do,' he breathed, taking her hand and pulling her into her parlour.

'Robert, calm down,' she told him when he started tugging up her skirts and pulling the pins from her hair.

The authority in her voice was such that he obeyed.

'I'm sorry,' he said. 'But Jane's heavy with child and it's been so long...'

Understanding filled her eyes. 'Ah, I see. Don't worry, it's perfectly normal for you to feel this way. I've attended to a lot of gentlemen in a similar state over the years.'

'The thoughts in my head,' he practically gasped. 'They're becoming so wild, I can barely see straight.' He decided not to tell her what those thoughts were because he didn't want her to send him away. Vivienne did not tolerate violence against herself or any of her girls. Anyone who broke this rule ended up smashed on the pavement by Corrigan. Despite his new boxing skills, Robert knew he was no match for that animal.

He thought he might faint with longing when Vivienne removed her dress, so she was naked before him. She might have been older than all her girls, but she was still so beautiful with the full breasts and curvaceous hips that he loved, fiery hair tumbling down her back.

Desperately he kissed her and pushed her back onto the bed while opening his trousers. Vivienne gasped as he slammed into her, running her fingers through his hair as he kissed her breasts.

'I see what April means,' she groaned beneath him as she became warmer and wetter. 'Oh, my,' she cried.

Corrigan was alarmed when he heard Vivienne scream. He raced down the hall and kicked open her parlour door to reveal her splayed on the bed, Robert between her thighs, both of them panting and covered in sweat.

'Please don't alarm yourself, Corrigan,' she called to him as Robert continued to kiss her breasts, unconcerned by the intruder. 'Believe me when I say that was a cry of pleasure.'

Corrigan glared at Robert, who raised his head to smile at him, mocking in his eyes. He left, slamming the door shut behind him.

'You should work for me, Robert,' breathed Vivienne, running her hand across his chest. 'We'd make a fortune. That's a real gift you've got.'

'I was taught by the best,' he smiled, kissing her before getting to his feet.

'Going so soon?' she purred as he started pulling on his clothes.

'I have to get home.'

'Feel free to stay longer. It'll be on the house.'

'Sorry, I can't. I don't want to be away from Jane for long.'

'Don't feel bad,' she said when his eyes filled with guilt. 'You're only fulfilling a need, one that is as vital as eating and breathing. You're not the first gentleman to do the same and you certainly won't be the last.'

'I want to ask you something,' he said as he pulled up his trousers. 'Does Benjamin Richardson come here?'

'I heard about your altercation with him at that ball.'

'How did you hear about that?'

'Your friends told me and no, he doesn't, although I do know that he frequents a discreet house in the Old Town, one that caters for men with different needs.'

He regarded her with interest. 'What do you mean by different needs?'

'It's a place for men who enjoy the company of other men.'

Robert's lips curled into an evil smile. If Benjamin did try to humiliate him again, he now had the perfect way to destroy him. 'Thank you, Vivienne,' he said, pulling on his coat. 'You were wonderful, as always.'

'Keep it,' she said when he placed some money on her dressing table. 'It's been a long time since I felt like that. Are you sure you can't stay longer?' she said, cupping his crotch when he bent over to kiss her.

'I'm sure. I feel much better,' he said before donning his hat and leaving.

Robert inhaled the air as he walked down the street. Some of the torment had eased, but not entirely. The thoughts still whirled around his head and he felt the heat in his blood start to rise again.

He turned onto a quieter residential street lined with fine townhouses. A young woman was coming towards him. Judging by her clothes, she was in service – respectable looking but slightly shabby. She caught him looking her way and smiled, appreciative of his dark good looks. Robert's hands curled into fists as the blood thundered in his head, the dark thoughts swirling faster, the screams echoing in his head...

The woman's smile fell and her eyes widened. She turned and rushed back the way she'd come, constantly glancing over her shoulder. Robert thought he must look wild, the madness in his brain reflected on his face.

'No,' he rasped to himself. He was doing so well, and he refused to go down that dark path again.

He rushed back to the main road and hailed a cab to take him to Alardyce, yelling at the driver to hurry.

The journey was torturous as he resisted his dark urges with everything he had. Rather than head to the house, he told the driver to drop him off in the village and he practically ran up the path to Magda's cottage, praying she was in.

Before he could reach the door, something large leapt out in front of him and he found himself face to face with a huge white wolf. One of its eyes was green, the other blue. Its lips were drawn back over its teeth, and it was growling.

He was relieved when the front door opened and Magda strode out, silver hair flowing behind her.

'Robert,' she smiled. 'I had a feeling you'd come.'

'I know we haven't always seen eye to eye, Magda, but I really need your help.'

'So I see,' she said, noting the way he constantly shifted from foot to foot, the perspiration on his brow despite the cold weather. She opened the door wider. 'Come in.'

'Er,' he said, pointing to the wolf.

'Let him pass, Fenrir.'

The wolf moved, even though he kept growling and snarling, those disturbing eyes locked on Robert as he sidled past the beast and inside. He breathed a sigh of relief when Magda closed the door behind him, leaving the animal outside.

'Isn't it a bit dangerous having a wolf for a pet?' he asked her.

'I hand-reared Fenrir from a cub. He's my companion and friend, not a pet. No one dare break in here with him on guard duty.'

She led him into her parlour, which was neat and tidy, the fire roaring. It looked like any country cottage.

'Expecting cauldrons and jars of foetuses, were you?' said Magda, noting his surprise.

'To be honest, yes.'

'Please sit,' she said, indicating the couch with an amused smile.

'Thank you,' he replied, slamming himself down onto the cushions, wringing his hands together.

She sat in the armchair opposite him and peered at him with her unnerving silver eyes. Her stare was so intense, he started to pine for the wolf.

'I see the darkness rising inside you again, Robert,' she said.

'I'm fighting it, but I think I'm losing.'

She looked down at his big hands flexing and unflexing. 'So it would seem.'

'It's because Jane's not able to... be intimate. I've managed for months, and boxing and hunting helped, but it's not working any more.'

'You've just come from a prostitute, haven't you?'

'What? No, I...'

'Don't lie to me. Your energy reeks of the brothel.'

'My energy?' he frowned.

'Don't worry, Jane and your parents won't be able to spot it. My gifts allow me to see deeper than everyone else.'

'Fine, you're right, but I was desperate. I was thrown out of my boxing club for beating someone to a pulp and the owner told me to go and see someone who could... alleviate the frustration.'

'But it didn't work.'

'Not really. I went for a walk afterwards and I saw this woman and... my blood started getting up again. Just the look on my face scared her and she ran off.'

'I'm not surprised. You really have no idea how wild you look when the urge rises.'

'You have to help me, Magda. I don't want to let my family down. Everything's going so well. Don't you have some potion that can help?'

'If I did, I would have given it to you months ago.'

He leapt to his feet and started to pace. 'Just something to ease the torment, to stop these thoughts going around my head,' he hissed, thumping at his forehead with his knuckles. 'Maybe some herbs or something?'

'I fear this is beyond herbs.'

He stopped pacing to look at her. 'What can I do?'

'Jane's not going to be physically ready for intimacy for at least another five weeks.'

'Five weeks? I can't go that long.' He closed his eyes, recalling the feel of his wife's bare skin against his, her hands running through his hair and down his back. 'Only when I'm with her like that do I know true peace.'

'She is a special woman. Why is it that only she can give you peace?'

'Because I love her so much.'

'That's certainly part of it, but could it also be because of what you went through together at Huntington Manor?'

'No. It's because she's the most beautiful and wonderful woman in the world.'

'Yes, I'm sure she is, but think about it, Robert – she was Matthew's niece, by marriage, of course. She lived with him, knew him...'

'I do not love her just because of that,' he retorted.

'Of course not, but you feel peace with her because she makes you feel close to the one thing you can never be near to again but that you long for – your real father.'

'That's not true,' he thundered, looming over her.

Magda looked up at him calmly. 'Your eyes have gone very black again, Robert. We're close to that pulsating wound inside you, a wound that was recently ripped wide open, making your condition worse. What caused that?'

The cold haughtiness returned. 'My sainted mother killed Matthew. Edward put the knife in him, but she tore it out and he bled to death.' He cocked his head to one side. 'Does that not shock you, Magda?'

'Why should it?'

'Because she's a killer.'

'People who live in glass houses shouldn't throw stones.'

'What's that supposed to mean?'

'You've taken life, more than once.'

'Whoever told you that is lying.'

'No one told me anything. No one needs to tell me. Remember, I see things deeper than other people. Anyway, the who and the why isn't important. Matthew's gone and he's not coming back, but you're still here.'

'And you won't tell anyone what you know?'

'What do I know? Nothing. I have no details and I'll thank you to remember that I'm not like the old fishwives around here who gossip about every little thing. I carry many secrets in my heart and I have never broken a confidence yet.'

Robert recalled that he wanted this woman's help and that his wife needed her to deliver their child safely, so he gave her a stiff bow. 'Forgive me, Magda.'

'No need to apologise.'

'But how do I rid myself of this urge? Even now, the screams echo in my head, the nagging frustration, the ache in my body... it's intolerable.'

'Actually, I have something that may help,' she said, getting to her feet. 'The effects will only be temporary, but it should alleviate the symptoms for a little while.'

'Oh, thank you. I would be most appreciative of anything you can do...'

He went silent, eyes bulging as her knee connected sharply with his groin. With a gasp, he sank to his knees.

'What did you do that for?' he managed to rasp when he could speak again.

'Do you still have the urge to attack a woman?'

He shook his head, skin pale. He was sweating again but for a very different reason.

'There's the temporary relief you were so desperate for.'

'I think I'm going to be sick.'

She retrieved a pot from the kitchen and placed it on the floor beside him.

Magda retook her seat and picked up her book. 'Let me know when you're able to stand again.'

With a groan, he collapsed onto his side, hands cupping his crotch.

Ten minutes later, Robert was able to drag himself onto the couch, where he sat looking pale and nauseous.

'Feeling better?' smiled Magda, putting down her book.

'I thought you were supposed to be a healer?'

'I healed you of your urge, didn't I? And you did say you were willing to try anything.'

'I'd no idea you were going to physically assault me.'

She studied him thoughtfully before replying. 'I want you to listen to me very carefully, Robert – these urges, they're the manifestation of a deeper darkness that dwells inside you, a darkness you inherited from your father. For now, Jane is enough to fend it off, but one day she won't be. When that day comes, you must be prepared to leave everyone and everything you love.'

'What? I will never do that.'

'You must. It's the only way to protect them from what you will become.'

'And what's that?'

'A monster, like Matthew Crowle.'

'That will not happen.'

'It already is. The shadows gather around you, Robert. You've welcomed them into your heart, you did that when you took a life, and you can never go back.'

He leapt to his feet, grimacing as pain shot through his groin and he was forced to take a few deep breaths before speaking. 'I refuse to go down that path. My life is perfect and I will do nothing to damage that.'

'Perhaps you're right. Perhaps you have a strength Matthew didn't possess.'

'What are you doing?' he said when she held out her hand to him.

'I do have some ability to see into the future. If you don't believe me, ask your mother. Unfortunately, my warning wasn't enough to save her, but it might help you.'

He stared uncertainly at her outstretched hand. 'You're not going to hit me again, are you?'

'I promise you'll be perfectly safe.'

Reluctantly he took her hand. Instantly warmth pulsated out of her and into him, racing up his arm and into his body.

'Everything is so dark,' she said in a voice that sounded several octaves below her own. 'The fire blazes through my body. Pain and fire are all I know. I can hear her but she's becoming fainter. I'm being taken from her and I can't stop it,' she wailed, voice filled with anguish.

Magda released his hand and slumped back into her chair, gasping for breath.

'I've never felt anything like that before,' she whispered, her eyes wide. 'It felt like I was really there.'

Robert recognised something he never thought he'd see in Magda's eyes – fear. The sight caused his excitement to spike, the dark thoughts overtaking the shock of her pronouncement.

Magda saw the way his eyes darkened, the curl of his lips, the way he tilted his head down, like a predator surveying its prey, and she wiped the emotion from her eyes. 'You think that fear belongs to me, do you Robert? Well, it doesn't. I fear nothing. The fear I felt was your own.'

'Sounds like a flimsy excuse to me, Magda,' he said, lips drawing back over his teeth.

She snatched up a hand mirror from the table beside her and held it out to him. Robert was so stunned by his own reflection that all the dark thoughts were forgotten.

'You see what dwells inside you?' she said, rising to her feet, still holding out the mirror.

He moved with her, taking a step back, the pain in his groin seemingly forgotten as the two halves of himself waged war inside him.

'You still have a chance to get off the path you chose when you took a life,' she said, lowering the mirror. 'Your salvation lies in the love in your heart for your family. Take refuge in it, nurture it and reject the darkness.'

'I try to reject it, but it won't leave me.'

'Your dark thoughts aren't out of control. You dream them because you enjoy them. Stop trying to deny the fact, accept it and remove the power they have over you.'

'You're babbling, old woman. I'm leaving before you infect me with your madness.'

'How can I when you're riddled with your own?'

He glowered at her over his shoulder before limping to the door.

'Let him pass, Fenrir,' she called when he opened the door to the growling wolf.

She stood at the door with the wolf, both of them watching Robert, who was trying to make a dignified exit but was hampered by the pain in his crotch.

'I know,' murmured Magda, stroking Fenrir's soft head. 'Unfortunately, there's nothing more we can do. That boy is mired in darkness. Such a shame in one so young. Still, he might surprise us. As long as he doesn't reject his loved ones, he may yet be saved, but I fear Amy Alardyce is in for a lot more heartache.'

12

Jane went into labour a week later, her waters breaking in the middle of the night. An anxious Robert tore open the bedroom door and yelled for his parents to come and help before rushing back to his wife and taking her hand.

'Robert, I'm scared,' said Jane.

'Don't be,' he replied. 'I'm here and I won't leave your side.'

'You promise? Because I know the husband isn't supposed to be at the birth. Convention dictates...'

'To the devil with convention. I won't leave you.'

'Thank you,' she breathed before releasing a cry of agony.

Robert had never been so pleased to see his mother. She rushed into the room, her hair in a long plait, a shawl around her shoulders. She was joined by Esther, who had arrived with William and the twins a few days ago in anticipation of the birth.

'It's all right, sweetheart,' Amy told Jane. 'I've sent one of the servants to fetch Magda in the carriage. She won't be long.'

'What if the baby comes before she arrives?' said Robert.

'That won't happen. Childbirth can be a long, hard process. Now try to keep as calm as you can, Jane, and breathe. We won't leave your side, you're perfectly safe.'

'She's right,' said Esther, standing beside her. 'I was in labour almost all day with the boys.'

Their calm, experienced tones soothed Jane and she started to settle down. 'Please don't send Robert away. He said he'd stay with me.'

'We won't send him anywhere,' smiled Esther, stroking her hair back off her face.

'Henry was with me for all three births,' said Amy. 'You know we care nothing for convention in this house.'

'Thank you,' Jane said, eyes wide with fear and pain.

Contrary to what Amy and Esther had said, the birth moved swiftly and by the time Magda arrived, the labour was well underway.

'How are we doing, Jane?' she smiled, plonking her big black bag down on the floor and leaning over to examine her patient.

'Can you give her something for the pain?' said a stricken Robert, clinging onto his wife's hand as she writhed on the bed, crying and moaning.

'Certainly. I have a preparation ready,' she said, opening the bag and producing a vial. 'A glass, please.'

Amy snatched one up off the bedside table, tipped out the water it contained and handed it to her.

Magda poured the contents of the vial into the glass and held it out to Jane. 'Drink.'

'Is that it?' said Robert. 'Don't you carry chloroform?'

'No, I do not,' retorted Magda. 'It's an outrageous thing to give a pregnant woman, it can damage the baby. My potion, however, is entirely natural and will cause no harm to mother or child.'

'I took this preparation myself during all three of my labours,' said Amy. 'Trust me when I say it works.'

'Give it to me,' rasped Jane, snatching the glass from Magda's hand and drinking it down. Within two minutes, her writhing and cries had ceased and she rested easier on the bed.

'All right, Jane,' said Magda, looking between her splayed legs. 'It won't be long now. You need to start pushing.'

Twenty minutes later, Jane pushed the tiny body into Magda's waiting arms and a loud cry filled the air.

'Congratulations,' said Magda. 'You have a healthy girl.'

'A girl?' said Robert. He closed his eyes with relief. 'Thank God.'

His eyes eagerly snapped open and he moved around Magda to get a closer look. The crying child with sparse blonde hair was covered in blood and birth fluids, but he'd never seen anything more beautiful.

Magda expertly cut the cord and wrapped up the child before placing her in her mother's arms.

'Hello, beautiful girl,' breathed Jane, tears filling her eyes. 'Welcome to the family.'

'Well done, both of you,' said Amy. She looked to Esther, who couldn't speak because she was so choked with joyful tears. Jane was her niece, but Esther had raised her because her parents had died when she was very young, so she was like a daughter to her.

Robert sat on the bed beside his wife and kissed her forehead. 'You did so well,' he said. 'Can I hold her?'

Magda gently took the baby from Jane's arms and placed her in his. He went rigid, terrified of dropping or damaging the child, but the love that swelled in his heart told him he hadn't yet become the monster Magda had said he might. Perfect peace filled his heart, and it was a relief to realise that this tiny bundle might be the one to save him.

'Have you decided on a name?' said Magda.

'Emily Clare Alardyce,' replied Jane. Her eyes started closing with exhaustion, but she forced them open, not wanting to miss a second of this precious moment. 'Clare was my mother's name.'

'It's a lovely name,' said Magda. 'Would you permit me to bless her?'

'Please do.'

Magda muttered something under her breath and waved her hands over the baby. 'She is protected from any negative energies. The first year is a vulnerable time for a child.'

None of them even blinked at what would have been called witchery by anyone else. All three of them found it reassuring. Only Esther found it a little odd, but because she knew of Magda's excellent reputation, she didn't comment.

'I'll give the family the happy news,' said Amy. 'They'll be on tenter-hooks.' She smiled at the sight of Robert and Jane together with their new baby, they looked so happy. She imprinted the image on her memory, it was one she never wanted to forget.

'Well done, sweetheart,' said Esther, kissing first Jane on the cheek and then Robert.

The last time Esther and William had seen Robert, they'd argued furiously. Robert had even threatened William, but they'd repaired their relationship and now all was harmonious again.

The two women quietly left the room and padded downstairs to the drawing room where Henry and William paced. The children – including the twins – had heard the noise and had got up too, all five of them looking pale and worried. The nanny was with them, her large round body encased in a tartan dressing gown, long snowy hair in plaits, a nightcap on her head. Rush was also in attendance in his dressing gown, placing a tea tray on the table.

'Jane's given birth to a girl,' Amy told them. 'Both mother and baby are fine.'

The children all let up a cheer while Henry pulled Amy into his arms.

'May I be the first to offer my congratulations?' said Rush.

'Thank you so much,' smiled Amy.

'What does she look like?' said Lydia. 'Is she cute or is she funny and squashed?'

Esther laughed. 'She's beautiful, with blonde hair and blue eyes, just like her mother, and a tiny mouth like a rosebud.'

'When can we see her?'

'In the morning.'

Lydia pouted. 'But I want to see her now.'

'Well, you can't,' said Amy. 'Jane's exhausted and they both need their rest. Go back to bed and you can meet her tomorrow, I promise.'

'Well, all right,' she sighed.

The nanny managed to shepherd the children out of the room and upstairs.

'Would you like some tea, my lady?' Rush asked.

'I'll pour, thank you, Rush,' said Amy. 'Could you arrange for some to be taken up to Robert and Jane? They'll be parched. Some sandwiches too, and give Magda whatever she wants, she certainly earned it.'

'I'll get Mrs Clapperton to arrange it.'

'She's awake too?'

'All the live-in servants are gathered together in the kitchen, my lady. We've all been anxious about this day. We wanted to be available in case we were needed.'

'That's very kind of you all,' said Henry. 'Give everyone, including yourself, 20 per cent extra in their wages this week for their loyalty and in celebration of the new arrival.'

'That is most generous of you, sir, thank you.'

'How was Robert?' Henry asked Amy when Rush had gone. 'He didn't faint, did he?' he added with an impish smile.

'No, he didn't,' she smiled back. 'He was wonderful, actually, a real rock for Jane. The love in his eyes for his wife and child gave me such hope.'

'He's been doing really well lately. This could be the impetus he needs to stay on the straight and narrow.'

'I admit he did surprise me in there,' said Esther. 'He wasn't lying when he said he loves Jane. Marriage has certainly matured him.'

'He's done very well,' said Henry. 'He has an excellent head for business too. I anticipate he'll make a great success of his life, as long as he keeps his urges under control.'

'Let's hope and pray he does,' said William.

After Amy had poured the tea, Magda joined them in the drawing room.

'Magda,' said Henry. 'I can't thank you enough for what you did for Jane.'

'No need to thank me, she did all the hard work,' she smiled. 'Thank you,' she added, accepting the cup and saucer Amy handed her. She took a seat in the armchair by the fire. 'Such a beautiful child. She'll have the sweet temperament of her mother.'

'We can but hope,' murmured Henry.

'So both Jane and Emily will be fine?' Esther asked her.

'Oh, yes. Emily is a very hearty child and Jane, despite her delicate appearance, is as strong as an ox. If there are any problems, you know where to find me, but I don't anticipate there will be any.'

'Would you like to spend the rest of the night here?' said Amy.

'Yes, please, that would be most satisfactory. Then I can examine them both before returning home tomorrow.'

They were joined by a beaming Robert. Amy had never seen him look so happy.

'They're both asleep,' he said. 'So I thought I'd leave them in peace for a little while.'

'How do you feel, darling?' said Amy, kissing his cheek.

'Amazing. I can't believe I'm a father,' he grinned as Henry shook his hand. 'Isn't Emily beautiful?'

'She's gorgeous,' said Amy.

'Jane was wonderful. She's so strong.' He looked to Magda. 'They will both be fine, won't they?'

'Absolutely,' she replied. 'You can rest easy, Robert.'

He breathed a sigh of relief and sank onto the couch.

'Tea?' Amy asked him.

'I could use something stronger, to be honest.'

'I think the occasion calls for a celebratory Scotch,' said Henry.

'What a good idea,' smiled Amy.

'I'll have a sherry, please,' said Esther. 'I've never shared Amy's propensity for malts.'

'Do you still not imbibe, Magda?' said Henry.

'No, I don't. Tea is fine for me, thank you.'

Henry handed round the drinks and they raised their glasses in a toast, Magda raising her teacup.

'To Emily Alardyce,' said Henry. 'May she live a long and happy life.'

'She will,' said Robert. 'I intend to see to that personally.'

'You seemed almost relieved she's a girl,' said Amy.

'To be quite frank, I am. I wanted a girl. I'd be too afraid of a son of mine having to live with the torment I've endured.'

'Oh, Robert,' she rasped, eyes filling with tears. She sat beside him and wrapped an arm around his shoulders. 'Things have been easier for you though lately, haven't they?'

He glanced at Magda and forced a smile. 'Yes, they certainly have, but it hasn't gone away. I never know when it will come back.'

'Just carry on as you are with the sports and simple diet and they won't. Plus you have a daughter to concentrate on now. She will keep you steady.'

'I'm sure she will,' he replied, glancing at Magda again, wondering if she would contradict that statement, but it seemed she was going to keep his confidence.

* * *

Jane and Robert remained at Alardyce House until the start of spring when the weather became milder, not wanting to risk taking little Emily on a journey while it was bitterly cold. The family was also enjoying being back together again.

'You don't have to leave,' Amy told them when it came time for them to depart. 'It's been wonderful having you all here.' Esther and William had already returned to London with their children.

'We've enjoyed it too,' replied Robert. 'But we want to get Emily settled into her home. You're all welcome to visit whenever you like, though.'

'You might regret saying that when Lydia is constantly coming round to see the baby,' smiled Henry.

'And she will always be welcome,' said Robert, kneeling down to hug his sister.

They all gathered at the front door to watch Robert and Jane board their carriage with their baby.

Something in Amy urged her to tell them to stop and get back inside the house, that they would be much better off staying with them, but how could she? They were both adults now, so she was forced to let them go.

* * *

Robert focused all of his attention on Emily and Jane and for a while the dark thoughts stayed away. Just looking at his sleeping daughter brought a peace to his heart he hadn't thought possible and once Jane was fully recovered from the birth, they resumed their activities in the bedroom with renewed vigour. He still fantasised about beating women and hearing their screams, but the urge didn't possess him like it used to. Apart from that one slip-up, he stayed away from Vivienne's, and he was much calmer in the boxing ring. His investments were still doing very well, and he anticipated that soon they'd be able to move to a bigger house.

However, the Richardson siblings wanted revenge and Robert didn't realise until it was too late. He hadn't seen or heard from them since the ball at Mary Walker's house. He encountered Benjamin at a gambling house in the Old Town. Robert wasn't really a gambler, he considered it to be a weak man's game. The little he did gamble was merely to be sociable because these dens were a good way to harvest information that could aid him in business. People were more likely to become loose-lipped when feeling reckless and in their cups. The dark, low-ceilinged room was thick with tobacco smoke and the smell of sweat, stale alcohol and desperation was prevalent. Robert always found it rather a depressing place, but he picked up lots of useful information, so he forced himself to visit two or three times a month.

Benjamin was slumped at a table, looking miserable after losing all his money at a game of cards. The whole city had heard how Robert Alardyce had turned the tables on him at his sister's fancy dress ball, so they all turned to eagerly watch.

'I see you've changed clothes,' commented Robert.

Benjamin sighed and looked up, sitting up straighter and plastering a confident smile to his face when he realised who was addressing him. 'You're the only servant they allow in here. This place is for gentlemen only.'

'There is more to being a gentleman than parentage. Knowing how to conduct oneself in polite company and behaving with dignity, for instance, as well as paying one's debts. How much will your parents have to pay to cover the debts you've run up this evening?'

'Debts? I've had a wonderful evening and won a big heap of money. Lady Luck is certainly on my side.'

'That's not what I've heard. Apparently, there are lots of debtors out for your blood.'

'You shouldn't listen to rumours, Robert.'

'They're far more than rumours. I recently spoke to one Mr Norris. Judging by how pale you've gone, the name rings a bell?'

'I haven't gone pale,' he scowled. 'The lighting in here is terrible.'

'He was raging about you. If he ever gets his hands on you, he's going to wring your scrawny neck. Those were his words, by the way, not mine. He told me you've owed him £200 for months but you keep refusing to pay.'

'Because he's lying,' he spluttered, leaping to his feet. 'I owe the man nothing.'

'That's right, you don't.'

'What?' he said, large forehead creasing with confusion.

'I paid the debt for you, so you don't need to worry about him catching up with you any more.'

'You did what?' exclaimed Benjamin, turning puce with rage and humiliation, which only deepened when Robert's lips curled into a sly smile.

'Aren't you going to say thank you?' said Robert. 'I've got a very violent individual off your back. Now you can pay me back at £10 a week. I'll only charge the same interest rate as the bank.'

'You bastard,' screeched Benjamin, everyone wincing as his voice reached an unpleasantly high octave.

'That's not very grateful after what I've done for you.' He smiled and shook his head. 'Fancy the great Benjamin Richardson being indebted to a footman's son.'

Benjamin stomped around the table, hands balled into fists. 'I'll kill you for this.'

Robert's grin increased. He was thoroughly enjoying himself. 'I try to do a good deed and this is my reward.'

'Good deed? The only reward you're going to get is a fist right in your mouth.'

'Really?' Robert thrust his face into his. 'If you want a fight, I'd be very happy to oblige.'

Benjamin blanched as he realised he'd gone too far. He couldn't fight Robert Alardyce, he'd be left a smear on the floor. However, he did know someone who could beat him. 'I hear you're one of Jackson Kinnaird's favourite fighters.'

'I have that honour,' he coldly replied.

'Prove it.'

'Prove what?'

'Your reputation. The White Hart in the Grassmarket has bare-knuckle fights in the back room, only for a select few. My man Tompkins is fighting there in three nights and he needs an opponent. Why don't you put your money where your mouth is and fight him?'

'Who is this Tompkins? I've never heard of him.'

'Oh, just a bare-knuckle boxer of some renown in the Old Town. Rather a modest man, really. I'm sure he'd be happy to give you a fight. What's wrong, Robert?' he added when he appeared uncertain. 'Don't tell me you're afraid?'

'Of course I'm not afraid,' he snapped when Benjamin's friends started to laugh.

'Then you accept the challenge?'

'I do.'

'Wonderful. Nine-thirty this Friday at the White Hart. Don't be late.'

'I'll be there,' Robert growled before turning and stalking away, grinding his teeth together as their laughter followed him out the door.

13

Robert went straight round to Jackson's to ask his mentor if he knew anything about Tompkins.

'That wee shite Benjamin Richardson,' snarled Jackson. 'I hate the fucking pig's prick. He looks like a death's head on a mop stick. I kicked him out of my club for being a big-gobbed shag-bag. And aye, I know Tompkins. He's a good fighter but you can beat him, I'll show you how. The good thing with bare-knuckle boxing is that you can fuck the Marquess of Queensberry's rules into the ground. I'm going to show you some of the nasty tricks of the trade,' he grinned, revealing several gaps in his teeth. 'It might be a good idea for you not to shag your missus until after the fight, it'll give you that desperate fury you turned on my fighter when she was up the duff.'

'You really have the soul of a poet, Jackson,' smiled Robert.

'Are you taking the piss, laddie?' he frowned.

Robert held up his hands. 'I wouldn't dare.'

'You'd better not. Right, get in the ring and I'll show you how to humiliate the pig's prick and his lobcock of a fighter.'

* * *

Robert didn't think it would be wise to tell Jane or his family about the fight. Deciding to take Jackson's advice, he told Jane he was feeling under the weather and slept in his own room for the three days before the fight on the pretext of not passing anything on to her. He didn't like lying to his wife, but he recalled the savage rage sexual denial had given him and he thought it would be a good weapon to employ against Tompkins.

After telling Jane he had to go out on some business and kissing both her and his adored little Emily goodbye, he left and took a cab, telling the driver to set him down a few streets away from the White Hart Inn. He had asked Jackson if he wanted to accompany him but he declined, not wanting the bad publicity if someone he'd trained ended up a bloodied mess on the floor.

As Robert walked to the pub, he looked at each woman he passed by, imagining them pinned beneath him, lying on their fronts, screaming as he striped their backs. He wasn't sure of the wisdom of deliberately stirring up his dark urges. They hadn't gone away, he still wrestled with them, but Emily and Jane helped him deal with them. However, he reasoned he'd get all his frustration and rage out in the fight.

He entered the pub by the back door and was surprised to find quite an audience had already gathered, crammed into the back room. There was no ring here, just a space left in the centre of the wooden floor, which had been stained by the spilt blood of previous fighters.

Everyone studied him as he walked in, sizing him up before turning back to each other and placing their bets.

'Thank God you're here,' said Robert, finding Andrew, Thomas and Daniel standing in a corner of the room.

'We wouldn't miss this for the world,' said Andrew.

'I only wish you were fighting Benjamin,' said Daniel, who for once wasn't drunk. 'I'd pay good money to watch you pound him into the floor.'

'No offence, Robert, but I'm putting my money on Tompkins,' said Thomas.

'Oh, thank you very much,' he retorted.

'Sorry, but I've seen him fight. He half-killed his last opponent. He's a big brute with fists like hams and a forehead so thick he could use it to knock down walls.'

'Well, Jackson knows him too and he's taught me a few moves to use against him.'

'What moves? Has he given you a cannon? Because if not, then we'd better tell Jane to lay out her best mourning dress.'

'Shut up, Thomas,' Andrew told him. 'Robert can handle that animal. I've every confidence in his abilities.'

'Thank you, Andrew,' said Robert. He scowled at his other two friends. 'At least someone believes in me.'

When Robert turned his back, Andrew shook his head at Thomas and Daniel and mouthed the word *Tompkins*, indicating where he was really going to place his money.

When the door opened again, everyone looked round to see Benjamin swan into the room.

'Good evening, gentlemen,' he called. Only the elite had been allowed into this fight, the riff-raff that often attended these backroom brawls temporarily banned. 'Thank you for coming out on this chilly night.' He smiled when he saw Robert. 'Mr Alardyce, you made it. I did have my doubts.'

'I don't know why,' he replied. 'I never turn down a challenge.'

The dark urges were still tumbling about Robert's mind, heat pounding through his blood. His savage gaze locked on Benjamin, who shuffled uncomfortably beneath the force of it.

Benjamin cleared his throat. 'Then you'll be ready to meet your opponent.' He turned to the door with a dramatic sweep of the arm. 'The Monster of Morningside.'

Robert thought the knuckle-dragging troglodyte that marched into the room looked like something that had escaped from Dr Campbell's hospital. The top of his head was square and flat, coated in thin black hair, and his lower jaw jutted out. He bore the typical mashed nose and ears of an experienced boxer.

'My God,' said Thomas. 'He looks like he was created in Frankenstein's laboratory.'

'Are you sure this is a good idea?' Andrew asked Robert. He caught the look in his friend's eyes and smiled. 'Are those impulses of yours causing mischief?' he whispered in his ear.

Robert nodded as he glowered at his opponent, who was removing his shirt to reveal a thick hairy torso.

As Robert removed his own shirt, Andrew moved through the crowd to find the man who was taking all the bets. When he told him to put all his money on Robert instead of Tompkins, the man looked at him as though he were mad but did it anyway.

Everyone started to cheer as the two fighters took their places in the centre of the room. Tompkins grunted and beat his chest in an intimidation display reminiscent of a mountain gorilla. Robert glared back at him, black eyes burning into his opponent's very soul as he gave the dark thoughts free rein, filling his head with images of blood and pain.

With a grunt, Tompkins lashed out first, Robert dodging to the right to avoid the blow. Jackson had warned him that he preferred to attack from that side. He kept moving, refusing to give Tompkins an easy target. Robert was twelve years younger than his opponent, giving him an advantage. Jackson had taught him that in bare-knuckle boxing it was vital to protect the bones of the hand, which were much more vulnerable without the gloves, so a lot of the blows were delivered with the heel of the hand instead. Robert dodged another punch and caught Tompkins in the side of the face with the meaty part of his palm. As he bent sideways from the blow, Robert followed with a heel hand uppercut that sent him staggering backwards, shaking his head.

The mood in the room changed as surprise overtook the onlookers. As Robert prepared to strike again, Tompkins whipped round with a right hook that knocked him into two of the spectators, bowling them over.

'Get up,' Andrew yelled at Robert, who remained crouched, shaking his head, feeling his left cheek swelling.

Robert got to his feet and reeled backwards, avoiding those massive fists. Benjamin's mocking laughter filled his ears, agitating the rage his dark impulses had built up inside him. Robert managed to bring up his forearm into Tompkin's face, scraping the bone across his face, bending him backwards, allowing Robert to drive a left hook into his cheek.

'Yes,' cried Andrew when Tompkins tottered backwards on shaky legs, only managing to remain upright by sheer will. The surprise in his eyes was comical. He'd expected to have put down this young pup by now.

The two fighters went at each other with renewed ferocity until the floor became slick with blood.

At the end of the fifth bout, the two fighters were given a breather. Robert closed his eyes and allowed all his violent thoughts to stream forth, calling on his deepest, sickest fantasies.

'Think of throwing her into the icy water,' Andrew hissed in his ear, referring to Mrs Grier's murder.

Robert recalled her scream as he threw her through the air, the crack as her body hit the ice, her terror as she sank beneath the murky waters…

With a snarl, he threw himself back into the fight, slamming his fists into Tompkins's face and torso, snapping his head from side to side, a roar leaving his lips.

'You can't beat him with punches to the face,' yelled Andrew. 'Look at him. His skull's so thick, you'd need to hit him with an anvil.'

Despite the dark place he was in, Robert heard his friend's words and understood the sense of them. He could hit this man all day and nothing would bring him down. There was only one way to stop him.

As Tompkins drew back his arm to deliver a punch, Robert stepped forward into the blow. When it made contact with his face, there wasn't enough power in the punch to do him much harm. Tompkins also hadn't had time to close his fist properly. There was a loud crack as a bone in his hand snapped and Tompkins bellowed with agony.

Robert was knocked back a couple of paces but he shook off the weak blow, watching with glee as Tompkins doubled over, cradling his injured right hand and screaming.

'He sounds like a little girl,' laughed Daniel.

The owner of the pub stepped forward to declare Robert the winner of the fight. Stunned silence followed this pronouncement before his friends broke into noisy applause.

'Have you nothing to say, Benjamin?' said Andrew.

But Benjamin was lost in his own world.

'Oh, dear. Did you put all your money on the troll?'

His blood still up, Robert marched up to Benjamin, grabbed him by the front of his jacket and slammed him up against the wall.

'Get him off me,' shrieked Benjamin.

After seeing this eighteen-year-old man take down an animal like Tompkins, everyone was reluctant to touch him. On top of that, there was something in his eyes that none of them liked.

'If you come near me again, speak to me or even look at me,' hissed Robert, 'I will kill you.'

'He threatened me,' cried Benjamin. 'You all heard it.' He felt like crying when everyone looked down at the floor.

Robert threw him aside and returned to his friends.

'Thank you, Robert,' smiled Andrew, tucking the large roll of money he'd just won into his coat pocket. 'I'll be very comfortably off for the next few months.'

Robert didn't reply as he wiped the blood off his face on a wet cloth the landlord handed him. There was a doctor on hand who tended to his cuts before turning his attention to Tompkins, whose screeches had turned into low moans.

'Have you thought of doing this on a regular basis?' the landlord asked Robert. 'You'd make a fortune.'

'No, thank you,' he replied as he pulled on his shirt. 'That was a matter of honour, nothing more.'

'Give the hero of the hour some peace,' said Andrew, clapping his friend on the shoulder. 'Let's have a celebratory drink.'

'All right,' said Robert. 'But just one. I want to get home to Jane and Emily.' He narrowed his eyes at Daniel. 'Was that a snigger?'

'God, no,' he said, holding up his hands. 'It's just so strange hearing you talk about getting back to the family.'

'Because they're wonderful. You should try growing up, you might enjoy it.'

After he'd finished dressing, Robert swaggered into the bar area, those who hadn't been permitted to watch the fight waiting to congratulate him, already having heard the news. A pint of beer was thrust into his hand. It wasn't his usual tipple, but he was so thirsty he drank it down. An elegant glass of wine didn't seem the thing after a bare-knuckle fight.

After slaking his thirst with beer, he ordered a whisky.

'How are you going to explain your ghastly appearance to Jane?' Andrew asked him once the four of them had seated themselves at a table.

'Is it bad?' His face ached, his left eye felt to be badly swollen and a tooth at the back of his mouth was loose.

'It looks like you ran head-first into a train.'

'I'll tell her someone tried to mug me and I fought them off. That will explain the damage to my hands,' he said, looking down at his knuckles, which were cut and bruised.

'They're not as bad as Tompkins's hand,' laughed Thomas. 'The bone came through the skin. You probably put paid to his boxing days, Robert.'

'Am I expected to feel sorry for the creature?'

'God, no. I have to say, I admired the way you used your own head to win the fight.'

'That was thanks to Andrew. I heard him yelling that Tompkins's skull was so thick I'd never win by punching him in the face. Stepping into the punch was a tactic Jackson taught me.'

'I must start going to his club. The man's a genius. I suspect tomorrow morning he'll have a queue of gentlemen wanting to join.'

Robert was only half-listening. The dark thoughts were still swirling around his head. Beating Tompkins had done little to appease them. He'd taken down the dam stemming them and now they refused to return to slumber.

'Robert,' called Daniel, his voice sounding far away.

His head snapped up. 'What?' he yelled at him.

'All right, calm down. I was only asking if you wanted another drink?'

'Oh, right. No, thank you, I want to get home.'

'You can't leave yet, this is your moment of triumph. Everyone wants to talk to the man of the hour,' he said, indicating the packed pub.

'Let him go if he wants,' said Andrew. 'He leads a grown-up life, one you couldn't possibly comprehend.'

'Thank you for coming,' said Robert as he got to his feet, feeling disconnected from everything as his dark thoughts took over. 'Your support is appreciated.'

Before his friends could say another word, he rushed out of the pub.

'What's wrong with him?' frowned Thomas.

'No idea,' replied Andrew, although he knew only too well what was bothering his friend, and he smiled into his beer.

14

Robert stalked the streets of the Old Town with his hat pulled down low and head bowed to hide the damage to his face. Fortunately, it was already dark and the night cloudy, the only light cast from the gas lights. In some parts of the Old Town, there was barely any lighting at all. These were the most dangerous streets, where few dared to tread after the sun had set, the shadows giving refuge to pickpockets and muggers, but even these ruffians sensed the wrongness about Robert as he strode down the street and they allowed him to pass by unmolested.

The dark thoughts were gaining intensity in Robert's mind until they felt to be possessing him completely. His assumption that the fight would appease them had been so dreadfully wrong. On the contrary, it had only stirred them up even more and they were desperate for an outlet. He didn't dare go home until they were once again contained, afraid he'd take them out on Jane.

The part of him that so abhorred these thoughts railed against giving in to them but the desperation to vent them was bursting out of his blood until his entire body was alive with an unbearable itch, as though insects were crawling all over him. Only a certain type of violence would appease it.

The women who passed him by were the lowest of the low, ragged and dirty, not even on a par with a serving maid, but they were all that were available. He couldn't go into the New Town with the better-lit streets because the damage to his face might give him away. Neither could he use his good looks to put them off their guard, not with his face the way it was, so he was forced to skulk in the shadows.

No one who passed him was suitable, they were either men or wretched women old before their time. The urge craved something specific, something young and vital who would struggle more.

Then he saw her – a girl of no more than twenty, tall with a long-legged stride. She wore a tattered wool dress and shawl, but her hard life hadn't yet had time to erase her looks.

The next thing he knew, he was dragging her down a stinking narrow wynd, his hand over her mouth as he forced her to the ground, pressing down on her head as he tore open the back of her dress. From the detritus discarded on the ground, he found a strip of wood from a broken crate and he used it to beat her bare back, the girl kicking and writhing beneath him. He enjoyed her feistiness, but she simply wasn't strong enough to throw him off. Sadly, he daren't remove his hand to hear her screams for fear of being overheard, but he still revelled in her fear and pain and her pathetic attempts to free herself. This was followed by sweet release over the backs of her thighs and finally he was liberated from the fire in his blood and the unbearable itch that had consumed his body.

He yanked her head back by her hair, his hand still clamped over her mouth.

'Remain silent until I'm gone and you will leave this alley alive,' he growled in her ear. He deepened his voice, made it gruffer and exaggerated his accent to disguise his voice. 'Make a sound and I will kill you and your family. Do you understand?'

The girl nodded, tears shining in her eyes, but as she looked back at him over her shoulder, there was a fierce hatred there too.

'Good girl,' he smiled before releasing her.

She remained quiet and compliant on the ground as he rose and adjusted his clothing before calmly exiting the alley. As he walked down the street, he kept expecting her to let up a wail, but she didn't and he escaped unhindered.

Elated, Robert inhaled the night air, enjoying how it cooled his fevered skin. He felt no guilt, only an enormous sense of his own power, as though he was an unstoppable force no one was capable of defeating. He'd cowed and humiliated the son of one of the wealthiest and most influential families in the city, beaten one of the best bare-knuckle boxers and unleashed his urges on a woman and nothing would happen to him for it. The power made him feel god-like.

The next thing he knew, he was standing at the gates of Greyfriars Kirkyard. Robert had no idea why he was there. Some irresistible force had compelled him to come to this place. He wasn't in the habit of visiting cemeteries, he hated to think of his own mortality, it scared him, but for some reason it felt right to be here.

To his surprise, the large wrought-iron gates were unlocked, allowing him to slip inside. The first thing he saw was food and sticks left by tourists for the deceased Greyfriars Bobby, the little dog who had supposedly maintained a vigil at his master's grave until he died. In Robert's opinion, it was a ridiculous tale designed to draw in gullible tourists. He had it on good authority that the dog had merely been one of the many strays who hung around graveyards because they got fed by the visitors and the legend had been encouraged by the caretaker of the cemetery. The story was that he replaced the original dog when it died with an imposter to perpetuate the myth and garner more tourism, earning himself more tips as he regaled anyone who asked with touching tales of the broken-hearted dog.

Robert moved through the cemetery, wishing he understood why he was here, but one thing he did notice was that he no longer felt the terror he usually experienced when confronted by anything to do with death. Confidently he strode through the tombs, past the rows of the slumbering dead, knowing nothing could hurt him. Some of the tombs were protected by iron cages over the graves, known as mortsafes, others were protected by caged lairs – iron bars cast into stone blocks to defend the dead from the resurrection men, whose nefarious work had been halted in its tracks by the Anatomy Act of 1832 that had made it easier for anatomists and medical students to procure bodies. He considered what a good body snatcher Andrew would have made; he was certainly wily and ruthless enough and would have enjoyed pitting his wits against grieving relatives and night watchmen.

Robert took the path that wound through the gravestones, some regal and eye-catching, others smaller and humbler, leading him towards the south end of the cemetery down an alley of mausoleums, their dark hulks rising up on either side, guarded by chained metal gates. Ahead of him was a dead end, the way barred by another mausoleum. This area was what remained of the covenanters' prison, where over a thousand people – who had opposed the interference of the Stuart kings in the affairs of the Scottish Presbyterian church – had been starved, tortured and executed over a four-month period in 1679, although a few had made it out alive either by escaping or being released. In the eighteenth century, what remained of the prison had been incorporated into the kirkyard.

Robert cared nothing for the history, but it was a place of suffering and death, which did appeal to him.

He turned in a slow circle, still experiencing that heady rush of invincibility, daring the dead to do their worst. Nothing happened save for the rustle of the breeze through the low-hanging trees, the wave of their branches scattering shadows across the gravestones. The sounds of the city failed to permeate here, there was naught but himself and the dead.

Now it became clear why he was here – because he'd realised that not even his fear of death could touch him any more. The evening's events had taken him far beyond ordinary mortal emotion and frailty. He was eminently powerful, no one could get the better of him. He was indeed a god on earth.

A mocking laugh echoed through the cemetery and it took Robert a moment to realise that he was the source of the sound. He peered into the darkest shadows, faced them head on and told them to do their worst, but they all retreated before him, recognising that he was too powerful, even for them.

With a smile, he strolled back towards the gates, sensing eyes burning into his back but not deigning to look around, not because he was afraid but because he'd transcended that pitiful emotion.

As he passed the mausoleum of Sir George Mackenzie, he stopped and turned to face the rounded vault, seeing the shadows slide across its sombre stone. This tomb contained the body of the man who had been responsible for the worst atrocities committed on the covenanters, his actions so horrific he'd gained a reputation as a monster and ever since he'd been known as 'Bloody Mackenzie'. It was said that he had failed to find rest and still roamed this place.

'Do your worst, Bloody Mackenzie,' he called, head bowed, lips drawing back over his teeth, hands curling into fists.

Nothing happened and the shadows retreated.

Robert turned and casually made his way towards the gates, confident that nothing and no one was capable of stopping him.

* * *

Jane anxiously kept vigil at the drawing room window, waiting for Robert to come home. He'd been gone for hours and she was starting to fear the worst, after all, the city could be a dangerous place. Robert had been unwell lately. What if he'd been taken ill again and collapsed in the street? She couldn't bear the thought of him lying helpless in the gutter, cold and alone with no one to help him. Every time a carriage approached, she would pull back the heavy curtains and peer out, only to let them fall back into place, dejected when the carriage passed by.

The slam of the front door had her rushing into the hallway to find Robert handing his hat and coat to the waiting footman, who had been forced to wait up for his return.

'Robert,' she exclaimed, racing up to him.

It was only when she was up close and could see his face in the lamp-light that she saw his injuries.

'My God,' she exclaimed. 'What happened?'

'I was attacked,' he told her in a tired, flat voice. Robert had spent a long time tramping the streets, ensuring he had himself completely under control before hailing a cab and heading home.

'Are you all right? Shall I call the doctor?'

'No need, I'm fine. It looks worse than it is.'

'Fetch some water, a cloth and diluted tincture of arnica for Mr

Alardyce's cuts,' she told the footman. 'And some cold vinegar for his bruises.'

'There's really no need...' began Robert.

'Yes, there is,' she retorted. 'If you won't see a doctor, at least let me tend to your injuries. I'm taking no chances with your health.'

He smiled and kissed her cheek, wincing at the pain in his split lip.

'Come and sit,' she said, taking his hand and leading him into the drawing room.

'I'm really fine, Jane,' he said. 'No need to fuss.'

She sat him down on the sofa to examine him.

'Look at your hands,' she gasped.

'I gave a good account of myself.'

'You must have done. Oh, where is Peters with the things I asked for?' She huffed with annoyance. 'Did you see who did it? Perhaps they can still be caught.'

'No, sorry. It was dark.' Robert gazed into her big blue eyes. He couldn't bring himself to lie to her. He wanted something pure left in his life. 'Jane, I...'

'I'll get you some brandy and water,' she said, getting to her feet and bustling over to the drinks cabinet. 'That will settle your nerves.'

'I assure you my nerves are quite settled.'

Nevertheless, she handed him the drink and watched until he'd drained the contents.

'Ah, finally,' she said when Peters reappeared with the items she'd requested on a tray. 'That is all, you may leave us.'

Peters placed the tray on a table, bowed and left.

'Now let's tend to these cuts,' she said, kneeling before her husband and taking his right hand.

He gazed at her as she gently dabbed at the cuts on his knuckles with the cloth, which she'd dipped into the diluted arnica.

'Actually,' he began. 'I wasn't attacked.'

'Then what happened?' she said, gazing up at him.

'I was in a bare-knuckle boxing match at the White Hart Inn.'

Her eyes widened. 'What?'

'It was Benjamin Richardson's fault. He challenged me.'

'Benjamin Richardson fought in a bare-knuckle fight?' she frowned, the idea ludicrous.

'The coward would never do something so risky. I fought a champion of his called Tompkins. And I won.'

'You beat a bare-knuckle boxing champion?' she exclaimed.

'Yes. I broke his hand. Andrew was the only one who bet on me winning and he made a small fortune. Are you all right?' he added when she just stared at him.

'Did you know you were going to end up fighting when you left the house this evening?'

'I did.'

'And you said nothing?'

'I didn't want to worry you.'

'I was worried anyway because you were so late home. I had visions of you lying broken and bloodied in the gutter.'

'I'm sorry, I thought I was doing the right thing for you.'

'I am not a child, Robert. I'm a wife and mother and I can cope with unpleasant truths.'

'Forgive me,' he said, enveloping her in his arms.

She struggled free of his embrace and, to his infinite surprise, shoved him in the chest. It barely had any physical effect on him, but it did astonish him as Jane was usually so meek.

'Don't you dare do anything so stupid again,' she said, rising to her feet, cheeks flushed with anger.

'It was a matter of honour,' he replied. 'If I'd refused, I would have been shamed.'

'How do you think Emily and I would have felt if you'd been killed?'

'It wouldn't have been allowed to go that far and I wasn't killed. I'm fine.'

'Have you seen your face? You certainly didn't get out of the fight unscathed.'

'This will soon heal,' he said, gesturing to his face. 'Oh, please don't be angry with me,' he said, pulling her to him. 'I can't bear it when you're angry with me.'

'Then don't do anything so stupid again. Emily and I need you. Did you think of us at all when you left this evening for your fight?'

'Of course I did. I was doing it for you two as well. You've already suffered because of my parentage and Emily will likely suffer in the future. I'm trying to protect you both by ensuring no further damage is done to my reputation.'

'And you think the best way to defend your reputation is by brawling in taverns?'

'After beating Tompkins, no one will dare insult me again. If I'd turned down the challenge, I would have been known as a coward, as well as the son of a footman, and the Alardyce name would have been tarnished again. I don't want Emily living with what I've had to endure from society.'

Jane's expression softened. 'Now I understand, but please know that I would rather endure the scorn of society than lose you. I couldn't bear it.'

He took her hand and cradled it to his chest, the love he had for this woman expanding his heart, dispelling the evil that still clung to him from his deeds earlier that night. Magda's words about finding refuge in the love he held for those closest to him made sense now. 'You won't lose me, Jane, because I couldn't bear to be parted from you.'

He kissed her, pressing her back onto the floor, her legs wrapping around his waist.

'But your injuries...' she began as he pushed up her skirts.

'Certainly aren't enough to stop me from making love to you,' he said, smiling down at her.

She smiled back at him, sliding her fingers through his hair and pulling his mouth back down to hers.

15

Robert's house practically shook from the savage blows that rained down on the front door. Even Forbes, their sturdy but solemn butler, was a little apprehensive about answering it and he told Peters to accompany him.

He pulled open the door, both men retreating a few steps. On the doorstep was a leviathan of a man with an enormous chest and furious green eyes. His massive fists had even managed to put a dent in the door.

'Is your master in?' he positively snarled.

'Please wait here, sir, while I ascertain if he is,' replied Forbes, not wanting to allow this thug over the threshold.

'That means he is,' said the man, stalking inside before Forbes could close the door in his face. 'Robert, where are you?' he yelled.

Recognising the voice, Robert emerged from his study. It had been almost a week since the fight at the White Hart Inn. The swelling to his face had gone but the bruises were a faded yellow.

'Here I am, Knapp,' he said. 'What do you want?'

'To talk in private. You don't want your lackeys overhearing what I've got to say.'

'Savage as ever, I see.' He indicated his study door. 'Come on through.'

'Shall I fetch some coffee, sir?' said Forbes.

'Do you want some coffee, Knapp?' Robert politely asked him.

'No,' he barked. 'This isn't a social call.'

'It never is where you're concerned.'

They entered the study, Robert closing the door behind them. 'So, what can I do for...'

Before he could finish the sentence, Knapp had grabbed him by the shirt front and shoved him back against the wall.

'I know what you did that night,' he spat.

'What night?' replied Robert.

'The night of the fight at the White Hart.'

'Ah, so you heard about that.'

'Aye, I heard about you beating that giant tulip Tommy Tompkins, but that's not what I'm referring to. I'm here about that lassie you dragged down an alley and beat with a plank of wood.'

'I did nothing of the sort.'

'Don't lie to me, boy.'

Knapp was startled when Robert threw him off and adjusted his collar.

'I'm not a boy any more,' said Robert. 'I'm a man now and I can have you thrown out of here if I wish. You can't bully me any more, Knapp.'

'I'm not here to bully, I'm here to protect every woman in Edinburgh from you and your disgusting perversions.'

'I've no idea what you're talking about.'

'I knew it was you as soon as I heard about the attack.'

'What attack? I've read nothing in the papers.'

'Because it wasn't in the papers. No one listens to women of Harriet's class anyway. When they have a problem, they come to me instead. As soon as she told me what had happened, I knew you were responsible. When she said your face was cut and bruised, it all made sense – you attacked her just after your fight with Tompkins.'

'Who on earth is Harriet?'

'What do you care? Your Majesty's too high and mighty to see her as a real person. To you, she's just a thing for you to use. I know exactly what happened that night – the fight got your blood up, but it wasn't enough for you to destroy Tompkins's boxing career...'

'Do you expect me to feel sorry for the brute?'

'God, no, the man's a prick, but you destroyed him and it still wasn't enough. You had to attack a helpless woman too, only Harriet's not as help-less as you thought because she knows me and I will get justice for her.'

'What are you going to do? Beat me to a pulp in my own study? Try it and I'll ensure you're thrown into prison. I'm a man of power and influence now.'

'You're nothing but a grubby little pervert who's so pathetic and weak he has to attack women to make himself feel big.'

'Actually, beating a bare-knuckle boxing champion and amassing my own personal fortune has done that for me and you are nothing. Now get out of here before I call for a constable to throw you out. I would hate to see you so humiliated, but I'm willing to take the risk.'

When Knapp lunged for him, Robert dodged and slammed his foot into his right knee. Knapp howled and hopped about on one leg.

'I noticed you favoured that leg slightly,' smirked Robert. 'I thought it might be an old injury. Judging by your rather girlish reaction, I was right.'

Eyes bulging with fury, Knapp drove his fist into Robert's stomach, folding him in half and knocking the air from his lungs. It took him a few seconds to catch his breath, by which time Knapp had grabbed his hair, yanked back his head and punched him in the face, sending him stumbling backwards.

'Tompkins is a fucking girl compared to me,' hissed Knapp, advancing on him.

Robert managed to stay on his feet and snatched up the poker from the fireplace. 'Come any closer and I'll smash in your massive ugly head.'

'Isn't a plank of wood more your weapon of choice? Put that down and fight with your fists, you coward.'

They both froze at the sound of shouting from the hall.

'What on earth is that racket?' they heard a voice demand. 'Why aren't you checking on your master?'

A few seconds later, the door was thrown open by Jane.

'What is going on?' she demanded of the men. 'Robert, why are you holding a poker?' Her eyes widened. 'Your face is bruised again.'

'Blame him for that,' he replied, nodding at Knapp.

'Who is he?'

'This is Knapp, the man my father sent to watch over me. Do you remember I told you about him? He was my jailer while I stayed at my uncle's house.'

'Yes, I do remember,' she replied, turning her outraged glare on Knapp. 'Don't tell me Sir Henry has hired you to abuse Robert again?'

'No one's hired me,' he replied. 'I'm here on a completely different matter.'

'And does that matter involve brawling in my home?'

'No, madam,' he replied, looking like an overgrown child who'd been caught doing something naughty.

'Then I would appreciate it if you would leave before you cause any more damage.'

'If that's what you want, madam.' He looked back at Robert. 'This isn't over.'

'Oh, yes, it is,' he retorted, dark eyes narrowed.

Knapp hesitated by Jane on his way out the door. 'Be very careful, Mrs Alardyce. You're married to an extremely dangerous man.'

'The only dangerous man I see is you,' she replied. 'Kindly leave.'

'He'll break your heart. You should get out while you still can. My name is Jacob Knapp. If you ever need me, just ask around, everyone knows where to find me. I hope you don't need me, but one day, I fear you will.'

His green eyes were rather sad as he left a lot more quietly than he'd arrived.

'What was that about?' Jane demanded of her husband.

'I have no idea,' replied Robert. 'The man's a lunatic.'

'Your cheek's swelling again.' She called for the servants to fetch cold water and a cloth to tend to his face. That achieved, she turned back to her husband. 'He must have some reason for coming here.'

'He was angry about me breaking Tompkins's hand in that fight.'

'Why? It was a fair fight, wasn't it?'

'Yes, but his boxing career is over, if you can call brawling in taverns a career. Knapp was furious.'

'Then he's no right to be. The man must be mad. Thank you, Peters,' she said when the footman fetched the water and cloth. He bowed before leaving.

'He is,' said Robert, sinking into a chair, enjoying his wife's gentle hands tending to his injury. 'He punched me and threw me about at my uncle's house. The man's a villain.'

'Something ought to be done about him.'

'He's gone now and he won't be back.'

'How can you be sure?'

'Because I am, don't worry. I'm so proud of you standing up to him.' And it was true. She'd looked magnificent putting that ogre in his place.

'I don't like anyone hurting you,' she said, eyes wide and sad. 'Between Benjamin Richardson, that fight and now this, it seems to be happening all the time.'

'It was inevitable, I'm afraid. I'm the son of a footman, I shouldn't exist in this world and not only am I surviving but I'm thriving and it's getting people's backs up. The cream of society expected me to stumble about before failing but I haven't and they're jealous of how well I'm doing in business, as well as the fact that I'm married to the most beautiful woman in the city,' he said, kissing her.

'It makes me so furious. I just want them to leave you alone.'

'They will soon, when they realise I'm not going anywhere.'

'I can't wait for that day,' she sighed.

'Don't worry. As long as we have each other, everything will be fine.'

'Yes, it will,' she smiled. 'Sounds like Emily's woken from her nap,' she added when the sound of crying filtered down to them from upstairs. 'I'll go to her, the nanny's gone out for a couple of hours. Keep that pressed to your cheek until the swelling feels to have improved.'

He took the cold compress from her and pressed it to the side of his face. 'You're tending to me so much lately, it feels like I have my own personal Florence Nightingale.'

She smiled and kissed him before rushing off to attend to their daughter.

When she'd gone, Robert scribbled a note and sent one of the servants out to deliver it. Knapp was becoming too dangerous and it was time he was dealt with.

* * *

Matthew Crowle had Hobbs, Henry Alardyce had Knapp and Vivienne had Corrigan, so Robert thought it was time he found his own thug on a leash, a right-hand man who would help him deal with the murkier things.

After careful vetting, he'd found Fraser, a big slab of a man who equalled Knapp in height, strength and ferocity. Best of all, Fraser possessed something Knapp did not – a brother called Will who was no less deadly, although he didn't possess Fraser's frightening proportions.

Robert had taken them out of the hovel where he'd found them in the Old Town and set them up in a pleasant flat in the New Town, paying all their bills and outfitting them in the best clothes. He'd given them everything and he could take it away in a moment, this fear ensuring he would always have their loyalty.

They never roamed far from their new home, just in case he needed them, consequently they were in when he knocked on their door.

'Come in, sir,' said Fraser, standing aside respectfully.

Robert walked into the flat, removing his hat and gloves. While Fraser was enormous and scarred, Will was small and reptilian with greasy dark hair plastered to his head. They didn't look at all like brothers but on closer inspection, it was clear they had the same light brown eyes, the same thick lower lip and thin upper lip, subtle hints as to their shared heritage. Fraser's speciality was brute strength and mindless violence, whereas Will's was his speed and skill with a blade. It was how he'd managed to survive the rough city streets despite being the runt of the litter.

'I have a job for you both,' said Robert. 'Jacob Knapp. Do either of you know him?'

Will's eyes narrowed into slits. 'Aye, we do. That bastard did this to me when he caught me robbing a house.'

Robert winced when Will tugged down his trousers and turned around to reveal a scar running across the top of his pale buttocks.

'What did he do to you?' frowned Robert.

'Caught me a cracker with a horse whip.'

'He must have hit you hard to leave such a scar.'

'The bastard did. Bled for hours, I did.'

'What do you want us to do exactly?' said Fraser in his deep growl.

'I want you to make sure that Mr Knapp doesn't bother anyone ever again.'

Will's lips curled into a smile revealing thick gums and crooked, broken teeth while Fraser merely nodded in understanding, as emotionless as a statue.

'Excellent,' said Robert, placing a bag of money on the table. 'This is to cover any expenses and for your time and trouble.'

'How do you want it to look?' said Will.

'As brutal as possible,' he replied, broadening Will's grin.

* * *

Knapp pulled up the collar of his coat as he delved once more into the city's underbelly, which he knew like the back of his hand. Many of his informants were the forgotten and ignored, consequently he knew everything that went on in Auld Reekie. It was how he'd discovered Robert Alardyce's latest atrocity, and he knew it wouldn't be the last, so he was keeping a close eye on things. Tomorrow, he intended to speak to Sir Henry Alardyce, who would be blissfully unaware of his stepson's fresh crime. If anyone could stop Robert, it was that man. He wanted to give Sir Henry more information to back up his accusation, so he was going to talk to those who were known to lurk around the shadowy wynd where Harriet had been attacked in the hope of learning something more.

As he reached the mouth of the wynd, a shadow darted out in front of him. His instinct was to hit it, until he realised it was just a child.

'Watch where you're going,' he told the girl. 'I nearly stood on you.'

The grimy girl flashed him a cheeky smile before darting away.

While he was distracted, an arm snaked around his neck and dragged him down the very wynd Harriet had been pulled down.

Knapp kicked and writhed but, as he was being pulled backwards, it was difficult for him to free himself. When whoever was pulling him eventually came to a halt, he attempted to drag them over his shoulder, but they were immovable. Left with no choice, Knapp threw himself backwards, knocking his attacker off balance, and they staggered back together. He surmised his attacker had fallen against a wall when they came to an abrupt halt. There was a loud grunt but still the iron band around his neck refused to let go. He drove his elbow into his attacker's ribs, making him yelp, and finally he was released.

Knapp whipped round and drew back his fist, but his attacker ducked and he met nothing but air.

There was a pain in the back of his left leg and Knapp dropped to one knee, feeling blood trickle down the back of his calf. It was then he realised there were two attackers, but he could only see one in the dark – a huge shadow looming over him. When the shadow tried to kick him, Knapp grabbed his leg and tipped him backwards, rising as he did so, sending the man crashing onto his back.

There was a disturbing laugh behind him, followed by a flash of pain in his lower back. Knapp whipped round, swinging his fists, once again meeting nothing but air. Was this a real man or a phantom?

'Too slow,' taunted a voice.

There was the glint of a blade and fire erupted in Knapp's chest. Putting his hands to the wound, he felt warm blood trickling down his front. It wasn't enough to kill him. Whoever was responsible was toying with him. They were enjoying themselves.

This time, he was ready, and when he spotted that fast-moving shadow, his hand shot out and he managed to grab them by the throat. The shadow was only small and at first he thought he'd caught a young boy, until he noted those evil eyes, the grimace of those thin lips and the ugly crooked teeth.

'Will Comyn, you nasty wee shite.'

Knapp was forced to drop him when Fraser charged into him from behind, knocking him onto his front. Knapp unknowingly snatched up a shattered piece of the same crate Robert had used to beat Harriet, turned and smashed it into Fraser's face. He released him and stumbled backwards, shaking his huge head to clear it. Knapp leapt to his feet and, deciding for once that retreat was the better part of valour, raced for the mouth of the alley. He knew this pair of old and he did not want to tackle them while they were together.

He'd almost reached the end of the alley when there was a pain in his back and he fell forward. Reaching round, he felt the knife sticking out of him. Will was as lethal with a blade from a distance as he was up close.

Using every ounce of his will, Knapp got back to his feet, feeling himself grow weaker from the wounds he'd already sustained, which were still bleeding. He was determined to go out fighting.

As he turned to face his opponents, Will ran by him, ducking out of reach as Knapp tried to grab him. His hands immediately went to his belly as he was sliced open. He slumped to his knees, blood pouring through his fingers, appalled to feel the pulsating warmth of his own innards attempting to exit his body.

Will's gurning face leered at him out of the darkness, black tongue licking his lips, his brother's immense shadow standing behind him, watching.

'Robert Alardyce says go to hell,' hissed Will before slashing Knapp's throat.

The big man finally fell onto his back, blood spurting from the savage neck wound, the last thing he saw the disturbing, twisted visage of his murderer, revelling in the pleasure of the kill.

16

Amy jumped awake in her armchair, looking around the room in confusion. She'd drifted off in her sitting room, warm and cosy by the fire. The book she'd been reading lay open on her lap. What had disturbed her?

Her heart sank when she saw her unwanted visitor sitting in the armchair on the other side of the fireplace.

'Matthew,' she sighed. 'You're back.'

She hadn't had any visitations from him since the night his own mother and Hobbs had attacked her and Robert and she'd thought it was over. Sadly, it didn't seem to be the case.

'I'm still asleep,' she said.

'Perhaps,' he replied with his self-satisfied smile, sinking back into the armchair, stretching his long legs out before him. With his dark hair, black eyes, sulky mouth and sharp cheekbones, his resemblance to Robert had never been more pronounced. 'Perhaps not. Why do you insist on making me out to be a figment of your imagination?'

'Because that's what you are.'

'No, I'm not, but you want me to be because you're afraid of the truth.'

'Was there a reason for your visit?'

'Why? Are you keen to get back to your urgent business of sleeping? You're getting old, Amy.'

'Doesn't everyone? Well, apart from you, but that's because you're dead.'

'And we both know whose fault that is, don't we?'

'Must we go over old ground again?'

'We must because our boy knows what you did to me and it's opened up a wound inside him.'

'I know,' she said, looking stricken. 'But you can thank your mother for that. Have you seen her, by the way?'

'Do you imagine we have dinner parties and balls on the other side?'

'I thought you might have been waiting for her when she crossed over.' She considered what a ridiculous conversation this was. 'Never mind all that. Has something bad happened? Is that why you're back?'

'The heat in our boy's blood is rising. Finally, he's becoming who he's meant to be.'

'You're right. He's a wonderful father and husband.'

'I'm not referring to all that sentimental nonsense. I'm talking about his dark urges, his personal demons. They're claiming him.'

'No, they're not. He's the old Robert again.'

His look was withering. 'Do you really think sports and vegetables can stifle something so powerful? Of course not. He may have had a temporary respite but that's all it is, and he's got up to far more than you know.'

'What do you mean? What has he done?'

Matthew's smile was wicked. 'I wonder if he'll tell you or if he'll be too ashamed? The day he no longer feels shame is the day he truly becomes what he was always meant to be. Remember that, Amy.'

'Tell me what he's done,' she insisted.

'I don't think I will. I don't want to spoil the surprise.'

'Robert's not done anything. You're just trying to stir up trouble because you've nothing better to do.'

'Am I really? Then I shall give you a little clue to get you started – the news your pasty fop of a husband is about to bring you is connected to Robert's wicked deeds.'

'Do not call Henry names. He's the best man I have ever known.'

Matthew rolled his eyes. 'How wonderful.' He regarded her with his head cocked to one side. 'Despite how you're ageing, Amy, you're still a very desirable woman. How I long for the day when we're reunited.'

'You mean the day I die?'

'Oh, yes. Don't forget, I'll be waiting for you.'

'And what if I don't want to go with you?'

'You will. We were always meant to be together.' He leaned forward in his seat, dark eyes full of threat. 'We will never be apart again.'

Amy gasped when there was a loud thud and she jumped in her seat for a second time. Her eyes flew open and immediately went to the armchair where Matthew had been sitting, sighing with relief to see it was vacant.

'Amy,' said Henry, walking into the room clutching a piece of paper. 'Are you well? You look hot.' His eyes filled with anxiety. 'You're not falling ill with a fever again, are you?'

'No, I'm quite well. I just had a bad dream... about Matthew.'

'Oh, he's not back, is he?'

'Yes, and he called you a pasty fop.'

'In that case, I got off lightly.'

'He also said that Robert is falling back into bad habits and you were about to bring me some news connected to that.' Her amused grin fell when he failed to smile, her eyes flicking to the piece of paper he held. 'What's that?'

'A letter from Knapp. I received it yesterday. It says he has some information he needs to share with me about Robert.'

'And you're only telling me about it now?'

'I wanted to hear what he had to say first before worrying you. The thing is, he was supposed to arrive an hour ago and he hasn't turned up.'

'He could be late or he could have forgotten.'

'I've known Knapp a long time, he worked for my father too and he has never once been late or forgotten anything. I'm worried something bad has happened to him. After what you said about the dream...'

'It was just a dream,' Amy hastily replied.

'We both know it's more than that. Matthew warned you when his mother and Hobbs broke into the house.'

'That could have just been my unconscious mind picking up on external clues my conscious mind missed. Please don't raise your eyebrow at me,' she sniffed when he looked sceptical.

'I'm sorry, but that explanation isn't very convincing.'

'But me being haunted by a fortune-telling ghost is?'

'I'm not sure. Magda's the one to discuss that with. My primary concern is Knapp.'

'There could be any number of reasons why he hasn't turned up, he does involve himself in a lot of nefarious activities. Anything could have happened to him and if it has, it doesn't mean it's connected to Robert.'

'Once I thought Robert incapable of overcoming someone like Knapp but after hearing how he beat Tommy Tompkins in a bare-knuckle fight, I'm not so sure.'

'You're rather proud of him for that, aren't you?'

'Yes, I am. I imagine Jackson gave him some training that isn't usually allowed in his club.'

'Probably.'

'It's all over the city. Jackson was particularly pleased when I went to his club yesterday. It's reflected very well on him and he's got some new customers.' Henry and Amy rarely went out into society, so if they did hear any gossip, it was usually from someone they employed. 'It's done Robert's reputation the power of good. He has now become a man to respect. I can't imagine anyone daring to mention his parentage in front of him ever again.'

'Then at least something good did come out of it, although I don't like the thought of my son brawling in pubs.'

'I'll make some enquiries, see if anyone's heard from Knapp.'

'I'd like to pay Robert and Jane a visit, it's been over a week since we saw them. We'll leave the children here and tell them we're going out to dine. If they know where we're really going, they'll want to come. We need to make sure Robert's sticking to the straight and narrow.'

* * *

Robert sat in his study, smiling into the flames of the fire. The Comyns had been successful and Knapp would bother him no more. How he wished he could have been there to see that bastard's final moments. The brothers had told him it had been brutal and bloody, but he couldn't risk getting caught up in any subsequent investigation. Knapp hadn't been some gutter rat no one cared about. He was highly respected throughout the city and there would be an investigation into his death. Not that it would get the police anywhere, the Comyns knew what they were doing.

He was a little surprised when Forbes announced his parents were here to see him. At first, he panicked that they knew about Knapp, then reasoned they couldn't as word hadn't had chance to spread. It had only happened in the early hours of the morning.

'Show them into the drawing room,' he smiled pleasantly. 'We'll need tea and cake.'

'Yes, sir,' said Forbes, bowing respectfully before leaving.

Robert crossed the hall into the drawing room and waited for his parents to be escorted in by the butler.

'How are you, darling?' said Amy as she walked into the room. She went straight to her son to hug him and kiss his cheek.

Her warm greeting reassured Robert. 'I'm very well, thank you. And to what do I owe the honour of this visit?'

'We haven't seen you in over a week, so we wanted to check everything was all right.'

'And to congratulate you,' said Henry, shaking his hand. 'I heard about the fight at the White Hart.'

'I expected you to be angry about that.'

'Why would I?' he smiled. 'It's a great achievement.'

'It certainly was,' said Amy.

'I'm glad you think so,' grinned Robert with relief. He was a little annoyed with himself when he revelled in the pride in his parents' eyes, it made him feel like a pathetic little boy.

'You've got some nasty bruising,' said Henry. His eyes narrowed at the sight of Robert's left cheek. 'That bruise looks very fresh.'

'It's taking a long time to heal,' said Robert, gently stroking the side of his face. 'Some teeth were loosened, which is contributing to the swelling.'

'I've experienced that myself in the ring more than once,' said Henry pleasantly, although the suspicion didn't leave his eyes as he continued to peer at Robert's face.

'Please, take a seat,' said Robert, gesturing to the armchairs. 'I've already asked for tea and cake to be brought in.'

'Lovely,' smiled Amy, taking the proffered seat, as did Henry. 'Where's Jane?'

'She's visiting a friend who's unwell.'

'I hope it's nothing contagious,' said Amy, worry filling her eyes. 'Not with Emily in the house.'

'Her friend fell in the park and broke her wrist, so don't worry, it's not catching,' he smiled. 'My wife is quite the ministering angel.'

Amy's heart swelled at the smile that lit up her son's face at the mention of his wife.

'Emily's upstairs sleeping, under the watchful eye of her nanny,' added Robert.

'I'd like to see her before we go.'

'Hopefully she'll wake before you leave, but I don't want her disturbed or she'll scream the house down for hours. Emily does like her sleep.'

'I wouldn't dream of disturbing her. I'll just peek around the door. So,' she said, looking around the room as though it could give her a clue as to what her son had been up to. 'How have you been?'

'Very well, thank you. Nothing much going on, apart from the boxing match.'

'I bet that was exciting,' said Henry with a knowing smile.

'It was, although painful.'

'Did he hurt you badly?' said Amy.

'Just some cuts and bruises. Tompkins went in assuming he was going to win. His overconfidence was his downfall.'

'Never underestimate your opponent,' said Henry sagely.

The footman brought the tea and as he was pouring, the nanny entered the room carrying Emily.

'Hello, beautiful girl,' beamed Amy, holding her twisted hands out for her granddaughter. She was glad the nanny Jane had hired was a matronly, middle-aged woman with a plump round face and spectacles. As Jane was nursing the baby herself, she didn't require someone to do that for her.

Amy was relieved, she would have been so worried had she hired a pretty young thing. Rush had recommended a lady's maid for her, a plain girl who hailed from Alardyce that Robert took absolutely no interest in. The kitchen maid was Mrs Clapperton's niece and was even more unattractive than the lady's maid. Apart from the stout elderly cook, the rest of the staff were male.

Amy took Emily from the nanny and gently rocked her, smiling when her eyes slid shut with contentment. 'I can't believe how beautiful she is,' she said as the nanny discreetly left the room.

'Me neither,' said Robert, gazing at his daughter with awe. 'I thought Jane was the only angel but now I have two.'

'Oh, Robert, that's so sweet.'

'I know we once said you'd make a terrible father and husband,' said Henry, 'but you've certainly proved us wrong.'

'I've never known happiness like this, Father.'

'I know exactly how you feel,' he replied, smiling at Amy.

As touching as all this was, Robert was still suspicious of this sudden visit. It could just be paranoia, but it seemed too timely with Knapp's murder occurring just a few hours ago. Perhaps they were here for the reason they'd said – they hadn't seen each other in over a week and they missed them and he knew how much his mother doted on Emily. He decided to believe the latter.

'I noticed you've got a new front door,' said Henry.

'Yes,' replied Robert, his paranoia raising its head again. 'The other one got dented.'

'How?'

'I'm not sure. One day the dent wasn't there, the next it was. I suspect the clumsy postman was responsible. He once fell into our rose bushes when he slipped on some ice. He probably didn't say anything because he didn't want to be liable. Besides, the new black door is much more tasteful than the gaudy red one. What are you looking at, Father?' he added when Henry continued to peer curiously at him.

'That bruise to your face really does look fresh. It could have happened yesterday.'

'Well, it didn't. It's just taking time to heal.'

'Don't snap,' Amy told her son. 'You'll disturb Emily.'

'I'm sorry, I'm not snapping, it's just that once again, he doesn't seem to believe me.'

Henry held up his hands. 'I believe you, Robert. I'm just concerned for your health, that's all. From experience, I know internal damage can be caused in the boxing ring.'

'My health is perfectly fine,' he pouted, folding his arms across his chest.

Henry had to force himself not to smile. Robert was a rich, successful man with his own family but on occasion he did resemble a sulky little boy.

When Emily started to cry half an hour later, the nanny came to take her away. Amy kissed her cheek before handing her back. 'Good timing, Emily, because we must be leaving.'

'So soon?' said Robert. 'You've not seen Jane yet.'

'I know and that's a shame, but Henry is expecting a visit from Knapp. He's due to come to Alardyce to discuss something with him.'

Robert forced himself not to react. 'That gorilla?' was all he said.

'Apparently he has some information for me,' said Henry. 'I asked him to look into Andrew Charteris, as you and I discussed. Knapp is very good at finding out people's secrets.'

Robert wasn't sure whether he was imagining the scrutinising look Henry gave him, so he didn't react to it. 'From my experience of Knapp, all he's good at is hitting people in the stomach and throwing them about the room. That's what he did to me at Uncle Abel's.'

'Never mind, you came out of it unscathed,' smiled Henry, clapping him on the shoulder.

'Tell Jane we're sorry we missed her,' said Amy, pulling on her gloves. 'You must come round to dinner on Friday. Bring Emily too.'

'We will. Thank you, Mother,' he said, kissing her cheek.

Robert walked them to the door to wave them off, only allowing his fury to show when he was alone in his study. They'd only come round to see how he reacted to the mention of Knapp's name. Obviously they'd heard about his murder and assumed he was responsible. It explained why Henry had kept staring at his swollen cheek so suspiciously and why he'd asked him about the door. Knapp must have informed Henry that he had information about his stepson, most likely about his attack on Harriet, but he'd wanted to break bad news like that in person, it certainly wasn't something he could put in a telegram. It was fortunate Jane had been out, or in her innocence she might have mentioned Knapp's visit. He must convince her not to speak of it to anyone.

Robert took a deep, calming breath. Everything was all right. Knapp was gone, taking everything he knew to the grave, and there was nothing linking him to the crime, the Comyns were far too careful for that. However, he couldn't prevent the ill will from brewing up inside him against his parents. They'd used subterfuge to try to trick him. Why hadn't they come straight out with it and asked him? That he could have respected. It was the sneakiness he couldn't bear.

Well, he was making plans to clear the city of all his enemies and the Richardson family were next. If his parents weren't careful, they would find their own names added to his list. One thing he'd learnt recently was to have faith in his own power. No one could bring him down.

17

'What did you think?' Amy asked Henry once they were back in their carriage.

'Well, he was very defensive about the bruise to his face,' he replied. 'I'm sorry, Amy, but that wasn't done a week ago. I don't care what excuses he gave about loose teeth, that just doesn't happen. He also seemed very touchy about his front door.'

'So you're saying Knapp barged into his home, dented his front door and punched him?'

'I think that's the most reasonable scenario.'

Amy peered out of the window. 'Where are we going? This isn't the way to Alardyce.'

'We're going into the Old Town.'

'Really?'

'Don't look so excited, Amy Alardyce. We're not plunging into the city's dark heart. We're going to Knapp's office.'

'Knapp has an office?'

'Yes. Why is that so surprising?'

'I assumed he worked out of some smoky tavern frequented by scarred individuals with no teeth.'

Henry smiled. 'Sorry to disappoint you, my dear, but he has a very respectable office on the corner of Fleshmarket Close.'

'What a thrilling name,' she smiled.

'And it's the closest we're getting to the city's underbelly.'

'I do hope you don't expect me to wait in the carriage.'

'I thought you might like to do some shopping while I go inside.'

'Why would I want to go shopping? I don't need anything.'

'You might enjoy it. You could get yourself some jewellery or a new hat.'

Her eyes narrowed. 'This is because I'm a woman, isn't it? I'm not qualified to walk into an office.'

'Not at all. I just thought you might prefer to visit the shops. It's not often we come into the city.'

'I have no wish to buy a hat or jewellery. I'm coming with you.'

The carriage dropped them off on the High Street at the entrance to the close, which wasn't far from Police Chambers. Amy winced at all the people teeming on the street and the carts rumbling along the cobbles and was reminded of why she rarely ventured into the city. She much preferred the peace and quiet of Alardyce.

Together they walked down the narrow wynd to a door halfway down the close. Henry pushed open the door and they ascended a flight of rickety stairs to the first floor into a surprisingly well-furnished office full of sturdy and practical yet ugly mahogany furniture. There was nothing decorative like a nice painting, vase or ornamentation of any kind. Everything had a purpose. Knapp didn't have time for fripperies.

'Hello, Frank. Is Mr Knapp in?' Henry asked the man who was sitting at a smaller desk at the opposite side of the room to Knapp's large imposing one.

'I'm afraid not,' replied Frank. 'To be honest, Sir Henry, I'm a little worried. He went out last night and I've not seen him since. Did he show up for his appointment with you this morning?'

'No, he didn't, which is why I'm here. I'm worried too. Knapp never misses an appointment.'

'I've been sitting here fretting about what to do,' replied the thin, agitated man. 'He doesn't like anyone checking up on him, but I think something's wrong. However, if all's well and I go to the police, I'm afraid of what he'll do.'

Amy could imagine this nervous creature lived in abject terror of Knapp.

'Does Mr Knapp have any other appointments today?' said Henry.

'Yes, sir. One this afternoon at five o'clock.'

'If he doesn't turn up for that, let me know, and I will instigate proceedings personally, then you won't be blamed.'

'Oh, thank you, sir. That would be wonderful.'

'Send me word when you hear about his five o'clock appointment.'

'I certainly will.'

'Do you know where he went last night?'

'He was going to speak to some informants in the Old Town.'

'Which part of the Old Town?'

'One of the roughest. He didn't specify which. I only know because he wore his cheapest suit, he always does when he ventures into those parts.'

'Do you know what he was going to talk to his informants about?'

'He mentioned some assault.'

'Assault, on whom?'

'He didn't say. All I know is that it happened a week ago.'

'What day last week?'

'Friday. I distinctly remember because he came in here on the Saturday absolutely furious. He was ranting and raving and throwing things around.' Frank indicated a dent in the wall just behind his head. 'He threw my paperweight. If I hadn't ducked, then that dent would now be in my forehead.'

Henry glanced at Amy before looking back at Frank. 'Thank you. You've been very helpful.'

With that, Henry and Amy left and climbed back into their carriage, which was waiting for them on the street.

'I don't like what Frank had to say at all,' said Henry as they set off back for Alardyce.

'Friday was the night Robert had that boxing match,' replied Amy. 'What if...' She trailed off, not wanting to put it into words.

'What if the thrill of the match excited him so much he got carried away and took it out on some poor innocent woman?'

She nodded, looking pale and a little afraid.

'I've been keeping a close eye on the newspapers and there's been no report of any more attacks on women.'

'If it occurred in one of the worst areas of the city, then perhaps the attack wasn't reported.'

'I do know that a lot of the poorer classes turn to Knapp for assistance rather than the police, who they don't trust.'

'So, if Robert did attack a woman in the Old Town the night of the fight, then Knapp could well have found out about it. The woman in question might have turned to him.'

'And Knapp realised it was Robert, hammered at his front door so hard he put a dent in it and punched him in the face.'

'What terrifies me even more than that,' said Amy slowly, 'is what if Knapp's disappeared because Robert wanted him to disappear?'

'He's already killed three people, so it's certainly not beyond him. However, even though he beat Tompkins, Robert could not have got the better of Knapp.'

'He wouldn't need to get his hands dirty. He has the means to pay others to do things for him.' She closed her eyes, a tear sliding down her cheek. 'Dear God, please let us be wrong.'

'We might be,' said Henry, taking her hand. 'For all we know, Knapp's fallen ill and is in hospital somewhere, the postman dented Robert's door and his face is just healing slowly, as he said. We could be jumping to conclusions.'

'I really want to believe that, but Matthew's visitation tells me otherwise. He said the heat in Robert's blood is rising, that he's becoming who he was meant to be and that he's got up to far more than we know.'

'Did he also say he'll be waiting for you when you pass?' said Henry, eyes flashing.

'Yes.'

'That's it, I'm talking to Magda.'

'Like you said, it could be my imagination.'

'You've changed your tune.'

'I just think we've got more pressing matters to attend to than

Matthew's spectre.'

'I still want to discuss it with Magda.'

'As you wish.'

Henry inwardly sighed. This would have to happen now, just as he'd decided to tell Amy about Edward's body resting in the family crypt. How could he drop that on her when she was going to have to deal with more of her son's perversions? Henry didn't think they were letting their imaginations run away with them. He was certain Robert had something to do with Knapp's disappearance and they'd just aroused his suspicions by their visit to his house. Every time life seemed to be getting back on an even keel something else happened to ruin their happiness.

* * *

Back at Alardyce, Amy went up to the schoolroom to play with the children and help them with their lessons to distract herself from her worries. Henry brooded in the library, anxiously awaiting news from Frank, which arrived sooner than expected.

Frank himself turned up at the house, pale-faced and wringing his hands.

'Oh, Sir Henry,' he said when he was led into the library by a footman. 'It's terrible news, terrible indeed.'

'Sit down,' said Henry. 'You look dreadful.'

'I feel it, I've had such a shock. Mr Knapp's dead, sir. They found his body mutilated down some stinking wynd in the Old Town.'

'Mutilated?'

'His stomach had been slashed open and his throat cut. It looked like he'd been in one hell of a fight too, pardon my French, sir. The police told me his innards were poking out of his stomach,' he rasped before closing his eyes and shuddering.

'My God,' breathed Henry.

He poured a whisky for himself and Frank, shoving the glass into the man's shaking hands.

'Thank you,' rasped Frank before gulping down the very expensive single malt. 'Who could get the better of Mr Knapp? I don't understand. He seemed invincible. My only thought is that more than one ruffian was responsible.'

'You could be right. What are the police's thoughts on the matter?'

'They agreed that they're looking for multiple perpetrators.'

'Have they any idea who?'

'It could be any number of suspects, sir, in that part of town. It might not have been personal. It could have been a mugging and he fought back.'

'Or it could be linked to a case he was investigating. Did Mr Knapp keep any records?'

'Sometimes, not always. It depended on the case he was working on.'

'I wonder if you could search the office, find if there's any record of what he was doing in the Old Town that night.'

'I can, but I think the police will get there first. There's some inspector who's very keen on finding who killed him. He was a good friend of Mr Knapp's.'

'What's this inspector's name?'

'Murphy, sir. He's Irish. Mr Knapp has Irish blood too. I mean had,' he ended sadly.

'If you hear anything of interest, please let me know as soon as possible. I'm very keen to help find who did this.' Henry opened a drawer in his desk, took out some money and pressed it into Frank's hand. 'Before the police know, if possible.'

'Leave it with me, sir,' he said, eyes lighting up at the sight of the money.

When Frank had left, Henry went upstairs in search of Amy. He found her sketching with the children. The governess she'd once been still existed inside her.

'I need to talk to you,' he said.

She caught the look in his eye and nodded. 'Carry on with your sketching, children,' she said. 'I'll be back to look at your work.'

They retreated into one of the spare bedrooms to talk. Henry relayed to her everything Frank had told him.

'Oh, God,' breathed Amy. 'Robert did this, didn't he? I just know it. He paid someone to kill Knapp because he had damaging information about him.'

'We don't know that yet. The police are investigating. A lot of crime goes on in the Old Town, it could have been a mugging that went wrong. The evidence indicates he was attacked by more than one person, he may have been overwhelmed.'

'You're right,' she said, taking a deep, calming breath. 'We can't accuse Robert unjustly. It might undo all the progress he's made.'

'Frank's going to see if he can discover why Knapp was in the Old Town that night.'

'What if he finds mention of Robert? He could use it as a blackmail opportunity or take it to the police.'

'He gave me his word he'd come to me first.'

'And you believed him?'

'Yes. He's one of those people who has a tremendous, if misguided, faith in the upper classes. He'll think I have a better chance of getting justice for Mr Knapp than the police.'

'And what if he does produce evidence of Robert's involvement? What will you do then, condemn him to the gallows?'

'Of course not, but better I have it than the police.' Henry took her hands in his own. 'He won't hang, I promise you, Amy, but if he is guilty, we have to do something about it. If he keeps getting off scot-free, his behaviour will only spiral even further out of control.'

'He only cares about Jane's good opinion. We could threaten to tell her.'

'She wouldn't believe us, just like she didn't believe us when we told her about how he attacked Daisy.'

'You're right and they might keep Emily from us.'

'We have to tackle this in a way that doesn't alienate them from us.'

'Just after they were married, Robert said he would keep from us any grandchildren they might have if we interfered in his life, and he will carry out that threat, I have absolutely no doubt.'

'Frank said Knapp's case is being investigated by an inspector called Murphy. I don't know him personally, but his reputation precedes him. The newspapers love him because he's a very tough, no-nonsense character who is ruthless when catching criminals. I fear what will happen if he gets on Robert's trail.'

18

Robert anxiously waited for Jane to come home, she seemed to take forever. When she finally strolled through the door at four o'clock that afternoon, he was almost beside himself.

'Where have you been?' he snapped when she walked into the drawing room.

She frowned. 'At Sarah's. I told you where I was going.'

'You've been gone all afternoon.'

'She's going mad with boredom stuck in the house while she recovers. I kept her company. Why, what's wrong?'

He sighed and took a deep breath, trying to calm down. 'I'm sorry for snapping but I do worry about you when you go out alone.'

'I was taken there and back in the carriage. It wasn't as though I was walking the streets.'

'I know,' he said, taking one of her hands and raising it to his lips to kiss it. 'Please sit. There's something I need to tell you.'

'Has something happened? Is Emily all right?'

'She's fine, it's nothing like that.' He led her to the sofa and sat down beside her. 'I need you to do something for me.'

'Anything, Robert, you know that.'

'Don't mention Knapp's visit here yesterday to anyone, not even my parents.'

'You mean that wild beast who burst into our home?'

'Yes.'

'Of course, but why?'

'Because he's dead.'

'What?' she gasped.

'The news is all over the city, he was a popular local character. He was found murdered in an alley in the Old Town.'

'But... that's horrible.'

'It certainly was a bloody crime by all accounts. Our family can't be linked to it in any way. We've endured so much scandal and finally we're coming out the other side but if the police find out he came here the day he died, it could lead to awkward questions.'

'You never did explain why he came here in the first place.'

'It's just something he liked to do every now and then, to intimidate me. He couldn't stand it that I'd got one over on him when I eloped with you. Often, he would catch up with me when I was out on business or on the way to Jackson's. Yesterday was the first time he had the nerve to come into my home.'

'I can see why you wouldn't want that news getting out. What about the servants? They might say something.'

'Not if they want to keep their positions, they won't. They know their place.'

Her eyes narrowed. 'He did seem very angry about something.'

'I was the only person who ever outwitted him. Worst of all, I was just a boy when I did it and it drove him insane. He saw it as a slur on his reputation. The more successful I became, the angrier he got. He was quite insane.'

'Surely it would be better if you approached the police with this information? They might find out anyway and it will look suspicious if you keep quiet about it.'

'Just imagine what the Richardson family would do if they heard I'd got wrapped up in a murder investigation. They're still smarting over my beating Tompkins. They will snatch any opportunity for revenge. I can't allow that to happen. It wouldn't just be me that would be affected but the entire family – you, Emily, my parents and brothers and sister. Emily and Lydia would be the worst affected, their lives could be ruined. No decent man would go anywhere near them. We would become the infamous Alardyces again, people would refuse us entry into their homes, no more invitations to balls and soirées...'

This bleak future was enough to convince Jane. 'All right, Robert, I won't say a word. It'll be as though it never happened.'

'It's the right thing to do,' he said, kissing her hand again. 'Things are finally going our family's way and we must do nothing to jeopardise that.'

'You're right,' she said with a small smile.

'Come in,' called Robert when there was a knock at the door.

Forbes walked in. 'There's a Mr Bruce to see you, sir.'

'Show him into my study, please.'

The butler bowed before leaving.

Robert looked back at Jane. 'I'm sorry to leave you but that's a business acquaintance of mine.' He kissed her before getting to his feet. 'I shall see you at dinner.'

Jane just nodded, watching him leave. When he'd gone, she remained where she was, pondering her husband's words. She could see the sense of what he'd said but something about the situation made her uneasy. Was there more going on than he was telling her? She forced the thought aside. She couldn't imagine her loving husband being wrapped up in murder. He was just trying to protect their family and their daughter's future.

Jane determined to forget all about it and get on with her life, but she couldn't rid herself of the nagging feeling that something wasn't quite right...

* * *

Mr Bruce was a man who knew things. He made it his business to gather all the nasty little secrets of the rich and powerful in Auld Reekie, information he would share for a very hefty fee. Robert had approached him after he'd learnt that Bruce had been doing some digging on him at the behest of the Richardson family and had offered to pay him double what they were paying him if he would feed them some false information.

Robert thought Mr Bruce a repellent creature – wiry, greasy and eyes constantly alight with cunning. A perpetually smug air hung about him as he considered himself to be more intelligent than everyone else. However, he was extremely good at what he did.

'So how did your meeting with the Richardson family go?' said Robert, reclining in his chair behind his grand gilded desk.

'Very well, Mr Alardyce,' replied Mr Bruce with his shark-like smile. 'They fell for my story about you wanting to buy the Edinburgh Insurance and Fire Trust Company. I told them it was the company of the future and whoever owned the majority share would be set for life. They're determined you won't profit from it.'

'So they're going to invest their own money?'

'Mr Richardson retired from business as he's old and infirm, but his son Benjamin was very keen to hear my news. He recently inherited a substantial sum, around £10,000, from an aunt who passed away a few weeks ago. By some miracle, he hasn't gambled it away and is looking for an investment opportunity. He said he was going to persuade his sister's husband to invest too. He thought that between the two of them, they could buy up all the company's stock. Benjamin has criticised his father for only investing in railways, factories, land and houses, things you can see and touch, which is the smartest way to invest, if you don't mind me saying, sir. He thinks stocks are the future and he said it's time their family joined the modern world and invested more heavily in the stock market. His older brother Innsbruck is in charge of the family's finances since their father decided to retire; however, he's also suffering from some ill health and he has quite a weak personality. Benjamin might be a fool, but he lets nothing get in his way and he's overruling Innsbruck in practically everything.'

'Excellent,' smiled Robert.

In truth, the Edinburgh Insurance and Fire Trust Company was Robert's own company, set up under an assumed name. He'd been careful to give it a very good pedigree, claiming other wealthy people had already invested and that all investments were protected by the banks. There were no laws against making such claims, even if they were untrue. He'd used fraudulent accounts and capital he'd personally invested to show the company was doing a roaring trade and increasing the price of the shares. Robert had gone to a lot of trouble to set his trap for the Richardson family, studying endless articles about frauds committed over the past few decades. The thing was, it was so ridiculously easy to do. No one asked questions when a new company was set up and no audits were done. The Limited Liability Act of 1855 meant there would be very little if no comeback on himself, not that he anticipated there would be. He'd set up the company under an alias he'd carefully cultivated.

When it was discovered the company was a scam – because it was part of his revenge that the Richardson family would learn that they'd been duped – Mr Terence Burgess would be the one everyone would look for and they would never find him. By the time Robert was finished with the Richardson family, they would no longer be the kings around here. It had been tempting to tell the police about Benjamin's sexual proclivities but that hadn't felt to be a very satisfying revenge. Everyone already knew and any simpleton could go whining to the police. All the planning of his fraud had been half the pleasure and he wanted to take everything from the Richardsons, including a considerable chunk of their wealth.

'You've done very well,' he said, handing Bruce more money. 'Have a bonus.'

'Thank you, Mr Alardyce,' he smiled, sliding the money into his jacket pocket. 'It's been a pleasure doing business with you.'

'And you, Mr Bruce. One more thing before you go – I wondered if you'd heard about that ghastly murder in the Old Town?'

'You mean Mr Knapp?' He nodded. 'Aye, I have. A terrible business. I knew him too.'

'Really, how?'

'Our paths crossed more than once and it was never pleasant for myself. He called me an odious little worm who should be dissected alive.'

'That sounds like Knapp.'

'You knew him too, sir?'

'He did some work for my father, which is why I'm interested in the case. I always thought he was a brute.'

'He was that. Once, he hit me so hard I was unconscious for two hours.

He just left me lying in the gutter. In my opinion, the world's a better place without him.'

'Oh, yes?' said Robert, allowing suspicion to flash through his eyes.

'Not that I was anything to do with it,' Bruce hastily added. 'I went out of my way to avoid him.'

Inwardly, Robert was laughing his head off. He wondered what this idiot would do if he knew he was talking to the man responsible, a man who had killed three people with his bare hands, including his own grandmother. That intoxicating sense of power swept through him again. He was becoming rather addicted to it.

'Well, don't let me keep you any longer, Mr Bruce,' said Robert. 'I know you're a busy man. If you hear anything else, let me know immediately.'

'I certainly will, Mr Alardyce,' he replied, shaking his hand before leaving, missing the way Robert's lips curled into a smile.

* * *

Mr Bruce hurried down the street, mistrustfully regarding everyone who passed him by, conscious of the large amount of money he carried. Even in the New Town, muggings did still occur. He resolved to go straight home so he could safely hide the money before making his way to Benjamin Richardson's residence. He was willing to bet he'd pay him a high price to learn of Robert Alardyce's plan to ruin him.

He rushed into his lodgings in a pleasant townhouse on the border between the New Town and the Old Town. His profession gave him a very comfortable living and his house was richly – if rather gaudily – decorated in brocade and Chinese patterned silk for curtains. His drawing room was packed with armchairs, console tables, sofas, screens, paintings, mirrors, books, china and silver. He loved money and he enjoyed spending it even more.

Mr Bruce pulled a leather-bound volume from the towering bookcase but, before he could retrieve the money from his pocket, he was disturbed by a sound behind him. He turned to see two individuals who looked to have stepped out of his worst nightmare. One was massive and appeared to have the strength of a shire horse, but his eyes were passive and dull. The other was small and scrawny, but his eyes glittered with viciousness.

'Who the devil are you?' demanded Mr Bruce.

'Mr Alardyce thought you might do this,' said the scrawny one.

'Do what, come home?'

'You've only come here to hide all that money he gave you. Then you intended to go to see Benjamin Richardson, didn't you?'

'I did not and may I ask what it's got to do with you?' This pair terrified him, but he determined to bluff his way out of the situation. He'd wound up in a lot of trouble in his life and his silver tongue had always got him out of it.

'You did,' said Will. 'The master always knows. Bloody clever he is, isn't he, Fraser?'

The big dumb one just nodded.

'Are you calling an eighteen-year-old boy master?' said Bruce.

'Aye, I am. We've already learnt that something nasty always happens to those who underestimate Robert Alardyce. You should have learnt your lesson before you betrayed him.'

'But I haven't betrayed him.'

'Not yet, but you were about to. We can see it in your heart, can't we Fraser?'

Another nod.

'But he's willing to forgive, if you do something for him.'

'What?' said Bruce warily.

He cringed when the skinny man reached inside his jacket pocket, sighing with relief when he produced a folded piece of paper.

'He wants you to copy this out,' said Will, opening it up and thrusting it into his hands.

Bruce scanned the document, which was covered in Robert's elegant script. His eyebrows shot up. 'He can't be serious?'

'I don't think that man's ever joked in his life. Copy it out nice and neat and we'll be on our way.'

'You mean it?' he said uncertainly.

Will's expression was more a grimace than a grin. 'Cross my heart and don't even think of tricking us. I know I don't look like it, but I can read.'

'I wouldn't dream of it,' said Bruce, sitting at his desk to write. Once the letter was completed as neatly as he could manage it, with his heart beating ten to the dozen, he handed it to Will and anxiously awaited his verdict.

'Very nice,' said Will, studying it before carefully folding it in half and slipping it into a blank envelope. 'Your hand's as pretty as any lady's.'

'Thank you,' he sniffed. 'Was there anything else?'

'Aye, just one more wee thing the master wants us to do.'

'And what's that?' said Bruce when he failed to elaborate. 'No,' he added, shaking his head and backing away at the malevolence that shone out of Will's eyes. 'You said if I wrote that letter, I'd be forgiven.'

'A wee lie. You should recognise one when you hear it after all the lies you've told.'

Bruce frantically scrabbled at his pockets as the two men advanced on him. 'Look,' he shrieked, producing the money Robert had given him. 'Take that and go, please. I won't say a word about this.'

'Thank you,' said Will, taking it from him. 'Very kind of you, sir.'

'You're a very smart man,' he said, trying not to sigh with relief.

'Too right I am and being smart is staying on the right side of Robert Alardyce. If we don't do this, he'll just get someone else to do it, then they'll come for us.' Will wasn't so stupid that he didn't think there were other people equally as dangerous as himself and Fraser in the city. He looked to his brother. 'All right, Fraser, do your stuff.'

Bruce tried to cry out, but a massive hand clamped down over his mouth and he was dragged into the bathroom. His eyes widened when he saw the noose ready and waiting, slung over a beam in the ceiling. He fought and struggled but he was incapable of throwing off his attacker, who felt to be made of marble. His legs kicked and thrashed as the noose was thrown over his head, his frantic breath cut off as the rope was tightened. Now he was incapable of crying out for help, Fraser released his mouth and hauled on the rope until Bruce's kicking feet were a couple of feet off the floor and tied the rope around a hook that had been hammered into the wall.

Will casually glanced up at their thrashing victim, whose eyes were bulging from his head, tongue lolling obscenely. He leaned against the wall, took out one of his knives and examined the blade while they waited for Mr Bruce to die. At one point, he even yawned.

'Is he going to take forever?' he asked his brother. Bruce was still writhing, but his movements were becoming weaker.

'Want me to speed things up?' said Fraser.

'Better not. We don't want to arouse any suspicion. Finally,' he said when Bruce went limp. 'Check if he's really dead.' Confirmation wasn't really necessary. Bruce's appalling visage was enough to tell them he'd gone, but they didn't want to take any chances.

Fraser took his pulse and nodded. 'Aye, he is.'

'Good. Let's set the scene, then.'

Fraser brought in a stool from the kitchen and lined it up with Bruce's feet, ensuring it reached them before knocking it onto its side.

'Another case of suicide in Auld Reekie,' said Will, looking up at the body. He shook his head. 'So sad.' He produced the money Bruce had given him. 'Here's your half,' he said, handing some of the notes to his brother. Robert had told them they could keep it as payment.

Fraser smiled with satisfaction and slid the money into his jacket pocket.

'Let's go to our favourite tavern to celebrate a job well done and don't get carried away,' Will told his brother. 'You need to keep your head. I get the feeling Mr Alardyce is going to keep us very busy.' He produced a pocket watch from inside his jacket and sighed regretfully. 'It's such a shame we can't keep this, but it's got a very important job to do.'

19

Henry was a little alarmed when Rush announced Inspector Murphy wanted to see him.

'What's he doing here?' demanded Henry.

'I'm afraid he wouldn't divulge that to me, sir.'

Henry wished Amy was here, but she'd gone to Magda's to discuss Matthew's visitations. 'You'd better show him in then.'

Inspector Murphy entered the study with a confident stride. He was a tall, broad-shouldered man with a thick dark moustache and a head of equally thick dark brown hair. His hat was tucked under one arm, and he extended his hand to Henry.

'Thank you for seeing me, sir,' he said in a strong Dublin accent.

'You're welcome, Inspector,' replied Henry, rising to his feet and shaking his hand. 'To be honest, I was curious to meet you. I've read about your exploits in the papers.'

'The press do tend to exaggerate,' the inspector replied with more modesty than Henry was expecting.

'Would you care for tea or coffee?'

'No, thank you. I'd like to get straight down to business, if that's all right with you, sir?'

'Yes, fine. That'll be all, Rush.'

The butler bowed before leaving, closing the study door behind him.

'Please, sit,' said Henry, gesturing to the chair before his desk.

'Thank you,' replied the inspector, taking the proffered seat.

'So, what can I do for you?' Henry asked Murphy while retaking his own chair.

'I take it you've heard about the murder of Mr Jacob Knapp in the Old Town?'

'I have. A terrible affair.'

'I believe you were acquainted with him?'

'I was. A very strong, dignified man. I admired him greatly.'

'As did I. We'd known each other a long time, so you can understand why I'm eager to catch his killers.'

'Killers, plural?'

'Indeed. One man could not have got the better of him.'

'That's a good point. So, any clues?'

'We're trying to ascertain why he was in the Old Town that night. In his pocket, we found a notebook that mentioned he had an appointment with you the next day.'

'He did, but he never turned up.'

'Do you have any idea what it was about?'

'I'm afraid not. He sent me a note saying he had some information I might be interested in, but that was all.'

'So you hadn't employed him to find anything specific out for you?'

'No.' Henry couldn't mention Andrew Charteris without dropping Robert in it.

'But you knew him?'

'Yes, he did some work for my father.'

'What sort of work?'

'My father was threatened by a business rival. Mr Knapp protected him.'

'And had you ever hired him?'

'I did. My stepson Robert went through a rebellious stage.'

'What form did this rebellion take?'

'Oh, nothing out of the ordinary. He got in with a dubious set, spent too much of his time and money at brothels. I sent him to stay with my puritan uncle in the city and, as my uncle is a blind old man, I asked Knapp to help him watch over Robert.'

'I see. And how long did this arrangement last?'

'Not long. My wife, Robert's mother, was poisoned by an insane servant who then killed herself. We sent for Robert to come home. The episode seemed to snap him out of his rebellion, so we didn't require Knapp's services again.'

'And how did Robert take to being watched over by Mr Knapp?'

'As you can imagine, he wasn't very happy about it, but he found my uncle's spartan home and religious lessons much more challenging.'

'So you don't think he harboured any grudge against Mr Knapp?'

'Certainly not. He was more furious at me for sending him away. Robert's now a responsible father and husband and is doing very well for himself. It was just a phase he went through.'

'I can understand that. My own son went through something similar. I put a swift halt to it, though.'

'I'll bet.'

'When did you last see Mr Knapp?'

Henry considered mentioning Robert and Jane's elopement to Gretna Green before deciding against it. Knapp had sworn he wouldn't tell a soul as they didn't want the scandal and Henry knew he'd taken his promises very seriously, so he decided to go with a lie. 'When Robert returned to Alardyce, Mr Knapp escorted him back.'

'And when was this exactly?'

'Just over a year ago.'

'And you haven't been in contact with him since?'

'Not until I received that note from him.'

Murphy thought carefully before saying, 'So the last time you employed Knapp was to do with your stepson. Could the note he sent you have had something to do with Robert?'

Outwardly, Henry didn't react but inwardly, panic shot through him. 'I really couldn't say. I don't see how, though, Robert's very happily settled. It could have been something to do with business. He worked for my father, so he knew what affairs our family's money is tied up in and he sometimes did give me information he thought I might find useful.'

'For a fee?'

'Sometimes, sometimes not.'

'When was the last time he gave you some business information?'

'About three years ago. It was to do with an investment I had in an insurance company. He told me the company was going under, so I withdrew my investment and saved myself thousands of pounds.'

'He was a very astute man,' said Murphy with a fond smile.

That fond smile disheartened Henry. It meant the inspector would not stop until he'd caught Knapp's killer. That was assuming Robert was anything to do with it, which hopefully he wasn't.

'He certainly was,' replied Henry.

They spent a moment in quiet contemplation of the man they'd both so admired before Murphy got to his feet and extended his hand. 'Thank you for your time, Sir Henry.'

'You're very welcome. Please let me know if I can be of further assistance. I hope you catch whoever did it very soon.'

'I will. Make no mistake about that.'

Henry wasn't sure if there was warning in the inspector's tone or not, so he just nodded. Only when he'd gone did he exhale with relief.

* * *

'I didn't think it would be so easy to get rid of Matthew's persistent presence,' said Magda once Amy had explained her latest encounter.

'The most frightening thing is that I think he's right, about Robert, I mean,' replied Amy.

They were ensconced together on the couch in Magda's cosy living room before the fire, drinking her homemade nettle tea.

'Why, what has he done now?'

'We're not sure, but we think he's up to something.'

'Probably. He would get bored if he wasn't scheming.'

If anyone else had said something like that about her son, Amy would have been offended, but she knew Magda understood the secrets of Robert's black heart. 'Sadly, you're right.'

'First, let us examine why Matthew is being so persistent. It's because you share a son. It's created a bond between you, a bond he is using to communicate.'

'What scares me most is that he says we're going to be together when I die, that he'll be waiting for me.'

'When we cross over, we go where we want to go, which is usually where the love is strongest. You have a choice, Amy.'

'The thing is,' Amy replied, looking down at her misshapen hands with shame. Magda was one of the very few people she didn't mind seeing them. 'I do love him. Well, part of me does. It's nothing compared to what I feel for Henry, but it's there. It happened in the last moments of his life, when he sacrificed himself to save me. It was born then and it's never left me and I feel so ashamed.'

'You shouldn't, it's perfectly understandable. He made the supreme sacrifice.'

'And I killed him for it.' She'd never confessed this to Magda before, but for some reason, it felt right to tell her. Amy raised her head when Magda failed to reply. 'You don't seem surprised.'

'I'm not usually one to break a confidence but I feel it's important you know – Robert came to talk to me when Jane was heavy with child. He was feeling a little... uneasy and hoped I could give him some herbs to help him. He told me about Matthew's death.'

'What do you mean, uneasy?'

'Jane was unable to be intimate with him and it was causing him some frustration.'

'And he was worried he'd be unfaithful?' Amy sounded hopeful because that would be infinitely preferable to him wanting to assault a woman.

'From what I could ascertain,' was all she said.

'Did you manage to help him?'

'I did, by connecting my knee sharply with his groin.'

Amy's eyes widened. 'What?'

'It worked, although I did warn him the effects would only be temporary,' she said, making Amy laugh.

'Matthew said knowing I was responsible for his father's death has ripped open a wound inside Robert. When I pulled that knife out of him, I was trying to protect my boy. Now I fear I've only made things worse for him.'

'Whatever Robert has done and whatever he does in the future is his own choice. He's a grown man capable of making his own decisions. He may choose to blame you to assuage any guilt, but it doesn't make him right.'

'And how he loves to blame me and Henry for everything,' she sighed. 'Have you heard about Knapp?'

'Yes. Most unfortunate. Despite his harsh and often dubious methods, he was a good man with a good soul.'

'It was such a shock. Oh, I'm sorry, Magda, you must be fed up with me coming here and dropping all my problems on you.'

'I don't mind at all. You're my friend and that's what friends are for.'

'You're my friend too, one of the dearest I've ever had. If there's anything I can ever do to help you like you've helped me, you've only to ask and I'll do all in my power to assist.'

'I appreciate that very much, Amy, but I don't have any problems or worries. I lose myself in mother nature and all her beautiful creatures. They're much less complicated than people.'

'Isn't that the truth? Sometimes I envy you, Magda, living a peaceful life in this lovely cottage, spending your time helping and healing people, surrounded by your animals.'

Magda thought that she had never once envied Amy her troubled life, despite all her wealth and the luxury she lived in. 'I will come to Alardyce House in three nights to see if I can sense Matthew's presence.'

'Is there something special about that night?' said Amy, knowing Magda did nothing haphazardly.

'Yes. It's new moon, when the energies are clearest and easiest for me to read.'

'What will you do if he is there?'

'I don't know yet. It depends on what I find.'

'You must stay with us for a few nights, I do enjoy your company and having you around the house.'

'In that case, I accept. I find it hard to turn down being waited on hand and foot,' Magda smiled, silver eyes twinkling.

* * *

Amy walked idly back to Alardyce House, wanting the time alone to consider what Magda had told her. She'd confirmed for her that Robert had felt the urge rising inside him again. Her boy was heading back down that dark path.

As she walked up the drive, she saw a dramatic figure wrapped in a long black coat and a black hat making his way towards her, silver-topped cane striking the ground with each step.

'Henry,' she said as they met halfway down the drive. 'I thought you had work to do.'

'I needed some fresh air to think,' he replied. 'Inspector Murphy has just been to see me.'

'About Knapp?'

'Yes. I was forced to tell him about Knapp watching over Robert at my uncle's house. I had no choice, or he would have been suspicious, but I said Robert just went through a rebellious stage – brothels, unsuitable friends, the standard thing most young men go through.'

'Did he believe you?'

'I think so. His son went through something similar. I didn't mention Gretna Green. I said after that I never heard from him again, until the note Knapp sent me, which I said I thought was something to do with business. He seemed satisfied and left.'

'That's a relief. What sort of man is he?'

'Upright, intelligent, determined to find Knapp's killer. He will not stop. Hopefully he'll find the culprit and it won't be anything to do with Robert.'

'I'm not sure about that. Magda said he visited her because he was feeling edgy when Jane was heavily pregnant.'

'Ah, I see.'

'What if he's been hiding his urges from us all this time? We know killing comes easy to him. I'm so afraid it's happening again but this time we have no control over him and he has a lot of resources at his disposal. Why did I give him that money all at once? I should have given it to him more gradually.'

'Even if you had, he would have trebled it. He has a tremendous head for business.'

'Which is even more worrying. He's wily and clever. Oh, I'm sick of thinking about it all. Take me to bed, Henry.'

'Now, in the middle of the afternoon?'

Her eyes filled with fondness. 'Yes, Henry. Let's be wild and untamed and make love in the middle of the afternoon. I'm sure it hasn't been taxed, yet.'

She linked her arm through his as they walked back to the house, laughing when Henry took her hand and they practically ran inside.

20

Robert was just about to leave the house to go to Jackson's when Forbes announced he had a visitor.

'Who is it?' he snapped. He was feeling tense again, the dark thoughts whispering in the back of his mind, and he wanted to get to Jackson's to take out his frustrations on someone else's face.

'Inspector Murphy, sir.'

'Inspector? You mean as in a police inspector?'

'Yes, sir.'

'What does he want?'

'He said he'd only discuss that with you.'

'Fine, show him in, but don't bring any tea because I'm due at Jackson's.'

Forbes bowed before exiting, leaving Robert to wonder why the hell a police inspector was in his home. It couldn't be anything to do with Knapp, the Comyns were too careful. He didn't employ idiots. It could be to do with his fight with Tompkins. After all, bare-knuckle fights were illegal and news of it was all over the city.

Robert had hoped the inspector would be a weak fool he could easily manipulate. His heart sank when a strapping officer with an enormous moustache and determined eyes walked into his study.

'Mr Alardyce,' he said in his heavily accented voice, extending a hand to him. 'Thank you for seeing me.'

'You're welcome but I'm afraid I can't give you much time or I'll be late for an appointment.'

'This won't take long. First of all, I'd like to congratulate you on your fight with Tommy Tompkins.' He smiled when Robert refused to reply. 'Don't worry, sir, that's not why I'm here. Personally, I enjoy a good bare-knuckle fight. I heard you fought in the Irish style.'

'Yes,' said Robert slowly. 'My mentor may be Scottish, but he trained with the best fighters in Dublin.'

'I know Jackson of old. You have the best teacher in the city.'

'I certainly do.'

'I'm afraid I'm here on a much graver matter. I trust you've heard about the murder of Jacob Knapp in the Old Town?'

Robert nodded. 'A terrible business. He did some work for my family.'

'I believe you were more intimately acquainted with him?'

Robert studied the man closely. His eyes were open and honest, but Robert could smell cunning a mile off and this man reeked of it. 'Yes. I take it you've already spoken to my stepfather?'

Murphy nodded, scrutinising him closely with his sharp eyes.

It was then Robert recalled Henry saying Knapp had arranged an appointment with him the day he died. His stepfather must have been top of this man's list to talk to and whatever Henry had told him had sent him here. He had no choice but to talk or it would cast suspicion on himself.

'My father sent him to watch over me while I was staying with my uncle in the city.'

'May I ask why he thought you needed someone to watch over you?'

'At the time, we weren't getting along very well. We argued a lot, mainly about my dissolute friends.'

'And who are these friends?'

'Forgive me if I seem reluctant, but I'm a respectable man now with a wife I adore and a beautiful daughter. Those friends are part of a past I don't like to think about.'

'I understand, but it could help my investigation.'

'How?'

'I'm talking to everyone who had any dealings with Mr Knapp. All routine, you understand, sir. It's nothing to be concerned about.'

'My friends only met Knapp once when he dragged me out of a brothel. I managed to sneak out of my uncle's house one night. Knapp came to tell me my mother was gravely ill and I had to return to Alardyce.' Robert was willing to gamble that this man knew nothing about the elopement to Gretna Green, Henry was far too good at hiding secrets. 'After that, I never saw him again.'

'I still need those names, sir.'

'Very well,' he sighed. 'Daniel Sweeney, Thomas McColl and Andrew Charteris. The only one I have any dealings with any more is Andrew because he's a respected medical man, although I did see the other two at the bare-knuckle fight.'

'I appreciate how candid you're being, Mr Alardyce.'

'Anything to help law and order. I heard Knapp's murder was very brutal. Whoever's responsible needs taking off the streets as soon as possible.'

'If only everyone was as upstanding a citizen as yourself, sir.'

Robert wasn't sure if Murphy was mocking him or if his paranoia was rearing its head again.

'So you've no idea who would want to kill Mr Knapp?' said Murphy.

'None whatsoever, I'm afraid, although I do believe he did interact with the less desirable members of society. It could have been anyone, especially in the Old Town.'

Murphy merely nodded. 'I have no more questions for you, Mr Alardyce, so I won't take up any more of your time. Thank you for seeing me.'

'You're welcome.'

Robert watched Murphy leave. The man was impossible to read. He wouldn't like to play cards with him, he'd end up losing a fortune. Neither did he like it that he came here asking questions, despite his claims that it was routine. He needed to find out all he could about Inspector Murphy.

* * *

As Murphy was escorted to the door by Forbes, he showed him a photograph of Knapp.

'Has this man ever come to the house?'

He could have sworn the butler's eyes widened slightly before the emotion was eradicated by professionalism.

'No, sir, not to my knowledge.'

'You're absolutely certain?'

'Yes, sir.'

He remained defiant in the face of Murphy's close scrutiny. The inspector sighed and shoved the photograph back into his pocket before leaving.

'How did it go, sir?' asked Sergeant Lees, his right-hand man, who had waited outside on the pavement.

'The interview was satisfactory, but I can't shake the feeling they were keeping something from me,' replied Murphy.

'They, sir?'

'Robert Alardyce and his butler. I'm certain the butler recognised Knapp's photograph, but he refused to admit anything.'

'What's Alardyce like?'

'I was expecting a wet-behind-the-ears boy but he's not, far from it, actually. He's clever and crafty and he knows more than he's saying. We need to keep an eye on him, Lees.'

Murphy stared thoughtfully at the house before sighing and heading down the street, the sergeant following.

* * *

Robert couldn't find anyone willing to fight him at Jackson's after he'd beaten someone to a pulp in the club's ring and then not only defeated a bare-knuckle champion but ruined his career too. He was almost tempted to challenge Jackson himself but decided he didn't want his brains knocking out of his head.

'I'll find someone to fight you,' Jackson told him. His trade had doubled thanks to Robert.

'But I want a fight now,' he told him, hands clenching and unclenching.

The dark whispers were growing louder in his head, taunting him, demanding release but he daren't, not after Knapp's murder in the Old Town.

'You can have a go at the punch bag,' he told him.

'I suppose I've no choice,' he sighed.

Robert pounded at the punch bag, unleashing all of his rage on it but, as it was incapable of releasing any cries of pain, it did nothing to assuage his rising fever.

He tore off the gloves, threw them to the floor and stormed through the club back to the changing rooms, everyone jumping out of his way.

He left the club and stalked the streets, considering going to Alardyce to ride and hunt. The exercise, fresh air and freedom might help, but he knew it wouldn't silence the whispers in his head. There was only one thing that could do that, but he was reluctant after his last attack had brought Knapp to his door. However, if he didn't do something, he knew he would commit a rash act that really would land him in prison.

The day was dark and grey, a thick yellow fog hanging over the city, the product of all the smoke and sulphur belched out by industry and household fires. Robert often pined for the fresh, clean air of Alardyce. The longing to possess that grand estate was starting to become firmly fixed in his mind. It was everything he wanted but it had been entailed to John as the eldest of Henry's biological sons. In recompense, Robert was to receive all of his mother's vast fortune. She'd given him £20,000 when he'd married but there was still another £30,000 to come when she died. This arrangement had never bothered him before, it had always felt to be a fair compromise but lately, as his ambition to possess his own estate grew in his mind, with it the desire to be master of Alardyce was rising.

He pushed those thoughts aside. The last thing he needed while he was in so agitated a state was to be around his parents, who would spot it immediately. Their judgement and condemnation would only make things worse. He had to handle this himself.

Robert considered going to Vivienne's but knew that would only provide temporary relief and if he unintentionally took his violence out on one of the girls, he would be banned for life. The restrictions and conventions of society felt to be suffocating him and a heaving sensation started up in his chest. Suddenly he couldn't bear all the rules and regulations of how to behave, of what you could and couldn't do. He wished he could grab polite society by the gilded chain around its neck and throttle it until it died in his hands and he was liberated.

The sensation was so overwhelming, he ducked down a quiet back street and doubled over, fighting for breath. His heart punched against his ribcage so hard he feared he might die, everything swimming before his eyes.

Then he felt it – a snap as the demon that dwelt inside him, enraged at being shackled for so long, finally broke its chains. Robert's eyes grew wilder and darker, hands curling into fists, an immense sense of power filling him.

He straightened up and threw back his head, gnashing his teeth, every muscle in his body popping out. So this was who he was meant to be. By God, it felt good.

A low chuckle to his left caused him to whip round, but no one was there.

'Father?' he breathed, certain he could feel Matthew's intimidating presence. The corner of Robert's mouth curled into a smile. His real father was here to witness the coming of age of his son.

Up ahead, he saw a woman walking alone. As her back was to him, she had failed to notice him.

Pulling up the collar of his coat and tugging down his hat, he followed her.

Robert intended to do his real father proud.

* * *

Murphy stared with dismay at Mr Bruce's dangling body. The face was bloated and distended, eyes popping out of his head, tongue lolling. It wasn't the first hanging victim he'd seen but he'd never got used to their eyes. He couldn't bear the way they bulged beyond the lids.

'Looks like it was suicide, sir,' said Sergeant Lees, indicating the kicked over stool. 'His poor landlady came up to collect the rent and found the door ajar. She walked in and saw this horror. She fainted, she's being looked after by the old lady on the floor below, another tenant of hers.'

'Was Mr Bruce behind with the rent?'

'Nope. He always paid on time and never missed a payment. It was routine that she came up on the first of each month to collect. Apparently, he was the ideal tenant – quiet, kept the place nice, never any trouble. He'd lived here for five years.'

'Judging by the place, he wasn't suffering any money troubles,' said Murphy. 'Some of this stuff is really expensive.'

'Maybe he overspent and ended up in debt?'

'That's something we need to look into. I won't feel easy about this until we find a motive for suicide.'

'You think it might not be, sir?'

'Cyril Bruce was an acquaintance of Jacob Knapp's. The two loathed each other but they did work together several times and exchanged information. I don't like Bruce's death so soon after Knapp's murder. Tell the police surgeon to look for any signs of violence on Bruce's body, no matter how small. I want to be sure he did this to himself.'

'Right, sir,' said Lees, who was a little shocked. He'd thought this was an open and shut case and had expected Murphy to agree.

'And search this place thoroughly. I want every nook and cranny checked and double-checked. Any skimping on that order will lead to my toe being booted up several arses.'

'Yes, sir,' said Lees, snapping to attention.

'There's more going on here than we know,' continued Murphy, talking more to himself than anyone else. 'And I will get to the bottom of it.'

'You might be right, sir,' said a voice.

A frowning Murphy turned to see a young constable standing behind him. 'Oh, how kind of you to agree. I'm so glad I have the expert opinion of someone who's been in this job six weeks.'

'I meant because of this, sir,' he said, holding up a gold pocket watch. 'It's Mr Knapp's.'

Murphy snatched it off him with gloved hands and turned over the timepiece to reveal the inscription inside – *To Jacob from Eliza 1887.*

'This was a gift from his wife,' said Murphy. 'She gave it to him the year before she died. Where did you find it?'

'In a drawer in the desk, sir. It was hidden under some papers.'

'Knapp carried this around with him everywhere he went.'

'Would he have taken it with him into the Old Town?' said Lees.

'Yes,' replied Murphy. 'Although he would have hidden it. He never left it anywhere and he was very confident of being able to defend himself against any mugger.'

'So Bruce here killed him, stole the watch and kept it. Makes sense because, judging by this place, he was a magpie. He liked pretty shiny things.'

'Can you imagine Bruce killing Knapp?'

'Well, no, sir, but he might have had help.'

'I don't know why he'd do such a thing. After their last falling out, Bruce went out of his way to avoid Knapp.'

'Maybe he thought he was protecting himself? He had the money to pay someone to do it for him. This watch might have been proof they did the job.'

'Perhaps,' said Murphy, continuing to stare at the watch, wishing it could speak.

'Then why hang himself?' said the constable. 'Sir,' he hastily added when Lees frowned at him.

'He couldn't live with the guilt,' said Lees. 'This was his only way out of the torment.'

'We found a lot of laudanum in a chest in the parlour,' said the constable. 'He could have taken the lot. It would have been a better way to go than this,' he added, grimacing at the body.

'That's a very good point, Constable,' said Murphy. 'One day, you might make a good detective.'

'I would love that, sir, it's why I joined up.'

But Murphy had already stopped listening, his mind working to put the pieces together.

21

Robert returned home in a much calmer frame of mind. The dark thoughts had retreated, as had the demon that lived inside him, but now it was free of its shackles, he knew it would be easier for it to spring back into life. For now, it was resting in a haze of contentment, enjoying reliving its victim's screams, the sight of her blood welling from the welts on her back and the feel of its hands around her throat. The woman had survived, but only just. Robert had released her neck moments before death approached.

'Robert, where have you been?' demanded Jane the moment he was through the door. 'We're supposed to be dining with Mr and Mrs Gregory this evening. If you hurry, you'll have time to change.'

He couldn't stand the thought of spending any time with that tedious couple. 'I'm not going,' he told her.

'But you have to. We said we'd go.'

'You can go if you like, but I'm staying here,' he said, sinking into a chair in the drawing room before the fire. The fever in his blood had died away, leaving him feeling cold and shivery but content.

'Robert, you have to come. You can't give your word then go back on it.'

'If I recall correctly, I didn't give my word. You gave it for me without asking and I'm not going.'

'But you have to.'

'I refuse to spend any time with those odious people.'

'But you said...'

He slammed his fist down on the arm of the chair. 'I'm not going,' he bellowed. 'And neither are you.'

She stared at him in astonishment. In all the time they'd known each other, he had never once shouted at her. 'Don't talk to me like that, Robert.'

'I'll talk to you any way I like. I am master of this house, not you. Send the Gregorys a message telling them we're not going. I don't care what excuse you give.'

Her eyes filled with hurt. 'Why are you talking to me like this? What have I done wrong?'

'I'm sick and tired of being badgered into spending time with people I cannot stand. I've had enough, Jane, and I'm not standing for it any more. Now send that bloody note before I go round there myself and tell them exactly what I think of them.'

He yelled every single word at her and when he'd finished, a terrible, shocked silence filled the room.

Jane's eyes were full of unshed tears, her chest rising and falling rapidly as she fought to contain the sobs while Robert glared at her with black eyes.

'Tell them yourself, you horrible beast,' she yelled back at him.

With that, she ran out of the room and upstairs, her sobs echoing down to him.

'Peace at last,' said Robert, getting up to pour himself a whisky.

He returned to the armchair, rested his feet on a footstool and gazed into the fire, revelling in that sense of power still pounding through his veins. Whereas before it had always raised its head before vanishing again, this time, it remained. He'd let Jane push him around too much, allowed her to force him into doing things he didn't want to do, but not any more. Finally, she'd been put in her place.

* * *

Amy noted Jane was rather subdued when she and Robert came for dinner two nights later. In fact, she seemed unable to bring herself to look at him, and fear filled Amy's heart. Robert seemed his usual self, in fact he was very jovial and doted on Emily, as always, but he practically ignored his wife. Amy saw Henry had noticed it too and she could tell he was as concerned as she was.

One thing Amy adored about her relationship with her husband was that they could communicate without words and, with a single glance, they came up with a plan between them to get to the bottom of the mystery.

After dinner, Henry took Robert into his study on the pretext of discussing some business. While Emily slept in Jane's arms, Amy's younger children played, leaving the two women free to talk.

'What's going on, Jane?' Amy asked her.

'What do you mean?' she replied, forcing a carefree smile.

'You can barely bring yourself to look at Robert. Have you had a falling out?'

'No, of course not.'

Amy noted the strain around the younger woman's eyes and the paleness of her skin. 'Please don't lie to me. I've been married for years, so I know when something's wrong between a husband and wife. Please tell me,' she added, placing her hand over Jane's when tears filled her eyes.

'It was two nights ago. We were supposed to dine with the Gregorys, who live three doors down from us. Robert came home late. I said if he changed quickly, we could still make it, but he refused, saying he didn't want to spend a moment in the company of that odious couple. The Gregorys aren't odious, they're very nice. They're one of the few families in the city who have never judged us. When I said that would be terribly rude, he said he wasn't going and neither was I, that he was master of the house and I should obey.'

'Did you go to the Gregorys?'

Jane shook her head. 'He wouldn't allow it. He was so beastly, he shouted at me. He's never shouted at me before.'

'And what did you do?'

'I said he could tell them himself and ran upstairs. I thought he'd follow me up and apologise, but he didn't. In fact, he hasn't spoken to me since. I don't know what to do, Aunt Amy, I've never known him behave like this before.'

'Do you know what's caused this sudden change?'

'I've no idea. I've thought and thought but I can't come up with anything. When I saw him earlier in the day, he was fine, my same darling Robert, but these past two days, he's been so different I hardly recognise him.'

'Has he shouted at you again or done anything else?' she said, almost afraid to ask.

'No. He's just treated me as though I don't exist.'

'How has he been with Emily?'

'The same doting father. I'm so afraid that now he has a child, he's lost interest in me.'

'I'm sure that's not true. A marriage can't be constantly harmonious. There will be ups and downs.'

'I know, but this is different. Something about him has changed and I can't put my finger on what.'

'Has he ever... hurt you physically?'

'Oh, no, nothing like that and he never would.'

'Thank God,' breathed Amy.

'It's when he ignores me that's the worst, I can't stand it. I'd rather he shouted at me, that's preferable to the silence.'

'I'll speak to him.'

'Oh, no, I think that might only make things worse. He's always so para-noid about people interfering with his business.'

'You can't go on this way. I'll talk to him and make him see sense. Now don't fret,' she added, patting Jane's arm when she started to cry. 'We can sort this out between us.'

'All right, Aunt Amy. I'm sure you know best.'

'I do. All will be well, I promise. Now have a sherry.'

'I'd rather have a Scotch,' she said, making Amy smile.

* * *

Amy was waiting for Robert when he exited Henry's study, both of them talking eagerly.

'Why are you lurking there, Mother?' said Robert.

She ignored the question. 'I take it you two had a good chat?'

'We're going into business together,' smiled Robert. 'Father's spotted an opportunity in South Africa.'

'Sounds exciting,' she replied, the tone in her voice not matching her words. 'Can I speak to you in private?'

'I am popular tonight,' he said, gaze turning suspicious.

'You can use my study,' said Henry.

Amy walked into the study without a word. Robert looked questioningly at Henry, who shrugged and headed towards the drawing room.

'Robert,' said Amy.

He sighed and followed her inside, closing the door behind him.

'Jane tells me you're ignoring her,' she opened.

He shook his head. 'So that's what this is about.'

'Why are you treating her so cruelly?'

'I am not being cruel, I'm annoyed. She's always pushing me into doing things I don't want to do, accepting every invitation we receive without bothering to ask me. For months, I've gone along with her plans, but what about what I want? She never listens when I tell her I hate going to parties and soirées.'

'I thought that was what you wanted, a reintroduction into society?'

'It is, but not for myself, for Jane and Emily and my brothers and sister.'

'So why, after all the trouble you've gone to in order to get that acceptance back into society, do you resent Jane enjoying the fruits of your hard work?'

'Because she insists on dragging me into it and I loathe all those fools. They're so boring and stupid and weak.'

Darkness flashed through his eyes, jaw tensing, muscles tightening before he forced himself to relax.

'It's only natural,' said Amy. 'You're her husband and she wants you by her side. I suppose this is my fault too. You were sheltered from society, brought up believing that as long as you have your family, you don't need anyone else, but Jane was raised differently. She was taken into society when she lived in London, she got used to attending balls and dinner parties and she enjoys it. You have to understand, Robert, that you have your businesses to occupy your time. Other than Emily, Jane has nothing except society.'

He sighed and nodded. 'I suppose.'

'The secret to a happy marriage is compromise.'

'I thought it was keeping things fresh and exciting.'

'That's half the secret. This is the other half. Talk to her, ask her to come to you first with invitations before blindly accepting them all. I can understand how that might get annoying.'

'I don't want to accept any of them. I just want to work and then go home to my family. I don't care about other people.'

'Unfortunately, other people are a side effect of life,' she replied, drawing from him a reluctant smile. 'You knew they'd be a part of the life you chose, so you need to learn to deal with them. Accept some invitations, turn others down and talk to Jane. Ignoring her will get you nowhere. You must make this up with her as soon as possible. Don't tell me you're getting bored of her already,' she said when he sighed again.

'No, of course not. She's still my angel, but I resent apologising when I've done nothing wrong.'

'But you have. You shouted at her then refused to speak to her for days. That's not how a mature man behaves.'

'I suppose Saint Henry would never behave in such a way.'

'He wouldn't dare.'

The corner of his mouth lifted into a smile. 'I'll bet, but Jane's not like you. No woman is.'

'Not many women have endured what I have, and I pray they never do. Make things up with her, Robert. It's not pleasant for Emily living in such an atmosphere. You can easily fix this with a word.'

'Yes, all right,' he muttered down at the floor.

Amy grabbed his chin and forced him to look at her. 'You're a man now, not a sulky little boy. Behave like one.'

'You're right, I am a man, meaning I no longer have to listen to my mother.'

'You will always have to listen to your mother, no matter how old you are, and this mother in particular will not take any nonsense. Make up with your wife, set things right.'

Robert nodded. 'I should. I've not enjoyed the past couple of days.'

'Haven't you?'

His eyes glittered. 'What do you mean?'

'You like control, just like Matthew did. You've enjoyed having power over Jane's emotions.' She scowled when he failed to reply. 'You're not going to deny it?'

'Why should I when it's true?' he said before knocking back his whisky.

'Don't you dare hurt that girl. Do you remember what Henry and I said to you before you decided to elope? We said you would eventually get bored of her and then you would destroy her. I swear to God, Robert, if you do, then you and I are finished. You might think you can get away with attacking women in the street...'

'I do not.'

'Don't treat me like a fool. Now you will go into the drawing room and you will behave like a proper husband. Do you understand me?'

He put down his glass and nodded. 'Yes, Mother,' he said, although there was a swaggering sarcasm in his tone.

Amy's eyes narrowed as she watched him leave. When he'd gone, she poured herself a whisky and drank it down in one go. Her control over her son was slipping. One day soon, he would choose not to listen to her. She was also starting to find his presence intimidating. Every day, he became more like Matthew.

She returned to the drawing room, the ice Robert had placed in her heart after their conversation melting when she saw Henry cradling Emily in his arms, looking out of the window into the gathering darkness. Jane and Robert were quietly talking on the sofa at the opposite side of the room and holding hands. When she walked in, Jane gave her a grateful smile before turning her attention back to her husband. She was happy again, but Amy knew it would only be fleeting. Robert would hurt her repeatedly until, one day, he would smash her heart to bits, and there was nothing she could do to stop it.

The doorbell rang and Rush escorted Magda into the room, to Robert's dismay.

'Sorry I missed dinner,' she said. 'But a woman in the village unexpectedly went into labour.'

'I didn't know you were supposed to join us,' said Robert.

'I was but sadly I couldn't make it earlier.'

'We can arrange some food if you're hungry,' smiled Amy, stepping forward to greet her friend.

'No, thank you. My patient's husband was so pleased with me safely delivering his new son that he fed me. If you don't mind, I'll have a cup of tea in front of the fire.'

'Of course. Rush, some tea, please.'

'My lady,' he bowed before slowly shuffling out.

'And how is this beautiful little lady?' Magda smiled at Emily. She held her hands out for her. 'May I?'

Henry handed her the baby and Magda cradled her to her chest. 'She's a strong, healthy babe.' She looked to Jane. 'She'll keep you on your toes when she starts walking.'

'I don't doubt it.' Jane smiled with pride.

Magda looked to Robert. 'And how are you?'

'Fine, thank you,' he replied.

Amy was amused by the mistrust in his eyes. Magda seemed to be the only person he was wary of any more.

'Excellent,' she replied. 'Ah, here's my tea,' she said when a footman entered carrying a tray. Magda handed Emily to Jane before taking the armchair by the fire.

'It's a bit late for a social call, isn't it, Magda?' said Robert. 'You'll have to be heading home soon.'

'Your parents kindly invited me to stay for a couple of nights.'

'Why, when you live so close?'

'Because we enjoy Magda's company,' said Henry.

Robert just gave Magda another of his mistrustful stares, and she looked back at him steadily.

'I had a police inspector visit me yesterday,' announced Magda before picking up her cup of tea.

Jane was a little startled by the effect this pronouncement had on her husband, who went rigid.

'You did?' he said.

'Yes,' continued Magda. 'Inspector Murphy. He asked me about poor Mr Knapp.'

'Why did he ask you?'

'He was asking around the village, seeing if anyone had met him.'

Robert noticed a look pass between his parents. 'You didn't know?'

'We had no idea,' replied Henry. 'He came to talk to me then left. I assumed he'd gone back to the city.'

Robert looked back at Magda. 'What did you tell him?'

'That I saw Mr Knapp once when he returned with you from the city. After that, I never saw him again. He asked other people in the village, but no one knew Mr Knapp, so he left.'

'I don't understand why this inspector is so interested in Alardyce,' said Jane.

'He's just following up on Knapp's movements, that's all,' said Henry. 'It's perfectly routine.'

Jane might have been innocent, but she certainly wasn't stupid. She glanced at her husband, who appeared to be deep in thought. She couldn't possibly have guessed that he was wondering if he could get the Comyns to remove the inconvenient inspector. Robert dismissed the idea as soon as it had occurred to him. With Knapp and then Bruce, a third death would look too suspicious, especially that of a respected inspector whose name was always in the newspapers. However, accidents could always be arranged.

* * *

Once Robert and Jane had left with Emily, and the children were being put to bed by the nanny, Magda unexpectedly announced to Amy and Henry, 'Matthew is very close to Robert.'

Amy gaped at her while Henry choked on his brandy.

'Excuse me?' he said between coughs.

'I felt Matthew's presence very strongly when I walked into the room. Now Robert's gone, it has dissipated somewhat.'

'I'm not surprised,' said Amy. 'Robert becomes more like him every day.'

'It's not just because of that. The darkness around Robert is drawing Matthew to him. He'll never be free as long as his spectre is around.'

'How do we get rid of him?'

'I fear any attempt I make will fail and I'm always reluctant to conduct exorcisms.'

'Exorcism?' exclaimed Henry.

'Sshhh,' Amy told him.

'Sorry,' he replied in a quieter voice. 'Exorcism? I didn't know that was what you had in mind.'

'Don't worry, Sir Henry,' said Magda. 'I don't intend to perform one. They can very often make matters worse. Relatively quiet activity can be increased tenfold.'

'What else can be done?' said Amy.

'I'm afraid that's down to you and Robert. You need to cast Matthew out of your hearts and minds.'

'I have done, repeatedly, and he refuses to go.'

'I anticipate that's because of Robert's strong connection to him.'

'So I must tolerate his unwanted presence?'

'Don't fear him. He has no power over you, only what you permit him to have. Also...'

'Yes?' said Henry when she trailed off.

'From what you've told me, Matthew gave Amy a very propitious warning. It may be handy to keep him around in case he has more warnings.'

'I can't believe I'm having this conversation,' sighed Henry.

'I suppose you're right, Magda,' said Amy. 'Matthew's much more useful in death than he ever was in life.'

She glanced over her shoulder, certain someone was standing behind her but seeing nothing. Amy stifled the shudder that ran down her spine.

22

'You're certain?' Murphy asked the police surgeon in the mortuary at the Edinburgh Royal Infirmary. 'There are bruises?'

'Yes, here on the right arm,' replied Sir Henry Littlejohn, a tall, regal-looking man with thinning grey hair and prominent cheekbones. A thick black apron coated in blood was wrapped around his slender frame. He was one of the foremost citizens in Edinburgh, whose work in hygiene reform was changing the lives of many of the city's residents for the better. He had a brilliant mind, and his expertise in forensic evidence had helped put away many a criminal. Murphy saw him as one of the leading lights in changing the way detective work was done. He'd learnt so much from this man, who had been part of the inspiration for Arthur Conan Doyle's Sherlock Holmes. Murphy loved those books and had adapted a lot of his methods from them, a fact he was careful to conceal from his luddite colleagues.

Poor Mr Bruce had been cut open, every part of him prodded and poked and assessed before being taken out and weighed, as per the inspector's instructions, before all his organs had been replaced and he'd been sewn back up. Littlejohn raised Bruce's right arm with his bloodied gloved hand to indicate the area just below the right wrist.

'You have the eyesight of a hawk, sir,' commented Murphy. 'That bruise is barely visible.'

'Because, in my opinion, he was grabbed through his clothing. There's also a very slight discolouration around the left side of his mouth, as though someone had put their hand over it.'

'To silence him?'

'It's very possible, but then again, those bruises could have occurred earlier in the day. He could have got into a scuffle with someone. Was he that type?'

'He was a seedy little criminal but he used his brain to commit his crimes, not his fists. Bruce certainly wasn't a fighter.' Murphy attempted to examine the tiny bruise at the corner of Bruce's mouth without looking at the rest of his face. Littlejohn had made no attempt to close his bulging eyes.

'He was also a physically slight man,' said Littlejohn. 'No doubt he was easy to overpower.'

'Any other signs?'

'I'm afraid not. If he was murdered, whoever did it knew what they were doing.'

Murphy returned to Police Chambers, feeling troubled. It would be so easy for him to write this off as suicide, claim Bruce was responsible for Knapp's death and tie up two cases that were very much in the public eye. Bruce's death had also made the papers, as it was known he did less than scrupulous work for the rich and influential of the city, but Murphy's instincts refused to allow him to take that line because he knew it was wrong. A third party was involved, he was now certain of it. The problem was finding the evidence to prove his theory.

'Sir,' said Lees, accosting him before he was even through the door. 'I've got something to tell you.'

'Not yet,' Murphy told him, indicating the journalists thronged outside the four-storeyed Police Chambers on the corner of Parliament Square and High Street on the Royal Mile. Murphy loathed journalists. To him, they were a bigger pest than the Scottish midge. He breathed a sigh of relief when he passed through the Doric-columned entrance into the cool interior, Lees trotting after him like a puppy. Only once they were inside the

building and the sergeant had closed the door behind them did Murphy
allow his colleague to speak.

'We've not found any records anywhere in Bruce's house,' said Lees. 'It
looks like he didn't keep any.'

'I thought as much. He had an amazing memory for facts and details.
He probably stored everything in his head.'

'We've also been contacted by some very influential people who are
concerned about Bruce's death.'

'You mean all the rich bastards who employed him and whose secrets
he held?'

'Yes, sir. They're worried about those secrets spilling out.'

'Let them stew. I've got more to worry about than those arseholes.'

'I'm afraid the chief superintendent doesn't agree.'

As they spoke, the man himself seemed to emerge from the very
walls of the building. He was a huge man, even bigger than Murphy,
with thick grey whiskers. Once he'd been a conscientious officer, but
now he preferred protecting his position to doing any real police work.
Murphy vowed he would never become like him. In his mind, Chief
Superintendent Battles was the opposite of what a conscientious officer
should be.

'Ah, Murphy. I'm glad you're here,' said Battles. 'I gathered the vultures
outside so you can tell them Knapp's killer will cause no more mayhem.'

'Knapp's killer?'

'Bruce, of course.'

'I really don't think he was responsible. I need more time to investigate.
If he was responsible, he certainly didn't do it alone, meaning the real killer
is still out there.'

'Are you forgetting that four years ago, Bruce attacked a prostitute with
a knife while in a drunken rage?'

'I haven't forgotten, sir, but that was very different to tackling someone
of Knapp's capabilities. Bruce was so physically weak, the prostitute took
the knife from him and punched him in the face, knocking him out. What
if the press get hold of that story, if they haven't already? That prostitute
could come forward at any time to tell her story and earn some money. It
would make us look ridiculous.'

Battles sighed and stroked his grey whiskers. 'There is tremendous pressure on us to put this sorry case to rest, Murphy.'

'I understand the people who used Bruce's services must be very anxious, but you can tell them he kept no records. Whatever secrets he knew he took to his grave, but you must let me look into this further, sir. If Bruce didn't kill Knapp – which I'm certain he didn't – then whoever did kill him strung up Bruce and made it look like suicide. They've already killed two people in just a few days and they might do it again. If we close this case too soon, we will end up with egg on our faces. Just give me a few more days, at least,' he pressed when Battles appeared to be wavering. 'If I don't turn anything up, then by all means, announce Bruce killed Knapp, and in turn killed himself because he was unable to cope with the guilt.'

Battles considered what he'd said, eyes turned thoughtfully up to the ceiling as he stroked his greying mutton chops, leaving Murphy rigid with anxiety. The inspector was sure he was purposefully drawing out his response just to annoy him.

'All right, Murphy,' Battles eventually said. 'You've got yourself a few more days.'

'Thank you,' Murphy breathed with relief.

'And I want real detective work, none of your usual fingerprint nonsense. That sort of evidence isn't even admissible in court.'

'Yes, sir,' he sighed, fighting the urge to roll his eyes, wondering what Henry Littlejohn would make of that ignorant statement.

'Right, time to disperse the vultures.' Battles ran a hand through his thick grey hair. 'How do I look?'

'The epitome of the professional police officer, sir,' said Lees, ignoring Murphy's disgusted look.

They watched Battles walk outside to deal with the waiting press.

'The epitome of the professional police officer?' Murphy scowled at Lees. 'Why don't you just follow him outside on your hands and knees and lick his puckered old hole?'

'I thought flattery would be the quickest way to get rid of him.'

'Never ever let me hear you speak like that again.'

'Yes, sir,' said Lees, eyes dancing with amusement.

'How goes the fingerprinting of Knapp's pocket watch?'

'The only prints on it were from Knapp himself and Bruce, as well as the constable who found it.'

'So much for him becoming a detective,' muttered Murphy.

'Anyone who reads the newspapers will be intimately acquainted with your techniques.'

'Damn journalists,' he spat. 'I'd love to go out there and kick each and every one of them squarely in the bollocks.'

'You and me both, sir. So, what do we do now?'

'For some reason, I keep coming back to Robert Alardyce. He was hiding something, as was his butler.'

'He could have just been nervous talking to a detective of such renown.'

Murphy scowled. 'What the hell are you doing?'

'Just brushing up on my flattery technique. We might need to fall back on it more to fend off the chief superintendent.'

'Do it one more time to me and it'll be *your* bollocks my boots will be pulverising.'

'Sir,' Lees winced, standing to attention.

'The problem is he's the stepson of Sir Henry Alardyce, who is a very wealthy and influential man, and if I push too hard, he might just use that wealth and influence to scare Battles into making me drop the whole thing, so I would prefer to do this more insidiously.'

'Right, sir,' said Lees slowly, not sure what *insidiously* meant but not wanting to risk a genital pulverising by asking. 'Robert Alardyce's biological father was a rapist and a murderer. If he hadn't died, he would have been hanged like Sir Henry's brother.'

'I remember the case well. It was a fascinating study into the criminal mind.'

'Criminals don't have minds. Something happens to their brains at birth and they fall out of the ears or something.'

'Shut up, Lees.'

'Yes, sir.'

'Matthew Crowle was an extremely clever – if deranged – man, despite his lack of education. He ran his wife's many businesses with great flair, swelling the family fortune, and by all accounts, his son is equally talented, especially for someone so young.'

'I wish I'd seen him batter Tommy Tompkins.' Lees's grin fell when Murphy's steely gaze settled on him. 'Oh, come on, sir. I know you enjoy a good bare-knuckle fight.'

'May I remind you, Sergeant, that bare-knuckle fighting is illegal,' he replied, although his eyes twinkled as he spoke. 'Robert Alardyce may only be eighteen, but that match proves we should not underestimate him.'

'If he is something to do with it, why would he kill Knapp or have him killed? Someone watching over you to make sure you don't go to a brothel isn't enough reason to commit murder.'

'I agree, but I think he's had more dealings with Mr Knapp than we know. However, after meeting him once, I know he's not the type of person to admit it, no matter how much pressure we pile on him. What we need is a motive. I'd like to talk to Lady Alardyce.'

'I've heard a lot about her,' grinned Lees. 'She's quite a woman, by all accounts.'

'I fear she'll be even tougher to crack than her husband and son. Any woman who voluntarily runs from a life of wealth and privilege to become a governess is not to be taken lightly. She's a survivor who's faced a lot worse than us, but I'm curious to hear what she won't say.'

Lees blinked, thinking he'd misheard. 'Sorry, sir?'

'She toiled as a governess for years simply so she could keep her child. She was then tortured to give up information about his whereabouts and resisted all attempts, despite being badly mutilated. Her instinct will be to protect her son again. Hopefully she'll be so busy defending him that what she doesn't tell me about him will be more revealing.'

'All right,' said Lees slowly, still not really following. 'But she hardly ever leaves the estate and her husband might stop you from speaking to her.'

'I know, which is why you will ask Sir Henry to come down here for an interview. While he's occupied, I will speak to his wife at Alardyce House.'

'They might make a complaint.'

'Let them. We're not breaking any laws and Sir Henry is too intelligent to stir up waves that might attract attention. This might give us the information we need. But first I would like to go back to the Royal Edinburgh Hospital.'

'Are you not feeling well, sir?'

Murphy's moustache bristled. 'I've never known a day's illness in my life. I want to speak to a member of staff there, one Andrew Charteris.'

* * *

Robert had decided against killing Murphy. It would be foolish and rash. He had hoped the police would believe Bruce was responsible and, even though he knew they'd found Knapp's pocket watch in his possession, they still hadn't blamed him for the crime, to his surprise. Things were complicated enough without throwing another death into the mix. What he needed was someone he could put the blame on for both crimes to nicely tie up all the loose ends.

In order to do that, he was back at the gambling den where Benjamin had challenged him to fight Tompkins. Benjamin himself wasn't there but a lot of business acquaintances were, who were a lot friendlier to him after he'd beaten Tompkins. He had a couple of drinks, gambled a little, even though he loathed it. He couldn't bear looking at his opponents as they played, the desperate hope in their eyes or the pathetic certainty that they would win a trifle. Why didn't they just put their brains to good use – because some of them did have brains – and earn their money rather than trying to win it? Personally, he preferred the heady rush when scheming and hard work paid off much more than a win on the turn of a card.

Benjamin arrived an hour later, and Robert was quite certain someone had informed him that he was there.

'Robert,' he smiled, prancing in wearing his usual silks, satins and bright colours. 'How wonderful to see you.'

'And where have you just come from, Ben? Tompkins's sickbed?'

Benjamin's smile briefly fell before being plastered back on. 'Actually, I've been celebrating. I've made an investment that's paying off very nicely.'

'Investment?'

'The Edinburgh Insurance and Fire Trust Company.'

'Oh, them.'

'I heard you were interested in investing yourself?'

'I was but fortunately I didn't go through with it. I certainly dodged a bullet there.'

Benjamin was too busy gloating to really hear his words. 'Sadly, I bought up all the stocks before you could... what did you say?' he said, the meaning of Robert's words finally sinking in.

'Haven't you heard? The director of the company took all the money and ran.' Robert frowned. 'You mean you don't know?'

Everyone had been listening to this exchange and watched Benjamin sink into a chair, mouth opening and closing.

'Oh, dear,' said Robert. 'It looks like you don't.'

'Run off?' he breathed.

'How much did you invest?'

'Te... ten thousand pounds,' Benjamin murmured, causing everyone in the room to wince.

'Painful,' said Robert.

'But... where has this man gone?'

'I've no idea. It seems no one does. He's left a lot of angry people in his wake. You never know, you might be lucky. Someone might catch up with him and you might recoup your money.' His lips twitched with amusement. 'Some of it, anyway.' Little did Benjamin know that his money was resting in three separate bank accounts set up by Robert under his own company name. He'd already ensured his financial records accommodated the extra amounts.

'All the money my aunt left me is gone,' said Benjamin, turning a sickly shade of green.

'So sad,' smirked Robert.

'No,' wailed Benjamin, jumping up and slamming his fists repeatedly against the wall in what was more a childish display of petulance than anything intimidating. However, he did strike the wall hard enough to cut his knuckles, smearing blood across the plaster.

'I didn't know you had it in you,' grinned Robert.

Benjamin groaned with anguish and slumped into a chair. Two of his friends rallied round him with reviving brandy.

'What am I going to do?' breathed Benjamin. 'My father... he's going to...' He closed his eyes and shuddered.

'Kill you?' smiled Robert.

Benjamin's head snapped up. 'You're enjoying this, aren't you?'

'You mean the devastating loss of your personal fortune? Oh, yes, I am. How does it feel knowing the son of a footman has more money than you?'

Robert was rather surprised when Benjamin leapt to his feet and charged at him. Coolly he rose to meet him and Benjamin, recalling what he'd done to Tompkins, halted in his tracks.

'I suggest you go home and speak to your father,' growled Robert. 'Before you get hurt.'

'Come on, Ben, let's go,' said one of his friends, tugging at his arm.

'I suggest you listen to your friend, Ben,' said Robert, eyes turning even blacker as the dark thoughts started to whisper in his head again.

Benjamin stumbled away from him, sensing the wrongness. Robert retook his seat, picked up his wine glass and smiled at his opponents at the card table. 'Ready for another hand, gentlemen?'

He glanced back at the door Benjamin had gone through. He might have found the puppet he needed to set up for Knapp's death, then his revenge would be complete on the Richardson family. Soon they would be the ones rejected by polite society.

23

Andrew slunk back to his lodgings in the old town from the hospital, so drained it was difficult for him to put one foot in front of the other. As he was new, his superiors worked him like a mule, getting him to do the dirtiest jobs, the ones they considered themselves too good for. He wasn't a surgeon, he was a glorified cleaner. His day had involved mopping up congealed blood and disposing of amputated body parts. They hadn't even allowed him to touch a surgical knife. His main duties were handing round the new rubber gloves they'd just started using for surgical procedures and sterilising the instruments. At least it was interesting being involved in these brand-new hygiene procedures. It was anticipated that because of these reforms, fewer patients would die of infection, so at least that was something, and he'd met the great Sir Henry Littlejohn on several occasions. But he wanted to get stuck in and it was frustrating that no one would let him prove his worth.

'Can I talk to you, sir?' said a voice.

'My God,' exclaimed Andrew, leaping backwards when a huge figure stepped out on the pavement before him. 'Who the devil are you and why are you trying to scare me?'

'I do apologise, I didn't mean to frighten you.'

Andrew peered at the man. 'You look familiar. Where have I seen you before?'

'My name's Inspector Murphy...'

'That's right, you're the detective I read about in the newspapers. How thrilling to meet you in the flesh. Well, if that's all, I'll be on my way. I'm very tired.'

'I'm afraid that's not all, sir,' said Murphy, blocking his way. 'I want to talk to you about Robert Alardyce.'

'Why?' Andrew frowned, genuinely confused.

'If we could talk in private, please?'

'Oh, very well,' he sighed. 'Can we talk while we walk? I'm eager to get home and collapse into bed.'

Murphy nodded and fell into step beside him, the older man easily keeping pace with Andrew's long-legged stride.

'So why are you asking about my best friend?' said Andrew.

'I'm curious to learn more about him.'

'Why? I don't believe you've taken a random interest in him.' Andrew's green eyes gleamed. 'What do you think he's done?'

'As yet, I don't think he's done anything.'

'But you think he might. I don't suppose important inspectors go around asking after people just in case they've been naughty.'

'I'm afraid I can't give out any details about an ongoing investigation.'

'So you do think he's been naughty,' said Andrew with something akin to triumph.

'How long have you known Robert?' said Murphy, evading the question.

'Er, about two years. We met when we were both sixteen.'

'Where did you meet?'

'At a certain, shall we say, discreet establishment.'

'You mean Vivienne's brothel?'

Andrew's smile was wicked. 'You know it?'

'I hate to tell you this, Mr Charteris, but it's not exactly a secret. Vivienne is quite the local character.'

'She certainly is. Funny, I don't remember seeing you there.'

Murphy refused to be drawn into a distracting conversation about a brothel. 'Have you ever met Robert outside Vivienne's establishment?'

'Oh, yes, we're good friends.'

'Have you ever spent time at Alardyce House?'

'I had the pleasure of spending a few days there not long before Robert got married. I must say, his mother is the most remarkable woman. Superficially she's not exactly a beauty, although she is still very attractive, but she radiates something I've never seen before. It lights her up like the sun. It's most fascinating.'

'Did any unusual incidents occur while you were at Alardyce?'

'I just missed the mad housekeeper poisoning Lady Alardyce and hurling herself into a frozen lake. Other than that, no. Oh, I tell a lie – I had an encounter with the witch who lives in the village. You do know she keeps a wolf as a pet, don't you? I'm quite sure that's illegal.'

'I've already spoken to Mrs Magrath and she told me all about you, sir. She said she caught you vandalising her garden.'

'Nonsense,' Andrew said, cheeks flushing when he realised he'd been caught out. 'That was some of the local children. I merely saw them off and she blamed me for the damage.'

'She was grateful to you because apparently all you uprooted were weeds, stinging weeds too.'

Andrew felt very foolish now he knew the supposed witch's curse had in fact been caused by a plant. 'Glad to be of assistance,' he mumbled.

'Did you ever meet Jacob Knapp?'

'The big brute who was recently murdered? Yes, at Vivienne's, when he hauled Robert out and then at Alardyce after he'd escorted him home from the city.'

'How did you get on with Mr Knapp?'

'Oh, fine, fine,' he replied, trying not to think about the names Knapp had called him. 'I didn't have much to do with him, to be honest.'

'And how did Robert get on with him?'

'Well, naturally he wasn't too fond of him after he'd been his jailer at his uncle's house, but beyond that, I don't think he thought very much about him. Robert was much more concerned with his mother when he got home after what had happened to her.'

'Did Robert ever see Knapp again?'

Andrew knew the Alardyce family had kept the elopement a guarded secret, so he was reasonably confident with his reply. 'Not that I'm aware of, and before you ask, I never saw Mr Knapp again either.'

'What's your opinion of your friend?'

'Well, I like him and very few people have managed to earn my good opinion.'

'He must feel very honoured,' said Murphy, causing Andrew's eyes to narrow at his sarcasm. 'And how did he manage to earn your good opinion?'

'Well, he is good fun and we just get along. It's hard to pinpoint anything specific. Some people you just sort of get along with.'

'And you two got along?'

'Oh, yes.'

'Two peas in a pod then?'

'If you like.'

'Does Robert confide in you?'

'Like I said, we talk, and if you're going to ask if he's ever confided any dreadful secret to me, then no, Inspector, he hasn't. Judging by your questions, this is to do with Knapp's murder. How intriguing.'

'Do you know Mr Cyril Bruce?'

'Is he the chap who hanged himself? I read about it in the newspapers. No, I'd never heard of him until I read that article. Why, should I?'

Murphy ignored the question. 'Are you related to James Charteris, the surgeon and mesmerist in London?'

'I'm his grandson. My father was raised by his aunt. She moved to Edinburgh to escape the notoriety after all the... unpleasantness.'

'James also studied at the Royal College of Surgeons?'

'He did and, by all accounts, he was very skilled. I take after him in a lot of ways.'

Murphy didn't like the pride in his voice as he spoke. He thought Andrew Charteris was definitely one to keep an eye on. 'Thank you for your time, sir,' said Murphy before walking away.

Andrew watched him go until he'd disappeared around the corner. He hadn't liked that at all. He sighed regretfully and looked back down the street. His lodgings were in sight, but he felt he must warn Robert. He was also curious to find out what was going on. Thanks to Robert's win against Tompkins, he could afford to take a cab, so he hailed a passing Hansom and told the driver to take him to Drummond Place.

As he journeyed into the New Town, Andrew stared enviously at the Georgian mansions, his spirits sinking as he considered his own dilapidated lodgings in the Old Town. Only yesterday, he'd opened his battered wardrobe and a rat had leapt out. He swore to himself that one day he would reside in one of the very best of these fine townhouses.

He was escorted into Robert's study by Forbes, who he was quite sure didn't like him, and was poured a Scotch before being left alone to await his friend. Robert appeared a couple of minutes later and extended a hand to him.

'Good to see you, Andrew. I wasn't expecting you.'

'I know, terribly rude of me,' he replied, shaking his hand. 'But I have some news you really want to hear. It's to do with Knapp.'

Andrew watched Robert's reaction to this statement carefully. His eyes narrowed a little but other than that, there was no reaction, to Andrew's disappointment, but then again, his friend was very good at concealing his emotions. He thought how much older Robert looked – not physically, he was still sickeningly youthful and handsome, but there was an air of gravity about him that would have been more appropriate on an older man.

'What about him?' was Robert's reply.

'I've just been accosted in the street by Inspector Murphy, you know, the darling of the Edinburgh police force. He wanted to ask me about my friendship with you. He also asked if I knew Knapp.'

'And what did you tell him?' Robert enquired, so casually he could have been asking the time.

'I told him we were the best of friends and that I only met Knapp at the brothel when he dragged you out and at Alardyce when he escorted you home. I didn't mention the elopement.'

Robert nodded. 'Good.'

'Is that all you've got to say, good?'

'What do you want me to say?'

'You can tell me what's going on, for a start. Why is this inspector so interested in you? Does he think you're something to do with Knapp's death?'

'I've no idea. He came here asking questions and he spoke to my father too. I think he's struggling to solve the case, so he's trying to blame the most convenient person.'

'Which is you?'

'It seems so. Why, I have no idea.'

'You once told me, Robert, that you wouldn't lie to me. I've never broken your confidence, nor would I, so you can trust me.'

'I do trust you, Andrew, and I'm sorry to disappoint, but I'm really nothing to do with it. I didn't like Knapp, but I had no reason to kill him. Besides, I wouldn't have been able to get near him. He was a lot tougher than Tompkins. My life is perfect, so why would I ruin it?'

Andrew had to own that his explanation was a convincing one and that he did seem to be being truthful. But then his friend was a changed man, and he might have just got better at lying.

'The newspapers are saying this man Bruce killed Knapp anyway,' added Robert.

'Yes, I did hear about that.'

'Perhaps Murphy was bluffing?'

'What do you mean?' frowned Andrew.

'I mean that maybe you're the main focus of his attention and he only asked you about me as an excuse to talk to you. Have you been up to anything, Andrew?'

'Me? Of course not. I'm perfectly innocent.'

'We both know that's not true,' said Robert, the corner of his mouth lifting into a smile. 'You haven't engaged in any more frauds, have you?' His eyes widened. 'You're not Terence Burgess, are you?'

'Who the devil is Terence Burgess?'

'It's the latest scandal. He set up an insurance scam and ran off with all the capital put into the business by his investors. The police are currently hunting him and I'm guessing their first port of call will be anyone with a history of fraud behind them, which includes you.'

Panic exploded inside Andrew. 'But that was years ago.'

'It was only three years, still fresh enough to be remembered, and everyone knows how clever you are.'

'It wasn't me,' he exclaimed.

'Then I suggest you lie low for a while and hope Murphy forgets all about you. Just bury yourself in your work and lead a quiet life. It might be best to avoid Vivienne's too until everything calms down.'

'Yes, you're right,' said Andrew, so afraid for himself he didn't question anything Robert had said. He downed his Scotch with a nervous swallow. 'I'd better go home. I think I'll have a quiet night in.'

'Very wise,' said Robert, clapping him on the shoulder. 'Don't worry, I'm sure they'll catch the fellow, then you can breathe easy. It might be a good idea not to go flaunting the money you won betting on me; the police might question where it came from and bare-knuckle fights are illegal. Just lead a dull, quiet life for the next few months and it'll all blow over.'

Andrew nodded, looking pale. 'I can't believe Murphy tricked me like that, the sneaky swine.'

'That's police officers for you.'

Robert smiled to himself as he watched his friend leave, so worried he didn't even say goodbye. Was there nothing he couldn't do?

He gave it ten minutes before leaving the house. It was time to celebrate. He would stalk the streets and find another woman whose back he could stripe. He deserved a treat.

Amy was taking a walk in the grounds of Alardyce House, lost in her own thoughts. Once again, the peace of her life had been shattered. There weren't many women who had to tolerate the toxic influence of their son's father over their child after he'd died. It was tempting to blame everything on Matthew, but she knew she couldn't. Robert did bad things because he liked doing them. The worst thing was she suspected she was helpless to stop him. He was too secure in his own power and success.

She stopped by the elegant stone building they used as a summerhouse. The old one, where Henry had witnessed her disgrace herself with Matthew, had been knocked down, and this new one held only happy memories of times she and the children had played together, and intimate moments with her husband. However, no matter how hard she tried, she could not shake off the spectre of the past. She would always be a haunted woman.

As she exited the front of the summerhouse, she thought the tall, dark figure striding towards her was another ghost, until she realised she could hear the rustle of his feet as he walked across the lawn. The man's demeanour was very determined and, for some reason, he looked familiar.

'Lady Alardyce?' he called.

His Irish accent gave her the final clue she needed. 'Inspector Murphy, I take it?'

'Yes, your ladyship. I wondered if I might have a word?'

Behind him, she saw a panting Rush appear from around the side of the house, for once looking a little frantic.

'Sorry... my lady,' he gasped, struggling for breath as he hurried to catch up with the policeman. 'He wouldn't wait... house...'

'It's quite all right, Rush,' she replied. 'You can go back inside. I'll talk to the inspector.'

'Yes... my lady,' he gasped, throwing Murphy a disdainful scowl before turning and making his way back to the house even more slowly than he would normally move.

'I'm sorry for upsetting your butler, your ladyship,' said Murphy. 'But this is police business.'

'Has something happened? Are my husband and children all right?'

'They're fine. I wish to talk to you about Mr Knapp.'

'Surely it's my husband you need to discuss that with? He's gone to Police Chambers...' She smiled when realisation struck. 'It's no coincidence he's asked to go there and then you show up.'

'One of my colleagues must have asked him to go in. I do apologise, I knew nothing of it.'

'I don't believe in coincidences, Inspector. Neither do I appreciate being lied to.'

Amy was so dignified that Murphy felt ashamed of his little deception. 'You're right. I'm sorry, but it is vital I speak to you in private.'

'And I would have granted you an audience had you just asked like a gentleman.'

'That is something I shall bear in mind in the future. I do hope you will give me a moment of your time now, although I admit I don't deserve it.'

'Very well, but we shall walk as we talk. I'm not cutting short my turn about the grounds.'

'You're very gracious. I don't often get to walk in beautiful gardens such as these. My life is taken up with the seedier side of the city.'

'I can imagine, but it's important to appreciate the beautiful things in life. It reminds us that the world isn't entirely lost.'

He glanced sideways at her as she spoke, the sadness clear in her voice. He bore in mind that this woman had just as much experience of the criminal element as himself. Murphy could see what Andrew Charteris had meant. She was a handsome woman, her coiled chestnut hair catching the light, reflecting a myriad of colours, and her figure was very upright and strong, her hips curvaceous and breasts large, which was what he liked, and he found he couldn't stop looking her way as they walked. There was something irresistible about her that demanded closer attention, although he couldn't have said exactly what that was. No wonder there'd been such a furore around this woman. That unnameable seductive something was bound to attract attention.

'I was very sad to hear about Mr Knapp,' opened Amy, surprising the inspector. He was used to people clamming up until they absolutely had to speak. 'I greatly admired him.'

'May I ask why?'

'He had a very strong sense of right and wrong.'

'How did you feel about him being sent to watch over your son? I assume Sir Henry arranged all that?'

'He did and I thought it was a good idea. Robert was being rather rebellious at the time and he needed a strong hand.'

'Forgive me for sounding rude, but was Sir Henry unable to be that strong hand?'

'Oh, no. Henry is a good disciplinarian, but he and Robert weren't getting along at the time and were constantly arguing. You could call it a clash of personalities, they are rather similar and it wasn't pleasant for our other children, so we decided Robert needed some time away from the estate. It worked, too. He was much calmer when he returned.'

'And he married his wife shortly after?'

Amy forced herself not to glance his way, afraid he'd read something in her eyes, she could feel how closely he was watching her. 'Yes.'

'Wasn't that rather quick for a boy who had been misbehaving?'

'I don't think so. He and Jane were very much in love and their separation only seemed to be making things worse. It was the right thing to do because getting married certainly calmed him down and he's an excellent husband and father.'

Murphy glanced at her sharply. Did he detect doubt in her voice? She seemed so calm and in control he decided he'd imagined it. 'No banns were read before the wedding.'

'We decided against it. You see, our family has endured so much scandal. When other people get a whiff of anything involving us, we're once again studied, judged, sometimes even ridiculed. Robert and Jane didn't want their wedding turned into a farce and neither did we, so we arranged a quiet ceremony here at Alardyce and the news was broken shortly after.'

Murphy was annoyed that this made sense. 'You must be very proud of your son,' he said, not taking his eyes off her as he spoke.

'I am.'

'He's been very successful in business and he beat Tommy Tompkins in a bare-knuckle fight. That's quite an achievement for an eighteen-year-old.'

'He's always been a very bright boy,' she slowly replied.

'His father had a very good head for business too.'

'Yes, Henry does,' she replied, wilfully ignoring his use of the past tense, seeing exactly where he was going.

'I was referring to Matthew Crowle.'

'I know you were, Inspector, but I have no wish to discuss him.'

'Does Robert miss his real father?'

Her blue eyes were as sharp as knives as she glanced his way. 'What a ridiculous question.'

'Is it?'

She came to a halt, turning to face him. 'His real father was a confidence trickster, rapist and murderer. None of us like to think about him and I refuse to answer any more of your questions until I know why you're asking about Robert.'

'I'm looking into the people Knapp was close to, who he interacted with.' He glanced down at her hands, which she wrung together. Although they were hidden by gloves, he knew the fingers were twisted and deformed thanks to Edward Alardyce and his mad compulsions.

'It's over a year since we last saw Knapp,' said Amy. 'In the time between then and his death, I'm sure he met with lots of different people, so I fail to see why you're harassing my family and friends. I know that not only have you spoken to Henry, Robert and now myself but you've gone around the village asking questions too. If you're trying to insinuate that Mr Knapp's death was something to do with my family – which I can tell you it's not – then I'd rather you just came out with it, instead of snooping around asking your devious questions.'

'Very well, Lady Alardyce, I can see that you're the type of woman who prefers to face things head on. I believe someone hired some thugs to murder Mr Knapp and I suspect that person was your eldest son.'

Amy's cheeks flushed with colour but Murphy spotted the fear in her eyes before it was replaced with indignation.

'How dare you,' she hissed. 'My son would never do anything like that. Why do people always have to try and drag him down? We've endured censure and ridicule from society and just when we're finally being accepted again – which is all thanks to my son, by the way – you want to drag us down. Well, I won't let you and if you dare slander Robert again, then my husband will ensure you're stripped of your position and set to work as a night watchman in the filthiest, most degraded slum in the city. Now get off my land before I have you thrown off,' she yelled before marching back to the house.

He took a moment to admire that fine figure of hers as she returned to the house, shaking with indignation. Judging by the way she moved, all the physical trauma she'd endured in her life hadn't adversely affected her.

Murphy left Alardyce, pleased with his day's work. He'd shown his hand, but he knew he wouldn't get any evidence against Robert for Knapp's murder because there was nothing to find. However, panicking people made stupid mistakes and if Robert knew he was being actively investigated, he might be pushed into making one.

24

Henry returned to Alardyce House after a rather puzzling and seemingly pointless conversation with a young sergeant at Police Chambers to be greeted by an extremely anxious wife.

'Thank God you're home,' said Amy, running into his arms when he entered the drawing room.

'What's happened?' he said, holding her close.

'Inspector Murphy came here to talk to me.'

'So that's what the interview at Police Chambers was about. I thought it was all very odd.'

'What did they ask you?'

'They just wanted me to confirm everything I'd told Inspector Murphy, which I didn't see the sense of. They didn't even get me to sign a statement. It was a complete waste of time. Now I know it was so he could talk to you alone.'

'He said he thinks Robert hired someone to kill Knapp.'

'My God,' he breathed.

Henry was forced to release her when she started to pace up and down the room.

'It's bad enough us suspecting him,' she began. 'But if the police do...'

'They have no evidence, that's why they're pulling tricks to talk to us.

They're hoping to scare us into revealing something and we must not play into their hands. Inspector Murphy is extremely clever.'

'What put him onto Robert in the first place?'

'He must have found out that Knapp visited him just before he died and that they quarrelled.'

'My boy can't hang,' Amy said, tears shining in her eyes. 'He just can't.'

'I fear it's worse than just Knapp.'

She stopped pacing to regard him, her skin turning pale. 'What do you mean?'

He picked up the newspaper off the table, searched through the pages and held it out to her. 'You need to read this.'

She took it from him with a shaking hand and scanned the article. 'Another woman attacked in the street and beaten. Sweet Lord, she was strangled.'

'Thankfully she was released before it went too far.'

Amy's hand involuntarily went to her neck. 'Matthew did that to me,' she rasped.

Henry's jaw tensed, hating the thought of anyone hurting her. 'It could be someone else doing this.'

'No, it's not. We both know the truth, Henry. I think it's time we had it out with Robert.'

'Perhaps we shouldn't.'

'Why not?'

'Remember what I said – Murphy's been pushing our family so Robert will make a mistake. If he had anything on him, he would have arrested him by now, but he hasn't. If we steam in there and get Robert riled up, which is what will happen, he may take some retaliatory action that will point to his guilt. We mustn't fall into Murphy's trap, so we will carry on as normal...'

'And pretend our son hasn't killed anyone and that he isn't attacking women?'

'As distasteful as it is to me to say it, yes, for now, anyway. Let all this die down first. It will also give us time to work out how to handle Robert. Yelling at him and banning him from doing something won't work any more. We must come up with a better way.'

'You're right,' she said, thanking God for her husband's wisdom and cool head. 'We'll carry on as normal and not see Robert.' She sighed. 'Sometimes I wonder whether we should protect him. He's only going to get worse. A monster stalks this city and we're doing nothing about it.'

'Only to save him from the gallows. My influence wouldn't be enough to stop him from being hanged. Knapp was very popular, especially in the Old Town, he was a champion of the people. If his killer escaped justice, there would be riots in the street and our family would become a target for their violence. We are isolated out here. They could burn the place to the ground with all of us inside before any help came. Even if we survived all that, the doors of society would be closed to our family again, ruining our children's futures, as well as Emily's.'

'Is it terribly selfish of me putting my own family before the well-being of everyone else?'

'No, Amy,' he said, taking her hands. 'It makes you a caring wife, mother and grandmother. There must be a way of putting a stop to Robert's activities without destroying all our children. We just need to find it.'

Amy rested her head on her husband's chest, the sound of his strong, steady heartbeat soothing her fraught nerves. His way was the right way to go. She would sacrifice the whole world for her children.

* * *

The news of the Edinburgh Insurance and Fire Trust Company spread like wildfire throughout the city, the Richardsons becoming a laughing stock for being so gullible. Robert basked in the knowledge that those bastards were getting a good idea of what his family had endured. But humiliating them and stealing a fortune from them still hadn't quenched the fire of vengeance that burned inside him. He'd attacked another woman, a pretty young maid who had left one of the finest houses in the New Town, dragging her down a back street and assaulting her. He'd beaten her even harder than the last two and throttled her, but he'd once again let her go before he'd taken her life. Not that he was afraid of taking their lives, in fact he wanted to, but he thought it wise to avoid any more deaths with Murphy sniffing around.

The attack had soothed his nerves and calmed his mind and now he could put into action the final stage of his revenge against the Richardson family. He'd prepared for this last step with the letter the Comyns had forced Bruce to write, and he was going to enjoy it. The irony was that Inspector Murphy's own actions had forced his hand. Terence Burgess's identity was about to be revealed.

* * *

Murphy returned to Police Chambers very pleased with how his interview with Amy Alardyce had gone. He'd rattled her cage. Now she would run to her son and tell him exactly what he'd said and that would force him to do something stupid.

'I'm glad you're back, sir,' said Lees as Murphy took his place behind his desk, which was stacked high with papers, mainly about new investigative techniques being implemented not just in other parts of the UK but around the world. The majority of his colleagues thought this study a waste of time, all they needed were their own wits, but Murphy disagreed. One day, police work would become a science, and sometimes the ignorance of his colleagues annoyed him.

'How did your interview with Sir Henry Alardyce go?' said Murphy

'He knew something wasn't right, but he remained polite,' replied Lees. 'He was quite pleasant actually, not a toffee-nosed arsehole like a lot of rich people. Did you speak to his wife?'

'I did. She's a very redoubtable woman.'

'So you were impressed with her?' Lees smiled knowingly.

'It's hard not to be.'

'While you were out, we had a report of another woman being attacked in the New Town. It was just like the last one. She was beaten and throttled, but her attacker let her go before he went too far.'

'It sounds like the same person.'

'Aye, I think so, sir. She's a maid who works for the Trenton family. They're very well-to-do and are appalled by what happened to a member of their staff. Fortunately, the maid's a feisty one and she managed to give us a description, despite her injured throat.'

'And?'

'It was a dark-haired man. She couldn't tell his age. He spoke with a rough voice and he sounded uneducated. She noticed he had cuts and bruises on his knuckles.'

'Robert Alardyce,' he exclaimed. 'His knuckles were cut and bruised from the fight with Tompkins.'

'I don't know, sir. He doesn't speak rough and uneducated.'

'Anyone can put on a funny voice. You do it all the time.'

Lees frowned. 'I do not.'

'Maybe not intentionally, but you do.'

Lees decided to ignore that comment. 'He also wore a ring on his little finger, a gold signet ring with the initial R.'

'There we have it,' said Murphy triumphantly. 'That proves it.'

'Did you notice Robert Alardyce wearing such a ring, sir?'

'Well, no.'

'Surely he'd wear a ring with the letter A instead, for his family name. Isn't that more what the toffs do?'

'Maybe, maybe not, but it's still not enough to nail the bastard to the wall. Did the victim have any more information?'

'No, sir, that was it, but she's furious. She wants her attacker to pay.'

'And he will, you can tell her that. I'll lock him up personally.'

'We mustn't rush into this, sir. If we move against a family like the Alardyces too soon, it could come back on us.'

'I know. We need to wait for his mother to talk to him. That'll light a fire under his arse.'

'There's news about Terence Burgess.'

'Who?'

'The Edinburgh Insurance and Fire Trust Company.'

'I'm not interested in all that nonsense. I couldn't care less about rich people losing their money in stupid, greedy gambles.'

'You'll be interested to hear about this, sir.'

'Get on with it then,' barked Murphy when Lees failed to elaborate.

'We've found trace of him and guess who he is?'

'Robert Alardyce?'

Lees was becoming a little concerned about Murphy's obsession with that man. 'Nope. Benjamin Richardson.'

'That prancing, pretentious little slug? He's not intelligent enough to pull off a fraud like that.'

'It seems he was, but he wasn't smart enough to get away with it. He was clever, see. He invested £10,000 of his own money and bought up the majority of the shares.'

'So he's guilty of stealing from himself?'

'No, sir, because other people bought shares in that company too, mainly his own brother-in-law, who invested £30,000. So not only did he get his own capital back, but he stole all that too. He would have got away with it if an informant hadn't come forward to denounce him.'

'What informant?'

'Mr Bruce.'

Murphy frowned. 'Did something heavy hit you on the head today, Sergeant?'

'We received a letter in his own hand detailing the entire plot. Bruce was instrumental in setting it up. It looks like he got cold feet and Benjamin found out he was going to drop him in it, so he had him silenced.'

Murphy shot to his feet so quickly he startled Lees. 'I want to see this letter.'

'The chief superintendent has it.'

Murphy ran out of his office, rushed across the landing to Battles's office and banged on the door.

'Come in,' called Battles.

Murphy burst in looking so wild that Battles frowned.

'What the devil is wrong with you, Murphy?' he demanded.

'I need to see that letter, sir.'

'Letter?'

Murphy wanted to throttle him in his impatience. 'The letter written by Bruce denouncing Benjamin Richardson.'

'Oh, that. Here you go,' he said, holding it out to him.

Murphy snatched it from his hand and devoured it with his eyes. 'It looks like Bruce's handwriting.'

'That's because it is.'

'With your permission, I'd like to get it analysed by a handwriting expert.'

Battles rolled his eyes. 'Why do you have to make everything complicated? This is a cut and dried case but, just to put your mind at rest, you may have it analysed. I don't want you picking holes in another case.'

'Thank you, sir. Has Benjamin been brought in?'

'He has and he's been interrogated by Inspector Grendal. Don't pull a face, Murphy, fraud is more his area. You do all the nasty murders, but you will get your turn with Richardson. He could be in the frame for Knapp's murder too. We think he discovered Richardson's little plot and was silenced.'

'Is there any evidence?'

'Naturally. Do you think I'd be so stupid as to accuse one of the Richardsons without any? Knapp's secretary told us Richardson visited Knapp at his office three days before he died.'

'Why?'

'He didn't know, Knapp never told him, but it gives us a link between the two men. We searched Richardson's lodgings. He doesn't live in the family pile, he has his own more modest home in the New Town where we found Knapp's notebook hidden under the sofa cushions. Richardson had him killed, took the notebook and pocket watch and planted the latter in Bruce's home to make it look like he was the killer.'

'Why would Richardson kill Knapp?'

'Because he discovered their plot. Benjamin Richardson has employed some nasty characters in the past. He got a group of dockers to beat up someone he owed a lot of money to. Why not pay them again to attack Knapp down a dark wynd? Only a group of angry dockers could get the better of that man.'

'I suppose that ties things up very neatly,' murmured Murphy.

'It certainly does. Oh, and one more thing – Richardson was brought in wearing a signet ring bearing the letter R.'

'You think he's responsible for the attacks on those women?'

'I'd say it's very possible. We showed the ring to the latest victim, who identified it as the one her attacker wore. That girl has an excellent eye for detail.'

'But it's rumoured that Richardson prefers male company.' Murphy sighed and shook his head. This didn't feel right. 'Were his hands cut and bruised?'

'Yes, but he blames that on punching a wall in a gambling den when he found out about the insurance swindle. A very clever blind, if you ask me.'

'Sir, I think it's very possible someone set up Richardson for these crimes. It's all too convenient.'

'Not convenient, Inspector, it just makes perfect sense. His family's influence may mean that we don't get a conviction, not unless we find more evidence, but it should scare him into stopping the attacks. If he does escape justice for Knapp's murder, then the angry mob may get its hands on him and he's no longer a problem. Either way, it works out very nicely for us. We've done some sterling police work and we've come out looking golden.'

'I don't think it's that simple...'

Battle's grey eyes hardened. 'If you're going to say something about Robert Alardyce, I don't want to hear it. He's only eighteen, for God's sake. Do you think he's capable of pulling off a coup like this?'

'After meeting him, yes, I do. He's clever, manipulative and much older than his years. Benjamin Richardson hasn't the wit to do all this.'

'I don't want to hear one more word about Robert Alardyce pass your lips, Inspector. Sir Henry Alardyce has made a complaint about you dragging him all the way down here on some nonsense so you could speak to his wife. Fortunately for you, he's a thoroughly nice man and hasn't demanded your resignation, which some of the other powerful men in this city wouldn't have hesitated to do. If you know what's good for you, you'll steer clear of anyone with the surname Alardyce. If you see one of them walking towards you on the street, you will turn and run the other way. You're a good officer, but it wouldn't trouble my conscience one bit to demote you. How would you feel having Lees as your superior?'

'I understand, sir,' Murphy sighed.

'Good. Now take that letter to your handwriting expert, not that I think it will do you any good. Then it will be announced that the killer of both Knapp and Bruce has been caught, as has the women's attacker and the good citizens of Edinburgh can sleep safely in their beds. Plus the reputation of the excellent Inspector Murphy will once again shine in the newspapers.'

Murphy knew when to attack and when to retreat, and this was certainly a time to retreat. Not trusting himself to utter another word, he turned and left, clutching the letter.

He returned to his office, slammed the door shut and pulled the blinds, wanting to be alone with his thoughts. This was too good to be true and bloody Battles had seized it with both hands.

Murphy paused to consider whether he was being obsessive. In the past, he'd seen the disastrous results of his colleagues getting a notion into their heads and ignoring all evidence that didn't fit their narrative. What if that was the case here? He would look into Benjamin Richardson and if the evidence pointed his way, then that was the direction he would follow. If he found something linking Robert Alardyce, he would follow that line of inquiry. It was vital he let the facts speak for themselves and not allow himself to be distracted.

Feeling better after deciding on a course of action, he carefully stowed the letter inside his coat pocket along with a letter Bruce had written to his landlady for comparison and set out to see his friend, who was an expert in handwriting analysis, as well as one of the few people he knew who was invested in advancing police investigative techniques. Dinosaurs like Battles certainly weren't. If his friend said the letter was a forgery, he would go straight for Robert Alardyce. His considerable experience was telling him that man was up to his neck in it.

On his way out, he saw Benjamin Richardson being led into one of their rancid prison cells. He looked the essence of misery, and his legs were trembling with fear.

'In here, your highness,' grunted a burly constable as he shoved Richardson inside.

'Wait,' Murphy told the constable before he could shut the door. 'I want to speak to him.'

'All right, sir, but it's a waste of bloody time. All that comes out of that thing's mouth is diarrhoea.'

'Leave us,' Murphy told him with narrowed eyes.

The officer shrugged and ambled off to make a cup of tea.

Murphy closed the cell door to give them privacy to talk.

'Hello, Mr Richardson. I'm Inspector Murphy. I hope you've been treated well.'

Slowly the prisoner raised his head, although it did appear to be an effort for him. 'I've been pushed about, humiliated and taunted, so no, I've not been treated well.'

'I'm sorry to hear that. I thought your father would be here?'

'He's taken a turn for the worse. Apparently, news of my arrest brought on a fit of some sort. My brother's also in his sickbed and my brother-in-law refuses to help me because he thinks I stole his money, but I didn't, I swear on my father's life. I've not done any of those things. Someone's framed me.'

'Who would do that?'

'Robert Alardyce,' he spat.

Murphy repressed a surge of excitement. 'Now why would he do that?' he replied, injecting just the right amount of scepticism into his voice.

'Because he hates me and all because I dressed up as a footman at my sister's fancy dress ball.'

'And you challenged him to fight Tommy Tompkins. You're fortunate that hasn't been added to your list of charges.'

'Right now, that's the least of my problems, and I didn't think in my wildest dreams that not only would Robert beat him but he'd ruin his boxing career too. This is a vendetta against me.'

'How can you be so sure he's behind all this?'

'I employed Mr Bruce to perform a little espionage on Robert, but I think he paid Bruce to feed me false information. Bruce was the one who told me about the Edinburgh Insurance and Fire Trust Company and that Robert was thinking of buying the majority of its stock. That was what compelled me to buy in the first place.'

'It's very convenient that Mr Bruce isn't alive to confirm that.'

'Convenient for who? Not me.'

'You silenced him before he could reveal your scheme, but you hadn't banked on him sending a letter.'

'He didn't send any letter. I can guarantee you that it's forged.'

'I might be able to prove that.'

'You might?' said Benjamin, eyes flaring with hope.

'I have a friend who's a handwriting expert. If it is a forgery, he'll prove it.'

'Oh, thank you, Inspector. You can't know how much I appreciate this.'

'Why did you meet with Knapp three days before he died?'

'I...'

'You're better off telling me,' he said when Benjamin trailed off and looked down at his hands.

'He caught me in... an illegal activity.'

'What activity?'

Tears filled his eyes. 'I can't say.'

'If you don't tell me, I can't help you and you're on your own.'

'Please don't go,' Benjamin cried, clinging onto his arm when he made to leave. 'Sorry,' he added, hastily releasing Murphy when he glared down at him. 'It's just that what I have to say could land me in even more hot water.'

'How about if I agree that I won't press charges for what you're about to tell me?'

'You promise?'

He nodded. 'On my life.'

Benjamin assessed Murphy and decided he was a man who kept his word. 'All right. He discovered I was keeping regular appointments with a man in the Old Town.'

'Regular appointments?'

Benjamin turned crimson. 'He... he was my special friend.'

'I see,' said Murphy slowly, moustache twitching.

'My friend tried to blackmail me. I refused to pay up, thinking no one would believe someone of his class, so he went to Knapp and told him.'

'And what did Knapp do?'

'Summoned me to his office and said I was never to see my friend again.

In fact, he didn't want me anywhere near the Old Town. My friend was only young.'

'How young?'

'Sixteen. Such a beautiful boy,' he said, starting to cry. 'I thought our relationship was real. No one I know is real, they're all such fakes. I wanted a genuine connection and I was betrayed. I can't tell you the pain.'

Murphy's stare was unsympathetic.

'I know this might get me put in prison, but I'd rather be put away for something I did do than for something Robert Alardyce set me up for.'

'Why are you so sure it was him? I've heard you have a lot of enemies.'

'Because he's the only one sly enough to come up with a plan like this. You can practically feel the cunning oozing out of him and if he did set me up, that means he was responsible for Knapp and Bruce's deaths. Mr Bruce might have been odious, but he loved life. He would never have given it up voluntarily.'

'If Robert Alardyce is responsible, where will I find the proof?'

Benjamin snorted. 'You won't, that's the problem. He's far too clever. I walked straight into his trap and even if I am lucky enough not to be put in prison, I'm still ruined, and all because I dared mock his parentage. Take my advice and stay away from him. That man's an infection. It's too late for me, but you can still save yourself.'

Murphy found himself starting to feel rather sorry for Benjamin. 'I'm sure your mother will work to set you free. She's a very redoubtable woman.'

'Oh, she is that,' he sighed. 'And you're right, she will work to have me released, but only because she doesn't want the family name tarnishing. Any emotion she might have felt for me died years ago.'

Murphy nodded and left, the man's despair embarrassing him. He hurried out of Police Chambers to visit his friend. If Benjamin was right and Bruce's letter had been forged, he might be one step closer to arresting the real culprit.

25

'Robert,' said Jane, entering his study carrying a gilded card engraved with elegant script. 'We've been invited to dine with the Trentons.'

He lowered the book he was reading. 'Who on earth are they?'

'They live on the next street. Nadia Trenton has a daughter Emily's age and we've got rather friendly.'

'Who's her husband?'

'He's called Richard, he made his money in banking. They're a very nice couple and I think you and Richard would get on very well. Shall I accept the invitation?'

'When is it for?'

'Tuesday evening.'

He paused to consider before shaking his head. 'No, I don't think so. I have no wish to spend the evening with people I don't know.'

Jane's instinct was to snap at him for being unfair, but she bit her lip, having learnt her lesson last time. 'We agreed that I would come to you with every invitation.'

'Yes, an agreement you have stuck to faithfully.'

'And you've turned down every single one.'

'Because none of them are of any interest to me.'

'But they're of interest to me. Nadia's becoming a good friend.'

'I'm not stopping you from seeing her. I just have no wish to meet her or any of her family.'

'You wanted to be welcomed into society, well, social calls are a part of that. You have to accept some invitations.'

'I will when we get one from someone who is actually interesting.'

'The Trentons are interesting.'

'I doubt it,' he said, returning to his book.

'If you don't accept this one, then I will send out invitations of my own to everyone we know.'

His gaze hardened. 'You'll do no such thing. I don't want strangers in our house.'

'We have to invite those who have invited us into their homes, that's how it works. If we don't, then we won't be welcomed anywhere ever again.'

'Fine by me.'

Jane snatched the book from his hand and tossed it onto the desk. 'This isn't fair, Robert. I'm going mad being cooped up in this house all the time. It's all right for you, you're in and out on business, but I have nothing to occupy my time.'

Robert's dark eyes glittered. 'Do not call our daughter nothing.'

'I'm not calling her nothing, but we have a nanny who does most of the work.'

'You pay calls to your friends during the day and you go shopping. What more do you want?'

'I want fun and excitement,' she exclaimed. 'I'm seventeen and I live the life of an old lady, only going out during the day, never going to parties or balls. It's ever since the night of Mary Walker's ball. It put you off, didn't it?'

'No. It's because all I see when I go into society is the stupid, the ridiculous and the useless. Every single one of them should have been euthanised at birth.'

'Robert,' Jane exclaimed. 'What a horrible thing to say. Many of them are thoroughly nice people, like the Trentons. You won't even give them a chance.'

'How many more times?' he sighed. 'I don't want to go. You can go on your own and tell them I'm ill,' he said with a dismissive wave of the hand.

'But I want to go with you. We're a married couple, we should be seen out together or people will start to talk.'

Now she had his attention and his eyes narrowed. 'Talk?'

'They'll think something's wrong with our marriage if no one sees us together. It might start rumours.'

Robert couldn't bear the thought of people spreading lies behind his back, not after he'd worked so hard to get everyone to take him seriously. 'All right, accept the invitation for both of us.'

'Really?' she beamed.

'Yes.' His smile was magnanimous. 'If that's what you want, then that's what we'll do.'

'Thank you, Robert,' she exclaimed, flinging her arms around his neck.

'You're very welcome. Why don't you buy yourself a new dress for the evening?'

'Can I really?'

'Yes, and some new shoes too.'

'But I already have so many.'

'And you deserve more.' He cradled her face in his hands. 'I want to give you the world.'

'I love you so much,' she breathed. She kissed him before straightening up and squealing excitedly. 'I'm going to my dressmaker's. I think something in emerald green.'

'You'll look beautiful, as always,' he smiled.

As she raced out of the room, Robert thought how child-like she was, her concerns only for parties and fashion. He supposed it was that air of innocence about her that he loved, but she could have quite stunning moments of clarity and depth that always surprised and intrigued him. He loved Jane so much but sometimes he would like to be a bachelor, free to come and go with no one to question him, able to turn down all invitations to dine and go to Vivienne's whenever he wanted. Then he considered how empty his life would be without her. They'd been so close since they were children, fallen in love over the years and he knew everything about her, but she could never know everything about him. He was sure she'd caught glimpses of his darker side, but it seemed she was choosing to pretend it didn't exist. She was compromising, so he supposed it was only fair that he did too.

Robert went upstairs to the nursery to see his little Emily, who was gurgling in her crib, the nanny watching over her.

'Go get yourself a cup of tea,' he told the nanny.

'Thank you, sir,' she replied, getting to her feet, stretching and heading downstairs.

'Hello, my lovely little angel,' he smiled, picking up his daughter and rocking her in his arms.

At the sound of the front door slamming shut, he went to the window to watch Jane get into their carriage, which had been brought round for her. She was smiling as she climbed inside, the footman closing the door behind her. Her happiness could still make him happy. He looked down at his daughter, content in his arms, smiling when she grasped onto his thumb with one tiny pink hand. The contradictions in his life never ceased to amaze him. These hands that so gently held his baby daughter had very recently been squeezing a woman's neck.

Robert banished those thoughts. He didn't like them anywhere near Emily. No matter how far he sank into darkness, he knew he would never hurt his daughter, who was his shining light, the purest thing in his life. Emily was his anchor, the rock he could cling to when the waves of evil tore at him, attempting to drag him into their depths.

'I wonder how Benjamin Richardson's getting on?' he murmured to his daughter. 'I suspect he's not having as nice a time as we are.'

* * *

Murphy left his friend's house feeling downcast. It had been confirmed that Bruce's letter wasn't a forgery, smashing all his theories and hopes. He stood on the street outside the house, wondering what he should do next, forcing passers-by to walk around him.

He couldn't tackle Robert Alardyce. Besides, he was hoping Sir Henry and Lady Alardyce would tell their son the police were treating him as a person of interest and he would panic and do something stupid. But that would take time and he was a man of action who couldn't bear to sit about doing nothing. Bruce was dead, as was Knapp, whose secretary could tell him nothing. Superficially, all the evidence pointed to Benjamin Richardson being responsible and Murphy had promised himself he would follow the evidence, but it galled him to follow breadcrumbs he was sure someone else had laid. Unfortunately, he'd reached a dead end. There was nowhere else to go.

Then it struck him – he might not be able to get anywhere in the investigation into Knapp's murder, but he might on the attacks on the women.

He returned to Police Chambers and arranged for the latest victim to come in and see if she could identify Benjamin. Fortunately, she was a strong, determined woman who wanted to see her attacker pay. She was younger than he was expecting, no older than twenty, pretty, with pale flawless skin and large dark eyes, but the resolute set of her heart-shaped mouth assured him she wouldn't quail from what he wanted her to do.

'Will I be in the same room as him?' she asked him, her voice weak and raspy after being throttled. She wore a scarf around her neck to hide the marks of strangulation.

'You will, Maggie,' he replied as gently as he could. 'But he's restrained and there are two constables guarding him. You'll be safe.'

Maggie took a deep breath and nodded. Despite her determination, he could see she was terrified.

'I'll be right by your side,' he added, wanting to make her feel better.

'Thank you,' she said, managing to raise a small smile.

He led her into one of the holding cells beneath Police Chambers. Usually prisoners would have been flung into Calton Jail by now, but Benjamin's family had managed to block that.

Two constables were already waiting inside. Benjamin was slumped on the rickety wooden slats that constituted a bed.

'Get up, you,' muttered one of the constables, nudging him in the ribs when Murphy and Maggie walked in.

Despite his abject misery, Benjamin saw a lady had entered the room and his natural politeness kicked in, allowing him to get to his feet and hold his head high. Murphy saw no recognition or panic in his eyes. He had no idea who this woman was.

'Is this the man who attacked you?' Murphy asked Maggie.

'What?' exclaimed Benjamin. 'It wasn't me, I have absolutely no interest in women.' He realised he'd practically shouted his sexual preference through Police Chambers, but he was too panicked to care.

'Shut it, you,' said one of the constables, clipping him around the back of the head, silencing him.

'All right, Constable, take it easy,' said Murphy. He looked to Maggie, whose trembling had stopped as she frowned at Benjamin.

'Can I see his hands?' she asked Murphy.

'Of course.' He nodded at Benjamin, who held out his pale, shaking, womanly hands that looked far too weak to wring a chicken's neck, never mind a woman's.

'It wasn't him,' said Maggie.

'Thank God,' breathed Benjamin, eyes filling with tears.

'You're certain?' said Murphy, attempting to hide his delight.

'Absolutely. The man who attacked me was bigger, stronger. This man's too thin and those aren't his hands. They were much more...' She shuddered, fingers brushing her neck. 'Powerful. His hair was darker too and his voice was deeper.'

'You're absolutely certain, Miss?'

She nodded. 'Aye. This isn't the man who attacked me.' A shadow passed across her face. 'And his eyes were dark, almost black.'

Benjamin's knees sagged and one of the constables had to grab his arm to keep him upright. He regarded Maggie with tear-filled eyes. 'Thank you.'

'You're welcome,' she replied before leaving with Murphy.

'Thank you, Maggie,' said Murphy once they were outside the cell.

'That poor man,' she replied. 'He was such a mess. What will happen to him?'

'He's facing charges in another case, so I really can't say at the moment.'

'He seemed like a lost little boy. It was so sad.'

Murphy had to admire her for showing such compassion to another person after the trauma she'd just endured. 'His family isn't without influence. Don't worry, he'll have help.'

'This means the man who attacked me is still out there, doesn't it?'

'It does, but I promise I will find him.'

'If anyone can, Inspector, you can. I've followed your exploits in all the papers.'

Murphy loathed the bloody newspapers, they'd made everyone think he had supernatural powers. 'I'll escort you out.'

As he escorted her to the door where Maggie's friend waited for her, a woman who resembled a yacht in full sail steamed her way inside, brushing aside anyone who got in her way. She was wrapped head to toe in dowdy rust-brown silks with the most absurd feathered hat balancing on her ornate grey coiffure. Her arched nostrils curled when she saw Murphy, creasing all the lines in her face.

'Inspector Murphy,' her voice boomed through the echoing stone building. 'Where is my son?'

'Lady Richardson,' he replied. 'I am at your service.'

'I demand to know why you've arrested Benjamin on these ridiculous charges.'

'I'm afraid it's nothing to do with me, your ladyship, I didn't arrest him. May I suggest you speak to Chief Superintendent Battles? He's in charge of the investigation. His office is on the first floor, second door on the right.'

'I shall speak to him immediately,' she announced before bustling towards the stairs. 'Out of my way, you ridiculous little man,' she barked at a constable coming towards her, causing him to leap aside.

'I don't envy Battles,' said Maggie, managing to raise a small smile. 'Thank you, Inspector, you've been very kind.'

'Please don't hesitate to contact me if you require anything else.'

Maggie nodded and left and he watched her go, a small, fragile woman with the heart of a lion. He wondered how he could manage things so she would get a glimpse of Robert Alardyce. After Battles's warning, he would have to do it very carefully and even if she did positively identify him, there was no reason why a jury – which would be made up entirely of men – would believe a maid's word over a wealthy and powerful man like Robert Alardyce, despite his family's chequered history.

'Inspector Murphy,' boomed Battles's deep voice, ricocheting off the walls like cannon fire.

He turned to see a red-cheeked Battles descending the stairs followed by Lady Richardson, who was glaring at his back.

'Yes, sir?' he said.

'Why on earth is Benjamin Richardson still locked up?'

'I couldn't say. As you know, Inspector Grendal is in charge of that case.'

'I don't care who's in charge of it. Set the man free, immediately.'

'Yes, sir.'

Lady Richardson pushed Battles out of the way and steamed towards Murphy. She tilted back her head. 'Where is my son?'

'He's in one of the holding cells, your ladyship. Perhaps you should wait here while I fetch him? It's an unpleasant place.'

'I'm not some weak, watery woman. Take me to my son. Now.'

'As you wish, your ladyship. This way.'

It boggled Murphy's mind that anyone could consider women to be the weaker sex. Or perhaps the fools who made such ridiculous statements had never met the likes of Amy Alardyce or Elizabeth Richardson? He thought of brave little Maggie too. There was certainly nothing weak about women.

He led Lady Richardson through the chambers and down to the cells, ordering the sergeant on duty to unlock the door.

'Good grief, the stench,' frowned Lady Richardson, her nostrils quivering with outrage. 'I'm disgusted that you've kept my son in this horrible place.'

'As I said, your ladyship, Inspector Grendal is in charge.'

'I'll be having words with that fool, make no mistake. Well, don't just sit there Benjamin, get up.'

'Mother?' he said, raising his head and blinking myopically. 'What are you doing here?'

'Sorting out this mess. Well get a move on. I'm taking you home.'

'Home?' he breathed, lower lip trembling.

Her gaze hardened. 'If you start to cry, I'll leave you here to rot.'

Even a man as hardened as Murphy was shocked by this statement. No wonder her son had turned out to be a nasty little tick.

Benjamin wiped away his tears on his sleeves, swallowed down all his emotion and got to his feet. 'I'm ready, Mother.'

'Good, because I don't want to spend one more second in this awful place. The shame you've brought on us, Benjamin. It's broken your poor father's heart, literally. You're the reason why he's at death's door.'

As she continued to rail against him, Benjamin looked back over his shoulder at his cell as though he wished he could stay.

'Good luck, Benjamin,' Murphy told him.

'I'm going to need it,' he sighed, eyeing his mother, who was still ranting at him, completely unaware the two men were talking. 'Thank you, Inspector. You're the only one who's shown me any kindness. I won't forget it.'

Murphy nodded, watching as he left with his mother, who was still beating him down verbally, the feathers in her hat bobbing up and down in time with her words, as though assisting their owner to scold him.

26

'My God,' said Henry.

Amy looked up from her breakfast to frown at her husband, who was sitting at the dining table reading the newspaper. 'What is it?' she asked him.

'Benjamin Richardson is Terence Burgess.'

'You mean the man who perpetuated that insurance fraud?'

'Yes. He's also been linked to Knapp's murder, as well as Mr Bruce's, who was found hanged.'

Amy's chest heaved as she was overcome with emotion, her hand holding the spoon shaking.

'Leave us,' Henry told the servants.

The maid and footman swiftly left, closing the door behind them.

'Thank God,' breathed Amy, letting her spoon drop to the table with a clatter. 'Thank God,' she repeated, burying her face in her hands.

'It seems Robert was innocent after all,' commented Henry, frowning at the newspaper.

Amy's head snapped up, eyes shiny with tears of relief. 'Are there any more details?'

'It's theorised Richardson hired some men to kill Knapp and Bruce.

He's a physical coward, so he didn't get his hands dirty. Unfortunately, they haven't managed to track down his accomplices.'

'What's the evidence against him?'

'The article's a bit vague, it just mentions personal items belonging to the victims have been linked to him, as well as a letter from Bruce to the police denouncing Benjamin as Terence Burgess.'

'Is that all the evidence they have?'

'The police are only releasing certain details and it's always hard to tell how genuine these stories are, but I don't think they would arrest a member of such a prominent family without solid evidence.'

'You're right,' she said, taking a deep breath to calm her fluttering heart. 'But it does make me uneasy that the person responsible for these crimes is the same man who insulted Robert. We know how personally he takes an insult.'

'You think this could be some elaborate revenge? If it is, it's an extremely complicated plot for someone of his age and limited experience to pull off.'

'Is it, though? He's been so successful in business, he has a natural flair for it. Would this really be beyond his capabilities?' She waved a dismissive hand and shook her head while her husband appeared thoughtful. 'I really am a terrible woman, continuing to think badly of my own son when the real criminal has been caught.' She caught Henry's look and frowned. 'What are you thinking?' she asked him.

He shook himself out of it and forced a smile. 'Nothing. All is well. The police have their man and Robert is exonerated. That pest Inspector Murphy should leave us alone now.'

'I do think you should have pressed for him to be disciplined.'

'Antagonising a man like that won't help anyone, especially Robert. It's much better to have a muzzle put on him, which is what the chief superintendent did. Robert is safe.'

'Is he, though? Women are still being attacked and he's graduated to throttling them.'

'We do need to find a way to contain him, make him so afraid that he'll never again indulge in his disgusting proclivities.'

'How can we do that? He will smash any cage we attempt to put him in.'

'I'm working on it and I hope I come up with something soon before another woman has to suffer.'

* * *

'My tie is fine,' muttered Robert, slapping away his valet's hand. 'Stop fussing, George. You can leave me now.'

'Sir,' bowed the valet before leaving.

George wasn't at all fond of his master, but he paid well, which was his only redeeming feature in the opinion of his servants. They had all thought they could run rings around an eighteen-year-old and have a cushy time of it, but they'd been proved very wrong. He wasn't a harsh or cruel master, just cold and aloof, and if the work was not done to his high standards, he wasn't shy about pulling them up about it. He kept them all on their toes and even when he wasn't around, they still felt as though he was watching them, as if he would somehow know if they didn't do the best job they could.

They were all very fond of their gentle, kind mistress, though, and they wondered why she'd married such a man, who they felt sure would only get worse with time. However, their employer had recently gone up in the estimation of his male employees, who enjoyed the status of working for Robert Alardyce. Working for such an infamous man used to mean they were looked down upon too, but things had radically changed since he'd beaten Tompkins. Now those of their own class could never wait to talk to them and buy them drinks, hoping to get some inside information about the notorious family, but none of Robert's servants were stupid enough to gossip about their employer.

Robert swept downstairs, not looking forward to the evening ahead, eyeing his cosy study with regret as he passed it by on his way to the front door. It was a chilly autumnal evening with spots of rain in the air and a biting breeze, and he would much prefer the company of his fire and all the papers on business he had to get through. To him, they were pleasurable reading. What could be more satisfying than learning how to make even more money? He loved money and he knew he would never have enough. Making more would always be his main purpose in life. He was aware that most men his age preferred the company of women and drink to books and cosy fires, but he seemed to get that part of his nature out of his system whenever he attacked a woman. This ensured he always remained calm and level-headed, which was how he had managed to so masterfully outflank Benjamin Richardson.

Movement at the top of the stairs drew his attention from his precious study and he saw Jane descending the steps, looking ravishing in the emerald-green dress she'd said she would buy.

'How do I look?' she smiled, enjoying the way his eyes sparkled.

'Like an angel,' he replied, kissing her cheek. He took a long black box from his jacket pocket and held it out to her. 'I bought you a present to apologise for speaking to you so harshly.'

'Oh, Robert,' she beamed, taking it from him and opening it up. She gasped at the necklace inside, the setting of which was exactly the same as the one her sapphire was in, only this one contained a beautiful big emerald. 'It's stunning.'

'I had the setting copied from your sapphire, so you have a matching pair.' He took the necklace out of the box and held it up to the light, so she could appreciate the jewel.

'That is so thoughtful of you,' she said, kissing him. 'Thank you.'

'You're very welcome. Why don't you turn around so I can put it on you?'

With a smile, she turned her back to him and he slipped the necklace around her long slender neck. As he fastened the clasp, he was almost overcome by the sudden, irresistible urge to put both hands around her throat and squeeze. He'd never experienced thoughts of violence against Jane before and it shocked him that the dark whispers were encouraging him to hurt her now.

'Robert, what are you doing?' she said. 'That hurts.'

He realised he was gripping onto her shoulders, fingers digging into her flesh. 'Sorry,' he breathed, snapping himself out of it and releasing her. He kissed her neck. 'You just look so beautiful, I was overwhelmed that you're my wife.'

'That is so sweet,' she smiled, turning to slide her arms around his neck and kiss him. 'Robert,' she added, tearing her mouth from his when he became more passionate. She glanced at Forbes, who was waiting at the door, staring straight ahead, professionally nonchalant.

'I want to take you to bed,' Robert murmured in her ear. The whispers had stopped but his blood was still up.

'We can't because we'll be late, but if you're good tonight at the dinner, you'll get a special treat later.'

'I can't wait until later,' he said, nuzzling her neck.

'Well, you must,' she said, half-heartedly pushing him away.

Forbes placed Jane's matching green cape around her shoulders and assisted Robert on with his coat before handing him his hat and gloves. They headed outside into the cold night to their waiting carriage.

'Do try to look more cheerful, Robert,' said Jane as the carriage set off. 'You never know, you might enjoy yourself.'

'We'll see,' he replied, frowning out at the dark streets, wishing he was in his study.

Jane didn't press him. She thought she was very fortunate to have got him this far and she didn't want him to change his mind and head back home.

Envy rolled through Robert as they pulled up outside the Trentons' home – a huge four-storey townhouse on the end of the block on Ainslie Place. It was bigger than their own house and Jane had already informed him that Nadia and Richard were only a few years older than them, in their early twenties. The house wasn't a grand estate like Alardyce, but it almost rivalled Mary Walker's home, although they didn't have an army of servants lined up outside to greet them.

The waiting footman opened the carriage door and they were escorted inside by a tall, thin but very erect butler. He led them into the grand drawing room where their hostess waited – an extremely attractive brunette in an elegant pale blue gown that accentuated her eyes, which were more violet than blue, raven hair piled atop her head. Robert forced himself not to stare, as she was one of the loveliest women he'd ever seen. He smiled when Jane stepped forward to greet her friend. His angel still outshone her.

Nadia greeted Robert cordially, saying what a pleasure it was to finally meet him, Jane had told her so much about him. Her husband Richard was an athletic man with a handsome, chiselled face, his good looks marred slightly by the fact that he was prematurely balding, all the hair down the centre of his scalp already having given up the ghost. He was relaxed and friendly and as he shook his hand, Robert studied him for any sign of derision, but there was none. The man gave off an air of relaxed amiability and Robert found himself uncoiling.

They had drinks in the drawing room before dinner, during which Jane and Nadia discussed their children while Robert and Richard launched into a dialogue about business. Richard was almost as clever as him and had some very useful insights into the future of stocks and the financial market in general. Robert went as far as to think that Richard might be ahead of his time, and he found himself enjoying the company of someone who wasn't a member of his own family or who didn't frequent Vivienne's.

When dinner was announced, they took their places around the grand table in the enormous dining room, the walls covered with swords and pistols.

'This is quite the armoury,' commented Robert.

'It's Richard's fascination,' said Nadia. 'Makes me feel like I'm dining in the middle of a siege.'

'It's very impressive,' said Robert approvingly. 'Where do you get them from?'

'Various antique shops in the city,' replied Richard. 'And I have a few contacts who were in the military. Some of these weapons have even seen some action. That Baker rifle there was used during the Napoleonic Wars.'

'It's very grim eating around objects that have taken lives,' said Nadia.

'More might be joining my collection,' said Richard with a morbid smile. 'Now it looks like we're on the brink of the second Boer war. Mark my words, it will break out.'

'Can we please not discuss war at the dinner table, Richard?' sighed his wife.

'It's a bit difficult not to when surrounded by weapons,' replied Robert.

'I don't know what the world's coming to with all its wars and hate,' said Nadia. 'Why can't everyone just get along? There always seems to be someone wanting to hurt some poor innocent. My own maid was recently subjected to a terrible ordeal.'

Robert's hand hesitated as he lifted the soup spoon to his mouth but only for a moment before he overcame his surprise and carried on eating.

'What ordeal?' said Jane.

'The poor girl was attacked in the street, had the back of her dress ripped open and her corset cut away with a knife. She was beaten and throttled.'

'Oh, gosh,' gasped Jane, a hand flying to her mouth. 'How awful. Is she all right?'

'Physically, yes. She sustained some injuries, but she'll recover; however, she'll never be the same. She's a strong, determined girl but it had a very debilitating effect on her. She doesn't like going anywhere alone and the other servants overhear her crying every night in her room. Such a shame because she's a sweet thing and a wonderful lady's maid.'

'The poor girl,' said Jane. 'Do the police have any idea who did it?'

'They thought it might be Benjamin Richardson, but they took her to see him at Police Chambers and she said it definitely wasn't him, not that anyone who knew him would think it was. We all know he has no interest in women.'

'Not surprising, really,' smiled Richard. 'His mother's a hideous woman.'

'She was certain it wasn't him?' said Robert. 'As I discovered, he has a thoroughly vicious character.'

'Oh, yes,' replied Nadia. 'He was nothing like her attacker. He was bigger, stronger. Nothing like Benjamin. He does wear a ring with the letter R like her attacker wore, but she was absolutely certain and she is a clever girl.'

'I hope they catch the animal soon,' said Jane. 'No woman is safe until they do.'

'Sadly the city's a dangerous place,' said Richard. 'And it gets more dangerous by the day. I don't mean to sound snobbish, but I'm glad this beast only attacks maids and the lower-class women because it means my Nadia's safe.'

Nadia smiled across the table at him. 'He worries about me terribly,' she told Jane.

'I understand what you mean, Richard,' said Robert, not wanting to be outdone. 'It's a worry each time Jane sets foot outside the door and not just because of this attacker roaming our streets. As you said, the city's a dangerous place and anything can happen.'

'Too true,' he replied. 'Just the other day, I saw a poor old man knocked over and killed by a tram. It was such a mess.'

'Please, Richard,' said Nadia. 'Not while we're eating.'

'Sorry, dear.'

'So the police are no closer to finding the man who attacked your maid?' said Robert.

'No, they're not,' replied Nadia. 'If he can be called a man. Such a creature must be so inadequate and pathetic to attack a defenceless girl walking alone.'

Robert's grip on the spoon tightened.

'I agree,' said Jane. 'He must be mentally incompetent, it's the only explanation.'

Robert felt the darkness rising inside him, wanting to punish these women for talking about him in such a disrespectful way.

'There are some people in this world who get a great deal of pleasure from causing other people pain,' said Richard. 'Obviously they're morally incompetent, but more than likely of low intelligence too.'

Robert slowly breathed in and out as he attempted to contain his rising rage. Once again, people were insulting and deriding him, even his own wife. He wanted to punish them all and it was taking him everything he had to contain it. The dark whispers started again, swirling through his mind, urging him to release the demon within.

'Robert, are you all right?' said Richard.

This brought him back to himself. 'Yes. I was just admiring that sword on the wall behind Nadia.'

'Oh, yes, that's an eighteenth Hussars officer's sword. It's about seventy years old.'

'Something else that's wrought death and destruction,' commented Nadia with distaste. 'Anyway, Maggie, my lady's maid, got to meet the famous Inspector Murphy.'

'Really?' said Jane. 'I've read all about him in the newspapers.'

'He took her to meet Benjamin when he was being held at Police

Chambers. She said he was a most impressive man and surprisingly sympathetic and that he has a quality about him that told her no one can escape him. He said he'd find her attacker and that she was a very strong and brave girl.'

'He has the best arrest record of any detective in the city,' said Jane.

'And he's trying to bring science to police work,' said Richard. 'Fingerprints, handwriting analysis, photography of the victim and crime scene, training officers so they don't blunder onto a crime scene and inadvertently destroy evidence. Apparently, he studied the Jack the Ripper case in London to learn from the mistakes of the investigating officers. Murphy thinks that if more modern techniques had been implemented in that case, they could have caught the culprit. Especially fingerprints, he's very keen on those. His efforts have been met with a lot of resistance, though. So many people can't bear change.'

'And have any of his modern techniques been useful in finding your maid's attacker?' said Robert.

'Sadly, no, but they could be in the future. I get the feeling this particular attacker will never stop.'

'You're more than likely right,' replied Robert with a smooth smile.

Nadia shivered. 'Can we change the subject, please? It's making me uneasy.'

Their soup plates were cleared and the second course was brought in. This time, a young maid was assisting the two footmen. Thankfully it wasn't Maggie. As she was a lady's maid, she wouldn't serve at the table, which was very fortunate for Robert; however, this one was also attractive. She was more sweet-looking than pretty, with a very appealing wide-eyed innocence. As she placed his plate before him and gave him a shy smile, the blood thundered in Robert's head. The urge to wrap his hands around her neck and squeeze possessed him again. Dear God, was he losing control? He'd had this urge twice in one night, but he was still able to push it aside and continue as though a war wasn't raging inside him, one between the light and the dark, and the light was slowly being smothered.

Magda's words came back to haunt him – one day, he would become too dangerous to be around those he loved and he would have to leave to protect them. Not so long ago, that had seemed a remote possibility, but now he wasn't so sure, his condition seemed to be progressing quickly. The maid moved away and the heat in his blood cooled a little. While all these thoughts raced through his mind, he managed to carry on eating and talking as though he hadn't a care in the world.

'You sound like you know Inspector Murphy personally,' Robert asked Richard.

'That's because I do, not that well, but I have met him at a few public functions. He's a very unique and interesting fellow and extremely intelligent.'

'Not a man to be taken lightly?'

'Dear me, no. I feel sorry for any criminal who has him on their tail.'

Robert just nodded before looking down at his food to hide the turbulence inside.

* * *

'You seemed to enjoy this evening,' Jane said to Robert on their way home in the carriage.

'Surprisingly, I did,' he replied. 'You were right, I did get on well with Richard.'

'You like him, then?'

'I do and he gave me an excellent tip on some stocks.'

'I'm so pleased, Robert. So, you wouldn't mind if we invited them to our house for dinner one evening?'

'Not at all, they're very welcome.' They could keep him up to date on the investigation into Maggie's attack. What Richard had said about Murphy's techniques had been very useful. So far, luck had been on his side and he hadn't left any evidence behind, but he must always be careful to wear gloves to avoid leaving fingerprints and think through what he was doing rather than just attack wildly. He would look forward to the challenge, it would be like a blind duel between himself and Murphy.

Robert wondered if he should do more to deal with Maggie. It sounded as if the girl was tenacious and didn't intend to stop until he'd been caught. Now he and Jane were friends with the Trentons, there was always the chance she might recognise him if he went to the house. He couldn't take the risk, but it might look suspicious if something were to happen to her just after he'd dined at the house where she lived and worked when Murphy was already suspicious of him. There must be a way of disposing of the girl without arousing suspicion. He immediately ruled out faking her suicide, even though that might work, as everyone knew how traumatised she'd been by her ordeal. No, this problem required an accident or death from natural causes, something that wouldn't arouse the suspicions of the authorities. He would speak to the Comyns and get Will's devious brain on the case. The girl had to go.

27

The next morning, Jane went into Robert's study to fetch some writing paper so she could compose a note to Nadia to thank her for the wonderful dinner the previous evening. She was delighted that Robert had enjoyed himself and was willing to socialise with the Trentons more. She hoped they would help bring him out of his shell a little.

She was unable to find any paper on top of his desk. In fact, there was nothing on his desk except for a large blotter, a letter opener and a glass paperweight. He liked things tidy and everything in its place. Sometimes it made her a little uneasy, as it reminded her of Matthew. He'd been the same, going into a rage if something wasn't put away, but her husband had never gone to those extremes. Neither could she ask him where the paper was because he was out on business.

The pile of financial documents Robert was always reading through to learn from were stacked neatly in one deep drawer. Trying the drawer on the opposite side of the desk, she found the writing paper she needed. Jane was about to close the drawer when something caught her eye. It looked like a ring. Excitement gripped her. Had he bought her more jewellery? He knew how much she loved it.

She almost closed the drawer, not wanting to spoil the surprise, but the magpie inside her was unable to resist, so she took it out. She gasped and almost dropped it in surprise when she saw it was in fact a man's gold signet ring with the letter R emblazoned on it. It looked identical to the one Benjamin Richardson always wore. Why on earth did Robert have this ring?

A thought occurred to her that froze the blood in her veins. Richard Trenton had said the man who attacked their maid had worn this ring.

All the warnings her family had given her when she and Robert had got engaged came screaming back – they'd said he was just like Matthew, who had enjoyed attacking and killing women. Now women in the city were being attacked and her husband was in possession of an item she knew the attacker had worn.

Jane stamped down these panicked, wild thoughts. She didn't know that was what was happening. For all she knew, Robert could have come into possession of this ring innocently. Perhaps it was Benjamin's and he'd dropped it somewhere and Robert had it so he could return it to him? Or perhaps stealing a beloved piece of jewellery from his loathed enemy was a pleasing revenge to him? But why would he keep hold of a piece of evidence that could convict Benjamin? Firstly, she had to ascertain if this was Benjamin's ring, which she was certain it was. She knew her husband and he was a good man, he treated her and their daughter very well. He wasn't cold and cruel like Matthew had been and she refused to condemn him before she understood the situation.

She replaced the ring in the drawer and quietly closed it before hurrying back to the drawing room clutching the writing paper, her palms sweating.

After anxiously pacing the room for several minutes, wrestling with herself and attempting to settle on a single course of action, she donned her hat and coat, rushing by the confused Forbes, who had just fetched her afternoon tea, without a word, and headed out the door. She didn't take the carriage, not wanting anyone in the house to know where she was going. She needed to keep this quiet, for Robert's sake.

She walked to Benjamin's townhouse on Albany Street, which was very nice but nowhere near the luxury or grandeur of his family's mansion. As it wasn't far from their own home, she was there in just a few minutes.

She raised her hand to knock on the door and hesitated, wanting to run back home and forget she ever saw that ring, but something inside her compelled her and she lifted the heavy brass knocker.

As she waited for someone to answer, the tension grew and she'd almost made up her mind to go home when the door was opened by Benjamin's valet.

'Yes, Madam?' said the squat but stately man with enormous flaring nostrils.

'Is Mr Richardson home?' she replied.

'He is.'

'Please could you tell him Imogen Day wishes to see him.' Jane had no idea what prompted her to give an alias, but it seemed the right thing to do, conjuring the name out of thin air.

'Yes, Madam,' he said, opening the door wider to allow her entry.

She stepped into the tiled hallway wringing her hands, her heart thudding.

'Are you all right, Madam?' said the valet with kindly concern.

'Yes, quite well, thank you,' she replied a little breathlessly, forcing a smile.

'Please wait here,' he told her before disappearing through a door on the right.

Jane had almost decided to bolt again when the valet returned and showed her into a pleasant sitting room. Benjamin was standing by the fire, and she was a little shocked by the change in his appearance. Dark shadows circled his eyes, his skin was pale and hair lank, flopping into his eyes. Neither was he clean-shaven. He looked like a man who was suffering deeply.

His curious look – for he had never heard of Imogen Day and had hoped his mystery guest would be someone who could help with his current predicament – was replaced by surprise.

'Jane,' he exclaimed. 'What are you doing here and why are you calling yourself Imogen Day?'

She didn't reply, her gaze fixed on his right index finger. She could clearly see the signet ring – gold and engraved with the letter R, identical to the one in her husband's desk drawer.

He followed her gaze to his hand before looking back at her with a puzzled frown. 'Why are you here? Is it something to do with Robert?'

'I...' Finally, she dragged her eyes off the ring and onto his face. 'I'm sorry, I have to go.'

'No, wait.'

She tore out of the room, down the hall past the valet, flung open the front door and ran down the street. A cab – which had just deposited a couple onto the street – was standing empty and she jumped in.

As the carriage started to move, she glanced out of the window to see Benjamin in pursuit.

'Please come back,' he called.

Jane ducked out of sight and clamped her hands down over her ears to block out the sound of his pleas. The driver urged the horses on and thankfully they left Benjamin behind.

The cab dropped her off at Queen Street Gardens, which wasn't far from her home. It was somewhere she could walk and gather her thoughts before facing Robert. What exactly had she learnt? That Robert possessed a replica of Benjamin's ring, and she knew that ring wasn't one just anyone could get hold of, he must have had it specially commissioned. Not even another member of his family owned one, it was a unique piece and had cost him a small fortune. Mary had told her all about it. Nadia's maid had been attacked by a man wearing that ring and she had told the police Benjamin hadn't been responsible. Only one other person in the world owned an identical ring and that was her husband, son of Matthew Crowle, whose own parents had said he'd attacked a maid at Alardyce.

Jane's head spun and she sank onto a bench before the small pond, swallowing down her tears. Was it possible she'd married a monster?

She thought it ironic that her Aunt Esther had discovered her own husband was a monster when she'd found Amy's locket in his desk drawer. Now she'd discovered the same about her own husband by finding the replica ring. But it was always possible there could be a perfectly reasonable explanation for the presence of that ring. The question was, how should she handle the situation? It was tempting to go to Alardyce and tell her Aunt Amy and Uncle Henry, place it in their capable hands and let them sort it out but, if Robert was innocent, that course of action could well ruin their marriage. He wouldn't take kindly to her going behind his back like that. He was her husband and they loved each other. They could work it out.

Decided on a course of action, she left the park and caught another cab back to Drummond Place.

'Is my husband home?' she asked Forbes as she handed him her hat and coat.

'Yes, Madam,' he replied. 'He's in his study.'

He hardly needed to tell her where he was. That was Robert's favourite room in the house.

'Would you like some tea, Madam?' he asked her.

'No, thank you. I want to talk to my husband in private, so we don't wish to be disturbed.'

'I shall let the other servants know,' he bowed before heading down the passage that would take him downstairs to the kitchen.

Jane stood before the door to Robert's study and took a moment to gather herself, smoothing down her dress and taking a few deep breaths before pushing it open.

She stopped in the doorway, heart warming at the sight of her very handsome husband working at his desk. He looked up and smiled, the warmth in his eyes reassuring her that she was doing the right thing.

'Hello,' he smiled. 'Where have you been?'

'To the park,' she replied. 'I needed some fresh air.'

'Did you enjoy your walk?'

'Yes, it was very pleasant. Can I talk to you?'

'You can always talk to me.'

His smile was so disarming, Jane relaxed.

Robert got up from behind his desk and they took the two armchairs either side of the fire, facing each other.

'I love this room,' he said with a contented smile, stretching out his long legs before him.

'I've noticed,' she replied.

'So, what do you want to discuss? Have we been invited to dine out again?'

'No, it's nothing like that.'

When he realised how nervous she was, he leaned forward in his seat and took her hand. 'It's all right,' he gently told her. 'Whatever's wrong, we'll sort it out.'

'Yes, you're right,' she smiled, raising her hand to touch his face. 'Our marriage is strong.'

'It is. Very.' He kissed her fingers and leaned back in his chair. 'So, what is it?'

'I found that ring in your desk drawer.'

'Ring?'

'The duplicate of Benjamin Richardson's ring. I wasn't snooping in your desk, you understand. I wanted some writing paper and I found it. I wondered what it was doing in there. Why would you have a copy made of his ring?'

Robert's calm countenance gave nothing away, although she did notice his eyes darken slightly.

'Is this why you needed to go out for some fresh air?' he replied.

His manner was casual, but inside he was seething. How dare she snoop through his things? She was as bad as his mother and Henry. Why could no one respect his privacy? All that about writing paper was just nonsense. He felt the anger rising inside him, but he was containing it as he hunted around for an excuse.

'Yes,' she replied. 'I was so shocked, I went to see Benjamin.'

His eyes flashed. 'You went to see him? Did you tell him why?'

'Of course not. I didn't say anything. I saw he was wearing his own ring and left.' She was a little startled when he shot to his feet and started pacing the room. 'What's wrong, Robert?'

'What's wrong? Why the hell did you go there? It was a bloody stupid thing to do.'

'Because I had to know,' she retorted.

'Know what?'

'If you used that ring to set him up. I know how much you hate him.'

'Why would I need to set him up? The fool set himself up with that insurance scandal.'

'Why do you have that ring, Robert?'

'It's nothing to do with him, there are plenty of those rings about. I bought it because it has an R on it for my name.'

'That's not true. Mary told me Benjamin had it specially commissioned. It wasn't one of a batch, it's one of a kind. So, I repeat, Robert – why do you have that ring?'

His gaze darkened. 'There are some things you're better off not knowing.'

'What do you mean?' she said, starting to get scared. 'What things?'

'I can't tell you.'

She got to her feet too, not liking the way he was looming over her. 'What have you done?' she rasped, almost afraid to ask.

'Just forget you ever saw it.'

'Nadia said her maid alleged her attacker wore that ring. Did you attack Maggie?'

She released a startled gasp and staggered backwards when he advanced on her, his eyes so hard and cold she barely recognised him. She grimaced when her back met the wall, jolting pain down her spine.

'No, I didn't,' he thundered in her face. 'Stop asking ridiculous questions.'

'They're not ridiculous. The way those women were attacked was quite similar to what Matthew did. That's why Inspector Murphy's been so interested in you.'

'No,' he cried.

'Is that why you didn't want me to tell anyone Knapp came here?' The way Robert avoided her gaze made her nauseous. 'My God,' she rasped. 'You killed him.'

'I didn't,' he exclaimed.

'Then you had someone do it for you.' Her eyes widened. 'You're Terence Burgess. You arranged that entire scheme to get Benjamin back for insulting you, didn't you?'

Every part of her husband she knew and understood fled from his eyes, replaced by an empty coldness. He looked so much like Matthew, she recoiled in fear.

'You're just like him, aren't you?' said Jane. Tears filled her eyes. 'The family tried to warn me, but I wouldn't listen because I was so blinded by love. Did I fall in love with the real man, Robert, or did he never exist?'

Emotion surged back into his eyes. 'Of course he's real and he loves you passionately.'

'Then how could you do this? Our life was so good, living in this beautiful house with our lovely daughter, and your businesses are very successful too. Why did you have to spoil it?'

'I've not spoilt anything. Nothing needs to change.'

'Robert, you had someone killed.'

'No, I didn't. I just didn't want Murphy to find out Knapp came here because it would give him another excuse to harass me. He's got it in for me.'

'You should tell him the truth. Only that will clear your name.'

'Don't be ridiculous, Jane. He'll use it to destroy me.'

'So you don't have anything to do with Knapp's death?'

'Of course not. Why would I?'

'Because he was beastly to you and, as you've proved, you enjoy destroying those who insult you. Or... oh, my God. Robert, are you responsible for all the recent attacks on women in the city and not just Maggie?' She started to cry. 'Please tell me it's not true.'

He took her face in his hands. 'It's not true,' he said ardently. 'You have to believe me.'

She gazed into his eyes and shook her head. 'You're lying.'

'I could never lie to you,' he said, kissing her face, her tears transferring onto his skin.

'Maggie's attacker wore Benjamin's ring and she said he wasn't responsible. You attacked her, you beat and strangled her,' she sobbed. 'How could you?'

'All right, I admit to doing it just that once. It was another attempt to set up Benjamin.'

'You hate him that much?'

'It burns inside me, all the time. Setting him up for fraud didn't feel enough, especially when the laws against it are so weak. I'd read about the attacks in the newspapers and thought I could set him up for those too, then he would definitely be thrown into Calton Jail to rot, but it didn't work.'

'Because of Maggie. What if she recognises you? You could hang.'

'That won't happen.'

'You're Matthew Crowle's son and Edward Alardyce's second cousin. Think about what would happen to you if everyone found out what you've done.'

His grip on her tightened, jaw throbbing with anger. 'But no one's going to find out, are they?'

'Robert, you're hurting me.'

'Sorry,' he said, releasing her. He took her hands. 'Listen to me, Jane – you can't tell anyone about this. If you do, I'll be in enormous trouble. I'll be arrested and the final nail will be hammered into our family's coffin. I'll dispose of the ring and we'll never speak of it again.'

'We can't just ignore this. What you did is very serious.'

'Which is why no one can know.'

'We can't simply brush it under the carpet. You attacked a woman and Benjamin could go to prison for something he didn't do.'

'That's the idea,' he said belligerently.

'How can you be so cruel? You didn't see the state he was in. He wouldn't survive prison.'

'Maybe it will teach him a much-needed lesson,' he said with a wicked smile.

'I can't believe you'd be so vicious as to condemn an innocent man to such a fate.'

'Why shouldn't I? What sort of fate do you think he would have condemned me to, given the chance? He would have had me humiliated and banned from society and when that didn't work, he attempted to have me pounded into the dirt by Tommy Tompkins. Why should I show him any mercy?'

'Because you're better than he is. Benjamin was raised by a cruel, uncaring mother, treated like the joke of his family, shamed whenever he tried to be who he truly is. You have no such excuse. You were raised by loving parents who have shown you nothing but kindness.'

'Kindness?' he snorted. 'Locking me up in that mausoleum Uncle Abel calls a home? Beaten and abused by Knapp? Kept from the woman I love?'

'And why did they do that? Because they were scared of what you'd become. They tried to stop the process in its tracks, but all their efforts were in vain. You're changing into the monster anyway.'

'Don't say that,' he snarled, chest heaving as he was overtaken by anger and fear.

'It's true. Even as we're talking now, the man I love is disappearing in front of my eyes. You have to go to Murphy and tell him the truth. If you allow Benjamin to be locked up for something you did, then you will slip away entirely and you'll never come back.'

Robert's hands clenched and unclenched into fists, he ground his teeth together and his eyes narrowed into slits. For the first time since they'd met when they were children, Jane was afraid of him. The urge to go to her child almost overwhelmed her and she started slowly side-stepping towards the door, his predatory gaze never leaving her.

'I'll never confess to Murphy,' he told her in a deep growl. 'And he'll never get any evidence against me. I've covered my tracks too well.'

Realising she wasn't going to convince him that way, Jane decided to try another tack. She just wanted to keep him talking so she could escape the room, get her child and leave, because only now did she realise that she'd made the same mistake as her Aunt Esther had when she'd met Matthew, only she hadn't been charmed by a handsome stranger. Robert was her closest friend. He'd completely pulled the wool over her eyes and it hurt so much.

'So you're going to let Benjamin rot in prison?' she said while slowly continuing to sidle to the door.

'He won't go to prison. His influential family will see to that. His mother's already got him out of Police Chambers.'

'After letting him languish there.'

'To teach him a lesson.'

'What lesson? He hasn't done anything wrong.'

'That man has done plenty wrong in his time and he'll do plenty more in the future. You shouldn't waste any sympathy on him.'

Jane had almost reached the door. All she needed to do was keep him talking a little longer. He'd moved across the room with her, but he was standing a few paces from her. She could make it. 'I will always feel sympathy for a fellow human being in pain.'

'You're too tender-hearted,' replied Robert. 'It's a cruel world full of cruel people like Benjamin Richardson.'

'And you.'

'I can be ruthless when I need to be, but you keep my heart good.'

'If I do, I've done a poor job of it.'

'It's not too late. We can sort this out.'

'No, we can't,' she said, reaching behind her to grab the door handle.

'I know what you're doing, Jane,' he said, eyes turning blacker. 'And I won't let you.'

'What am I doing, apart from trying to save my husband?'

'You're going to leave me, aren't you?'

'I'm taking Emily and we're going to stay at Alardyce for a while.'

The darkness fled from his eyes, replaced by panic. 'No, please don't go. Without you two, I'm truly lost.'

'You're already lost. What Benjamin's done is nothing compared to your viciousness. You attacked that poor maid and if you think I'm foolish enough to believe you didn't attack those other women too, then you don't know me at all. Why would I want to be with a man who assaults women? For all I know, you could one day turn on me.'

'No,' he cried, wrapping his arms around her waist and pulling her to him. 'I would never do that. You and Emily are the best and purest things in my life, and I would never sully you.'

She tore herself from his grip. 'You convinced me you're someone you're not, just like Matthew did with Aunt Esther. You betrayed me, Robert.'

'I haven't,' he cried, attempting to pull her back to him, but she slapped his hands away, stunning him. She had never been anything but gentle and loving before.

'What makes you think you have the right to go around treating people this way?' she cried.

'Because I've had to fight my entire life just to be accepted by bastards like Benjamin Richardson.'

'You never had to fight with me. I always accepted you, Robert. I wouldn't have cared if you were the son of a pig farmer, I still would have loved you. This obsession you have about your parentage has led to this. It's blackened your heart and forced you to commit horrible crimes just to prove you have power and control. You want to punish the whole world because your father was a footman,' she yelled. 'And now look what you've done. You've ruined everything.'

'I haven't, we can still fix this. I need you, Jane. Without you and Emily, I'm lost.'

'And whose fault is that?' she said, before turning the handle and pulling open the door.

In his panic, he lashed out, catching her a glancing blow across the left side of the face and she fell to the floor, out cold. Robert stared down at her, stunned by what he'd done.

'Oh, God, Jane,' he cried, kneeling by her side. 'I'm so sorry, I didn't mean it. Please wake up.' When she failed to respond, the panic started to completely overwhelm him and he gently shook her, tapping the undamaged side of her face, her cheek already bruised and swelling. Then he saw the rise and fall of her chest and realised he hadn't killed her. 'Thank you,' he breathed, although he wasn't sure who he was talking to because he certainly didn't believe in God.

The panic receded and he remained crouched by her side, calming down as his cool, logical brain finally took over. This wasn't his fault, it was hers. She was going to leave him and take their daughter and he refused to lose his angels. He could fix this.

Taking the key out of the back of the door, he exited the study and locked her in before striding determinedly towards the stairs leading down to the servants' hall. Thanks to his real father, he already knew what he had to do.

28

Amy was attempting to embroider in her sitting room, but she had to keep putting down her work because of the pain in her hands. Every year, it got worse, thanks to Edward Alardyce and his torture. Magda had given her a tincture to rub in which did alleviate the pain for a while, but it would always come back. She only used to experience the pain in cold weather, but it was starting to occur throughout the year now and she dreaded the day it became so bad she was unable to indulge in her favourite hobbies of embroidery and watercolours. Already she'd had to abandon the more intricate embroidery designs and settle on simpler patterns, but it still gave her a lot of pleasure and she determined to enjoy it while she could.

'Yes, Rush?' she smiled when he walked in. 'What's wrong? You look rather put out.'

'I am, my lady. We have a visitor. He came by the servants' entrance but he insists on speaking to you.'

'Who is it?'

'Mr Forbes. He says he's butler to Master Robert.' Rush made this pronouncement in a way that indicated he thought it was all a falsehood to gain access to the lady of the house for a nefarious purpose.

'What does he want?'

'He refuses to tell me and says it's for your ears alone.'

'Very well. Show him in.'

'In here?' he said, shocked.

'I'll see him in the drawing room if it makes you feel better,' she replied with a fond smile.

'Well, it does a little, but he does have a rather villainous aspect and his boots are muddy.'

'Then you can tell him he must leave his boots downstairs. Is that an acceptable compromise?'

'I think so, my lady,' he bowed before leaving. 'But I refuse to fetch him any tea.'

'Quite right,' she said, breaking into an amused smile when Rush turned his back.

Amy pondered what Forbes could want as she wandered into the drawing room. Obviously it was something to do with Robert, it was the only link between them, and she dreaded to think what news he might be bringing.

A few minutes later, Forbes entered the drawing room in a pair of polished shoes Amy surmised Rush had furnished him with. He stood on the threshold of the door, anxiously turning the brim of his hat in his hands. Rush stood at his shoulder, frowning at him disapprovingly.

'Hello, Forbes,' she smiled, attempting to put him at his ease. 'Please come in. Thank you, Rush, you may leave us.'

'Are you sure, your ladyship?'

'Yes. I'll be perfectly fine.'

He bowed, throwing Forbes a mistrustful glare before leaving.

'What brings you here on this inclement day, Forbes?' Amy asked him.

'Forgive me for turning up like this, your ladyship, and I know you don't usually receive servants in your drawing room, so I appreciate you seeing me but I didn't know what else to do. Someone must know.'

'You might not be aware that I used to be a governess, so I don't have any pretensions about not allowing fellow human beings into my home. Now please, tell me what's wrong.'

'It's Master Robert, your ladyship. He's run mad.'

'Run mad?' she frowned.

'He had an argument with Mrs Alardyce, and it became very heated.

Their quarrelling became so loud, we could hear it downstairs in the kitchen, although it was too muffled to make out the words. Then there was a bang and everything went silent.'

Amy gripped onto the table beside her. 'What sort of bang? Like... a gun?'

'Oh, no, nothing like that. It was more like something had fallen and hit the floor. We didn't know what to do, we were so confused and scared. The footman and I had decided to go up there and check on Mrs Alardyce when the master stormed into the kitchen and dismissed the lot of us. He told us to clear out our things and get out. He gave us only one hour and said if we hadn't left by then, he'd get the police to throw us out. We had no choice but to do as he said, but I'm not here about myself or the other servants, your ladyship. We're all terribly worried about Mrs Alardyce. She's a gentle and kind mistress and we're all very fond of her. We're terrified something bad has happened to her. I thought the best thing to do would be to come here and let you know.'

'Yes, you did the right thing,' Amy breathed, her head spinning as she attempted to understand this fresh shock. 'What about Emily?'

'The master dismissed the nanny, but she was safe and well in her crib when she left.'

'Thank you for bringing me this information, Forbes,' she said, her mind racing. 'Rest assured that I will sort it out and your mistress will be well.'

Amy strode to the door and flung it open to find Rush pretending to arrange the vase of flowers on the hallway table, a job usually done by the maids, but she knew he was only staying close to ensure she was safe. 'Take Mr Forbes down to the kitchens, feed him and give him something to drink,' Amy told him. 'I have to go out.'

'May I enquire where, my lady?'

'To my son's house. As soon as Sir Henry comes home, inform him of where I've gone.'

'Yes, my lady, but wouldn't you like myself or one of the footmen to accompany you?'

'I appreciate your concern, Rush, but this is something I need to do alone. Order the carriage to be brought round for me.'

'Yes, but...'

'Now, Rush.'

He bowed. 'Yes, your ladyship.'

* * *

Robert was pacing back and forth in his study when there was a knock at the front door. He froze, hoping the unwanted visitor would give up and go away, but they persisted, knocking again and again. He sighed when he realised it could only be one person, his suspicions confirmed when the shouting began.

'Open up, Robert, or I'll fetch a constable to break down the door.'

He huffed and rushed to open it before the entire street heard her.

'Mother,' he said. 'What are you doing?'

'Why are you answering your own door? Where's your butler?'

'I had to sack him. I caught him stealing.'

'Then why didn't your footman or maid answer my knock? Men of your calibre don't normally open their own front doors.'

'Because, like you, I don't have such pretensions.'

'Oh, yes, you do,' she said, pushing past him inside.

'Please do come in,' he said sarcastically before closing the door.

'Where are Jane and Emily?' she demanded.

'Out for a walk. Jane's taken Emily to the park.'

'And the nanny?'

'She's gone with them.'

'And the rest of the servants?'

'They're around somewhere. I don't keep track of them every second of every day. They're all very good at what they do and fortunately don't require any watching.'

'I insist on speaking to one of them right now.'

'Mother, are you quite well?'

'I've just received some very disturbing news.'

'Is it Henry? Or my brothers and sister?'

'No, they're all well. Apparently, you've dismissed all your servants and, shortly before you did that, they overheard you arguing with Jane.'

Robert was furious. One of them had gone blabbing to his parents. He'd thought they were too afraid of him to ever do that. 'Who told you these outrageous lies?'

'It doesn't matter, but I'm going nowhere until I've seen Jane and Emily.'

'What the hell do you think I've done to them, Mother? Locked them up like Matthew did you?'

'I really couldn't say, but I refuse to leave until I know they're safe.'

'How can you think so badly of me?'

'Because I know you're responsible for the attacks on those maids, and don't even bother to deny it,' she said when he opened his mouth to respond. 'Now why don't you have one of your servants fetch some tea while we wait? Well?' she added when he just stood there. 'Aren't you going to ring for one of them?'

Her challenging gaze met his and mother and son stood facing each other in the hallway. Robert refused to speak.

'I'm going to ask you again, Robert, and this time I want the truth – where are Jane and Emily?'

'As I've already told you, they've gone out for a walk.'

'In that case, you won't mind me checking.'

'There was a time when my word was enough for you.'

'That was before you started telling lots of lies,' she said, checking the drawing room before peering into Robert's study and then the small parlour.

'Satisfied?' said a smug Robert.

'Not by a long way,' she replied before heading upstairs.

'No one's up there,' he said, rushing after her.

'Then what does it matter?' she retorted.

Amy flung open the first door, which led into one of the guest rooms. The room was empty.

'See,' smirked Robert.

'I've not finished yet.'

Amy opened every door on that level but found no one, each room immaculate, no sign of a struggle anywhere.

'Now do you believe me?' said Robert.

There was a thud from above and Amy looked up. 'The nursery.' When she looked back at her son, she was dismayed by the panic in his eyes. 'They're up there, aren't they?'

'No. We've got a rat problem.'

She studied him hard. 'I don't believe you.'

At the sound of another thud from the floor above, she made for the stairs that would take her up to the third floor.

'No, Mother,' he said, placing himself before her, barring her way. 'You can't go up there.'

'Why not? What will I find?'

'Nothing,' he replied a little uncertainly.

'Out of my way,' she said, shoving him aside but only because he allowed her to.

He watched her hurry up to the top floor where the nursery was, the dark thoughts whispering in his head. No, he couldn't allow her to discover what he'd done.

Amy's heart thudded as she heard Robert tear up the stairs after her, but she reached the top floor without incident, lunging for the nursery door, finding it was locked.

'Jane,' she yelled, banging on the door with her fist. 'Are you in there?'

She heard a muffled shout and another thud.

'Open this door,' Amy told her son.

Robert shook his head. 'No, Mother.'

'You've locked up your wife and daughter, haven't you?' gasped Amy, so breathless with fear she found it difficult to speak.

'Jane was going to leave me.'

'Why?'

'She knows.'

'Knows what?'

'I can't say.'

'Are they all right?'

'Yes. I wouldn't hurt them.'

'Thank God,' she breathed. 'Now open this door.'

'I can't. If I do, they'll leave.'

'Right now, I don't care what's happened. All I want is to check on them. Will you do that for me, Robert?'

He shook his head.

Amy was appalled as she watched the darkness gathering around her son in the same way it had around Matthew, his eyes turning black. 'You can still come back from this,' she told him. 'Not all is lost, but you have to open that door.'

'I'm not losing Jane and Emily, I can't.'

'Whatever's happened, I'm sure it can be worked out, but you will most definitely lose them if you keep them locked up.' Amy was fighting against the alarm wanting to claim her as horrible images of what had been done to her daughter-in-law and granddaughter flashed through her mind. Why hadn't she brought her coachman up with her? He was a strong, sturdy fellow. Because, in her arrogance, she'd assumed she could handle her son and only now did she realise that she couldn't.

She held her hand out to him. 'Give me the key right now.'

'No, Mother. You should leave before...'

'Before what?' she said when he trailed off.

Robert looked so murderous, the blood froze in Amy's veins and the panic finally won out. 'Jane,' she cried, hammering on the door. 'Jane, are you all right?'

A wail set up from inside the nursery, so strong and hearty that Amy was assured that Emily at least was unharmed.

A flustered Amy turned back to her son, breathless and red-faced. 'Open the door,' she yelled at him in frustration and fear.

'Now you know what's happened, you can't leave. You'll come back with others and take them from me.'

'Robert,' she said, backing away from him. 'What are you going to do?'

'You can't leave,' he repeated in a strange monotone, fingers twitching, eyes unblinking. 'If I lose Jane, I'm lost.'

When he lunged for her, Amy snatched up the vase on the hall table and smashed it as hard as she could into the side of his face. His head snapped sideways and he dropped like a stone.

Amy stood over him, shocked by what she had done to her own boy, her hands shaking, tears rolling down her face. She was reassured that she hadn't killed him when she saw the rise and fall of his chest. There was a cut to the side of his head that was bleeding a little.

'I'm sorry,' she whispered.

Emily's cry snapped her out of it, and she knelt by Robert's side and began searching his pockets, praying he stayed unconscious for at least a few minutes. She found the large key in his jacket pocket and jammed it into the lock. Her hands throbbed with pain as she turned the key. She threw open the door and rushed inside, being careful to remove the key from the lock so she couldn't be locked in. She came to a startled halt when she saw a gagged Jane tied to the bed, regarding her with pleading eyes, one side of her face bruised and swollen. She'd managed to attract her mother-in-law's attention by banging her slippered feet off the metal bedframe.

'My God,' breathed Amy.

After ascertaining that Emily was unharmed, just upset, Amy freed Jane, cutting her bonds with a pair of scissors she found in a drawer, the action worsening the ache in her hands.

'Don't worry,' Amy told her. 'Emily's fine.'

The moment she was free, Jane flung her arms around Amy's neck.

'Thank you,' she said, clinging onto her.

Jane released her and got up off the bed, taking a moment to rub her hands to bring the sensation back to them before going to her child and scooping her up.

'We have to leave right now,' Amy told her.

'Where's Robert?'

'Unconscious outside the door. We have to go before he wakes up. My carriage is waiting outside. Is there anything you need to take?'

'Just some spare nappies for Emily.'

Amy snatched up the pile of linen nappies and the two women rushed to the door.

'He's bleeding,' said Jane when Amy pulled open the door to reveal Robert still sprawled on the floor.

'It's only a small cut,' replied Amy.

They skirted around him, afraid to take their eyes off him.

They tore down the stairs, Amy leading the way, Jane following carrying Emily, who had stopped crying now she was back in her mother's arms.

As they reached the first floor, they heard pounding footsteps from above.

'Run,' cried Amy.

She never thought she'd see the day when she was in mortal fear of her own son, but she'd seen in his eyes that he would do anything to stop his wife and daughter from leaving.

Robert must have been a bit woozy from the blow to the head because she heard his footsteps stagger, followed by a thud as he hit a wall.

They reached the ground floor and ran for the front door.

'Get back here,' roared Robert, causing them to jump and run even faster.

Amy fumbled for the catch on the door but her aching, deformed hands were unable to manage it.

'Get the door, Jane,' she told her as Robert raced down the last few steps.

Amy stood before Jane and her granddaughter and snatched up the heavy walking cane propped up in the stand beside the door.

'Are you going to hit me again, Mother?' snarled Robert, a line of blood trickling down the side of his face.

'If I have to,' she replied.

Behind her, Jane had managed to pull open the door.

'Don't go, Jane, please,' cried Robert.

She glanced over her shoulder at him, eyes sad. 'You went too far, Robert. I'm sorry.'

'No,' he howled as his wife rushed out of the house with their daughter.

'I tried to stop this day from coming,' Amy told him. 'But you wouldn't listen. You did this to yourself.'

Robert's face twisted with anger and when he lunged for Amy, she drew back the heavy stick, causing him to recoil.

'Don't think I won't,' she told him. 'Now we're leaving and you're not going to stop us,' she added before backing out of the door.

Once she'd stepped out of the front door, she let the walking stick drop and rushed to the waiting carriage. Jane and Emily were already inside, the door standing open.

'Run, Aunt Amy,' cried Jane when she saw Robert pursuing her.

Amy got into the carriage, but she was unable to pull the door shut as Robert had grabbed onto it.

'Go,' yelled Amy, hammering on the carriage wall.

Jane retreated into the furthest corner of the carriage with Emily when Robert attempted to grab her.

'Don't leave me, please,' he cried.

'Leave us alone,' she screamed, eyes filled with terror.

The carriage picked up speed, finally forcing Robert to release the door. He stood in the middle of the street watching them go, head bowed, eyes black, chest heaving.

Jane and Amy watched him through the rear window, sighing with relief when they turned the corner and he disappeared from view.

'He's going to punish us for this,' murmured Amy.

29

On their return to Alardyce, Amy called for Rush and told him to assemble all the male servants in the study, including Forbes, who was still in the kitchen. Jane took a very distraught Emily upstairs to one of the spare bedrooms to calm her down. Amy ordered the two footmen, the heftiest of the stable lads, the coachman and Henry's valet to remain upstairs at all times because they were expecting trouble. She refused to say what form this trouble would take, but Rush and Forbes had already guessed. She also told Rush to tell the female servants to stay downstairs in the kitchen and make sure the doors were kept bolted.

'Where are the children?' Amy asked Rush.

'They're in the village with the nanny and under-nanny, my lady,' he replied.

'Thank goodness. Have you heard anything from Sir Henry?'

'I'm afraid not.'

She turned to the second footman. 'Ensure all the doors are locked,' she told him, knowing he would do the job a lot faster than Rush.

'Yes, my lady,' he said before rushing out of the room.

Amy told Frederick, the first footman, to stand guard outside the room Jane and Emily were in and not to allow in anyone but her. Standing at six foot two, he was the biggest and sturdiest of all their male staff, which was why she'd selected him for this job. Because of his height, he was paid a very hefty wage, as height was how the worth of a footman was judged.

Amy dismissed the rest of them, except Forbes. 'I expect you're in need of a new position?' she asked him.

'Yes, my lady.'

'You've proved yourself to be trustworthy and intelligent. Rush is due to retire soon, and I need someone I can rely on to take his place. Are you interested in the position?'

'Yes, my lady,' he said, delighted. 'But you should know that I've never worked in a house this large.'

'That's very honest of you, which convinces me even more that I've made the right decision. It's no different, really, and Rush is an excellent teacher. Until the position starts, which won't be for another six months, you'll be under-butler and you'll be paid double what my son paid. You will also have your own room in the servants' quarters. Are those terms acceptable?'

'Y... yes, my lady,' he breathed, a little overwhelmed. 'Very much so. Thank you.'

'Excellent. We'll sort you out with a uniform but that can wait because very soon we're going to have an unwanted visitor.'

'Mr Alardyce?'

She nodded.

'May I enquire if Mrs Alardyce is well?'

'She is and she'll be very grateful for your concern. Emily needs her nanny. Do you know where she is?'

'Yes. She went to her sister's house in the Old Town.'

'Could you give her address to the coachman so he can fetch her, please?' She thought it safe to let the coachman leave because she had plenty of capable male servants to see off Robert.

'My lady,' he bowed.

Forbes exited the room, leaving Amy to stare out of the study window down the drive. Robert would be on his way, and he would be more furious than ever.

She decided to check on Jane and Emily while they waited for the inevitable storm to descend on them. On her way to the stairs, she passed the second footman, who assured her the rear of the house was locked and that he was on his way to check the front. Amy thanked him and moved on. She wondered if the servants knew who they were taking these precautions against. They weren't stupid, no doubt they'd already guessed, but they were loyal and would act like the professionals they were.

Amy had almost reached the bottom of the stairs when a voice behind her said, 'Hello, Mother.'

She stopped and slowly turned to face her eldest son. 'You've never looked more like your father,' she told him.

'Why, thank you,' said Robert, with a smile devoid of anything pleasant. He'd wiped the blood from the side of his face, but it was still congealed in his hair and his normally immaculate clothes were rumpled. But it was his eyes that were the most frightening. Memories of what Matthew had put her through started assailing her.

'You look frightened, Mother,' he said, advancing on her.

'I will never be afraid of my own son,' she replied, standing her ground. 'How did you get in?'

'I broke a window in the conservatory. A room composed of glass can never be secure.'

'You won't win Jane back by breaking into houses. Go home and allow her to calm down. You frightened her.'

'I didn't mean to.'

'You hit her,' she exclaimed. 'How could you?'

'It was an accident. You don't understand what she's been like since Emily's birth. She's become paranoid, thinking people are out to get her.' He sighed heavily. 'I didn't want you to find out like this, it's why I had to keep her locked up for her own safety. She threatened to take Emily and run off. I couldn't allow her to put my daughter in danger...'

Robert was silenced by a slap to the face.

'Don't you dare,' spat Amy, so furious she was able to ignore the pain shooting through her right hand. 'Don't you bloody dare. Matthew tried the same cheap trick to take me away from you, telling Esther I was going mad and needed locking up, and it's an insult that you think I'd believe it. There's nothing wrong with that girl except for the fact that she's terrified of her own husband, and I can't blame her for that. She told me everything in the carriage ride back here. I know what you did to Benjamin Richardson as well as to all those maids and that you were probably in on Knapp's death too. This isn't anything Henry and I haven't already considered, but it's still a shock to have it all confirmed.'

She grimaced when he wrapped his hand around her throat and pushed her back against the wall.

'You've dictated to me for the last time, Mother. I am master of my own life, not you. I'm taking my wife and daughter home and I promise you'll never see them again.'

'Don't think you scare me,' she snarled back. 'I've faced worse than you.'

'Matthew's not here to save you this time, and where's Henry when you need him? Not around, as usual.'

'Go on then, Robert, strangle me like you did those poor girls, but I swear to God I will give you one hell of a fight.'

'I always did admire your feistiness,' he said before casting her aside and making for the stairs.

Amy hit the floor hard, landing on her back. Fortunately, the worst of the impact was absorbed by her corset. She dragged herself up to a sitting position.

'He's here,' she yelled in warning. 'Robert's here.'

He paused. 'Calling for your servants, Mother? The second footman is currently unconscious in the billiard room, the valet's locked in a cupboard and Rush is lying winded on the library floor.'

'You hit a defenceless old man, you coward?' she cried, getting to her feet. 'The darkness has entirely swallowed you, just like Magda said it would.'

'I might just pay your witch friend a visit on my way home with my wife and daughter.'

'I hope you do. You'll never get the better of her and Fenrir.'

Robert just glared at her before continuing on towards the stairs, smiling when he saw Forbes blocking his way, armed with a poker.

'I might have known it was you who came telling tales,' said Robert.

'I won't let you hurt Mrs Alardyce,' he told him. 'She's a kind, gentle woman who never did anyone any harm.' He tilted back his head defiantly, but his trembling voice betrayed his fear. Robert might be half his age, but he was the most intimidating man he'd ever met.

He was knocked sideways by a punch to the face and fell to the floor unconscious, the poker falling from his hand.

'I never did like him,' said Robert, staring down at Forbes with distaste.

Amy snatched up the dropped poker and placed herself before the staircase. 'You're not going anywhere near Jane and Emily. I refuse to let you do to them what Matthew did to me.'

She yelped when Robert grabbed her arm and twisted, forcing her to drop the poker, his other hand wrapping around her throat.

'Let... go,' she grimaced as he started to squeeze.

Robert looked into his mother's eyes and recalled all the happy times they'd shared when he was a boy – her soft voice as she'd sung him to sleep, held him when he was afraid, clinging onto her after they'd fled Huntington Manor, terrified he'd lose her again. Her deformed hands clawed at his arm, and he saw the flesh where her nails had once been, torn out because she'd refused to tell Matthew where he was.

'Robert,' she rasped, her eyes filling with tears because of the pain in her neck.

He found himself dragged backwards, forcing him to release her. He was whipped round and a fist was slammed into his stomach, folding him in half.

Robert gasped and looked up into the furious eyes of his stepfather.

'You little bastard,' snarled Henry before punching him in the face, knocking him onto his back. Henry looked to his wife. 'Amy, are you all right?'

She nodded, shakily sinking onto the bottom step, a hand to her neck. 'Fine,' she replied, her voice coming out weak and strained.

Robert was back on his feet quicker than Henry anticipated and attempted to punch him, but Henry dodged and drove his palm into the side of Robert's face in a classic bare-knuckle move.

'Do you think you're the only gentleman Jackson taught to fight bare knuckle?' Henry told him when Robert regarded him with surprise.

The two men charged at each other, fighting savagely, the Marquess of Queensbury's rules entirely forgotten as they clashed with the brutality of the most savage of bare-knuckle fighters, tumbling from the hallway into the study.

After beating Tommy Tompkins, Robert had thought he could beat anyone, but he found himself hard pressed against Henry. He'd always known he was tougher than he looked, felt the brute strength in his wiry body every time they'd clashed in the past, but he hadn't been prepared for the sheer ferocity with which he fought, and Robert understood it was because he'd seen him throttling his wife.

Robert managed to get the upper hand slightly. He was younger and stockier than Henry and sent him reeling with a blow to the solar plexus, causing his stepfather to gasp for breath.

Robert loomed over him and drew back his fist, ready to deliver the punch that would end this fight, when Henry suddenly straightened up with surprising speed and struck him with his forearm, pain erupting in Robert's face as he felt Henry's arm bone drag across the lower half of his face. As he was bent backwards, Henry delivered a right hook that sent Robert crashing to the floor. As he fell, he shook off the dizziness trying to claim him, snatched a poker from the fireplace and lashed out, catching Henry in the left thigh, making him yelp with pain and stagger backwards.

Robert got to his feet and advanced on him with the poker.

'Did you really think you could beat me, old man?' said Robert, drawing back the poker.

Henry scrabbled for his walking cane propped up against his desk and pulled it apart to reveal a lethal blade that Robert had had no idea was there. He drew himself up to his full height and pointed the blade at his astonished stepson's chest. 'Actually, yes, I did.'

Amy staggered into the room, shocked by the scene before her. 'Stop it, both of you,' she yelled.

'Has he told you his secret, Mother?' Robert asked her, not taking his eyes off Henry.

'Don't, Robert,' Henry told him.

'What are you talking about?' said Amy.

'The secret in the crypt,' continued Robert. 'The one I discovered after all the Hobbs unpleasantness.' He smiled at the wrath in his stepfather's eyes. 'I see you still haven't told her. And I thought you kept no secrets from your wife?'

'Will someone please tell me what's going on?' demanded Amy.

'He put Edward's body in there. He was interred there straight after his execution and he never told you.'

As Amy stared at them both in shock, Henry dared to take his eyes off his stepson to look at her. 'I'm sorry, Amy, but I couldn't let my father's son be buried in a disgusting prison pit.'

'Why did you never tell me?' she said.

'I kept meaning to, but the right time never seemed to come.' Shame filled his eyes. 'Then it was too late. I promise I'd made up my mind to tell you when we got back from Riverwood, but then all this happened with Robert and I couldn't bear to break your heart even more.'

'That's right, Henry,' said Robert. 'Blame me, as always.' He was smiling, certain he had finally come between his mother and stepfather.

'I don't care,' announced Amy.

Robert's smirk fell. 'What?'

'I don't care if he has put Edward in the family crypt because that is nothing compared to what you've done. Now put that poker down right now.'

Furious, Robert's head snapped back round to face Henry and he drew back the poker with a snarl while Henry drew back the blade.

'Stop it,' screamed Jane, appearing in the doorway.

The sound of her voice brought Robert back to his senses. He turned to look at her and the distress in her eyes managed to touch his heart and shake him out of the grip of the dark thoughts. He recalled Magda's words and knew what he had to do.

He let the poker drop with a clang, although Henry kept the blade pointed at him.

'I'm sorry,' he told them.

The regret was so clear in his voice that Jane took a step towards him. 'Robert.'

'No, don't come near me,' he told her. 'I'm poison. I have to go.'

'What do you mean, go?'

'If I stay, I'll hurt you even more. I must leave.'

'Where will you go?' said Amy.

'As far as I can from you all.'

Jane shook her head and started to cry. 'Don't do this.'

'I have to because I love you,' he said, looking from her to his mother. 'I don't want to hurt you, but the demon inside me does.' He took one long last look at them. 'Goodbye,' he said before flinging open the window and jumping through it.

'Robert,' cried Jane, running after him.

'Let him go,' said an exhausted Henry, replacing the blade in the walking cane and letting it drop to the floor.

Amy ran to her husband and took his face between her hands. 'Are you all right?'

'Bruised and sore, but I'll be fine. Robert packs a hell of a punch. Now I understand how he beat Tompkins.'

The three of them went to the window to watch Robert charge by on his black horse. He paused to look back at them, Jane pressing her hand to the glass before he urged his horse on and disappeared down the drive.

'He's never coming back, is he?' she said, tears rolling down her face.

'He will one day,' said Amy. 'When we're least expecting it. Sit down,' she told her husband when he grimaced.

Henry sank into an armchair, still breathing hard and drenched in sweat. 'I think he may have cracked a rib.'

'Shall I have someone fetch Magda?'

He shook his head. 'There's no need to bother her.'

'Jane,' said Amy. 'Jane,' she repeated louder when she continued to stare out of the window. 'Could you arrange for some water and bandages to be brought in?'

The girl nodded and rushed out of the room, still crying.

Amy knelt by her husband's side to examine his injuries.

'Did you mean what you said?' he asked her, stroking her cheek with his thumb. 'You don't care about Edward's body?'

'Well, I admit I was furious at first. I only said I didn't care because I didn't want to give Robert the satisfaction, but I could have lost you today had you not been so capable. I've lived here all these years with his body on our land and it's not done me any harm.'

'I'll have him disinterred and reburied somewhere else.'

'It's really not necessary.' She took his hand and kissed his fingers. 'I recall how distraught you were after his execution. Despite what he did, he was still your brother, so let him rest where he is.'

'That really is too generous of you.'

'You're in this state because of my son and my past mistakes. It's the least I can do.'

'Thank you. I'll have the crypt sealed. No more Alardyces will rest there. We'll buy a plot in the village kirkyard instead. I don't like the thought of any of us resting alongside Edward.'

'That's fine by me. How did Robert find out?'

'He guessed when he saw the coffin with no name plate in the crypt.'

'And he's been holding it over you ever since?'

'Yes, and revelling in it. I was going to tell you, I swear, but I couldn't bear to do it after the whole Hobbs and Mrs Crowle incident, you'd gone through so much and then things kept happening and it never felt the right time...'

'It's all right, you don't need to explain. I understand. We've been through too much together to allow anything to come between us, and you saved my life today. I really believed Robert wasn't going to stop squeezing my neck.'

'That's the impression I got too. I'm sorry to say this, Amy, but he's a lost cause.'

'Perhaps. Jane confirmed all our suspicions. She found out what he's been up to, which was why he was keeping her locked up.'

'Locked up?' he exclaimed.

'Of course, you don't know.'

She was forced to go silent when Frederick walked into the room with a bowl of water, some bandages and a cloth.

'How are Rush and Forbes?' Amy asked him.

'Fine, my lady,' replied the footman. 'Mr Rush has recovered from the blow to the stomach and Mr Forbes is downstairs with some steak pressed to his eye.'

'And Samuel?'

'He's been given some ice for the lump on his head. They'll all be fine.'

'Robert said he locked Donald in a cupboard.'

'He did and he's been released. I heard him banging on the door.'

'That's a relief. And Robert hurt no one else?'

'No, my lady.'

'Thank you. Tell Rush, Forbes, Donald and Samuel they can take the rest of the day off and yes, Forbes is now a member of our staff.'

'Your ladyship,' he bowed before leaving.

'Forbes?' frowned Henry. 'Isn't that Robert's butler?'

'He was until Robert sacked his entire staff. He'll be the ideal replacement for Rush when he retires. He's more than proved himself. He was the one who alerted me to the fact that Robert was keeping Jane and Emily locked in the nursery.'

'I can't believe he locked them up,' he sighed.

'He'd even tied Jane to the bed and gagged her.'

'He was the one who bruised her face?'

'Yes.'

Henry growled with anger.

As Amy tended to his injuries, she related everything Jane had told her.

'My God,' said Henry. 'Robert was Terence Burgess. He's taken the entire business world by storm. He pulled off quite a coup, especially at his age. He is frighteningly intelligent.'

'But I don't think he's entirely lost. He chose to flee because he knew if he stayed, he'd only hurt us more. That indicates there's some goodness left inside him, doesn't it?'

Henry's smile was tender. 'Yes, Amy, it does. He's not entirely gone.'

'We must somehow prove that Benjamin Richardson isn't Terence Burgess without landing Robert in hot water.'

'We can't do both. If we want to free Benjamin, we must tell the police the truth. Besides, financial crime doesn't carry such a heavy penalty because the laws against it are so weak. Benjamin's only in trouble because they think he's responsible for Bruce and Knapp's murders.'

'Which Robert was responsible for. We're not sure how, although he must have had help, and they will pursue him for the murders and the attacks on the women. Inspector Murphy is relentless and he already suspects Robert is the real culprit.'

'But we can't help Benjamin without giving up Robert.'

Amy sighed with frustration. 'Robert said he was going to go far from here. Let's give him a few days, then we'll speak to Murphy.'

'And our family will be disgraced again.'

'We can't allow an innocent man to be hanged.'

'They would never dare hang a Richardson, although he might be thrown into Calton Jail.'

'We can't let that happen either. I couldn't live with myself.'

'Leave it with me. I'll find a way around it.'

Amy decided to let that topic of conversation go for now because Henry was clearly in pain.

He sat back to enjoy her ministrations before his eyes snapped open again. 'Our children...'

'Are in the village with the nanny and under-nanny.'

'So they didn't see their older brother like that?'

'They didn't.'

'They'll be distraught when they find out he's gone.'

'We'll keep it from them for as long as we can, although they will ask why Jane's here. She can't go back to that house. She must stay here while she decides what she's going to do.'

'Of course. Poor Jane, this is going to destroy her.'

'We need to let Esther and William know what's happened.'

'And how do you feel about Robert leaving?'

'Sad, but my heart isn't breaking. After seeing what he'd done to Jane, I know this is the right thing and we won't have to deal with him any more. I'm just so tired, Henry.'

He embraced her, Amy being mindful of his cracked rib as she leaned into him, allowing her tears to stain his shirt.

After tending to his injuries, Amy gave Henry a brandy and he fell asleep in the armchair a few minutes later, so she left his side to find Jane. She found her upstairs in one of the spare bedrooms with Emily, who was asleep in the middle of the bed.

'How are you?' Amy asked her. 'Do you need Magda to look at your face?'

'No, thank you, it's fine,' Jane replied in a soft, faraway voice. 'He's really gone, hasn't he?'

'I think so, but with Robert you never can tell.'

'He truly loves us. He left to protect us.'

'Yes, he did,' said Amy gently.

'I wish I'd never found that stupid ring. Then I'd still be at home with my husband and we'd still be a family, but he's gone and I might never see him again.'

'I think you will, one day.'

'But... what happens in the meantime? I'm a wife with no husband. What will become of me? Will Emily have to grow up never knowing her father?'

'Try not to worry, you'll be fine. You can stay here until you decide what to do. Robert owned the townhouse, so you can stay there if you want to.'

'And have everyone whispering behind their hands, wondering why my husband's abandoned me? I couldn't bear the shame.'

'I'm going to contact Esther and William. No doubt they'll be on their way the moment they hear the news.'

'I can't believe he's gone. We've only been married a year.'

Jane descended into tears, Amy holding her as she cried on her shoulder. She allowed herself to weep too for her lost son, but she knew she would see him again one day. The question was – what would he be when he returned?

30

Robert stormed into his house, slamming the door shut behind him, the noise echoing through the empty building. He stood in the hallway, dripping wet, as the heavens had opened on his way back. Even though he knew he was alone, he still half-expected Forbes to approach and take his hat and coat or for Jane to rush up to him with a welcoming kiss. How he longed to hear Emily's gurgle or her wailing for him to hold her. But the house remained silent because they were gone. He'd driven them all away. Everything he'd gone through to build this life for himself with the woman he loved – his precious daughter, the beautiful home, servants, a thriving business and a large fortune – and he'd destroyed it in a single day. The memory of him throttling his own mother returned, only intensifying his pain. How could he have done that to her, of all people?

Robert hung his head and his shoulders slumped, ashamed when tears filled his eyes. Men did not cry, but he was appalled when the hot tears started to fall and he was helpless to stop them. Robert Alardyce, who had ruined his enemies and stolen a fortune from the wealthiest and most influential family in the city, was bawling like a baby in his own hallway.

The dark thoughts started to whisper, urging him to attack a woman to make himself feel better. His head snapped up and rage filled his every pore.

'It's your fault this has happened,' he whispered to his demon. 'If it hadn't been for you, Jane and Emily would be here and my mother would still love me. You've destroyed my life and I refuse to enable you any longer.'

Robert charged up to his bedchamber, dragged out his trunk from the corner, threw open the lid and began to toss his clothes inside. He'd never had to pack for himself before. His mother had always done it for him, until they'd moved to Alardyce House, when servants had taken over, so his packing was haphazard. He had no idea where he was going, so he didn't know what it would be best to pack. He threw in his warm woollen suits as well as lighter ones more suited to a warmer climate. A few other essentials joined the clothes, but he didn't want to take too much. Travelling light would be much more sensible.

Before leaving, he hesitated to look at the photographs in their silver frames on the windowsill. He snatched up the ones of Jane holding Emily, which they'd had taken just days ago, others of his brothers and sister and his mother, before throwing them to the floor. Instantly full of regret, he retrieved the images from the tangle of metal and smashed glass, and carefully placed them inside his coat pocket, not wanting to crease them.

Robert produced his father's watch from his waistcoat, the one his mother had gifted to him for his birthday all those years ago. It was tempting to smash that too. After all, Matthew was the reason why he was the way he was, but some weak sentiment urged him not to, so he replaced it in his pocket.

Robert kept a large bundle of money in the safe in his study. After retrieving all of it, which amounted to several hundred pounds, and safely stowing it on his person, he heaved his trunk downstairs.

He harnessed his horse to the carriage and drove it himself to Waverley Station, where he knew there was a train that would be leaving soon and which ran to Carlisle and then on to London. He wanted to put as much distance between himself and Alardyce as quickly as possible.

At the station, he paid a lad to drive the carriage to Thomas's house. Hopefully his friend could sell the carriage and horse and pay off some of his debts.

Fortunately, the train was on time and Robert's trunk was loaded onto a first-class carriage. He'd bought all the seats in the carriage so he could be alone with his thoughts.

Robert exhaled with relief when the train left the station. He'd been taunted by the hideous notion that the intrepid Inspector Murphy would arrest him before he could leave. He wouldn't be surprised if Henry reported him to the police for breaking into Alardyce House and assaulting the inhabitants.

Leaving Edinburgh was painful, and as the distance between himself and home increased, the pain in his chest intensified, knowing he was being taken further and further from Jane, Emily and his mother. It would be hard being parted from his siblings too. He thought of Lydia's pretty little face, his brothers' mischievous smiles and the hot tears threatened once more; however, he held them back with his iron will. He refused to cry ever again. If only he could rid himself of the dark thoughts and become a normal man, he could return to them and be the husband, father, brother and son they deserved. The only person he wouldn't miss was Henry, although he did have a lot more respect for him after that fight.

The journey to London was long and arduous. Robert was tempted to get off at Carlisle but he was afraid of Murphy realising he'd left Edinburgh and chasing after him, so the fear propelled him to remain on the train all the way to London. He was familiar enough with the city, having visited on business, and he'd even attacked a pretty little maid down one of the city's stinking alleys.

He found a cab to take him to the Royal Victoria Dock at Plaistow Marshes, where several of the huge iron-hulled steamers waited to commence their journeys to exotic locations and the colonies. Robert's troubles were momentarily forgotten as he took in the scene. The dock was half a mile long and had its own railway to transport cargo to and from the waiting ships. It was a veritable hive of activity as ships were loaded and unloaded. Fruit, frozen meat, tobacco, grain and luxury goods were stored in the enormous warehouses and granaries that had been built along the dock, along with the new refrigerated warehouses that had only increased trade.

He made his way through the hustle and bustle, the porter he'd enlisted to carry his trunk struggling beneath the weight as they made their way towards the passenger steamers, dodging in and out of sailors, dock workers, carts, horses and travellers. It was a noisy, colourful place and had he more leisure time, Robert would have liked to take it all in, but he had to get out of the country. He swore to himself that he would get on the first steamship that had space for him, no matter where it was going. Glamorous-sounding places such as Australia, Canada and America flickered through his mind. The first steamship he found was going to Argentina, so he booked himself a cabin, which certainly wasn't as luxurious as he'd imagined, but it would do. Robert had no acquaintances abroad, he would be completely alone, living on his wits, but he was good at that.

He remained in his cabin until the ship departed, when he went up on deck, still wary of Murphy catching up with him. His heart ached as he was taken further and further from land and his family, wondering when or if he would ever see them again. The ship could sink before it reached dry land and they wouldn't know what had become of him or that they had been constantly in his thoughts. He would miss out on Emily growing up. He would miss her first steps, her first word. The pain became so bad, he was tempted to hurl himself over the rail, swim back to the dock and tear back up the country to Edinburgh, until he recalled his hands wrapped around his own mother's throat. He was doing this for them, not himself. It was the only way he could protect them from the devil that dwelt inside him.

Robert took a deep breath before resolutely turning on his heel and stepping back into his tatty cabin. During his time away, he would wrestle with this devil and either he would cast it out of himself or it would kill him. Either way, he swore he would not return home until it was gone from him, even if that meant he was separated from those he loved forever.

* * *

Amy sat on a bench close to the house, gazing out at the grounds but not seeing them. She was thinking of Robert, wondering where he was, what he was doing, if he was even alive. Rumours had spread like wildfire around Edinburgh about the reason for his sudden disappearance. Some thought it was because he was Terence Burgess, while others considered him to be too young and inexperienced to pull off such a clever plot. Some people thought he'd been responsible for the attacks on the maids in the city – after all, he was Matthew Crowle's son – while there were other rumours that he'd been untrue to Jane and had fled to avoid a whole host of angry husbands. This latter one hurt Jane more than anything, and she and Emily had gone to London to stay with Esther and William to escape all the gossip. Amy had the feeling they would remain down there and she would only get to see her granddaughter sporadically. Not that she could blame Jane. Edinburgh held only bad memories for her, and Amy had no right to demand anything of her, not after what her son had put Jane through.

Her thoughts were interrupted by Rush's voice.

'My lady,' he said. 'Inspector Murphy to see you.'

Amy sighed heavily.

'Shall I send him away?' said the butler determinedly.

'That won't be necessary, thank you, Rush. I've been expecting this.'

The butler bowed and slowly returned to the house. Amy looked up at the inspector, who stared down at her grimly.

'Please, sit,' she told him, gesturing to the space on the bench beside her. 'I have no wish to injure my neck looking up at you.'

'Thank you, your ladyship,' he replied, taking the proffered seat. He gazed out at the view, the grounds of Alardyce seeming to roll out endlessly before them. 'This really is a beautiful place.'

'Please dispense with the small talk and get to the point,' she said in a hard voice. 'I have a lot on my mind.'

'So I believe. I heard your son has left Edinburgh.'

Amy just nodded, her gaze fixed on the garden.

'Where is he? There are some matters I wish to discuss with him.'

'I wish I could tell you, but I have no idea.'

'With all due respect, I don't believe that.'

'I care very little about what you believe.'

'Why did Robert leave?'

'Family differences.'

'Such as?'

'That is absolutely none of your business.'

'I'm afraid it is. Robert is still a suspect in the attacks on those women.'

'By all means, discuss the subject with him, if you can find him.'

'Where should I start looking?'

'As I said, I don't know. He could be anywhere.'

'Abroad?'

'Perhaps, perhaps not.'

'I find it odd that he would flee just as he has it all – a beautiful wife, a baby, wealth and a prosperous business. Something terrible must have happened to encourage him to leave it all behind.'

'I couldn't possibly comment.'

'Lady Alardyce, I appeal to you as a woman who has suffered much. Your son is a dangerous man and he may well put other women through what you went through. Can you really sit back and let that happen? You must tell me where he is.'

'I am the wife of a rich and influential man, so I don't have to do anything.' Amy turned to face him, and he was surprised by the softness in her large blue eyes. 'You're a good man, Inspector. That is plain to see. You're one of the rare breed that genuinely wants to help others, but you will have to admit defeat in this case. Robert is gone, no one knows where and he'll make sure he can't be found. You're wasting your time here, but there is something you should know.'

'Oh, yes?' he said, trying to hide his eagerness.

'Benjamin Richardson is innocent of the charges levelled at him. You have to release him.'

'He was released this morning. The evidence against him – Mr Bruce's letter – mysteriously vanished.'

'That is good news,' Amy breathed with relief. 'But how did this happen? Was it some accident?'

'I very much doubt it,' he said, eyes flashing with anger. 'There are certain officers at Police Chambers who will do anything for the right amount of money and Richardson's family is extremely wealthy.'

'In this particular case, Inspector, you can rest assured that justice has been done. Benjamin is innocent.'

'Which tells me your son set him up.'

Amy turned her gaze back to the garden and refused to respond. Murphy wanted to burst with frustration. He knew Robert Alardyce was Terence Burgess and was responsible for attacking those maids, as did this woman sitting beside him. She could provide him with the evidence he needed to pursue Robert to whatever rock he was hiding under, but she refused to cooperate and there was nothing he could do about it. This was one of the very few failures in his career and he knew it would always haunt him.

'Robert will return to Edinburgh one day,' he told Amy. 'And when he does, I'll be waiting.'

'Perhaps he will, perhaps he won't,' she replied. 'My son is enormously unpredictable.'

'You're shielding him and I understand that, you're his mother. It's your instinct to protect him, but you're doing Robert and the women in this world no favours. How much more pain will be inflicted on others because of your obstinacy?'

Amy was unmoved. Murphy was right, she would do anything to protect her son, even though he was a monster. 'Thank you for coming, Inspector. I expect you're eager to return to Police Chambers, you must have so much work to do.'

With that, she rose to her feet and walked back to the house.

'Lady Alardyce, please,' he said, hurrying after her.

Henry appeared from around the side of the house, striding determinedly towards them. 'There you are, dear,' he told his wife. 'Have you forgotten that we have that important lunch engagement we can't miss?'

Amy was quick to spot the ruse. 'Of course, how foolish of me. I must go and change.'

Henry looked to Murphy. 'If you will excuse us, Inspector, unless there was anything you wished to discuss with me? Although I do recall Chief Superintendent Battles informing me that you were told not to come near our family again. I can't think why,' he added with a pleasant but knowing smile.

Murphy sighed. He was a stubborn man, but he wasn't stupid, and he knew when to concede defeat. 'I was just taking my leave of Lady Alardyce, sir,' he said. 'Enjoy your luncheon,' he added before leaving, taking the path that led around the side of the house to the front. His stiff gait told them both he was annoyed.

'That was excellent timing,' Amy told her husband.

Henry wrapped an arm around her shoulders. 'Rush sent one of the footmen to inform me Murphy was here. I take it he wanted to discuss Robert?'

'Of course. He never talks of anything else, but I gave nothing away.'

'Good. That should be the last we see of him.'

'Until Robert returns. I have the strong feeling that he will, one day.'

'More than likely. I just hope we're prepared for when he does land on our doorstep.'

'Murphy said the letter written by Mr Bruce naming Benjamin Richardson as Terence Burgess mysteriously vanished, so at least he won't be punished for something he didn't do. No doubt Benjamin's redoubtable mother arranged it.'

'Actually, that was me.'

Amy's eyes widened. 'Henry,' she exclaimed.

'I couldn't allow Benjamin to suffer for Robert's sins, so I bribed the woman who cleans Battles's office to steal it from his desk drawer. She gave it to me and I destroyed it.'

'That is a relief, but what if the woman talks and gets you into trouble?'

'I very much doubt she will. She's a sweet, quiet creature who doesn't want any trouble. She was, however, struggling financially, until I gave her some fiscal assistance,' he said knowingly.

'But how did you find out about this woman?'

'I discovered another agent in the city who is almost as efficient as Mr Knapp and he did some digging for me. Please don't worry. All is well.' Henry smiled. 'Now perhaps we can enjoy some peace and quiet until Robert decides to grace us with his presence once more.'

Amy's eyes filled with pain. 'I can't believe he's gone. Whenever I think of him, I don't recall the man he became, the one who enjoys inflicting pain and violence on others. I think of my sweet little boy whose heart was so full of love.'

Henry's smile fell. 'I miss that little boy too.'

Amy's gaze turned distant as she looked out over the gardens. 'This separation from his family will mean one of two things – either he will overcome his inner demon, or it will claim him completely, as it claimed Matthew and Edward. We won't know which until he returns, the thought of which makes me rejoice as well as shudder,' she murmured, fingertips brushing her throat as she recalled the feel of Robert's hand around her neck.

Anger filled Henry as the memory of his stepson attempting to throttle his wife returned. He could have happily killed Robert in that moment. 'We'll just have to make sure we're prepared for it but in the meantime, let's relax and recover. How about we go away for a while? Get away from Edinburgh until things settle down.'

'I think that's a lovely idea. Let's go back to the Lake District. We were so happy there.'

'Then that's where we'll go,' he said, wrapping an arm around her and pulling her to him.

Amy buried her face in her husband's chest, taking comfort in his strong, calm presence. Her oldest son was gone but she still had so much. She hoped only for peaceful, contented years ahead.

Until Robert returned with a monster on his back, to destroy it all.

MORE FROM HEATHER ATKINSON

We hope you enjoyed reading *His Fatal Legacy*. If you did, please leave a review.

If you'd like to gift a copy, this book is also available as an ebook, hardback, large print, digital audio download and audiobook CD.

Sign up to Heather Atkinson's mailing list for news, competitions and updates on future books.

http://bit.ly/HeatherAtkinsonNewsletter

Explore the rest of Heather Atkinson's chilling Alardyce Series...

 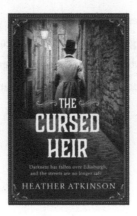 

ABOUT THE AUTHOR

Heather Atkinson is the author of over fifty books - predominantly in the crime fiction genre. Although Lancashire born and bred she now lives with her family, including twin teenage daughters, on the beautiful west coast of Scotland.

Visit Heather's website: https://www.heatheratkinsonbooks.com/

Follow Heather on social media:

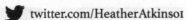 twitter.com/HeatherAtkinso1
instagram.com/heathercrimeauthor
bookbub.com/authors/heather-atkinson
facebook.com/booksofheatheratkinson

THE *Murder* LIST

THE MURDER LIST IS A NEWSLETTER DEDICATED TO SPINE-CHILLING FICTION AND GRIPPING PAGE-TURNERS!

SIGN UP TO MAKE SURE YOU'RE ON OUR HIT LIST FOR EXCLUSIVE DEALS, AUTHOR CONTENT, AND COMPETITIONS.

SIGN UP TO OUR NEWSLETTER

BIT.LY/THEMURDERLISTNEWS

Boldwood

Boldwood Books is an award-winning fiction publishing company seeking out the best stories from around the world.

Find out more at www.boldwoodbooks.com

Join our reader community for brilliant books, competitions and offers!

Follow us
@BoldwoodBooks
@BookandTonic

Sign up to our weekly deals newsletter

https://bit.ly/BoldwoodBNewsletter

Ingram Content Group UK Ltd.
Milton Keynes UK
UKHW042010210323
418912UK00001B/7

9 781804 158029